P-TOWN SUMMER

P-TOWN SUMMER

Lisa Stocker

KENSINGTON BOOKS
http://www.kensingtonbooks.com

KENSINGTON BOOKS are published by

Kensington Publishing Corp.
850 Third Avenue
New York, NY 10022

All Kensington titles, imprints and distributed lines are available at special quantity discounts for bulk purchases for sales promotion, premiums, fund-raising, educational or institutional use.

Special book excerpts or customized printings can also be created to fit specific needs. For details, write or phone the office of the Kensington Special Sales Manager: Kensington Publishing Corp., 850 Third Avenue, New York, NY 10022. Attn. Special Sales Department. Phone: 1-800-221-2647.

Kensington and the K logo Reg. U.S. Pat. & TM Off.

Library of Congress Card Catalogue Number: 2003101658
ISBN 1-7582-0296-2

First Printing: September 2003
10 9 8 7 6 5 4 3 2 1

Printed in the United States of America

This book is dedicated to JoAnn:
My love, my life,
My reason, my answer,
My muse, my first fan, and
My "woofit" always . . .

ACKNOWLEDGMENTS

No doubt it was the cumulative effect of many dear friends—Scott, Suiter, Emily, Michael, Deb, Mychelle (who told me long ago I had at *least* one book in me!), Travis, John Paul, Kate, and many others—who sought to persuade me over the years that I actually *could* write a book if I put my mind to it, that laid the necessary groundwork for this effort. But it took the tenacious persuasion of Douglas Mendini (with a little help from Hiram Walker that night!) to *finally* convince me. Without his ongoing encouragement, support, guidance, and invaluable friendship, this page and all that follow would be blank. My most profound thanks.

Once begun however, I had the expertise, direction, and care of my editor, John Scognamiglio, to thank for making the process painless and gratifying.

To my mother, whose belief in all I could be never wavered, and my father, who blazed the trail first and granted me the benefit of his genes, thank you both. As for the dear ones at 28-28 Jordan (past and present), thank you for making—and at times suffering through!—the journey with me. Your love, belief, and patience carried me through . . . how lucky I am to have such a family.

Without a story and inspiration, however, there can be no book. Lucky again for me, I had both in abundance in the persons of Grisella Ramos and Chris Santiago. Not to mention their help, enthusiasm, insight, and constant encouragement from beginning to end. Most importantly, though, I have had the gift and blessing of their friendship all these years . . . my heartfelt thanks, ladies—for *everything*.

CHAPTER

1

"Sorry, girls," Claire intoned as she slowed the minivan from an idling roll to barely a crawl to a dead stop. "I'm afraid it's time to give the poor AC another break."

For the third time that morning, Claire and the three other women in the car wearily reached for the power window buttons and braced themselves for the onslaught of heat. Fortunately, it was still early in the day so that the heat machine that is August in the New York City environs hadn't yet cranked itself up to full power.

Claire looked at her watch and shook her head in frustration as she waited for the cars ahead to show signs of any forward momentum. She stretched her long body, arching her back and wiggling her toes to try and get the blood flowing again after the long sit in the driver's seat. "I'm sorry, guys. Really, it's usually not nearly this bad. " She took a swig of tepid McDonald's coffee. "Of all times for traffic to be so shitty . . ."

And it *was* shitty. It was already 7:30 and they were barely halfway through Connecticut—having been on the road since six. In the morning. If it had just been Claire and her partner, Rita, it would be one thing. After three years of making this same trip, they were more or less used to the frustrations of the drive up. I-95 was always a horror on summer weekends—especially in Connecticut, amidst the *never*-ending road construction—which could make the trip seem to take forever, particularly given the anticipation of what lay at the end of it. And this year they were even more eager to not only get where they were going, but, also to have everything be as ideal as they had described it to their new friends, Kit and Sabi, whom they were initiating in the time-honored gay summer ritual of making the pilgrimage to Cape Cod and the gem that lay at its farthest reaches: the gay mecca of the East Coast, Provincetown, Massachusetts. So far, things weren't exactly turning out to be the rollicking kick-off to sun and fun that Rita and Claire had hoped.

"Hey—not to worry. You can't help the traffic," Kit assured them. "Maybe there's an accident up ahead and we'll get moving soon."

"Didn't you say that an *hour* ago?" Sabi, Kit's "other half," interjected.

"Well . . . it still *could* be. With this mess, it'd take a while for anything to get cleared up," replied Kit.

"All I know," Sabi said, resituating herself in her seat, "is we'd better get to an exit with some sign of civilization pretty soon, or my bladder's going to explode—and we'll be swimming way before we see the ocean!"

Rita chuckled. "Well, it wouldn't be any worse than that awful, hundred-degree pool in New Hope!"

They all groaned, remembering one of the signal incidents on their first trip together earlier that summer.

"Aw, Jesus! It was like diving into piss water!" Kit, with her usual delicacy, added between sputtering laughs.

"STO-O-O-P!" Sabi half laughed, half whimpered. "I'll pee my pants right now if you make me laugh!" She saw Rita's shoulders shaking with silent laughter and burst out in the raucous laugh that seemed so incongruous with the super-feminine look and persona she so carefully cultivated. Then again, some of her actions were a little at odds with that as well. She leaned forward and slapped Rita on the back. "And you, too! You're supposed to be my *friend!*"

The traffic finally picked up some speed. Not flying, by any means, but moving.

"You know," Sabi shouted over the increasing noise of the wind and radio, "I wasn't kidding about the rest stop bit!"

"I know, I know," said Claire. "My God—you're worse than a kid! We finally start moving and you have to stop."

"I told you at breakfast that coffee would go right through me. And it's always worse when I'm away from home. *Everything* goes right through me!"

"Oh God. Now that's a threat! I'll keep my eyes open—you guys help. These assholes keep slamming on their brakes, so I need to watch."

They had driven a bit longer when Rita touched Claire on the shoulder. "Honey? There was just a sign for an exit with gas station and restaurant symbols. I guess now's as good a time as any."

"Oookay. Here we go!"

They turned off the highway, and the exit curved down to the right and ended at a stop sign.

"Alright, kids, which way?" Claire asked.

"You guys see any likely signs of life either way?" Kit asked.

"Not exactly," Rita replied.

"Oh, for God's sake—just pick a direction and let's go! I'm gettin' desperate back here . . ." Sabi pleaded, rolling her eyes in mock despair.

"Okay, let's give left a try; it makes me feel like we're making northward progress, no matter how pointlessly! Just let's remember how we're going so we can find our way back to the highway, okay?" Claire offered, giving Rita an imploring look. "But why am I telling you?" Claire smiled tolerantly at Rita. "My little navigator with no sense of direction. We just might have to adjust the 'cockpit' seating arrangement on the return trip." She gave Rita a little pat on the knee as she turned toward the back. "Kit, *you* keep track of where we are."

"I'll remember that. You just wait," Rita retorted as Claire turned on to the two-lane highway.

Ten minutes later, nothing. "Any bright ideas, crew?" Claire asked a little anxiously.

"I'm tellin' you guys, I'm jumping out of this car at the next house if we don't find something soon," Sabi said.

"There's always that field over there if you're really desperate," Claire chided.

"Yeah, right. I don't *do* the outdoor peeing thing. That's more for you, uh—how you say—sturdy, rugged types. I have my standards, you know."

"Well, my mom's hardly 'rugged,' but when the time came and we were out fishing, she went wherever there was to go! You need to re-think this lesbian stereotype thing, Sabi—especially when it comes to basics like an exploding bladder!"

"Hey!" Rita chirped in the nick of time. "I think that's a Texaco sign over to the right. It looks like it's down the next road."

"I hope you're right for *all* our sakes," Claire half-muttered as she made a right onto a blacktop road that no one had even bothered to paint divider lines on. "Jesus, if this is what that little gas station symbol meant, they gotta be kidding!"

Sure enough, about five miles up, there was the Texaco station—all two pumps of it.

"Ahhhh, superhighway convenience: easy off, easy on," quipped Claire. "I don't know about you guys, but I'm hearing strains of 'Dueling Banjos' here. Since this is for your benefit, how about you go in and check out the facilities, Sabi."

"Don't worry, babe—I'll go in with you." Kit said. She pitched her voice lower, adjusted her baseball cap and did her squaring-the-shoulders bit. "I wouldn't let anything happen to my little lady."

"Oh, for Christ's sake! I'll have knocked 'em out with my purse by the time you're done doing your macho-girl thing," Sabi huffed as she opened the door and got out. She looked back in the car. "The hard part's gonna be keeping my dignity if I don't make it inside in time!"

As the altogether-too-stereotypical attendant approached the car, Claire decided they might as well fill up since the gas was definitely cheaper than on the highway. The attendant came to the window and grunted what sounded like a single word version of what'll-it-be, and Claire gave him a fill-er-up straight from her Midwestern roots. Rita and Claire figured they might as well grab a Pepsi—though Mountain Dew seemed the more appropriate choice—and went over to the soda machine to see what was available. Claire spied a Beer Nuts display inside and went in to avail herself of the rarely seen treat, at least in the East anyway. "Jeesh—this place really is like something out of the old days back in Ohio," she remarked to Rita as they lingered waiting for their friends to reappear.

"So? Is it safe?" inquired Claire with a raised eyebrow when Sabi and Kit returned.

"Well, it ain't no dee-luxe, food court rest stop, but, with enough toilet paper and if you don't touch anything, it'll do," Sabi assured them, in a Brooklyn-accented half-assed attempt at a drawl.

"Okey-dokey. Here we go," Claire replied as she took a deep breath.

Rita and Claire went off to do their respective things and rejoined the girls a few minutes later.

"Did you get gas?" Kit asked Claire. "Looks a lot cheaper here."

"Yep. We're ready to rock and roll."

The women piled back into the car as two pickups pulled in, blocking their exit.

"Ooh. It's getting busy!" Claire jockeyed the car around to try to get out. "Like they couldn't see us ready to leave," she added in exasperation.

Sabi looked back to make sure Claire cleared the bumper of one of the trucks. "Ah, you gotta love country hospitality. Jethro there's waving goodbye!"

"How nice. But I'd keep my voice down. The windows are open, and I don't think 'Jethro' would take well to your New York sarcasm," Claire said. "Let's boogie!"

And they were on their way again, humming a not-half-bad four-part rendition of "Dueling Banjos."

"My God, that's a shitty road," Kit said as they approached the stop sign to get back on the road to the interstate. "My teeth feel loose from all the bumps."

"Well, between that and all the stuff we've got crammed in this poor little van, we're bound to do some bouncing," Claire replied.

"I don't know . . . did you check the tires by any chance back there?"

"No. We had the whole car checked out Wednesday—didn't we, Rita?"

"Ye-e-es," Rita said tolerantly. "It was checked off my list of chores."

"Don't worry, honey," Sabi said, reaching over the seat to pat Rita's shoulder. "I get the same thing. They're the generals and we're the lowly privates."

"Alright you two," Claire said. "But you're right, I think, Kit. It does feel a little funny."

"Well, why don't we pull over and check before we get all the way to the highway?" Rita suggested. "Though we are almost there."

"Yeah, right. You and your sense of direction. We've got another five or six miles to go," Claire said. "So-o-o, we'll pull into this . . . whatever the hell little place this is and take a look."

Ahead on the right was a small ramshackle building. As they got closer, they could see a sign that said Bait, Bullets and a Bite. "Oh, great—now we get the real cream of the crop," Claire moaned. "If that's what the restaurant symbol meant, God help somebody looking for a McDonald's." She pulled the car over in front of the shack that was the store, and she and Kit got out to take a look. The proprietor strolled over to the car.

"Well, little lady, looks like you're gettin' yourself a flat there."

"Yeah. It does, doesn't it," Claire said with a tight smile.

"And I'll bet you were heading for the highway right here."

"Right here?"

"Yep. About five hundred feet around that curve." Claire and Kit looked at each other and shrugged.

"There's no service station for about fifteen more miles on the highway. But there is one back up the road apiece. You just turn right at—"

"Yeah, I know. We were just there," Claire said heading back for the car. "Thanks anyway. We'll just head back."

"Jethro" was standing by the pumps, looking a little smug as they pulled in.

"Thought I might see you girls again," he said with smirk. "Tried to stop you when you was leaving last time, but you just peeled outta here. I was gonna tell you that tire didn't look so good."

Kit leaned over to Sabi. "Waving goodbye, huh?"

Forty-five minutes later, they were back on their way to the highway. As they passed the other roadside establishment, their friend was sitting outside—and *did* wave as they drove by.

"Well! I hope that ends the unforeseen surprises for the day—actually, make that for the *week*. If I wasn't ready for this vacation before, I am now," Sabi said.

"You said it," Claire replied. "With any luck, the only surprise from here on out should be you guys seeing the Cape for the first time.

And then it's one whole week of just us, the ocean, frosty summer drinks, great food, and peace and quiet. Except, of course, for the hundreds of other gay people there with us!"

"Now if we can just *get* there," Rita said wearily.

"Don't worry, honey. Traffic's moving now, so it shouldn't be too bad," Claire offered optimistically as they got up to a nice, seventy-miles-an-hour cruising speed for maybe the second time that morning. "Besides, it looks like the worst of it's cleared out in the meantime."

"Nice try, Claire," came Kit's voice from the back. "If it wasn't for Little Miss Mini-Bladder back here, we'd probably be in Rhode Island by now. Odds are good we picked up a nail on that cow path of a road." The harrumphing sound that came from the back was *definitely* not Kit. "Aw, come here, honey," Kit said leaning over to give Sabi a kiss that was intended for elsewhere but ended up on the back of her head. "I love your little mini-bladder just like I love everything about you," she cooed.

"Alright, you two lovebirds. Enough with the new-lovers baby talk jazz," Claire said with mock exasperation. "You're gonna put ideas in Rita's head, and I'll have to start having to come up with all that lovey-dovey shit again!" Claire ducked in advance of the hand.

"You're just lucky I've put up with you all these years," Rita snapped playfully. "You just *think* you're blessed with irresistible charm!"

"How long did you guys say you were together?" Sabi asked.

"Gee, it's so long, I've lost track. Hey! Enough with the hands!" Claire shouted as she started to duck again. "I learned early on that it's suicide to forget the anniversary deal! I'm no idiot. Alright, I know what you're going to say, so don't!" Claire gave Rita a sidelong glance. "Let's see . . . this May was eight, wasn't it, honey?" asked Claire, eyebrows raised in an attempt at innocent questioning.

"Well, since we got together in '80, it's not too tough to figure out," Rita parried back. "And eight *glorious* years it's been."

"Aw, come on. It hasn't been *that* bad!"

"No, honey, it hasn't—not at all," replied Rita, mellowing and taking her hand to give it a squeeze. "The truth is, I wonder what I would've done if she hadn't come along," she continued with a tender look at Claire. "Seriously, I was so miserable with Rick that I'd forgotten there was anything *but* being miserable. So I thought I was okay. And with the kids, you just figure that's what life is, so you make the best of it."

"My God, Rita. I don't know how the hell you lived like that so long. I mean, I dated from the time I was fifteen, and was even engaged for a while. Who knew? I wasn't ecstatic with any guy, but I wasn't miserable either. I'll tell you one thing— *no* one ever got by with cheating on me. That's for sure. His little *cojones* would be in serious jeopardy. But, God knows, I never even *considered* the idea that I might be a . . . lezzzzzbian! But once my little honey showed me the light, well, let's just say calling off the engagement seemed like a *pretty* good idea!" Sabi leaned over and gave Kit a peck on the cheek. "See? You saved me from a life of despair, *mamita.*"

Kit smiled. "Come to think of it, I guess I did," she replied a little proudly.

"I don't know," Rita said thoughtfully. "It's just what everyone I knew *did*. A good Italian wife just accepted those things because 'that's how men are' and 'he's a good provider, isn't he?' is all you heard otherwise. But then . . . everything changed. And though it hasn't been easy, I wouldn't change a thing." Rita reached over and stroked Claire's cheek.

"Aw, come on—you're embarrassing me," Claire protested. "But neither would I. It's just that it was obvious you deserved better. And it *became* obvious something was going on with us. I'm just glad I did something about it before anyone else did."

"And, frankly, pal, given what a hottie your honey is, it's a good thing you didn't waste any time," Kit added.

Claire looked to her right and smiled. Kit was right. Rita was, indeed, a veritable "hottie." Besides being "endowed" with two obvious assets—the 38 double Ds that would do a twenty-five-year-old proud, let alone a forty-year-old—and a great figure otherwise to complement them, Rita had a number of other definite assets. She was attractive in a soft, Northern Italian sort of way: medium height, fair skin, soft brown eyes, good cheekbones, and a smile that radiated kindness and warmth—almost a Julie Andrews look, with a

Neapolitan flair. The only aspect of her features that betrayed the
Sicilian half of her heritage was her mother's Mediterranean nose.
But it added to her accessibility by being the one feature that *wasn't*
perfect. The other thing she had her mother to thank for was her
very prematurely gray hair—but Clairol had come to the rescue
there: number 114, light ash brown was what her short bob was
these days.

Then there was her amazing cooking, her maternal nature that
was a more profound part of her than just *being* a mother could ac-
count for, and a rare kindness and slowness to anger. It was no surprise she was so beloved by her family. And friends—that rarefied
company who had managed to win her trust and get by a certain
wariness she had with new people, a function, it seemed, of not having strayed very far in the past from the large, close-knit family she so
treasured. But for those who broke through the shell, the prize was
worth the effort. Claire smiled a little wider. Definitely worth it, she
thought. Especially if you were the lucky object of the smoky passion
that was the ultimate prize.

"Yeah, I know why *you* think Rita's a hottie—but mine are *almost*
as big as hers," Sabi said, cupping her hands under her own perky, little mounds.

"And you guys are together, what, two years now?" Rita asked,
clearly redirecting the conversation and at the same time jolting
Claire from her reverie.

"Yep," Kit retorted cheerily. Then added quietly, "Two years . . .
going on forever."

Everyone in the car—including Sabi—let out a loud groan.

"Aw, man, you're *really* workin' it, kid!" chided Claire. "Somebody
wants to get lucky toni-i-i-ight," she added in a singsong voice.

"C'mon. I mean it," Kit replied with wounded gravity. Then she
grinned and re-adjusted her baseball cap. "But, hey, a girl's gotta do,
what a girl's gotta do!"

"Oh, yeah. You're gettin' some tonight," Sabi shot back as she
crossed her arms.

"That's okay," she laughed. "My friends'll keep me company!"

"You better hope!"

"I do have to tell you two, though," Kit continued, "it's pretty neat finally being able to *be* with each other with other people—especially another couple."

"Alright, alright, don't get all serious on us. This is vacation!" Claire said over her shoulder.

"No, I'm serious. If you hadn't come out to me and we all hadn't gotten together—forget getting along so well—I don't know when we would have ever have gotten around to getting to know other gay people, let alone another couple. Really. It was getting *real* easy living in our own little world. We've been pretty isolated these last couple of years."

"We'd have been the same way if it wasn't for Claire making me get out of my shell and deal with other gay people. I was used to family—period. And I've got *lots* of family. But my popular little honey, here," Rita looked over at Claire, "convinced me there was something to be said for friendship. And she was right."

"Excuse me, ladies," Claire interjected. "But I would like to call your attention to the fact that we are approaching the Rhode Island border which we should be crossing . . . right . . . about . . . now!" Cheers all around. "Which means, that after Providence, we should be crossing over into Massachusetts in about twenty minutes or so if traffic stays nice and clear like it is now. Now—excuse me. You were saying, dear? About how wise and wonderful I was??"

"Despite your sarcasm, you are. And I love you for it. If it weren't for Claire pushing me when I needed it, I wouldn't know *any* of her friends—including you guys. I really didn't see the point of all this friend stuff. But that's changed over the years—like so much else!"

"Well, *I'm* certainly glad you got over that," Sabi replied, "because I can't imagine not knowing you. Claire's cute and all that, but she's no fun to talk to about girl stuff. And besides, I don't know anyone else who's as bad a swimmer as I am!"

"You two can knock yourselves out," Kit countered. "Claire and I'll have *fun,* and you two can do your little chitty-chatty thing and get manicures!"

"Ditto for me," chimed Claire. "Hey! Here's Mass. We're gettin' there!"

It was another half hour or so before they saw the first of the signs for Cape Cod exits. Sabi started getting excited. "We're almost there, we're almost there," she chanted.

"Well, we're almost to the *Cape,*" Claire corrected.

"And that means we're almost there!" Sabi happily chimed back.

"Well, not exactly. I keep forgetting you haven't done this before. P-Town's at the *end* of the Cape."

"Whadya mean, 'the end'?"

"Well, if all goes well on Route 6, we'll be there in about an hour."

"Awwww . . ." Sabi moaned. "I thought we were *there.*"

"Almost. But trust me when I tell you that it'll all be worth it when we *do* get there. Right, honey?"

Rita smiled and put her head back. "She's right. I don't know if it's the sight of the dunes or the smell of the ocean or the fact that, for a change, there's more of *us* than *them,* but it's heaven."

"Oh—that reminds me," said Kit. "Speaking of 'them,' I hope you guys don't mind, but a friend of mine from college—a straight friend, which, of course, were the only people I knew up till now—is in Boston on business, and when I told her where we were going, she wondered if it'd be alright if she came out to say hi."

Claire looked at Rita and shrugged. "It's alright with us. And, now that you bring it up, I was gonna check with you guys to see if you'd mind if an old friend of mine did the same thing. Grant—well, her name is actually Georganna Grant, but she's *definitely* not a 'Georganna'— is *from* Boston and was planning on coming out for a few days anyway. Bad break-up recently—time to check out the summer babes. Anyway, she called to chat the other night and was pretty hyped that we'd be out here at the same time. So, I tentatively told her we could hook up at some point—if it was okay with you guys."

"Just a minute," Sabi interjected. "I know you two social butterflies like to have your adoring public around you. And I like Diane, Kit's friend. But I'm here on vacation, which I am *very* much looking forward to. So, if you two make sure this doesn't become some sort of babysitting deal, that's fine. But I'm not arranging my schedule around 'the friends.' Got it?"

"Oh, thank God," Rita sighed. She turned to look at Sabi. "Bless you. This one always feels like it's her sacred duty to play social director for everyone she knows. Not me. I'm with you. I'm on vacation—and that means *I* get to relax and not do my usual 'good wife' entertaining and hostessing duties!"

"That's not fair!" Claire shot back. "I do my part."

"Oh, I forgot. That's right—you pick out music and make drinks and get the right subdued lighting. Forgive me."

"Not to worry. Kit and I will make sure you ladies are not inconvenienced in the slightest. Right, Kit?" Claire said, ignoring Rita's dig.

"Right. We'll be good. A couple of cocktails, a little conversation . . ."

"I know you, Kit Summers. And I know what a couple of cocktails can turn into. Don't make me embarrass you," Sabi warned

"Jeesh, I feel like I'm seventeen."

"That's only because most of the time you act like you're seventeen!"

"Okay, okay. We get the message, you two," Claire interrupted. Now, if you'll sit back and start taking note of the scenery instead of being difficult, you might notice that it's starting to change just a tad."

As they'd driven along Route 6, the scenery had indeed begun to change. The tall pine groves on either side of the road had given way to scrub pine blown into gnarly, almost sculpted shapes, while the loamy soil got perceptibly sandier. The still, summer air was now getting cooler, with a touch of a light breeze . . . a breeze with a scent to it that already called to mind the waves and surf that lay just ahead.

Conversation ceased as they took in the vista that greeted them as they made the last long curve out of Truro—a sight that two of them had come to treasure and that the other two were now experiencing for the first time. Golden, windswept dunes stretching off toward a horizon that shimmered with a silvery blue glint. And just beyond that, a little notch in the blindingly blue sky.

"That, ladies, is Pilgrim's Monument. You are in Provincetown."

CHAPTER
2

For a moment there was utter silence in the car.

"Oh—my—God," Sabi said quietly. She rolled the window down and stared, totally taken by the sight. "It's gorgeous."

Claire slowed the car a bit, the better to appreciate the sweeping vista, as they neared their destination. Off to the left, little white bungalows dotted the shoreline, one moment blending in with the white of the breakers and then popping into bright relief against the steely blue of the sea. To the right, the dunes continued on and on, broken here and there with hillocks of dune grass and half-buried picket retaining fences, the sand blowing into ever-new swirls and shapes as they watched. And up ahead, the tiny notch in the sky loomed larger as it became the towering landmark it was.

"So? Worth the drive?" Claire asked.

"Uh, yeah, I'd say so," Kit replied. "I've seen some impressive ocean views, between living in Virginia and Florida, but this is pretty spectacular."

"And we're *just* getting started," Claire said as she eased the car into the left turn lane. "I think we should take the long way in, whadya think, honey?"

Rita just nodded, lost in her thoughts. Then she sighed deeply. "It always feels like coming home."

The car was quiet as Claire took what the signs had said was the first of three exits to P-Town. Straight ahead, the horizon undulated slightly, covered with brilliant, dancing specks of light and little foamy patches of white.

As they approached a stop sign at the end of the road, Claire gestured out the window: "And that's the bay you'll wake up to every morning." Sighs were the only responses. As she stopped the car, she added, pointing to their left, "That's the Holiday Inn where we spent our first weekend here. It'll always have a little sentimental value for us, right, babe?"

"It sure will," Rita said. "Though Grant and Lynn—her ex—constantly battling almost ruined that weekend. But if that was the price for discovering this place, it was a bargain. We do have Grant to thank for that."

"So, when was that?" Sabi asked.

"Hmmmm . . . let's see. About five years ago?"

"Yeah. That sounds about right," said Rita. "We'd been in Boston for a long weekend visiting them and came out here on a Saturday morning for the day. We were *supposed* to beat the traffic, but if you think *this* was a rough trip, try coming from Boston along with all the other day-trippers. We sat on that damned bridge for an hour just getting on the Cape."

"Okay, enough about that." Claire turned right. Her deep, alto voice took on the dulcet tones of a radio announcer: "Ladies, you are now at the beginning of famous Commercial Street, the main drag of P-Town. Now, the first thing you need to know for future reference is to reorient your perspective: this is the East End even though it *feels* like east should be on ahead of us since we're still heading out. But remember," and Claire raised her right arm as if to make a muscle, curving her fingers in, "this is the shape of the Cape, so we've really curved around and are now heading west, back toward the mainland across the bay."

"Huh?" said Sabi. "Look—you two worry about the geography lesson. I'm more interested in what's here than where it is!"

"Well, my friend *Kit* is probably interested in knowing which way is which. Right, pal?"

"Right. Ignore her. Just point her in the direction of the stores, and she'll be happy."

"You're damn right—and remember you said that. I've saved up my nickels and dimes, and I intend to spend every last one of them," Sabi shot back.

"Like I don't know that," Kit mumbled.

"Don't start, you."

"I'm not, I'm not! I just know you. And it always makes me break out in a cold sweat when I think of doing the bills later."

"Oh, Sabi. Wait till you see the Christmas shop," Rita gushed. "And there's a great New Age book store and, oh my God—Zeus . . . the most amazing crystal and gorgeous gifts, and—"

"Excuse me!" Claire interrupted. "There's plenty of time for all that. Right now, take a look at some of these houses."

All along Commercial, there was one cottage more beautiful than the next. Traditional Cape Cods, of course, perched next to expanded bungalows overlooking the water, Victorian confections painted in salmons and teals, little saltboxes, most of which showcased front yards and gardens that were exploding with beauty and dazzling color. Interspersed were former homes, schoolhouses, and churches that had been converted into art galleries.

"Did you ever see gardens like that?" Claire said dreamily, half to herself. "The colors are amazing. You know, that's the reason this started out as an art colony—they always talk about the special, unique light out here. Of course, that's not all that's unique and special!"

The private homes started to give way to a more, well, *commercial* look.

"There's one of our favorite restaurants, Franco's. Very deco, thirties-ish kind of place with incredible food." Claire cruised slowly, so they could savor their first impressions. "And there's Womancrafts, the obligatory lesbian bookstore, and The Mews, another great restaurant and . . . well, just soak it up. We'll have plenty of time to hit 'em all."

As the number of stores increased, so did the number of people strolling, almost aimlessly, down the middle of the street. Claire slowed the car to a crawl.

"That's the other thing about this place. Sidewalks don't mean a whole lot. Everybody just goes where they want. It's a *very* laid back kind of place."

"Jesus Christ! Look at all these women!" Kit burst out.

"Down, girl. Take a deep breath. Just remember—looky but no touchy."

"Oh, stop. That's not what I mean. I've just never seen so many gay people in one place before. And everyone's holding hands, with all these straight people around!"

"Welcome to P-Town."

"I know how gay you said it was, but I somehow thought that meant *all* gay."

"Nope. That's the neat thing about this place. It's the only place *I* know of where the whole gay/straight thing is pretty much a non-issue. I guess the Village is the next closest thing. But even there I don't typically feel all that comfortable walking hand in hand with Rita. Except, of course, on Gay Pride Day. But here, it's kind of Gay Pride Day all the time. And the straight people keep bringing their babies in their little carriages like everything's just fine. Which of course it is—like it really *should* be all the time everywhere."

"Wow, how cool." She paused, watching the families ambling happily along. "Huh. Can't you see my folks strolling along in a place like this?" Kit said looking at Sabi.

"Yeah, right. They could barely bring themselves to walk in our house. And that's when they only *suspected.*"

Outside the car, the street was now packed with people of every shape, size, color, and persuasion. Among the gay contingent, there was every imaginable variation on a theme: big dykes, little dykes; ultra fem, "truck drivers"; boys with pink tank tops, boys with muscle shirts—and the muscles to go with them; quiet, shy-looking couples who were clearly from the heartland and loud, very "out" couples in from Boston or New York; pink hair, understated Wall Street coifs; pierced nipples and dangling earrings (male and female of each); cut-off jeans and faded tees; drag queens and motorcycle mamas; boys prancing coquettishly and women striding purposefully. It was beautiful.

"Okay, guys, there's our regular parking lot. Stella has a deal with the crusty old guy you see sitting there on that chair by the office. Every year, same get-up: straw hat, pipe, short sleeve beige shirt. And I guarantee the conversation will be the same when we pull in after we get our room receipt." She shifted to a New England accent: " 'Sooooo, wheah you girls from? New Yahk, eh? Traffic bad comin' up, eh? You say you're from Stella's Seaside? Now, what room you in this ye-ah? Yes, yes, that's a dandy. Ah-huh. You just leave this ticket in the

window while you're he-ah so I know you're one of the weeklies.'
And a fairly close version of that entire thing every time we go out!

"But first, to see how much of a hassle Stella will give us *this* year
about being here before three. The rooms are *always* cleaned by
11:00, but," Claire frowned and said in a low, growling tone, " 'girls,
check-in's not till three, like it says on the brochure, ya' know'!"

They stopped at a small but busy corner, and Claire signaled for a
left turn onto what seemed to be the sidewalk but was actually the
top of a wide, steep driveway leading down to what looked to be a
dead end.

"Where *is* this place?" Sabi asked as they waited for the throng to
let up. "You're not gonna tell me we have to *back* up that ramp once
we go *down?*"

"You'll see. It's just one of the many charms about this place. O-o-
kay, here we go."

They inched down the steep incline, avoiding people walking
back up the driveway. Claire stopped three-quarters of the way
down, put the car in park, pulled the emergency brake, and announced, "Okay, kids. We're here!"

The foursome got out of the car and stretched after the long haul
as they took in the approach to their home for the next week. The
blacktop incline ended a few feet in front of them leveling out and
broadening into a quaint, little plaza. On the left was a sandwich
shop, and on the right side of the blacktop sat a shed-like structure.
Straight ahead, spanning the area between, was a white picket fence
that looked as if it could do with a fresh coat of paint and a couple of
new slats. It was backed by bushes and trees grown a bit wild that
created a sense of remove from the hubbub of the street for the
buildings that lay beyond. Claire beckoned to the two newest guests
and led them toward a gate in the fence. A loud bonging stopped
them in their tracks.

"That would be Stella," Claire said as she smiled and looked up to
her left.

Looking out from the second floor above the sandwich shop was
a woman who stood about five-foot-two, with a weathered, deeply
tanned face and black-rimmed glasses, circa 1960. She was dressed in
navy blue men's workpants and a man's plaid blazer, with a black

wool fisherman's cap pulled down on her head, her grizzled gray hair poking out the sides. And she was yanking the hell out of a ship's bell mounted at the end of the balcony.

"Where *is* that boy?" they could hear her muttering as she looked back beyond the fence and bushes. "Den-nis!" she intoned. "I told you to get the laundry up on the street or we'll miss the truck!" She clanged the bell again. "Den— oh." She stopped short and squinted down at the women. "Don't tell me you girls are here to check in!"

"Hey, Stella," Claire yelled up. "It's Rita and Claire—we were here the last two years?"

"I have people in and out of here every damned week. I can't re- member everyone."

"A real charmer, isn't she?" Claire muttered under her breath. "Her bark is definitely worse than her bite—and everyone has to go through this. Consider it part of your initiation to P-Town."

Claire looked up, took a deep breath and then smiled her broad- est smile. "I know, I know—we're a little early. But we love it here so *much* we couldn't wait to get here!" She turned around and winked.

"Huh," Stella growled as she started down the steps of the bal- cony and disappeared from sight.

"We'll meet you in the office," Claire cheerily called after her, rolling her eyes. "Let's go," she said to the others.

They went in through the gate and headed to what looked like one of the units on the left. Instead, it was Stella's office, a cramped little room that was filled mostly by a mammoth oak desk, every inch of which was covered by papers, ledgers, knickknacks, unopened mail, and an antique lamp that provided the only light in the room. Postcards and notes and ancient nautical posters covered three of the walls, with a large shellacked board on the other wall to their left that was covered with cup hooks on which hung numbered tags and room keys. Stella was sitting at the desk in a classic swivel office chair, hands clasped on the desk in front of her, looking like some backroom politician.

"Who'd you say you were again?" she asked them gruffly.

"Claire Griffith, and this is my partner, Rita Campanella. And these are the two friends we talked into coming up with us this year, Kit Summers and Sabi Ramirez."

"Hmmm . . ." Stella adjusted her glasses and ran her finger down a page of a large, well-worn journal-type tome. "Claire and Rita . . . yes, you two do look familiar." She suddenly stopped her search and looked up at them. "Ye-e-e-e-s," she said thoughtfully, stroking her chin. "The big, tall blonde who doesn't *look* like she's from New York and the Italian that doesn't *act* like it. Too nice," she muttered, looking back at her book. Then she stopped again and looked back up at them. "Say, aren't you the two I had a birthday drink with last year at the Pilgrim House?"

"There you go!" Claire said, brightening. "I knew you'd remember. We're fellow Leos! We came up earlier last year—closer to all our birthdays?" she encouraged.

"Well, if you've been here before, you should know that check-in's at three o'clock. I can't have people showing up whenever they feel like it. That's no way to run a business!"

Claire could tell without looking that Kit and Sabi were looking around the "office" and wondering the same thing.

"I know," Claire said quietly, "but it's so hard to judge traffic and how long it's going to take, and then there's the mess on Route 6, and juggling all those cars checking in together, and—"

"Alright," Stella said, still annoyed but conceding. "It's already 1:30, so I guess I can let you—this time. But don't you go telling any of the other guests I let you in here early. I have more than I can handle keeping this place running right without more problems like this!"

"Thanks, we really appreciate it."

Then the drill began: $5.00 room key deposit, " 'cause I can't be running out and having keys made every fifteen minutes"; "no grilling on the deck—the whole damn place is wood and it could go up like that," with a sharp snap of her fingers; "one fan per room—it's not the damn Ritz, you know—electricity's not free"; "and keep your showers to fifteen minutes—the fresh water wells are gonna run dry any day out here." Oh. "And be sure you read the rules—(!)—in your rooms and abide by 'em!"

"Okay, here are your keys and receipts. If you show your receipt to Mr. Ayers up the block, he'll give you a discount on the parking. Now . . . I think that's it. Clean towels on Wednesday, so have the old ones out and ready by 10:00. Any questions, ladies?"

Claire just *knew* what Kit was going to do. She whipped around and shot her a look just as she was lifting her arm to salute.

"No, I think we're fine. We'll unload the car and get settled in. Thanks. We'll see you around. In fact, why don't we toast your birthday a little late sometime during the week?"

"Well, uh, we'll see," Stella said, a bit taken aback. "Running this place sucks the life out of me—it's a twenty-four-hour job, you know."

"No problem. We'll check with you later." Claire turned to the group. "Okay—let's do it, girls!"

"Jeesh, she is *some* piece of work," Sabi said as they went out through the gate to the car. "But the place does look cute—and at least they have maid service."

"Uh, yeah, they do," Claire said as she looked over at Rita and smirked.

"I can't *wait* to get in the room, take a nice cool shower, and maybe see what stations they get here. Do they have cable?"

"Not *exactly*. As we told you, they're efficiency apartments. So, you have a little kitchenette—and stuff. Remember, I told you this place is big on charm rather than amenities."

"No problem. Actually, maybe I'll just soak in the bath rather than a shower."

"*Maybe* we should just focus on getting everything in first," Claire responded and gave Kit a nudge. Kit looked over, and Claire covered her mouth in mock laughter, shaking her head. Kit grinned and nodded, starting to get the picture.

Rita and Sabi got to the car first. Sabi grabbed her makeup case and pillow, while Rita picked up the boom box and the bag of potato chips she'd brought in the car.

"Hey, you two! There's a lotta shit here!"

"Excuse me?" Rita said looking at Claire. "As I recall, I'M on va-CA-tion!"

"Oh, yeah, right!" Claire growled as she hauled out the crate of food. "Like Kit and I aren't."

"You know the rules—for one week I get to lie on the beach and cook. That's it."

"Alright, alright," Claire said with a resigned air. Then she slowed to let Rita catch up to her. "But don't let her go in the room till I'm there!" she whispered.

This time when they walked through the gate, they bore to the right along a bricked path, at the end of which Kit and Sabi stopped and took in the view: the bay up ahead of them and the heart of Stella's Seaside, a large weathered deck that was a sort of central "plaza" for the complex; the two levels of rooms, all covered in what one might politely call "rustic" shakes; and the riot of flowers in planters and in every exposed patch of dirt. Outside all the rooms were signs with the rooms' names—all named for stars, since Stella was short for Eustella, Greek for star—and what were once brightly painted pictures of the corresponding heavenly bodies. Above the signs were outdoor lights that looked like they were right off the Titanic—before or after it sank was open for debate. At the end of the deck were big Adirondack chairs, an over-sized picnic table and a twenty-foot ship's main mast with a full compliment of semaphores, topped with the stars and stripes, of course.

"Oh, you guys, it really *is* charming," Sabi said, looking around her as she walked down to the end of the deck by the picnic table and looked out over the bay and the little beach just ahead. "Granted, things aren't exactly brand new. But this view! I could plop right down here and not move for the whole week, I swear."

"Not just yet, sweetie," Kit said to her, putting her arms around her from behind. "But I agree, it's great."

"I know, I know. Gotta get the stuff in," Sabi said with a resigned sigh. Then she brightened. "But first I want to see our room. I bet it's adorable!"

Claire walked up to them with her second load as they were turning around to go to the room. "Looks like I made it here just in time," Claire said under her breath to Rita.

The four of them walked over to Mercury, Kit and Sabi's room, which fronted onto the deck a couple of doors back from where they'd been standing.

"We had your room the first year we were here. You can actually hear the waves lapping the shore when the tide's up at night," Claire said.

Sabi broke into a smile and squeezed Kit's hand.

Kit put her load down and fished the key out of her pocket. The door opened with a creak.

"No sneaking in late for you!" Claire teased, nudging Kit.

Claire and Rita crowded in quickly behind their friends and waited for the reaction. For a minute neither of them said a word. Then Kit started to grin while Sabi's face slowly collapsed into a look of combined astonishment, disbelief, and apprehension. Shock might be more apt. The room itself was *just* big enough to contain its contents. Immediately beyond the swing of the door was a round "table" made of the heavily shellacked wood top of an ancient cable spool suspended from the ceiling by a thick ship's rope, with two director's chairs on either side of it. Maybe a foot or two to the right of it was the end of a double bed, covered with a white chenille spread (minus a few nubs), that extended to the back wall. Above it hung another version of a ship's lantern, containing what looked like a red light bulb. Immediately to their right at the foot of the bed was a chest of drawers that had been painted a sort of sky blue and then decoupaged with old cruise ship brochures. A lamp with a faded lampshade sporting flying seagulls sat on top of it. Beyond the hanging table was what one might call a *junior* refrigerator, a two-burner stove that abutted a tiny sink and an equally tiny counter. The walls were planking, painted a faded bluish gray and decorated with a veritable armada of pictures of ships and schooners as well as a large wooden whale overlooking the bed. The wooden floor had been painted *many* coats of battleship gray and was dotted with mismatched scatter rugs.

"Well. It's . . . certainly . . . nautical, isn't it?" Sabi finally offered. "And it does have character. Definite character."

By now it was all Rita and Claire could do to keep from dissolving in laughter. Claire cleared her throat and swallowed the impulse as she strolled, as best one could, around the room. "We loved this room when we had it. It's so cozy and warm and . . . well, you're right—nautical!"

"Oh, I'm sure we will, too," she replied a little too quickly, realizing how she looked and flashing a quick less-than-convincing smile. "Right, honey?"

"Oh, babe," Kit said as she hugged her, "yes we will. I know you're more the Hilton type, but I think the girls are right. This is the kind of place you tell stories about later—not those places with the little fancy soaps and dumb bottles of complimentary shampoo."

Sabi looked at her with genuine horror. "Oh, my God. The bathroom. Don't tell me it's like the rest of this place. Are you serious? I can deal with no—oh, my God. There's no TV!" She scanned the room quickly. "And no phone! Where the hell have you brought me?" She dropped her makeup bag and ran to the only area *left* for a bathroom and opened the door. Again, she said nothing. The bathroom consisted of a metal shower stall—white canvas curtain, no glass door—a towel rack with two rather thin-looking, clean white towels hanging over the bar, a john, tiny sink and vanity with a metal medicine cabinet hung a bit askew over it.

They all waited out in the room for Sabi to rejoin them—or at least to *say* something. Suddenly they heard guffaws coming out of the bathroom. Kit frowned in puzzlement and shrugged her shoulders, walking toward the bathroom. Sabi came stumbling out, doubled over in laughter.

"What's so funny?" Kit asked her.

Sabi couldn't speak she was laughing so hard. "I was gonna bring *candles* to put around the tub for our romantic baths together!" she sputtered. "With the scented bath gel I was going to find sitting right beside my complimentary hand cream!" She gasped for breath and held out her hand. "Somehow these shitty little Ivory soaps that look like they're a hundred years old and that'll maybe last for one shower just aren't the same!" She collapsed on the bed, and was greeted by the loud squeaking of springs. She was engulfed by another paroxysm of laughter and sat up, wiping tears from her eyes from laughing so hard—which by this time was the case with all of them. "Oh, that makes it complete! Squeaky bed, no tub, and how the fuck are you supposed to eat on a table that swings?" She cackled again and then paused a minute and got up off the bed. "Tell me there's at least a closet."

"Uh, you passed it on your way out of the bathroom," Claire said, trying in vain to stifle another outbreak of laughter.

"No fucking way." Sabi was hooting again before she even got to the louvered doors across from the bathroom door. She opened one, which sagged a bit from the missing hinge on the top, and peered in at four lonely hangers on the three-foot bar. "Yep. We got a closet all right!"

"You should have seen *me* when I saw the 'kitchen'!" Rita choked out between laughs. "All those romantic dinners *I* had planned that year! Right! At least upstairs in Jupiter I can actually cook two things at once!"

"And you . . . my *friend*—*!* I can't believe you didn't prepare me for this! Letting me go on and on about cable TV and baths." Sabi stopped and thought a minute. "I did at least see an outlet in there for my hair dryer, didn't I?"

Rita shook her head yes, now unable to talk herself. When the two of them dissolved again, Kit and Claire looked at each other, nodded and headed back to the cars to retrieve the rest of the week's supplies. As they walked out the door, they heard Sabi say, "I don't believe this. No wonder you guys didn't go into detail about the actual *rooms*. I mean, *look* at this place! Hilton? Are you kidding me?" She tried to get her breath. "Oh, my God. Stories? Oh yeah, we're gonna have stories!"

CHAPTER
3

Stories . . . that was maybe the *only* element missing from this already close-knit foursome. Which made it all the more surprising that they'd become so close in the few short months they'd known each other; something unique and imperceptible and profound had happened *without* the benefit of much in the way of the embellished tales and experiences lived through together that it normally takes to make genuine friends out of two couples. Individuals can "click" for any number of reasons, though that's rare enough; for *four* individuals to forge the kind of friendship that existed between these women, individually and collectively, it usually takes a trickier, more delicate, time-proven formula. But from the beginning, the sense of inevitability about their quartet and the immediate trust and comfort between them all, as though they'd known each other for years, had the smack of kismet about it. It had taken them all rather by surprise.

It wasn't long after Claire started temping at White Ryerson Advertising that she noticed Kit. Having been "out" since college, Claire had a practiced eye for noticing the stray lesbian that crossed her path—and when Kit came striding down the aisle beside Claire's cubicle, looking noticeably uncomfortable in her stockings, business suit, and *reasonably* "sensible" pumps, Claire had smiled to herself. This was clearly a woman who was much more at home in a tee shirt, jeans, and sneakers. It wasn't that Kit was particularly dykey or mannish; *boy*-ish was more the descriptor Claire would have used. Especially that heavy, leggy stride that was so incongruous with her five-five-ish, lean frame; like a ten-year-old boy who's trying to walk like the big guys. Even her hair had a boyish quality: a decided brown but with a stray light-blondish tress here and there born of lots of time spent outdoors in the summer sun. A couple of cowlicks that clearly refused to be tamed regardless of the cut—which was a short, neat one that complemented her natural wave—completed the boyish impression. Later, Claire learned that it was only with the help of Kit's ubiquitous baseball caps—of every conceivable color, style, and team affiliation—that those rebel locks of hair could be contained. Or so she said.

At the office, though, all these elements were well hidden from the casual eye by her impeccably professional demeanor. Her colleagues clearly considered her capable, solid, and no-nonsense—that is, until it was cocktail hour. Then that impish, Little League quality could hardly be contained. She was the first with the latest joke, her eyes practically disappearing as her face crinkled into a smile in anticipation of the punch line. Her youthful handsomeness glowed as she became engrossed in sports talk—especially any that involved either North Carolina State or UNC, both of which she'd attended—and got just a little too loud and a little too boisterous, thanks, in part, to the beers. But even then, it was perceived as the understandable letting-her-hair-down of a team player—if they'd only known what team!

That Kit and Claire had hit it off really wasn't so surprising. The first time Kit invited Claire to join the regulars for happy hour, they'd spent hours debating politics. Then they'd somehow stumbled onto a discussion of Star Trek, a mutual passion they shared. And then there were those oblique and careful references to their respective "friends"—a specific, female friend in each case. Claire knew what *she* knew; she just didn't know if *Kit* knew.

Shortly after their first lunch together, Claire had come home and told Rita about the woman she'd met a couple of cubicles away.

"I'm telling you she's *gay*," Claire had insisted as Rita rolled her eyes and continued frying chicken cutlets.

"Uh-huh. *Everybody's* gay according to you."

"Well, I was right about *you*, wasn't I?" Claire said into Rita's neck as she put her arms around her waist from behind and nuzzled her. "And how crazy was *that*, according to everyone I knew? Right, a nice Italian lady—an older woman, no less!—with three kids and an ex-

Marine husband. Showed them." She moved her arms up from Rita's waist and lightly cupped her breasts. "Mmmm . . . glad I did, too."

"Hey, stop that!" Rita shivered a bit at Claire's touch. "Rick'll be bringing the kids home any minute."

"Alright, alright!" Claire chuckled, kissed Rita on the cheek, and leaned back on the counter. "But I'm telling you, Kit's gay. And I *do* know these things—I have very finely tuned 'gaydar,' I'll have you know. Besides, she's got the walk, the stance, the not-really-masculine-but-in-control kind of attitude, dresses in that tailored-clean-lines way, and never wears any make-up—not that she has to. I swear to God, she barely looks twenty-one, let alone twenty-nine. And she's got amazingly blue eyes. Nice-looking kid. Oh—*and* she's got this picture on her desk of a hot little chick in a slinky red dress, with this 'come hither' look. Definitely the Latin type. I'm thinking it's not her sister."

"I'm just telling you, you better watch yourself. Someday you're gonna be wrong and get yourself in trouble. Besides, you're new there, and what if this is someplace you want to stay? That'd be a great way to start, saying something stupid to some young girl there who may have no idea what you're talking about. That'd be a great first impression."

"Relax. First of all, I doubt very highly I'll stay there. Furthermore, trust me, Kit's *not* as naïve as you make her sound. And I have no *intention* of saying anything stupid. We'll just have a drink down in the Village and see where the conversation goes. My God—sometimes I can't believe you've lived in New York all your life. You sound like you're the one from the heartland instead of me!"

"I'm just telling you that not everyone's as open as you are. You don't always have to be the one jumping in with both feet. If you're smart, you'll take my advice."

Of course, Claire didn't.

The drink went well; actually, the *many* drinks went pretty much as Claire had expected. As the night wore on, the story came out, Kit showed Claire pictures of her partner Sabi and told her how great it was to finally have someone to talk to about the woman who was the love of her life, and how did Claire and Rita deal with all the hassles, and what about Claire's parents—did they know—and. . . . It was a *long* evening. But by the time they left, the seeds of a friendship had taken root. For Rita and Sabi, a little more weeding, tilling, and copious amounts of verbal fertilizing were required to prepare those "fields" for the same "seeds."

Rather like Rita, Sabi also had been skeptical about Kit's recent "coming out" event and resultant friendship with Claire. And the whole idea of *her* becoming a part of the equation didn't sit particularly well. Besides, she had her doubts about this newfound friend that Kit kept talking about and insisting Sabi had to meet, regardless of her supposedly equally "involved" status.

"I told you when we first got together, I'm only interested in being with you—not in getting involved with a bunch of bra-burning, protesting, crotch-scratching, motorcycle-riding *lesbians*. We both *have* friends and, God knows, plenty of relatives between us. Things are fine as they are."

"Wow. Where the hell'd all *that* come from? Who said anything about crotches or motorcycles or bras, for that matter? I think all *I* mentioned was a drink and maybe dinner with two women who have been together for years and might be worth talking to since we were both pretty clueless when we got into this. And as for friends, you know as well as I do that they're either bullshit acquaintances from work or people we haven't had much to do with since our lifestyles *changed*. Which means *we* don't have any friends. And, they might actually be fun—heaven forfend!"

"Well . . . I don't know what there is to find out. I love you, you love me, and that's all that's necessary as far as I can see. Besides, I know what I've heard; and that's that lesbians—I still don't like that word—are always screwing around with each other *and* each other's lovers and I certainly don't need that kind of shit. And how do you know that this 'Claire' isn't interested in you, anyway? I mean, she took you to a *gay* bar. And God knows you came home drunk enough—you probably don't know what the fuck she even said to you!"

"Jesus Christ! I don't believe you. Trust me when I tell you Claire is not the least bit interested in me. She's *with* someone. And we're definitely two of a kind, if you know what I mean. *You,* maybe . . ." A mixture of annoyance and panic flashed across Sabi's eyes as she glared at Kit. "Just kidding. You have no idea how ludicrous you sound, because you HAVEN'T MET THEM. That's the point. If you don't like them, that'll be that."

"Fine. I'll go."

"I gotta tell you, from the way Claire describes Rita, I think you'll like her."

"Right."

Of course, she did.

The four of them rendezvoused at Broadway Baby, the same bar where Claire and Kit had had their talk, the two of them having decided that they'd better stick with the good vibes that had marked their meeting. Claire and Rita got there first and waited for the girls. And went through their *own* version of the Sabi/Kit conversation.

"It just amazes me how you never know how or when you're going to run into people who could end up being major parts of your life," Claire mused, smiling in a pensive sort of way. "I mean, think of who I know—half of 'em I met in job situations where it would have been just as easy, and likely, *not* to have met them. Of course, there were other settings, too; which *maybe* we should just leave alone." Claire grinned and gave Rita a sidelong look as she took a drink of her bourbon and Seven. "I don't know . . . it's just neat how often you 'happen' to run into the right people."

"And I suppose Kit and . . . what's her 'friend's' name again?" Rita asked.

"Sabi."

"Right. Sabi. What kind of name is *that?* What is she . . . Puerto Rican or something?"

"Rita . . ."

"As I was saying, I suppose you can somehow just *tell* that these two virtual strangers are 'the right people.' "

"I dunno. I just automatically felt comfortable with Kit, and she's great fun to be around. And since she and I both come with 'wives,' it seemed a reasonably good idea for the two of you to meet."

"Claire, all these years I've accepted the *entourage* you seem to need to have around you. I get along with everyone, and I genuinely do *like* everyone. But you know that's not my thing. I just don't need friends like you do. Now it's a special *couple* we have to meet. A couple that's younger than *you* for, God's sake. What in the world do you think I have in common with kids who aren't even thirty? Forgive me if I feel like I'm being set up here. It was one thing meeting your 'group' and whoever they were with at parties or when everyone got together for drinks or whatever naturally came up. It wasn't this kind of big deal. Like I *have* to like them."

"Oh, for Christ's sake. This is hardly a big deal. We're having a *drink*. You were coming into the city anyway. Just relax and try to be friendly. I know it's a stretch. And keep the Brooklyn biases in check. Okay?"

"That's not fair, and you know it." Rita picked up her seltzer sheepishly and took a sip. "Of course, I'll be friendly—and polite. Just don't expect much else."

About that time the door swung open and let in a welcome rush of warm spring air that momentarily cleared the smoky cloud around the bar. Along with it came the street sounds of the Village—cars passing, people laughing and talking, the rhythmic clinking of a dog's leash—that clashed momentarily with the show tunes playing inside. Two young women walked into the bar.

Claire squinted against the glare of the sudden sunlight. "Hey, you made it!"

Rita looked up, exerting a conscious effort to maintain a bland, neutral expression. It was wasted energy. The two women were about the same height, but that's where the similarities ended. Though Sabi was objectively the more striking of the two—with her dark ethnic beauty, manicured, coifed, rouged, mascaraed, and dressed within an inch of her life—it was Kit that Rita noticed first. Even with that determined stride, there was a spring to her step and a sense of life, energy, and confidence she fairly exuded. And despite the almost cognitive dissonance between the "business drag" she sported and her very evident and contradictory persona, such that one was inclined to chuckle, the impression she made wasn't at all comical or funny. Rita shocked herself thinking what a cutie she was. When she glanced over at Sabi, she thought she glimpsed a hint of something resembling fear beneath the glamour. But, above all, she was struck by what a fitting and handsome couple they made.

Despite herself, she found herself smiling—and looking forward to their joining them.

"You didn't think we'd stand you up, did'ja?" Kit replied.

"Hell, no. Figured you were just timing it so the beers'd be cold!"

Kit and Sabi perched on stools around the curve of the bar next to Claire and Rita as the bartender strolled over to them. "What'll it be, ladies?"

"Ah, yes. First things first," said Kit. "I'll have a Lite. Sabi?"

"Ummm, a Cape Codder, I guess."

"Miller Lite okay for you?" he asked Kit.

"Sure. Just so it's cold and wet and beer."

As the bartender headed for the cooler, Kit swung around a bit to face the other couple. "Well. The 'other halves' finally meet! Sabi—short for Isabella—Ramirez, this is Claire Griffith and . . ."

"This is Rita—Rita Campanella," Claire offered, jumping in to pick up her side of the introductions. "And, as you might have guessed, this is Kit Summers," Claire said to Rita. Sabi and Rita both leaned across their respective partners and shook hands, polite little smiles plastered on their faces.

"You didn't have any trouble finding this place again, did you?" Claire continued.

"Nah. Not really. Though things look a little different down here in the daylight. And, given the shape I was in the last time I was here, I did wonder a couple of times if I was headed in the right direction. But when it comes to me and bars, a sort of sixth sense kicks in!" Kit said with a smile.

"Half the time I think that's the *only* sense that kicks in with you and bars," Sabi shot back as the bartender put their drinks in front of them.

"Oooo. *Good* one. So, is this how you know the honeymoon's over?" Kit asked Claire.

"Oh, I don't know," Rita chimed in. "As I recall, this one almost blew the *courtship* when she used to call me from Ohio half loaded. Slurred speech is *so* romantic."

"Hey! I think I like you already!" Sabi grinned slyly as she reached over the bar to shake Rita's hand again for emphasis. "So, do you get the 11:30 phone calls from the station, where they're speak-ing-so-dis-tinct-ly that you *know* they're plowed, and the big excuse is, 'But honey, we were talking and having a couple of drinks and I just didn't realize what time it was!'? Yeah. Go jerk somebody else off will ya'?" she said with a dismissive wave of her elegantly manicured hand.

Rita smiled broadly this time. She didn't know what she'd expected Sabi to be like or how to interpret the fear she'd thought she'd seen. But whatever it was, it wasn't this. Rita had rather gotten used to being a sort of oddball in Claire's cadre of friends; the one who was more traditionally feminine in everything from general appearance to her willing—and preferred—role as keeper of hearth and home, at least on a daily basis. Claire was the *project* person. She figured it was a generational thing; having just missed being a baby boomer, Rita likewise missed—or had been too busy being a Mom to notice—the whole feminist mindset. And there were all the years she'd played the nice straight wife and mother. But here was a woman some thirteen years younger than she, who, by the look of her, was as comfortable with her lipstick, nail polish, and heels as Rita was. In fact, more so.

Instead of the tailored business suit that Kit and Claire favored, Sabi had fairly sashayed into the bar in a low-cut, clingy, chiffon blouse and tight-fitting print skirt. She was one of those women who knew it when she looked good—it was evident in the way she carried herself and glanced around to see who was noticing. In the style of the day, her very curly black hair probably reached a little below her shoulders when it wasn't teased and sprayed within an inch of its life in a big Jersey-girl do. Even so, unlike the types across the river, she pulled it off with a classy look rather than the gum-snapping, cheap effect. That was likely due to the fact that, while she certainly liked her makeup kit, it was done with a keen eye to enhancing rather than disguising her distinct Hispanic features, a very pleasing mix of Spanish and other contributors to the Puerto Rican ethnic mix. There was a little slant to her brown-black eyes that always seemed alert, missing nothing; high cheekbones; a small, well-shaped nose that perfectly fit her heart-shaped face; and a wide, bright smile enhanced by deep red lipstick. It was a smile that seemed to hover between polite—masking a certain dark look of combined distrust, skepticism, and boredom—and uninhibited, unguarded amusement and joy. It was the former Rita had sensed earlier. She was definitely glad she was now eliciting the latter.

If there was a key difference between them, it was that while Rita tended to be the silent, less forthcoming observer, Sabi, once she knew you, was definitely not one to hold back what she thought— and it was usually well peppered with all the New York slang and pro- fanity that marked true Brooklyn natives.

"I don't know if this was such a good idea after all," Kit moaned in mock anguish to Claire. She turned to Sabi. "Aw, c'mon. I don't do that all the time. You're gonna make poor Rita here think I'm a bad influence on Claire!"

"Me cajo en los pelos de tu madre!"

Rita, uncharacteristically, given her natural reserve, broke up laughing. "Whatever that was, I agree! I'm also beginning to think this was a *very* good idea." She smiled warmly at Sabi. "And as for your being a bad influence, I doubt that. Though, it is pretty scary thinking of the two of them out together."

"Hey—is that a touch of 'Brooklyn' I hear?" Sabi said to Rita. "Whatever" had come out more like "whatevuh," and "idea" like "idee-ur."

"Uh-huh. Born and bred. At least for the most part; we moved to Queens when I was about ten."

"Me, too! Well, not the Queens part. So, where in Brooklyn?" Sabi asked, with that upswing at the end of the sentence that verified her roots.

"You know Knickerbocker Avenue? Or Starr Street?"

"Do I *know* them? Of course, I know them! We used to get all our bread there, though I was raised in Williamsburg."

"So, how'd you know about the bakeries over there?"

"Hey, smart Puerto Ricans paid attention to their Guido neigh- bors—especially when it came to food. I was raised with a neighbor- hood full of Italians, Jews, and Puerto Ricans." Sabi stopped and smiled to herself. "Gee, I haven't thought about that in years."

"Well, it can't be very many years. You're a baby."

"Oh, for God's sake, I'll be thirty my next birthday."

"Sabi, your birthday was just three months ago," Kit said.

"So, am I wrong? Will I be thirty my next birthday?" she said, glaring at Kit.

"And I'll be forty-two this summer. Trust me, you're a baby."

"And what does all this have to do with Brooklyn? So, when's the last time you were in the old neighborhood? Can you just *die* thinking about that bread? We used to get it and bring it home when it was still hot."

"But it's got to be the semolina bread with the seeds."

"What else?"

And that was that. A lock. A done deal. A night that went on *much* later than any of them had planned, and inaugurated something new and unexpected for them all: a friendship where the whole truly was as valued and important as, and, indeed, sometimes greater, than the sum of the parts. Not the usual situation of two friends dragging their spouses into an expected, social foursome. Four friends. There would be the misunderstandings, disagreements, clashes of expectations and the like that naturally occur between people who care deeply about one another. For the moment, however, it was more than enough to sense—to be certain—that there was just something *there,* woven through and linking the very hearts of all of them. And they felt it embrace them that night. The stories would come.

CHAPTER

4

Once they got past the room trauma, Kit and Sabi were as wide-eyed and wowed at all the town had to offer as Rita and Claire had been their first time. The rest of Saturday and most of Sunday had been devoted to introducing the two novices to what was on tap for the rest of the week. They'd checked out the little beach on the bay (one of the *only* luxuries of staying at Stella's) and met one of the other couples staying there; did an initial reconnaissance of the vast shopping opportunities, including a far too marvelous jewelry shop that catered to the gay clientele; took a romantic sunset dune trip; and had their first cookout—grilling down in the sand and *not* on the deck, per Stella's rules—as well as dinner at one of Claire and Rita's favorite restaurants. By Monday, they'd decided that it was time for a little of the *relaxing* part of the vacation. A phone call from a friend of a friend of Claire's sealed their plans for Monday: a day of sunning in lounge chairs and sipping cocktails poolside on the deck at Provincetown's premiere gay resort hotel, The Boatslip. Just what the doctor ordered.

The day was perfect—eighty-five degrees, cerulean skies, beautiful bodies in Speedos (male *and* female). And *this* pool was an appropriate temperature, for a change. Plus there was an added bonus to spending the day at The Boatslip: the nominal lounge rental fee (and having purchased pina coladas all day!) entitled you to stay and enjoy afternoon tea dance, *sans* cover charge. An ideal way to spend an afternoon.

By two-ish, the sun had them all feeling a bit on the crispy side, so the girls packed up their respective summer reading and migrated to the umbrella-shaded tables next to the pool where Jimmy Shea, the friend of the friend, had said he'd meet them. No sooner had they claimed a table, ordered a round of drinks, and settled in for an even more intense round of people watching, than they noticed someone approaching their table.

Claire smiled. Jack's description of Jimmy left no doubt as to who it was. Jimmy looked to be in his late fifties, with gray, close-cropped hair and a round, open, still-boyishly handsome face. Though his girth was a bit more ample than that of the young actor Jack had described knowing years before, he still had a theatrical flair that marked his walk and general demeanor.

"Well, since this is the only table of attractive ladies—the *bona fide* kind, that is—I feel reasonably certain that one of you must be Claire!" quipped the new arrival.

"And I am *absolutely* certain you must be Jimmy!" Claire retorted, standing and offering him her hand.

He stopped dramatically, hands on hips, and leered at her with mock menace. "Why? What has that evil Jack told you?"

"Only the most glowing things," she said with a smile and a little deferential nod. "Among which was that a cocktail and news from the Big Apple, and you'd be putty in our hands."

"I do so hate him. He knows me too well," Jimmy said with a little pout as he pulled over a chair from the adjoining table. "But he's right. Where's a damn pool boy when you need one?"

Claire made introductions, and Jimmy was off and running. Within fifteen minutes, the conversation had touched on a dizzying range of topics, from politics and theatre to local restaurants and who should and shouldn't be wearing those Speedos. As Jimmy launched into yet another monologue, Claire spied their waiter.

"Excuse me. 'Tom,' isn't it?"

An absolutely astounding looking young man stopped short and trotted backwards to their table.

Jimmy looked up. "Oh *yes,*" Jimmy said, looking up at Tom with a slightly raised eyebrow. "That would definitely be Tom—'Tom the Tease,' as I like to call him. How are you, gorgeous?" Jimmy said, batting his eyelashes.

Tom rolled his eyes. "How'd you nice ladies end up with *this* old queen?" He smiled at Jimmy.

"Why, Thomas. You cut me to the quick," Jimmy said, hand held to his chest.

"Pay no attention to him," Tom said. "If I've told him once, I've told him a thousand times, his many charms are wasted on me. The truth is," he looked down sheepishly, "I'm straight."

Dramatic gasps around the table.

"No!" said Claire. "Then it's true—you all *are* taking over P-Town! Straight waiters at The Boatslip?"

"Have no fear. I'm the only one. It's not easy," he sighed with feigned melancholy. "And I don't tell just *everyone,* mind you. You guys don't have the monopoly on closets, you know." He winked and flashed them a dazzling smile as he walked to the bar for Jimmy's drink.

They all laughed, and Jimmy returned his attention to the women. "He's a good kid. But he's just so damned *pretty!* Someone's got to give him a hard time—as it were! And I've accepted the responsibility. That, and making sure none of these tacky faggots around here really *do* give him a hard time. I may not have much of a right hook, but I can kick and claw with the best of 'em!"

Tom returned in short order, and Jimmy took a sip of his drink. "So. Since I've managed to dominate the conversation since I sat down, tell me how your week's going so far."

Claire and Kit took turns recounting the story of the fraught trip up, and then both paused and looked at one another when they got to their arrival at Stella's.

"Oooh! That's right—I forgot you were staying at Stella's. First time?" he said with a slight smile.

"Not for us," Claire said, looking over at Rita. "But the whole P-Town thing, including Stella's, is a first for our friends here."

"And?" Jimmy said looking over at Kit and Sabi.

Sabi beat them to the punch.

"I gotta tell you, when I looked up and saw Stella standing on that balcony in her little man's blazer and *trousers,* I was already starting to wonder what was up with the place. But then I see *these* two," Sabi crooked her head and nodded sideways at Claire and Rita, "grinning like Cheshire cats as they walk us to our 'apartment.' " She paused as she took a deep drag on her cigarette and a sip of her Key West

Lemonade. "You don't know me," she said, leaning in and looking earnestly at Jimmy, "but trust me when I tell you that I am *not* your rustic type." She waggled her perfectly manicured nails at Jimmy. "My idea of 'roughing it' is no heat lamp in the bathroom of my nice, air-conditioned hotel room." Jimmy chuckled and leaned back in the deck chair to get out of the sun. "So, I'm walking along making an ass out of myself talking about how I love those little scented *soaps,* taking a nice hot *bath,* maybe relaxing with some *TV* before we go down to the beach—and these bastards don't tell me a thing!" Now everyone was laughing while Sabi took another sip and a puff. "And then I walk into this . . . *place.* I nearly died! I tried not to look so shocked—they *did* keep telling us this place had a lot of *character,*" she leaned on the word as she looked over again at Claire and Rita and stuck her tongue out at them. " 'Character'? To me, that means one of those places where they think a room stuffed with mismatched antiques is chic!"

Jimmy was hooting. "Oh, that's rich. You really had no clue about *lovely* Stella's Seaside? Come on . . ."

"Are you kidding? I sure as hell didn't think my room would be this dark little closet done in elegant . . . *planking,* I guess you'd call it, that looks like it was part of the goddamned Mayflower! And then I look around at the tasteful décor—that ancient ship's lamp with the *lovely* red light bulb hanging over the bed and some sort of bizarre table strung up on ropes that I can't imagine we can actually manage to eat on without our food flying off onto the bed! Hell, you can sit on the *bed* and eat at the damned thing." She paused. "Hmmm . . . now that I think about it, maybe it's not for *that* kind of eating after all—!" She winked at Kit, then whipped back around. "Because *regular* eating presumes you could cook on that oversized hotplate she calls a stove!" Another puff and sip. "My favorite, though, is the bathroom—remember the bit about the perfumed soaps? Perfumed, hell! I'd kill for a nice, big bar of Ivory instead of those cheesy little domino-size bars you could loose in the crack of your ass!" Everyone was rolling.

"Aw, c'mon, Sabi. It's not *that* bad. Remember . . . all those stories we're gonna have to tell in our old age?" Kit replied with a big grin.

"You betchur' ass—the first one will be about how I hitchhiked the hell outta here." She smiled slyly as Kit put her arms around her and gave her a kiss on the cheek.

"Aw, you wouldn't desert me on our first real vacation together?"

"Well . . . I guess not. But I better not hear one word out of you when I start shopping. It's the *least* you can do to make it up to me."

"Oh, here we go!" Kit sighed in mock exasperation.

"Well, I must admit, Stella's is hardly the Waldorf," Jimmy added, "but, dear, you *are* staying at one of P-Town's best-loved little dyke hideaways. And, you must admit, it does have its charms." Sabi sighed and rolled her eyes. "Besides, you're in *P-Town,* darlings!"

"Yes," Sabi sighed as she closed her eyes and reclined as best she could in the upright chair to catch the waning rays of the sun, "we *are* in P-Town. And for that, I suppose I can put up with Stella's stupid ship's bell clanging to call that poor kid who's her slave for the week, and towels you can practically see through, and her nine million rules. Actually, I'm getting to like that dumb red light—it's kinda sexy," she said as she squeezed Kit's knee.

"I have to say," Jimmy said, "we've all been taking bets for *years* on when that whole damn place is going to go crashing into the sea. She's tighter than a new shoe! It just kills that woman to spend one damn dime she absolutely doesn't have to."

"Well, I'm just glad she still even bothers to run the place. She's no kid. Anyway, *I* love the old place, especially *because* it has a few warts. Even so, it's close to everything on Commercial Street and has its own little beach on the bay. And, even if the stoves are a *tad* on the modest side, we can cook and not have to spend a zillion dollars on dinners if we don't want to," said Claire.

"All I know is that for all we went through and as much as they talked about this place, I was expecting more. Not, as I say, that it's not growing on me, too. But, man . . ." Sabi lit a cigarette and looked at Jimmy with a raised eyebrow. "Do you know they practically made us *audition* to come here??"

"Oh, God. I know where *this* is going," Claire intoned conspiratorially to Jimmy. "These Latina types are *so* dramatic."

"Hey, little blonde Anglo girl! You don't want to piss this little Puerto Rican off! Besides, it's a good story."

All four of them chuckled. "I'm gonna need another drink for this one," Kit said. "See if you can get Tom's attention the next time he struts by."

"Will do," Claire said. "I'm about ready, too."

"I'm sure you are," Rita replied with a bored but edgy tone.

"Shhh. Let Sabi tell her story."

"Actually, you tell it better, Claire. Go ahead. I want to make sure my honey's not enjoying the 'sights' around here too much," Sabi said as she put her arm around Kit and looked around to see if there were any bikinis doing too much wiggling within Kit's view.

"Okay. Get me a Corona if you see him, Kit." Kit nodded. "One of the nights we were all out, we heard some women talking about New Hope, Pennsylvania, which, it turns out, is a very gay little town not far from New York. On the Delaware River, lots of nifty shops, gay dance clubs, bars—sounded ideal for a weekend. So, Rita and I had already booked our week here, and had heard another friend mention that Stella might be having a cancellation. And we immediately thought of the girls here. But before we committed ourselves to a whole week with the little Latin spitfire over there and her *wonderful* friend—" she smiled solicitously at Kit, who smiled back.

"Hey! Don't talk about my *friend* like that!" Rita shot back as she put her arm around Sabi, who smirked and nodded at Claire.

"As I was saying, before we *doomed* this burgeoning friendship—a week can be a *very* long time with the wrong people—Rita and I decided a little 'test run' wouldn't be a bad idea."

"Yeah. We had to 'pass muster' to qualify for *P-Town,*" Kit said dramatically, but with a knowing smile.

"Sounds like a good idea to me," Jimmy said. "Dear God—I can't imagine spending much more than dinner and cocktails with more than one person . . . and at least one of them better have a helluva cute ass if he thinks he's gonna 'rack' up overtime with me, as it were!"

"Anyway, we suggest the weekend, they agree, and we're off. The drive down was great, we're laughing and goofin', and having your basic 'road trip' good time. So, we get to the motel where we'd booked the room."

" 'The' room? Jesus, you *shared* a room??" Jimmy asked in horror.

"We had to—we found out as soon as we started calling around that we weren't the only gay folk in the area who head to New Hope for a summer weekend. So, this really would be the ultimate test of compatibility!

"I think we all were a little nervous. We'd been to their house a time or two, but had never done the concentrated-time-together bit before."

"It really was strange," Kit added. "It was like we were getting to know each other all over again."

"Really. We were all trying to make a good impression. So, Kit, unbeknownst to us, had brought champagne—which she proceeded to drop on the concrete steps as we're walking up to our rooms. Of course, the Moët was the bottle that ended up shattered!"

"Aw, swe-e-tie," Jimmy said in feigned dismay. "Not the good stuff!"

"No problem—she had another bottle. Sadly, *not* Moët. But the tension broke along with the bubbly, thank God. And then we had a whole *new* bonding moment cleaning up the mess it made on the steps.

"We get ourselves settled and decide to take to take a nice, relaxing dip in the hotel's big, beautiful pool—remember how hot it got all of a sudden in June? Well, that's when we were there. It was an absolute sauna when we got there, and we were totally wilted. So, down we go, claim a couple of chairs, and head for the pool . . ."

". . . and dive into frigging soup!" Kit interjected between sputtering laughs. "That's what it felt like. I swear to God, that pool had to be a hundred and ten degrees. It was hotter than we were! Gross."

Rita's shoulders started to shake with silent laughter.

"Stop that!" Sabi half laughed, half whimpered. "I should've gone to the bathroom before she started telling this. You know what happens to me when I get laughing!"

"Aw, jeesh. Didn't we have enough of that comin' up here?" Claire groaned.

Sabi burst out in laughter as she realized Rita still couldn't talk. "Stop that!"

"I can't help it," Rita gasped, trying to catch her breath. "It's just thinking about the look on your face—going down that ladder, bitching and complaining about how hot you were, prepared for that first little shiver, and then plopped your little—butt—in—that—water!" Rita was dissolved again.

"Yeah? Well, that wasn't half as funny as those two show-offs down by the *deep* end, *diving* in like pros and coming up with those idiotic looks on their faces!" Sabi's guffaws turned into something resembling a cackle and set everyone off again.

"But it was worth it," said Claire, as she, too, got her breath. "Talk about a great weekend. Kit singing her own inimitable version of 'Red, Red Wine,' dancing, great food, teaching you guys how to play Euchre—good stuff." Claire took a drink of her newly arrived beer. "Needless to say, they passed with flying colors."

" 'Passed,' huh?" Sabi shot back slyly. "You guys don't think you were the only ones doing some 'testing,' do you? After that, *we* decided we'd keep *you* as friends!"

"Tou-ché, girl" said Jimmy.

"And here you all are, soaking up the sun and the booze and having a *fabulous* time at the lovely Boatslip, thanks to your competent and caring waiter." Claire looked up, shielding her eyes from the sun, and smiled at Tom.

"Surely someone as gorgeous as you doesn't need to boost his own ego!"

"No, not really, but it sounded good, huh?" Tom flashed a smile that definitely went with the whole beautiful package.

"Like I said before, he wouldn't have to if he'd give us *boys* a chance," Jimmy said with a little pout.

"Now, Jimmy. We just have to accept that Tom is one of those misguided," Claire cupped her hand by her mouth and her eyes darted back and forth, *"heterosex-x-xuals!* But he's amusing and fun to look at. Which is all that counts out here in public anyway. I think you should try harder to treat him as though he were normal, like *us.*"

"Yeah. What Claire said!" Tom shot back.

"So, you were listening to our war stories?"

"Well, I couldn't really *miss* it going back and forth by the table. Your voice carries, you know." Claire rolled her eyes and nodded. "And that laugh!" He looked at Sabi. "Jesus, they heard that over in

Truro!" He cleaned up the empties that were scattered around the table. "But I have to say, it really is great that you guys are so close. I've seen groups of girls come through here, 'best friends' and all that. But there was practically bloodshed when two of them had their eye on the same chick. And some of them weren't exactly single when that old eye started roving."

"Tom, dear, we don't want to jinx these lovely ladies." Jimmy turned to them. "Pay no attention to this evil boy. Make that evil *straight* boy!"

"Not to worry," Sabi answered. "No 'roving eyes' allowed around here. Well, I guess you can *look*. But that's where it stops. Right, honey?"

"Right, dear."

"I got news for you, Tom—shit like that doesn't just 'happen,'" Claire said. "It *happens* if you come here looking *for* something . . . not just looking. Which, thank God, is not the case with any of us. Besides all this nifty 'best friends' stuff, we've all had a rough few months. So the only things *we're* looking for are nice tans, good meals, and no hassles. Between family shit, work shit, ex-husband shit, you-*name*-it shit, we all need to chill, decompress, and simply 'not deal' for an entire week. That's all we ask. Hell, this is the most conversation we've had outside our little quartet since we got here."

"I feel so honored," sniffed Jimmy, wiping away fake tears.

"Alright. Maybe it does sound melodramatic. But it's true. I think the only other people we've talked to are a couple of women who were out on our little beach when we first got here. Nice enough, but that was sufficient. From here on out, it's the four of us in our little summer cocoon. And we'll stop by and see you boys from time to time."

"You're forgetting one thing, my love," Rita said leaning over toward her.

"What?"

"Our soon-to-arrive visitors? Thanks to you and Kit."

"Oh, hell, they don't get here till Wednesday. And Grant'll be too busy cruising for a new girlfriend to be bothered with us. Anyway, she'll be out at the Holiday Inn, so it's not like she'll actually be 'with' us."

"Did you call her yet about trying to hook up with Diane and take the ferry over together?" Sabi asked.

"No. I was gonna do that on our way back. Why?"

"Well, now that you mention the Holiday Inn bit, maybe you could ask her if her friend the manager could get Diane a room there. Then we don't have to fart around with all that when she gets here."

"Good idea," Kit added. "I can't wait to see her, but I hope she's got as much work to do as she said. She can perch by the pool at the motel and work her little heart out. Claire's right—I definitely need to veg out."

"Well, you didn't *have* to ask her to come out, you know. Just because she was in Boston didn't mean you had to play hostess while we're on vacation," Sabi said.

"Oh, please. Why do you think Claire's friend Grant's coming out? Because she just can't resist playing social director," Rita added.

"Two little peas in a pod, those two," Sabi said.

"Ah, c'mon," Claire said, looking at Rita. "You know she's been through a tough time. Trust me, it'll be fine."

"Yeah. And I haven't seen Diane in almost three years. It just seemed like the right thing to do."

"For whom?" Sabi asked, with a dead-eyed stare. "Yeah, that's what I thought. One of these days maybe you'll think about what's 'the right thing' for us."

"Oo-oo-oo! What's that I hear? Sounds like classic disco to me!" Kit perked up in her seat, head akimbo with her hand to her ear.

"Nice try, *chica.*" The music had cranked up more than a few notches, and, even in her pique, Sabi couldn't ignore the thumping bass of "It's Raining Men." "Alright. Maybe it is time to shake a little booty."

CHAPTER
5

The dance floor at The Boatslip was packed. While Sunday afternoon tea dance is a long-standing tradition in gay clubs everywhere, in P-Town—in keeping with the prevailing spirit that more isn't just better, it's *fabulous*—*daily* tea was the norm. And The Boatslip was the unrivaled host club. Every day at 3:00, the crowd that had been at The Boatslip since morning, sunning in hundreds of rented beach chairs, sipping cool, sweet cocktails and soothing incipient sunburn in the pool, began to dissipate and was replaced by new arrivals casually strolling in to see and be seen—oh, and to dance. The vast deck was cleared of strap chair lounges, and tanned bodies filled in where the chairs had been. By 4:00, the deck was getting pleasantly crowded and burbling conversation filled the cooling air, while the dance floor was just beginning to be populated by the early, *serious* dancers. Singles and couples leaned on the railing that faced the ocean, staring out in differing poses of feigned nonchalance, hoping to command the attention of the one they were with or capture that of the interesting—and hopefully *interested*—passerby. As the oranging sun slipped further behind the headlands to the west, the music got louder, the drinks went down more smoothly, and the couples—newly linked and long established—started to drift inside to take a place on or around the dance floor.

Kit and Claire finished packing their respective beach bags, all of them having donned tea-appropriate shorts and tees over their dry bathing suits, while Rita and Sabi continued chatting with Jimmy.

"So, you usually make the trek from Boston later in the week?" Sabi asked.

"Yes, but I could tell yesterday it was going to be absolutely *dead* this week. Who the hell wants to go house hunting in hundred-degree weather? And who the hell wants to put *up* with anyone who would? Not this fairy. I'll sell those Beacon Hill babies another day. So, it was out to the Cape for me."

"And I'm so glad you did," Claire said. "I can't tell you how many times Jack told me to be *sure* to look you up when we got here. Of course, per the norm with Jack, he neglected to give me your phone number the last time I saw him, and his damned answering machine was broken when I called. So, thank God, he told you where we'd be." She smiled warmly at the thought of always-a-little-distracted but ever-endearing Jack.

"Oh, honey, he's been like that for the last thirty years."

"Wow. I didn't know you guys knew each other *that* long."

"Oh, yes—since we were sweet young things. Well, *I* was a mere *boy,* while he was the dashing older man. Ah, the days when twenty-seven was an 'older man' . . . dear God, the stories! When we were the toast of New York, St. Maarten, L.A., here—back when being gay was *truly* bohemian. My, oh my, what fun!" Jimmy said as he did the limp wrist bit for emphasis. "But that's for another time. I have *plans* this evening," he said, batting his eyes flirtatiously, "which will require a major toilette. So, let me run, and you girls go have yourselves a wonderful time out there with all those sweaty bodies." He licked his lips and winked.

"Well, I'm so glad we got to meet you," Sabi said as she got up and gave him a big hug. "And despite that whole conversation before, I hope we can get together again before we leave."

"*Absolutment,* my dear. Why don't you all give me a call as your plans for the week shake out, and maybe you can come over to my place or we'll go grab a bite. Speaking of a bite! Patricia, darling! Where the hell have you been, you mean old dyke?" Jimmy exclaimed as he skittered—at least the best he could "skitter" with a girth that belied his rather indulged lifestyle—over to the fence surrounding the pool area.

"Jimmy! You nasty faggot! I haven't seen your face darkening the door of the store lately, so don't give *me* shit!" A woman looking to be in her thirties, with medium length sun-lightened brown hair and a slightly crooked, easy smile that called to mind Jodie Foster, was leaning over the fence hugging Jimmy warmly.

"Ladies, here's someone you absolutely *must* meet. One of the lavender doyennes of town, a veritable Sapphic princess—pun intended, darling—Pat Williams. If you're a fan of lovely baubles—the kind you *wear*—this is the woman to know. Pat's one of the owners of Sapph-ires, P-Town's premiere, yet quite reasonable, *queer* jewelry store."

An introduction wasn't needed. Sabi stiffened a bit and forced a pinched smile. They had already discovered Sapph-ires on one of their first strolls down Commercial Street. Sabi had spied a ruby ring that made her positively drool . . . which is what Pat had nearly done when she'd zeroed in on Kit, who made the inquiry about the ring.

"Pat, meet my new best friends for the week." Jimmy proceeded to make introductions. "They're practically Little Women incarnate, these four—a *very* close-knit bunch. Except in this version, they're 'sisters' of a, shall we say, different kind?"

"I've seen you guys before, haven't I?" Pat asked, frowning a bit in thought, trying to place the women. Then she spotted Kit, who was returning from checking under their beach chairs for any forgotten items. *"Yes.* Now I remember. Hey, blue eyes," Pat said, greeting Kit. "You guys decide about that ring yet?"

"Actually, she was looking at it for *me,"* Sabi retorted, a definite edge to her voice.

"Y-eaahhh, that's what I thought," Pat said, with just the slightest hint of testiness at the accusation implicit in Sabi's decidedly unsubtle claim of female turf. "Just lookin' to keep the merchandise in mind. Never hurts to be nice to the lady doin' the buyin', know what I mean?" She looked at Kit. "That little ruby ring would look nice on her. It'd match those blood red fingernails," she said, giving Sabi a sidelong look. Then her face cleared, as though she'd shrugged off the remainder of a potential exchange between them. "Anyway, it's nice to have names to go with faces I *hope* I'll see in the store again. Really. In fact, you should definitely stop back in. I've got some new pieces that should be on display tomorrow. And, uh, maybe I can give you an even better deal on the ring." She nodded at Kit—and then Sabi. "And you, you pain in the ass," she said giving Jimmy a light punch on the arm. "Surely there's someone you need a little trinket for."

"Check with me after tonight," he responded slyly, eliciting the intended oohs and chuckles around.

Pat disappeared in the crowd, while Jimmy lingered, gathering his things. "My, my, my. Maybe it's different with girls," he said, looking in Kit and Sabi's direction, "but when we boys choose an attractive *amour,* we know damn well that others might agree with our good taste. It's a badge of honor when someone else notices, don't you think? You might want to watch those claws, sweetheart. Save 'em for the real thing. Pat's just your basic natural flirt. Though she has been a bit more forward about it lately since she and her business and 'otherwise' partner broke up. Trust me, she's okay. One of the only people in this town I'd actually trust."

"Well, maybe I'm new to all this, but coming on to my girlfriend before I've even met you—and in my face!—is no way to say hello in my book."

"Would you rather it be behind your back?" Jimmy replied as he slung his tote over his shoulder. Before Sabi could respond, he walked over and gave her a kiss on the cheek. "Tut, tut, tut! That's it for Ann Landers tonight. You all just get on in there and have a gay old time! Later." Jimmy situated his canvas tote on his shoulder, slipped into his flip-flops, and headed for the exit—checking out the smorgasbord of male bodies along the way.

"Well, I don't care what he thinks, I didn't like that shit with boyfriends, and I certainly don't like it now that it actually matters." Sabi crossed her arms and lapsed into a pout.

"C'mon, honey. What matters is what *I* do about it. And nobody here—or anywhere," she added quickly, "can hold a candle to you, sweetie." Kit put her arms around Sabi, arms still crossed, and kissed her in a way that left no doubt as to her unrivaled position. "There. Now can we go dance?"

They all set out for the canopied back deck, the main entrance to the interior of The Boatslip, and sidled their way through the crush of tanned arms and bared thighs to find a place to perch alongside the railing that bordered the dance floor. The music filled every inch of airspace and reverberated off all the glass surrounding them. Not so loud you couldn't talk—at a certain volume—but loud enough that you felt the bass in the pit of your stomach. It entered your head and vibrated through shoulders, hips, and feet that couldn't help but keep time with the irresistible beat. By the time they found a spot to sit their drinks and bags down, their heads were bouncing rhythmically and they were clapping along with the dancers on the floor. People were dancing on the strip of floor behind the railings, some with such abandon that bodily harm—to the *observers*—seemed imminent.

"Oooo!" Sabi squealed over the din. "They're doing another disco song!"

"You know, honey," Kit said with a slightly weary tone, "it's been ten years since *Saturday Night Fever*—1990's not far away. Don't you think it's time to move on already?"

"Let's go!" Sabi shouted to Kit. She grabbed her hand and they inched their way into the mass of bodies, eking out their own two-by-two piece of dance floor. They looked good together, Sabi and Kit. Pint-size Sabi, with her curly, black hair, gleaming smile, and seductive little salsa moves insinuating herself against softly handsome Kit, who had that look that says "She's *mine*," undulating in response against her.

"So?" Claire shouted to Rita, raising her arms and snapping her fingers in time with the music.

"You know I can't dance," Rita shouted back over the music.

"Ah, gee," Claire said back, doing the feigned pout thing. "You don't have to *dance* dance. There's no room! Just move around."

"Maybe later," Rita said, sitting down on the ledge by the wall-sized windows that looked out on the pool.

"Nuh-uh. Come on!" Claire grabbed Rita's hand and literally dragged her up off the ledge. Rita conceded and allowed herself to be led to the dance floor. Between her natural tendency to be more reserved than the others and a self-consciousness about dancing anything other than a nice, predictable Lindy, her dancing was confined to a side-to-side two-step that was designed to be as unobtrusive as possible. But she was a good sport and hung in for two dances.

At the end of the second, Claire smiled and gestured toward the window ledge with her head. Rita willingly took her hand and led them through the crush of bodies back to their spot.

"You're so cute," Claire said, smiling at her and holding her head a minute and looking into her eyes. Then she kissed her and laughed. "Okay. You're off the hook for a while with the dancing. But there's no one I'd rather dance with, you know. Just let me know if you have a change of heart later." Claire leaned on the railing to watch the dancers. Kit and Sabi soon waved to get her attention and flagged her over to where they were dancing. She looked over at Rita, who motioned her to go.

Rita got up and leaned on the railing herself. She'd always preferred watching Claire dance to actually dancing with her. Besides not being much of a dancing fan, she liked the opportunity to simply observe her in a way one usually can't in everyday life, without the observed party wondering *why* she's being watched. Claire was grinning with that little-too-broad smile of hers at Kit and Sabi as they all danced, abandoning herself to the movement and the music. Rita watched Claire's body, thinking of those strong arms holding her at night and her large hands delicately, knowingly touching her in a way that had so totally changed how she thought about lovemaking. It was moments like this that Rita remembered all over again why she'd fallen so in love with Claire.

Altogether too typically, theirs had been an attraction of opposites. Rita, the good, Italian wife, and the tall, blond, blue-eyed Germanic Claire, long-time lesbian. Demure, smiling Rita, the loud, laughing Claire. Cynical New Yorker and liberal Midwesterner. The homebody and the life of the party. Rita, so used to deferring to the domineering males in her life, and Claire, who was sure of herself and confident. Rita, cautious and not so sure about most people, and Claire, trusting and committed to the good in people. And it worked.

It had been an odd reality for Rita to realize how similar Claire was in some ways to her ex, Rick, and yet *not* like him at all. They both thrived on people, were never at a loss for words, loved the spotlight, and were as outgoing and embracing as Rita was reserved. But with Claire, there was a warmth and lack of guile. That hadn't been the case with Rick. In all things, Rick had to be superior and show that he knew more. With Claire, there were certainly areas where Claire really *did* know more and had skills superior to Rita's. But Rita always felt challenged and encouraged and proud . . . even when Claire's ego got a little out of hand. Not embarrassed and lacking like Rick had made her feel.

Rita smiled at the thought of contentedly cooking away in the kitchen, while Claire was out in the midst of guests, choosing just the right music, mixing everyone's favorite cocktails, and recalling a personal story or an article she'd read that would have some bearing on each person's favorite topic. Where Rita was more comfortable keeping her own counsel in the midst of a debate, Claire forged ahead with definite, informed opinions. And if Rita was inclined to quickly judge and dismiss the ill-considered opinion or ludicrous comment—and the person offering it—Claire typically considered the thought and tried to suggest a different perspective that would leave them both feeling more or less justified, though the other party often walked away with knitted brow, still chewing on the implications of Claire's response. Her little social butterfly . . . always bringing home new ideas and thoughts—and often the people that went with them!

In short, life changed from being what happened day after day to something Rita looked forward to every day—*and* every night. That had been a major stumbling block in the beginning as she tried to figure out the unexpected and intense feelings Claire called up in her. It shocked and surprised Rita when she was finally honest enough with herself to admit that there were unmistakably sexual feelings involved; that there was an entirely different level of desire and attraction and arousal going on when she saw or thought of Claire. And yet, because those feelings were so new, so powerful, so unlike the feigned interest and acquiescence that had marked her long marriage to Rick, the prospect of actually acting on them had terrified Rita. But when the moment finally, unmistakably, presented itself, it was Rita who decided to make it happen. She never looked back.

Now, making love was altogether different. Every time she rolled over and kissed Claire hungrily, demanding her attentions and aching for her touch, she was still a little shocked at how much everything about her life had changed. Now it was . . . well, fun. And exciting. And wonderfully unpredictable. Dear God—here she was standing in a gay disco, actually feeling flushed and moist watching her partner dance, sipping her *third* cocktail of the day! Who'd a thunk it, as Claire liked to say.

Claire danced through the crowd to where Kit and Sabi were and joined in the grand mass gyration on the floor. A contented smile filled her face as she closed her eyes and gave in to the music and hypnotic movement of bodies. She opened her eyes and kept smiling, enjoying the sights of the dance floor: the perfectly-muscled, naked chests of the boys who lived to flaunt them, and the pale, doughy, less-than-perfect bodies of guys who were there to see them. Hard-edged butch women in muscle tees and cut-off jean shorts, and the handsome professional types in the exact same outfits but with well-cut hair and a hint of mascara. Flaming queens whose hips and arms moved with a sassy grace, and lipstick lesbians dressed to the nines. Big women whose hip action bordered on the dangerous, and women slender and lithe as gymnasts. It always made Claire happy—and as their sub-cultural slogan enjoined, *proud*—to see the endless variety of people who comprised the gay populace, contrary to what so many outside their ranks still believed. And it made for an even deeper satisfaction to make that observation in a place where all those types and kinds could fully "be" in their own wonderfully unique ways.

The DJ segued artfully into another tune with the same compelling bass line and they kept on, hot and sweaty and energized. Claire loosened up even more, hands clapping above her head, and backed toward a vacant patch of floor just as another woman had the same idea. Claire recovered enough to prevent an outright collision and turned to smile in apology. It was the woman from Stella's— Dara. Claire felt an almost adolescent tingle run through her body, lodging in the pit of her stomach, as well as lower down. They both smiled and nodded in recognition, and then in time with the music . . . and then, in the understood way that happens naturally on the dance floor, just *kept* dancing—with one another. Claire was again struck, as she had been that first afternoon on their private beach behind Stella's, by Dara's refined beauty: bright greenish blue eyes, perfect eyebrows, sun-streaked honey blond hair, a well-defined jaw, and a smile that, because it was not an easy one, was all the more brilliant when it broke through her subdued demeanor. Before Claire had even seen that face, she had noticed the woman lying in a sand chair, slender, nicely proportioned, stretched out in what had struck Claire as a somehow self-assured, almost commanding way, soaking up the late afternoon sun. As their little group staked out a roomy square of sand, Dara had roused and looked over at them from under her hand. She'd greeted them and chatted a bit about what a gorgeous day it was, ultimately introducing herself and the woman with her: she was Dara Winston and the woman lying next to her was Becca Knight. They, too, were veteran renters at Stella's, which explained how they'd managed to score one of the two waterfront rooms just off the deck. As the conversation continued, they learned they were former, long-time partners, who were now good friends that still traveled together. Though that was pretty much the extent of the conversation, Claire had found it hard not to glance over at her whenever an unguarded moment—when neither Dara *nor* Rita would notice—presented itself. They made the usual noises about getting together sometime during the week as they all packed up their beach things at the end of the day. And now here they both were.

Claire regained her composure, hoping her look of recognition hadn't belied her pleasure and excitement at the encounter—again, to either Dara or Rita. God knows, she wasn't in any way looking for anything; but it sure was fun to look and fantasize and flirt just a little. And what a woman to be the object of her mental dalliance! Jesus. She was outstanding.

The music changed again, but this time to something that shifted the dynamic on the floor, and a few people started to drift back to the sides to reclaim drinks and half-smoked cigarettes. As Dara and Claire both stopped dancing, Dara brushed her hair back and took a deep breath.

"Whoo! That was fun!" Dara said, as she wiped the sheen of sweat from above her eyes. "And I guess it's true that sooner or later you run into everybody at tea! So, you girls having a good week so far?"

She was so casual and direct that Claire was torn between feeling embarrassed and disappointed, given her private reverie while they were dancing. And maybe just a little relieved as well.

"Absolutely. How could you not here? What about you guys?" They reached the spot where Claire had left Rita, but only their beach bag and her drink were there. Claire quickly scouted the immediate area but didn't see her. She turned back to Dara.

"Oh, pretty good." Dara scanned the room, her focus lingering at one point, as she nervously peeled away the label on her beer bottle.

"I'm sorry. I didn't mean to keep you," Claire said quickly, realizing that Dara's change in attitude since they left the dance floor might be impatience to get on with whatever, or whomever, had occupied her before.

"Oh, God—no, I'm sorry. That's not it. I apologize. I'm not on my way anywhere at all. I just saw Becca over there, and it put me in a strange mood . . . which I certainly don't want to bore you with."

"Well, actually I'm just sort of hangin' until Rita gets back or our friends collapse from exhaustion out there!" She smiled and nodded her head at Sabi and Kit still going on the dance floor, though a little slower than before. "What's going on? You guys seemed pretty civilized when we met you on the beach."

"We were—and we have been for *years* now. *And* we've been coming here together before and since we broke up, just to relax and get our 'fix' of the atmosphere here to keep us going out in the real world. But this year, I made up my mind it was time I kept my eyes open . . . just to see what's out there. It's been a while, you know?" Claire nodded her understanding, and took a *long* drink of her beer. "And, amazingly, Becca's got a real problem with it. Which sure shocked me. I mean, it's been three years since we broke up, and it's not even like much has *happened* since I've been, well, looking; a conversation here, a drink there. But whenever I see Becca, she's pouting and I feel like a schmuck. Not to mention incredibly frustrated—'cause there are a lot of *very* nice-looking women here this year." She shook her head defeatedly and took a drink of her beer, staring out onto the dance floor.

Claire lit a cigarette, took a deep drag, and shook her head, too. "In a word, that sucks." Dara chuckled wryly and kept staring. "However, it seems to me you can do one of two things. Either continue doing what you're doing—God knows, you have a right to, it sounds like, though you don't seem all that happy. Or there's another option. I'm of the opinion that situations like this are more about the other person's jealousy that you *found* someone else—not that you're *with* someone else. 'Course, the problem is what to do about it. That could be tricky." Claire thought for a minute. "You don't know any of the locals here after all the years you guys have been coming up here?"

"Well, we know a couple of the bartenders at The Pied . . . and a woman who works at the Pilgrim House downstairs." She stopped and mused on what she'd just said, nodding as she let the thought and resultant possibilities settle in.

"There you go!" Claire replied emphatically. "I say you stop by the Pied on your way back tonight—alone—and have a quick cocktail and a conversation with whoever you know there. Bartenders are pros at doing the 'fixing up' thing. Then you and Becca stop in later and see what's what. Even if she only has a conversation or a dance with someone, it could be enough of an ego boost if she's feeling left out."

"Wow. Lucky I bumped into you out there. It's not every day you get a great dance *and* great advice from the same person—and practically at the same time, no less," Dara said, smiling warmly at Claire. "Thanks."

Claire found herself studying Dara's perfectly shaped eyebrows and lips, afraid to look at her eyes. Her mind clicked back into gear. "What can I say? I'm just an incredibly multi-talented woman—and humble!" said Claire, smiling broadly, hoping to inject some levity into the moment. "Just let me know how it turns out."

"Oh, I will," Dara replied, tilting her head slightly to catch Claire's eyes. They could only have been looking at one another for a few seconds when Claire half-heard someone walk up behind her and stop. She quickly shooed away the butterflies in her stomach and re-connected with reality. When she turned around, the previous moment and the rush of sensations that it had provoked were hidden behind a quick smile and feigned surprise. Or so she hoped.

"Hey, babe! *There* you are." Claire put her arm around Rita and turned back to Dara. "You remember . . . Dara, isn't it? One of our fellow residents at Stella's?"

"Yes. Hi. You were on the beach the day we got here, I think." Rita was cordial enough, all smiles. But the probing glance she gave Claire reminded her of the occasional ambivalence she felt about having someone as in tune as Rita for a partner; there were times it was a blessing, then there were times . . .

"We literally stumbled across one another out on the dance floor," Claire explained. "And we were catching up on how our respective weeks were going so far."

"I guess you must be having a good time—or at least an interesting one. You two seemed to be having a pretty in-depth conversation." Rita's enigmatic smile and focus on Dara remained unchanged.

"Actually, it was more illuminating, I guess, than in-depth," Dara responded, totally unfazed. But, then again, Claire thought, what was there to be "fazed" about? It was a conversation, period. "And definitely helpful. Claire was being a 'good neighbor' and trying to help me out with an awkward situation I've found myself in. And I think she has." She smiled a totally benign smile at Claire. "And I think I shouldn't waste any time taking her advice. Thanks," she extended her hand to Claire, who shook it genially. "You really have been a help." She picked up her drink. "You guys have a great evening," she said, and started to move away into the crowd, when she suddenly turned back. "By the way, you eating out or cooking in tonight?"

Claire looked at Rita quizzically and then turned back to Dara. "Well, we haven't decided for sure, but we were talking about getting a bite out tonight."

"If you do, you should try Anna, Anna, Anna. It's back toward the center of town, next to Zeus, across and this way from The Cactus Garden. It's off the street, back along a little path, so you have to look for it. But it's worth it; fabulous Italian food and a great atmosphere. It's my favorite restaurant find this year—so far, anyway," she said with a warm smile.

"Thanks. We'll keep it in mind," Claire responded.

"Great. I'm sure I'll see you guys around," Dara said as she turned and disappeared into the crowd.

Rita stood looking at the dance floor, eyebrows slightly knit, peering at the dancers. "So, where have Sabi and Kit gone to?" she asked nonchalantly.

Claire hated moments like this. Was it best to go along with the change of subject and let the whole Dara conversation slide until Rita brought it up, or address the immediate question and then ease into a conversation about Dara's dilemma so Rita would be less inclined to bring it up later? Possibly in an unguarded moment, which might *not* be to Claire's benefit? Up front and out of the way—that's the ticket. But what if that's exactly what she expected her to do? On the other hand . . . aw, hell.

"I don't know," Claire said, genuinely puzzled. "They probably went to get a drink at the bar—and find a quiet little corner. You know them—'young love.' " Claire took a sip of her drink and then looked at it. "I'd get another one, but we probably should find them and decide what we *are* doing for dinner." She paused. "So, what's your vote: you want to eat out or in tonight?"

"I don't care. We'll ask the girls," Rita said evenly.

"The place Dara mentioned sounds kinda good." Claire lit a cigarette. "I feel bad for her."

"Who?" Rita asked.

Claire gave her a bored look. "Dara. You know who. Seems she's decided that after all these years of not being with Becca, she's ready to take advantage of being in the midst of so many likely prospects. Can't blame her. But Becca's doing the territorial thing. A little late, if you ask me."

"Well, it can't be a comfortable position for Becca. Even if they're not together, who wants to have that shoved in your face?"

"Aw, c'mon. They're here as friends."

"So? They were lovers—for a long time, I gather. It seems a little callous to me."

"You would say that."

"Yeah, I would. And you *would* side with Dara."

"What's *that* supposed to mean?" Claire challenged back. "Oh, never mind. It's not worth fighting about. Actually, I feel bad for both of them. With any luck, maybe they'll both find someone to add a little spice to the rest of the week."

"Oh, that's great. What'd you do, encourage Dara to find a 'fling' for both of them? My God, Claire. How tacky."

"I forgot—you're the lesbian Mother Teresa."

Mercifully, Kit and Sabi walked up.

"Hey, guys? Whatcha talking about?" Kit asked cheerfully.

Rita and Claire looked up simultaneously, a little too quickly.

"Ooh. Never mind. I don't think I want to know," Kit said.

"No, you don't. But your timing's excellent." Claire took a deep breath. "We started *out* talking about what we should do for dinner. Which is a topic I think we should return to."

"Well, is there anything on the agenda for later tonight?" Sabi asked.

"I kinda wanted you guys to see Big Ed at some point during the week. And there's Jimmy James and Lea DeLaria, both really good shows, too," Claire said.

"Okay. Here's my suggestion," Sabi said. "The sun pretty much wore me out today, so why don't we go to dinner tonight and talk about when we want to do what. We'll catch up on our 'cook in' nights later on. "

"Sounds good to me," Rita said. "You guys want to dance some more, or are we ready to get out of here?"

They all agreed there was plenty of time left in the week to do more dancing, so they gathered up their things and went out on the deck to get some air and reconnoiter. Claire told them about Dara's suggestion, which definitely appealed to sun-and-swimming-enhanced appetites, and they set out for Anna, Anna, Anna.

They found the restaurant easily, thanks in large part to the sign out front. Dara had been right about its being hidden away off the main thoroughfare. But it only added to its quaintness that one had to follow a cobblestone path back to a set of stone steps leading down to a sort of cellar entrance door, which opened onto a wonderfully charming entrance done in flagstone and rough-hewn timbers. The hostess sat them right away, as it was only a little after six; practically mid-afternoon in a town that catered in large part to the metropolitan customer base from New York and Boston, for whom dinner was definitely an after-seven consideration.

Though they were hardly necessary yet, the wonderfully tacky candles in Mateus wine bottles, complete with countless layers of multi-colored wax encrusted on the sides, set the ideal relaxed mood as they flickered and sputtered in the melting wax. The waitress brought their drink orders and proceeded to read them the evening's specials. As she walked away, Claire sighed contentedly and leaned back in her chair as she raised her glass.

"Well, ladies, to our first true *sun* day in P-Town!" Everyone smiled, clinked glasses and took a sip. "We've been out on our little beach in back a couple of times, but today was the epitome of basking. So let's see. We've done a day at The Boatslip, had brunch at Café Blasé, took our sunset dune ride yesterday, walked Commercial Street a few times," Claire leaned close to Kit and said under her breath, "(with minimal financial damage!) and are about to *hopefully* have our first new P-Town restaurant dining experience. There's *always* a wonderful new restaurant here to try every year. *And* we're all together." She took another deep breath. "I'm not sure it gets a whole lot better." She took another sip of her martini, lit a cigarette and leaned on the table. "So, what do you think, girls?" she said, looking over at both Kit and Sabi.

"Now *that's* a stupid question," Sabi said. "Do we look like we're hating it so far?"

"Just asking. You could be acting nice just not to hurt our feelings," Claire said with a little smile.

"Well," Kit said, taking a deep breath and settling back in her chair as she resituated her baseball cap on her head, "there is one thing." Everyone looked up. "We don't really have to *leave* on Saturday, do we??"

"Oh, way to go. Talk about ruining the moment," Sabi snapped at her.

"Okay. We forgot to tell you the cardinal rule when you're here," Claire said, adopting a stern look. "You are NOT allowed to mention the 'L' word or the day the 'L' word is to occur. Got it?"

"Got it. I won't make that mistake again! Instead, we probably should talk about what we want to do in the meantime."

"You guys *have* to see Big Ed. I swear, I've never laughed so hard," Rita said. "And we've already seen him two or three times already! He usually does two shows every evening, so we've got some flexibility. We'll have to check the magazine to see what nights the other shows are on."

"So, we've basically got four nights left to plan for after tonight," Kit said, thumbing through the Provincetown Magazine that she'd stashed in her beach bag. When nobody answered, Kit looked up to see everyone staring at her. "Wha'd I say?"

"I think it's the way you said it; it almost crossed the line into 'L' day territory," Claire said, raising her eyebrows in mock disapproval.

"Alright, alright! Let's see . . . tomorrow we're going to the beach, right?" Nods around. "Okay. Then maybe we want to cook at home tomorrow night and do either Jimmy James or Lea DeLaria in the evening. I was just thinking that it might be fun to go to Big Ed with Diane and your friend. The more the merrier kind of thing, since you guys said he does a whole audience bit."

"Sounds cool to me," said Claire. "You guys?" she asked, looking up at Rita and Sabi.

"Su-u-ure," Rita replied coolly, looking over at Sabi, who raised her eyebrows.

"Listen, you two, I know where you're getting ready to go with this," Claire said, jumping to Kit's defense. "But just because Kit was thinking ahead to what might be fun for all of us to do together *doesn't* mean we're planning around *them*. It was a perfectly reasonable thought—and I, for one, think it's a great idea," Claire said with a firm nod of her head in Kit's direction.

Rita looked over at Sabi with an exaggerated look of puzzlement on her face. "Did you say something I missed?" Sabi shook her head. "And I think all I said was, 'Sure.' Nothing about anybody that I re-call." The two "innocents" looked at each other and laughed, while Claire and Kit grumbled on their side of the table.

"Ha, ha. Very funny. Why don't we let Kit continue."

"Actually, honey, that poor waitress keeps peeking out here to see if we're ready to order. Why don't we do that first?" Rita suggested.

"You're absolutely right, hon."

They all perused their menus and talked about what looked appealing. And there was *lots* that looked appealing. The waitress had told them that there really *was* an Anna who was famous for her marinara sauce, and who was out in the kitchen doing the cooking herself. So, they were all looking forward to the meal. Claire looked up and over to where the waitress was standing patiently and got her attention.

"He-e-re we go," Rita said, rolling her eyes and looking over at Claire with a tolerant smile. "Honey, don't drive the poor waitress crazy."

"I don't know how asking to hear the specials again is driving her crazy. And I also want to know about this roasted garlic thing. I've never heard of it."

"Fine. But when she tells you, pay attention," Rita said with a pleading tone. "And try not to take another twenty minutes making up your mind." Rita, Sabi, and Kit all looked at each other and then over at Claire, all shaking their heads.

"WHAT?!?" Claire's attempt at righteous indignation and a straight face didn't last long. Soon they were laughing as the waitress approached their table and took their orders.

Another drink arrived for Kit and Claire along with more Italian bread and olive oil for dipping, a new and very pleasant variation on the usual rock hard pats of butter.

"So, where were we?" Claire asked.

"I think I was up to tomorrow when I was ambushed by those two over there," Kit said, giving Sabi and Rita a sidelong look. "Anyway, I still think Big Ed or Lea DeLaria would be more fun with a whole group of us. I guess Thursday or Friday we could see whoever we don't see tomorrow night."

"Two things," Claire interjected. "One, I think Thursday night is Carnival, which is a *BIG* deal here."

"Yeah, I'd say so," Kit said, looking at a splashy ad in the magazine. "It's right here. Wow—a parade and everything, huh?"

"*And* the competition for Miss Carnival 1988. Every drag queen for miles around will be here! So I don't think we want to miss that. Second, anything you want to do Friday, we better make reservations for. For reasons we've agreed not to speak about," Claire gave them a mock serious eye, "it's a popular going out night. Oh, and there's a number three. You'll probably need time to do one last whirl for souvenirs or whatever, so keep that in mind."

As appetizers arrived, they agreed on yet another tentative plan for the week. At *least* three others had been proposed over the last two days as Sabi and Kit saw, heard, and read more about what P-Town had to offer by both day and night: the different beaches, horseback riding (high on Kit and Claire's list), the many art galleries, a major flea market (*only* on Rita and Sabi's list), cabaret shows, other dance clubs, special concerts, dance cruises . . . and then there was the *original* plan to do absolutely nothing and finish those trashy novels they'd started today. For now, however, tomorrow was to be a beach day—at Herring Cove, the gayest of the local lot—followed by a possible cookout on the beach, then off to see what was supposed to be one of the best drag performers around, Jimmy James. Wednesday they'd do the Big Ed thing with their arriving guests and maybe have a drink afterward to bring them up to speed on what they—Diane and Grant—might find fun to do for their respective times there. Thursday was Carnival—maybe another appropriate group endeavor—and Friday there'd be reservations for the four of them to see Lea. The days they'd play by ear. Of course, this whole grand plan could change by mid-morning at the beach, but it worked for now.

The veritable feast that was dinner wound down. The marinara sauce had definitely lived up to its reputation, and Rita, no shabby cook herself, had all sorts of ideas about wonderful new dishes she could concoct based on what they'd eaten. A little "Death by Chocolate," allegedly created by Anna herself, split four ways, a couple of brandies with after-dinner cigarettes, and it was more than time for a leisurely stroll back to their rooms. After calling Anna herself to their table so they could lavish her with compliments about their very satisfied taste buds, they exited the restaurant to find an evening as perfect as the meal they had just consumed.

As they walked along Commercial Street, they could hear the competing strains of music from the various shows and barroom jukeboxes. A warm, light breeze from the sun-baked dunes carried the music off to the sea where it lingered and floated back. Another lighted display window seemed to wink on with each gentle gust, until the stores were alive with colors and shapes, appealing in a way they weren't in the sun's glare.

As they walked along, the women took note of spots they planned to revisit another day. Tonight, the only thing on either couple's agenda was the comfort of a double bed, windows open to the sounds of lapping waves and distant foghorns, and the feel of familiar curves and cradling arms.

CHAPTER
6

Rita stood by the railing at the end of the deck, looking out over Stella's Seaside's "back yard"—the cozy little beach that gave onto the private boat section of Provincetown's marina. To the right, what would be equal to a block or two away, was the official marina and the wharf that serviced it, which extended out about a quarter of a mile. There it met a large rock breaker that in turn jutted east another quarter of a mile or so to the left, a main element of the horizon as one looked out from the deck. The water was dotted with various outboards and rowboats and anchoring buoys that bobbed lazily in the slight current, a soothing nautical foreground. A few of the buoys were belled; the signature harbor sound of rhythmic gonging in time with the lapping of the waves on the sand was mesmerizing, especially at night.

Rita picked up her coffee cup from the railing and took a tentative, testing sip. As usual, she was the first one up; and also, as usual, she was enjoying the first sights and sounds of morning, the best part of which was the *absence* of sounds. Human ones, anyway. This nearly dawn ritual was one she'd come to value over the years, mixed blessing though it was; sometimes she truly envied Claire's typical sleeping mode, a peaceful oblivion that could last *well* into the morning. On the other hand, mornings like this—tranquil, beautiful, peace-filled in a different, conscious way that sleeping couldn't rival—were something she wouldn't trade for the world. Growing up in a household with five siblings all vying for attention, physical and emotional, left precious little time for any one child, let alone the competent, care-taking, eldest one. So, like her father before her, the early morning alone-time was something she treasured.

However, just like those childhood mornings and the ones that followed as she raised a family of her own, the reverie never lasted long enough. As she stood looking out over the little piece of the harbor that she thought of as *theirs* and watched the pier awaken— the rumbling engines of the fishing and whale-watching boats coming to life, the shouts of the crews, the squawking of seagulls diving for their breakfasts, the constant lapping splashes of the tide crawling up the beach, a buoy bell ringing here and there—she heard the squeak of a door and knew she was no longer the only one up. Oh well . . . at least there had been that couple of hours or so of quiet, special time to say good morning to another P-Town day.

At the creaking of the deck planking, she turned around and assumed her "people" face. Sabi was walking slowly towards her, yawning and carefully balancing her cup of java. Even half awake, moving slowly, Sabi had a sexy walk that was *way* more hip-powered than leg-powered—and that accounted for a certain allure that always seemed to make people take notice. That, and, as the Cowardly Lion sang, "that certain air of savoir-faire." However, her hair standing up in fifty different directions sort of negated the "savoir-faire" part of it first thing in the morning.

"Good morning, sweetie," Sabi said warmly as she stifled another yawn. She joined Rita and rested her arms on the railing, cradling her coffee in her hands. For a few minutes she, too, simply took in the same calming, morning sights. She sighed deeply and took a sip of her coffee. "Not so bad to wake up to, huh?" she said softly.

"No. Not bad at all."

"How long you been up?"

"Oh, I don't know, an hour or two maybe?"

Sabi shook her head in disbelief. "I still can't get over how early you get up on vacation. You're supposed to *relax.*"

"You know I'm an early riser. This is late for me. Anything past five is late for me!"

"Uggh. Not me. I always tell myself I'm going to get up to catch that first, brisk smell of morning, but sleeping here is just too wonderful. If it hadn't been for that damn ship's horn a few minutes ago, I think I could've slept till noon."

"Gee. I didn't even hear it," Rita said almost dreamily as she con-

tinued to look out over the water. She shook her head a bit, returning to the moment, and smiled warmly. "But it is nice having company at this hour." She frowned a bit. "What time is it, anyway?"

"Oh, I guess almost eight."

"Wow. It's later than I thought."

"I hardly call this late," Sabi replied with a stifled yawn. "But I
don't mind getting a fairly early start on the day. I can't believe it's
Wednesday already. My God, the time flies here. And I don't want to
waste a second of it."

"I know. But don't confuse relaxing with wasting time. That's why
we're here. Even getting up at my usual early time is a luxury here—
'cause I can do just what I'm doing now: nothing!"

"You said it, sweetie," Sabi replied, patting Rita's back. "But
there's relaxing and there's *relaxing*. The other two seem to be mas-
tering that last version pretty well. So, when do we think they'll be
moving?"

Rita smiled and chuckled. "If I know Claire, we could be *well* into
the next pot of coffee before she's moving!" She smiled. "Besides,
after those heroics last night on the beach and all the bourbon it
took to memorialize the event, I suspect it could be a late morning—
even by her standards!"

"Same for Kit," Sabi added. "She can always pack away the beers,
but I'd forgotten how much she likes the hard stuff once she gets
going." She chuckled. "Ah, yes, our two brave protectors." She took a
sip of coffee. "Protectors, my ass. *We* had the good sense to save ourselves and head for the car."

"Yeah, well, it makes a better story their way!"

"Jesus, I haven't laughed that hard in years. Which I definitely
needed. And Kit even more than me. It's so good to see her relaxed
and happy. God, she was so wiped last week. I can't tell you how
much she needed this vacation. It's been a hard year—at work and
otherwise."

"Well, from what you've been telling me lately, it hasn't been fun
and games for either of you for a while."

"Yeah, I only have my crazy mother to deal with. And at least she's
on our side. But poor Kit . . ."

"I know," Rita said consolingly. "No, I take that back—I *don't* know. I can't really even *imagine* how it feels having to deal with that kind of rejection from your family. Especially that whole bit with her father."

"Yeah. It hasn't been easy for her. To say the least. Or me either, frankly, having to see her so upset." Sabi took a drink of her coffee and lit a cigarette. "And even though this promotion at work has been exhausting for her, at least it's certainly kept her busy—which has been a blessing. Less time for her to dwell on the whole fucked-up situation."

"Good, since it doesn't sound like there's much she can do about it at the moment."

"No, there's not. But being with you guys really does help. Not to mention being here. It's just so wonderful being someplace where you feel absolutely normal. Hell, fuck 'feel' normal. Where we *are* the norm!"

"Alright. What are you two evil girls plotting so early in the morning? More expensive shopping excursions maybe? When what you *should* be doing is cooking up a nice, tasty breakfast for my friend and me?!?" Claire strolled casually toward the two women with a devilish grin. Her blond hair was bent in directions impossible to intentionally create. "We liked to have exhausted ourselves last night with all that intensive grilling and then defending you against swarming killer mosquitoes!"

"Yeah, right. Now you can just dig into some nice cold cereal while *my* friend and I enjoy the lovely breakfast that I have planned!" Rita retorted. She turned away in mock annoyance as Claire put her arms around her and playfully tried to find a spot to kiss her while Rita twisted and turned to fend off her "advances." Then Claire found the ticklish spot on her neck. "Stop it, you! Now you're risking not getting lunch as well!"

Claire snuck in a quick peck on the lips and put her arm around Rita, joining them in surveying the bay. "Ah . . . this is how every morning should start," she said, closing her eyes and taking a deep breath. "Just smell that ocean air. It's absolutely wonderful."

"It must be to get you up and at 'em this early," Rita said with a little smirk.

"God knows, I love to sleep. And nothing's better for it than Cape

Cod nights. But, by the same token, it's a sin to miss mornings like this." Claire took a sip out of the mug of coffee she, too, had brought out on the deck. "Besides, without you lying beside me, what *possible* attraction could sleep hold?" she said dramatically, looking at Rita with eyebrows raised innocently.

"Right. That sure never stopped you any other morning!"

"Ah-h-h, don't be mean," Claire said, sticking her lower lip out in a pout. She smiled and shifted to a perkier mode. "So, what *were* you guys talking about?"

"My God, you're like a dog with a bone," Sabi said, rolling her eyes.

"Whatever. I just want to make sure I protect my friend's and my interests here. You two being conspiratorial can be dangerous." She lit a cigarette and grinned at each of the women as she exhaled her first puff. "Besides, you had that hunkered-down-serious-topic air about you—which is really kind of hard to do in the midst of such a gorgeous morning. So, I figured it had to be something juicy."

"Not really," Sabi answered, her tone mellowing. "We were just talking about Kit and her lovely family."

"Oh. Yeah. They really have a unique take on the idea of unconditional love, don't they?"

"That's what *I* keep telling her," Sabi said. "But Kit's always bought into her parents' idea of their picture-perfect little family. And, as the oldest, they've really dumped her with some sort of weird, warped sense of responsibility for keeping it that way. Talk about pressure. Kit calls the sibs. Kit relays all the important family news—read: the parents' wishes. Kit's who they call if there's a problem. Kit's house is where everyone comes when they need a place to crash. Kit even *speaks* for the sibs. And yet Kit's a piece of shit now that she's told them she's gay. But they still expect her to do what she's always done—and just not *notice* that they totally reject who she is. Not to mention me." She drew deeply on the cigarette she'd just lit from the previous one. "Talk about messed up. Especially the father. That whole ambush when she was down there in the spring was a real treat. I told her his lovely, 'Christian' comments after he saw that news blurb about Gay Pride Week coming up in New York should've told her something was up."

"I have to admit, I might not have launched into my coming out speech after that. But I understand why she did it," Claire added. "Sometimes the anticipation is worse than when people really have something to deal with. Like they're obligated to work extra hard to fend off even the possibility of that evil curse, ho-mo-*sex*-u-ality. And you hope that once it's a *fait accompli,* they at least know and can *start* moving toward some sort of acceptance. I mean, at that point, it's what it is. Granted, I wouldn't have expected them to jump up and down for joy and start waving little rainbow flags! But I can't help but believe it'll get better now that they have something concrete to work with."

"I know. And maybe that's how it is with other people. God, we all wish we could be as lucky as you've been with your Mom. But you saw Kit's face yesterday at the beach when you asked how things were with her family. She *so* wants to believe that's how it can be. But I could tell she was thinking about the looks on their faces that day. And I've seen those looks when we've been there together—*before* they even knew. I just don't think that's how it's going to go with the Summers clan."

Rita and Claire both looked around as Sabi was finishing talking.

"Okay, okay. What'd I miss?" Kit said as she came shambling towards them, adjusting her pre-contact-insertion glasses.

"Ah, come here, *mamita,*" Sabi said as she pulled Kit to her and gave her a good morning kiss. "I just love your groggy morning face," she said giving her another hug. "We were just talking about the wonderful woman I'm so madly in love with."

"Yeah. Okay." Kit added her cup of coffee to the row of cups on the railing. "Ooh! Shit!" She reached down and scratched her leg. There were at least a dozen red welts on her legs. "I can't believe how those little bastards feasted on me last night!"

If anyone had been watching, they would have seen quite a sight. It started out as a good idea: a sunset cookout on the beach, complete with romantic music on the boom box, champagne, a blanket if they got chilly, the works. Everything was downright idyllic—the coals were glowing nicely, they'd gotten some great sunset pictures and shots of each other clowning around. That is until the steaks got cooking, the champagne was uncorked, and Claire decided to get a shot of the other three relaxing with their drinks. As she tried to focus the picture, first Rita moved, then Sabi jumped and slapped her leg. Next, Kit was flailing in the air. Annoyed, Claire thought they were being cute and told them all to hold still, when suddenly the air itself seemed to be moving in front of the viewfinder.

And then all hell broke loose. There were swarms of mosquitoes *everywhere.* Millions of them. In their eyes, noses, ears, everywhere. Sabi and Rita's contribution to the escape effort was standing there swatting the air and screaming. Kit shouted orders so that they at least grabbed the boom box and their shoes and the blanket, which they promptly put over their heads as they scaled the dune behind them in mere seconds and ran screaming for the car. Poor Kit and Claire were left to deal with gathering up the remainder of the stuff—portable grill, cooler, half-cooked food, camera, shoes, and God knows what else—while trying vainly to breathe without a mouth- or noseful of insects. Amazingly, as soon as they cleared the dune and were off the beach, the onslaught disappeared. Kit and Claire stopped to figure out if they had everything, the other two long gone. They realized almost simultaneously that the coals they'd dumped were still live. Looking at each other pathetically, they pulled their sweatshirts over their heads and headed back down to take care of the situation.

By the time they got to the car, Rita and Sabi were collapsed in hysterics *inside* the car, refusing to open the doors lest more mosquitoes get in. Kit and Claire were not amused.

"I know, honey. You were so brave last night," Sabi said, stroking Kit's head.

"Brave, my ass. I was a fucking chew toy for those damned mosquitoes! And you two weren't very damn much help!"

"Hey! That's not fair! You know how much I hate bugs!"

"Oh, and I love 'em, huh?"

"Alright, alright—it sounds to me like we're all awake enough to be ready for a little breakfast," Rita interjected. "What sounds good to everyone?"

Part of what had cemented the couples' relationship was the easy, unforced way the simplest or most complex of tasks flowed. Whether it was installing a ceiling fan at one of their homes or preparing a meal together, the job was accomplished almost wordlessly. Certainly *conversation* was always a main component of time spent together doing anything. But the kind of explaining usually needed when people work together—explaining that typically includes having to point out the obvious (Okay, I need the screwdriver now; Could you set the table?; No, the *other* wrench; Ummm, I think the garlic bread is burning), and that more often than not reveals what's missing and consigns most friendships to the casual, overt entertainment level—was mercifully *not* part of these friendships. Theirs was graced with the kind of intuitive consideration and commonsense anticipation of needs that made any activity or the most traumatic or mundane of circumstances into a shared moment.

Granted, each *set* of friends had its forte—stereotypes usually *do* have some basis in fact. Kit and Claire definitely gravitated to tackling the ceiling-fan-installation-type chores together, while Rita and Sabi dealt with the shopping-as-therapy and what's-for-dinner arena. The lines were not so indelibly drawn, however, that overlap didn't occur. Mealtimes were a case in point.

The women headed up to Claire and Rita's larger apartment to rustle up some breakfast. Rita, the undisputed chef of the foursome, had decided omelets were on the morning's menu and proceeded to pull together the ingredients. Sabi got another pot of coffee going while Claire and Kit stirred up some Bloody Marys and mimosas. While continuing to recall the evening's events, which had culminated in seeing the terrific female impersonator, Jimmy James, they all wordlessly gravitated to what needed to be done next. Sabi peeled and chopped the onion Rita had gotten out, Kit got the bacon out and started frying it, Claire cleared and set the table, while Rita toasted some English muffins. In no time, they were sitting down.

"Jesus, Rita, I don't know what you do to make even an omelet taste fabulous," Kit exclaimed. "Granted, Claire makes a mean Bloody Mary, but I don't know if that would have been enough to seal the deal about vacationing together!"

Claire put her fork down quietly and wiped her mouth. "You cut me to the quick. My friend. Huh." She hung her head in feigned anguish.

"Ahhh, now look what you've done," Sabi said sympathetically, patting Claire's hand. "You know how delicate Claire is."

"Hey! I think I deserve a compliment now and then," Rita shot back indignantly. "Besides, it's nice hearing it from someone other than my kids!" she added with her own hangdog look.

"Oh, yeah—like I never compliment you!" Claire said. "Why, I spend most of my time telling you how wonderful you are!"

The table erupted in groans.

"Well, I do!" she said playfully.

"Speaking of the kids, what's going on with Amy and her dad?" Sabi asked.

Though Rita had been divorced for some six years, that had not ended her ex-husband Rick's negative influence. Even in his absence, he managed to create trauma in their lives. The two oldest kids, Maria and Robbie, had pretty much written him off. His tantrums at the least perceived slight, an ego that led to center-of-attention embarrassing moments with their friends, ongoing insults about their mother and Claire, their mother's hardships dealing with unpaid child support, and too many missed weekends had proved too much for the sixteen- and eighteen-year-old to deal with. Though Claire continued to be insistent that they respect their father and honor the every-other-weekend visit schedule, Rita had long ago decided they'd be better off without him. Amy, on the other hand, the youngest at fourteen, had not given up. She'd been "daddy's little girl," while simultaneously being the one closest to Claire. Combined with the usual travails of adolescence, it made for just a *little* volatility at home. To top it all off, Rick had remarried a year ago, and the *new* Mrs. Campanella had *no* interest in sharing her—or her husband's—affections with his youngest child. The latest incident had involved Amy overhearing an argument between them about her having overstayed her weeknight visit—by fifteen minutes.

"Amy. I really don't know what I'm going to do. She's so crushed with Rick's caving in to that . . . that . . . *bitch's* demands," Rita sputtered. "God knows, I want nothing to do with him. But I even broke down and called him about it last week. Of course, even though I really *did* try to stay calm, all he had to do was start to shush me and tell me how badly I was raising Amy since she was so overemotional at everything, and I exploded. *I'm* doing a bad job with these kids! That son-of-a-bitch. How dare he!"

"Honey, you can't let him get to you like this," Claire said comfortingly, taking Rita's hand.

Rita pulled it back. "And you keep encouraging her to see him! All of them. Like they haven't had enough."

"I just don't want them to ever look back and regret their teenage actions, *or* resent me and think I ever tried to influence them against him. *Especially* Amy. She's got to be very ready to write him off. Or we'll all pay for it in the end."

"Well! I guess that pretty much tells me how things are going," Sabi said, half apologetically.

"Oh, stop," Rita said quietly to Sabi. "I'm glad you asked. Really. Amy loves you so much—both of you. It's just such a frustrating situation. And I have such a hard time reconciling this cruel man with the father that absolutely worshipped Amy. I mean, he practically raised her when I started back to work when she was five. It's unbelievable . . ."

"Yes, it is, honey. But we just have to hang in there until she's decided she's had enough. Amy still wants to see him. That's that." Claire got up and hugged Rita from behind her chair.

"I know," Rita said, relaxing into Claire's embrace.

"I don't know how you guys do it," Kit added. "We've thought about adopting or one of us having a kid, but I don't know if I could deal with the whole thing. God, it's . . . so *big.*"

"That it is, my friend," Claire said. "But don't let our horror stories put you off the whole being parents thing. There's a lot of good stuff, too. Without a doubt."

"Hey! Don't encourage her," Sabi interjected. "The whole gay thing is new enough to us. Remember, we're both novices at this. I'm not so sure my little honey's sown all her wild oats yet." She gave Kit a sidelong look. "I think it'll be a while before we're ready to seriously think about adding any third parties to this relationship."

"What the hell's that supposed to mean?!?" Kit shot back angrily.

"Oh, *mama,* I'm just teasing you!" Sabi leaned over a planted a big kiss on an unresponsive Kit. "Now you're going to pout." She stroked Kit's face. "But you do need to know I'd have to kill anyone who even *looks* at you."

"Oh, that makes me feel much better," Kit said, rolling her eyes. Then she smiled. "You don't have to worry, baby. I'm a one-woman woman."

"Damned straight you are!" Sabi said, then thought for a second. "Or-r-r-r whatever. You know what I mean!"

"Now, girls," Claire intoned. "I think that's enough serious conversation for one morning. It looks to me that we have another round of Bloodys and mimosas that need drinking. I say we get our refills and take our respective beach books down to said beach at our doorstep and relax until we have to greet our guests in a couple of hours." She got up to start the preparations. "Even though it's a little on the cloudy side at the moment, I'm betting there'll be some nice sun pretty soon. And we shouldn't let it go to waste."

"Shit. I forgot all about that," Sabi said. Rita nodded in silent agreement. "Time to take care of the emotionally 'walking wounded.' "

"Come on, Sabi," Kit said with more than a trace of exasperation. "Diane's fine. Just 'cause she goes through men faster than I can keep up doesn't make her fucked up."

"And every single one of them is the love of her life. Yeah, that's normal." It was Sabi's turn to roll her eyes as she proceeded to clear the table. "Didn't she tell you she'd just broken up with someone when you talked to her about coming out here?" Kit nodded sheepishly. "Well, then I'm not too far off base, am I? When did she *not* look to you to pick up the pieces after one of her break-ups? Huh?"

"Alright, alright. Point made. We'll just have to keep a lookout for some cute guy to take her mind off it." All three women stopped and looked at her. "Oh, yeah. Not so easy here, is it? But Tom's straight, right? And 'they' all do tend to hang out together, right?" Everyone chuckled. It *was* nice to turn social stereotypes on their heads every now and then.

"Well, hopefully she and Grant will have had time to thoroughly rehash their love traumas on the ferry ride over," Claire said by way of smoothing the situation over. "Grant's just coming off a bad one, too. She's another one who can't seem to find anybody who's on the same wavelength. Though she *is* pretty intense, I have to say. God, she had a crush on me for a while. That was weird."

"Oh, *really,*" Sabi said with sudden interest, tossing the dishtowel aside and turning around with her arms crossed and a look of out and out nosiness on her face. "And what did my friend Rita have to say about all this? You inviting an ex-lover on your vacation?!"

"Please. She's *hardly* an ex-lover. I said she had a crush on me, not that we were torrid lovers. And Rita not only *knows,* we've been to see her and she's been to New York. So, put your claws back in. Nothing juicy there."

"Damn. I was all ready for a story."

"Sorry, not really. Just your basic misguided and fortunately short-lived infatuation," Claire said with an apologetic smile. "But now that you bring it up, I certainly hope Grant *heard* me when I told her that Diane's straight. Not that I didn't tell her—a couple of times. At first I think she thought I was suggesting something when I asked her to get Diane a room at the Holiday Inn. But I set that straight—literally."

"*That'd* be great. Like poor Diane isn't insecure enough already about her dating prospects. All we need is for her to get propositioned by a woman. She'll totally throw the towel in!" Kit said.

"I wouldn't really worry. Grant's not totally stupid. It's just that she likes a challenge. So I'll be keeping an eye on her," Claire hastened to add.

"Hey, you two!" Sabi shouted, holding the door open and leaning in. "You've managed to screw around just long enough for Rita and me to get all our shit together, including yours. Think you can get your*selves* down to the beach?"

CHAPTER

7

By about eleven o'clock, the morning practically exploded into an ideal, crystalline Cape day. The clouds blew out to sea, the air fairly glistened it was so clear, the sky was an indescribable shade of blue, and the temperature had climbed to about eighty degrees—hot by P-Town standards since the sun was markedly more intense out at this far eastern end of the continent than back on the mainland. When it got up into the eighties here, it was *decidedly* hot. But it made for a classic summer day. People seemed to glide down Commercial Street, contented smiles on every face. Perfection.

It was nearly noon as Kit arrived back at the driveway to Stella's with her newspaper. An inveterate "news junkie," even on vacation Kit had to have her journalistic "fix" every day. Though she'd been gone almost an hour already, she lingered a moment just watching the constant stream of people passing, which was pretty much what she'd been doing for most of the time she'd been out. Even though they'd been there four days already, Kit still couldn't get over the idyllic atmosphere that pervaded the place. It seemed to be the one little spot in the world where people truly lived and let live. Who knows how they behaved back home, wherever that might be; when they were here, the notions of straight, gay, black, white, male, female, singles, couples simply didn't matter. Granted, the day-trippers from "down Cape" would occasionally indulge in gawking and pointing. But even they seemed to eventually absorb the bonhomie that was in the air.

And the throngs of gay people—! It was dazzling. Kit had never been around that many "members of the club" in one place *ever*. It was heaven. The smorgasbord of women, in particular. Not that she was in any way unhappy with Sabi; she was truly the woman Kit had always imagined being with. That is, once she even realized it was a woman she'd wanted to be with. And Sabi was the woman who brought that reality crashing down on her.

There had been women in college—and probably even high school, if she was honest about it—that she'd noticed, even had major crushes on and nursed full-blown fantasies about in the privacy of classroom daydreams and late-night reveries. But other than what she now recognized as unusually intense friendships with substantially higher quotients of "accidental" physical contact, comforting hugs, and irrational jealousies, she'd had no true lesbian "encounters" to speak of—or to confirm her own half-formed suspicions about her romantic preference.

But then she'd walked into the junior high school social studies class to do her bit for a career day—and saw the teacher. As she delivered her presentation, she realized she was much more focused on impressing Ms. Ramirez than selling the class on the virtues of the ad business. In fact, when Ms. Ramirez suggested they lunch together, the somersaults her stomach was doing and the smile she couldn't seem to wipe off her face made her feel much more like a hormone-addled junior high student than a twenty-six year old professional woman. By the time Kit left that day, they had definite plans to meet for drinks later in the week and tentative ones to go to an upcoming Stevie Nicks concert.

It was the providential snowstorm the night of the concert that sealed their respective and mutual fates. The concert was in Long Island, not far from where Kit lived; Kit's invitation to spend the night rather than risk the icy roads back to Brooklyn had met with instant agreement from Sabi. And thanks to the spin-out they did avoiding a stalled car on the way to Kit's, Sabi was more than open to the massage Kit offered to relieve the tension in her neck and shoulders. Had either of them been any less naïve and realized they were taking a page from Classic Lesbian Seductions 101: The Backrub, the evening might have gone very differently. Fortunately, that was not the case.

As Kit rubbed and kneaded Sabi's back, the tension *she* felt was anything but in her back and shoulders. Straddling Sabi's back, it was all she could do not to gasp each time Sabi moved under her, clearly enjoying Kit's every touch. Kit looked down at her small breasts, mortified to see that her nipples were also anticipating something yet to come. Kit took a deep breath and tried desperately to think clearly. *Is this an invitation or just someone enjoying a back rub? How do I know? Do I want to know? Either way, what do I do next? Especially if this is what I hope it is? Or do I hope it is? Dear God, maybe she thinks I know what to do. What do I do? She's engaged, for Christ's sake. But I almost was, too. Oh my God—what if I fuck this up? Either way? What the hell is she thinking . . . and feeling?*

Suddenly, Sabi turned her head around as far as she could. Kit realized she'd stopped massaging her as she'd become absorbed by her inner debate. "Hey," Sabi said softly. "Something wrong?"

Kit sat there, paralyzed, just looking down at Sabi. Sabi shifted her weight and flipped over onto her back, Kit still sitting on top of her. As Kit registered the position they were now in, she jumped, averting her gaze and mumbling some sort of apology and shifted to get up. Sabi grabbed her wrist and held it. She reached up with her other hand and turned Kit's head back around so that Kit could not avoid the dark eyes looking up at her. Kit returned the gaze, as afraid of what hers might reveal as of what Sabi's might not.

Sabi peered at her, searching for something. Then she reached up, and touching Kit's lips very softly asked, "Hey, my usually talkative friend. What is it?"

Before she could think, Kit had closed her eyes and kissed the finger on her lips. As she realized what she'd done, she flinched. "I, uh, I think I should go in the living room and sleep on the couch."

Sabi had not released her grip on Kit's arm. She continued looking at her very calmly, almost dreamily, a small smile on her lips. "I don't think so. I think you should stay right where you are . . . and continue doing just what you were doing." She let go of Kit's arm and put hers under her head, stretching a bit in the process and revealing the two hard nubs under her sleep shirt. The other hand she left extended toward Kit's face.

"But—I, I don't know, I never—and what about Joe and—"

"Kit . . ." she said in a voice that was a cross between a sigh, a moan, and a whisper. And then she arched her body a bit, pressing herself against Kit.

Kit started with the fingertips in front of her face and continued kissing Sabi until she'd arrived at the hollow of her neck, and then she paused and lifted her head. As they looked into each other's eyes, each searching for the final assent to the moment, instinct was taking over the rest of their bodies, the hungry, demanding rubbing and thrusting finally answering the question for both of them. Kit closed her eyes for a moment, overwhelmed by the electric intensity and feeling that was overwhelming her. When she opened them again, Sabi gasped at the certainty, power, and fire she now saw in them. Kit fell to Sabi's lips and kissed her with such passion that Sabi had to stop her for a moment to take a breath.

"Oh, my," she said, exhaling deeply and taking another deep breath. "Well, I guess that's it."

Kit froze above her, panic stricken. "Oh, my God. I am so sorry." Kit's voice was quivering with a combination of emotion and terror. "But I thought . . ."

Sabi laughed. Not her usual loud guffaw, but a deep, throaty, seductive laugh. "Relax, *mama*. You don't see me leaping out of this bed, do you? Oh, no. I'm not going anywhere. I think we've got some unfinished business here, and I may just melt into a puddle if we don't, uh, get to it pretty soon. What I meant was after all those times of you looking at me till I forgot to breathe—even that first day in class—and brushing against each other that left my skin actually hot. . . . well, I didn't know what to think, and I didn't know if you really felt any of it, too. Or what I would do if I did know. But now, with that kiss, I guess we both just crossed the border into somewhere. I don't exactly know where . . . but I don't think I want to go back. Not to Joe or anyone else. Not if this is what's on the other side." She pulled Kit back down on her.

They were a little clumsy at first, neither knowing what was expected in this particular situation. But in the amazingly empathetic, deeply knowing way that takes over when two women first touch one another's flesh, they simply followed the inner sense that leads one woman's hands and lips and tongue to do what it is she most loves done to her. The Sexual Golden Rule. And, while neither one knew what guided her, each of them followed it into the damp, musky, hidden parts of the other. The gasps and moans and whimpers of rhythms and swollen needs discovered was all they needed to take one another to the edge of explosive ecstasy and on into the welcome chaos of utter surrender to it. They never slept alone again.

Kit smiled to herself, recalling that first night. In retrospect, they had both laughed at just *how* clumsy and ignorant they both had been. Granted, it had been one helluva night. But more due to how much need and desire and plain, old lust they'd both been keeping tamped down deep in their respective psyches. The sex had only gotten better—as had every other aspect of life—with every passing day together. But Kit couldn't help but wonder if things were as great as they thought. There was no point of comparison, no way to know just how *gay* normal they were or weren't. Kit also couldn't help but wonder, in the midst of so many attractive women, how her life might have turned out if she'd come to a place like this before they'd met; if she'd been honest with herself years ago when, in fact, she'd known there was nothing of real substance happening with the string of guys she'd dated in college and after. What if she'd had the opportunity to really find out on her own about what being a lesbian meant? Had the chance to run wild with women as she'd done with men in her I'm-straight-and-I'll-prove-it days? She smiled as she thought about Pat's flirting with her. She had to admit it had been fun. It was kind of nice knowing someone else thought her attractive. Very nice, in fact.

Since she got to know Claire and some of her group, Kit had gotten much more comfortable in her identity and had quit trying so hard to hide a natural tendency toward, well, butchness. Not that she was some diesel dyke—God knows, she'd run into women here that actually made her look twice to figure out gender. She had no interest in being a man or trying to act like one. Even so, she knew she had traits that definitely fell within the scope of the traditionally masculine and had been wondering how she was regarded now that she was just being herself. Given Pat's reaction—and some sidelong glances she'd noticed walking around that morning—it appeared she was as desirable now to certain female eyes as she had been to male eyes when she'd gone the makeup and skirts route.

She shook her head. If she enjoyed that kind of attention too much more, she'd have a full-blown "situation" on her hands with Sabi taking on all comers! Her little honey was *definitely* territorial—the scene at The Boatslip was still fresh in her mind. Oh well . . . looking was still allowed, if done subtly. As for the other questions, well, there was always the old adage about not fixing what ain't broke. And given the last few nights, things might be a little tender but they sure weren't broke.

She sighed and headed down the driveway. Before she got to their apartment, she noticed the other three women sitting around the picnic table.

"Hey, you slugs! What'd you just come up off the beach? Anybody bother to check the time? If anyone's thinking about showers and whatnot, you might want to get busy. The girls'll be here at one, you know."

"Excuse me?" Sabi said as she looked up, one brow raised quizzically. "If you'd look before you start barking orders, you might notice that we've all done the 'shit, showered, and shaved' thing. All, that is, except *you.*"

"Yeah . . . well . . ." Kit sputtered, "I just wanted to be sure we didn't have to wait on you girly-girls to do the whole hair and makeup bit."

"Nice try, sweets," Sabi replied as she turned back to touching up her fingernail polish. "So, where have you been?"

"Having coffee with my new girlfriend," Kit said calmly.

Sabi's head whipped around to catch the smug smile on Kit's face. "Ha, ha. Very funny," she replied, returning to a look of nonchalance.

"Had *you* going!" Kit sat down. "Actually, I walked around just taking everything in. Convincing myself this place is real."

"Yeah, the first time here, it's pretty overwhelming," Claire added. "But you'll get used to it—then you go back and can't believe out *there* is real."

"Alright, alright! Let's not go there! It's too gorgeous a day, and I'm too mellow right where I am, thank you." Kit turned her face upward to the sun and slowly stretched.

"Speaking of showers . . ." Sabi said, looking at her watch.

"Yes, ma'am!" Kit sprang to attention, saluted, and headed back toward the stairs. "I'll be back before the second coat is dry!"

True to her word, Kit was back outside in under twenty minutes, her shock of short, wavy brown hair still wet, with little wet spots on her tank top from having donned it over her still-damp skin. When the ocean breeze hit her, it was obvious that some of her quickness came from having *only* donned the tank top.

"Well, that *was* quick." Sabi gave her a once-over. "You, uh, looking to catch someone's eye out there?"

Kit gave her a bored look. "C'mon. You know I never wear a bra on the weekends at home. And this is like one big long weekend. Besides, you haven't worn a bra all week And I don't have any more to worry about than you do. Now if it were *Rita . . .*"

"Uh oh," Claire said, looking over at Sabi then at Kit. "I don't think that was your best tack to take."

The standing joke of the week was Sabi's pet fantasy that she was *really* a buxom Spanish beauty. The Spanish beauty part was right; the buxom . . . well, not exactly. But she'd appear all decked out in some slinky, hot number, loudly complaining about how hard it was to find the right outfit to set off her "bodacious ta-tas"!

Sabi gave Kit a withering glance and then turned her attention to Rita. "I don't know what she's talking about—they're *huge!*" she exclaimed, rearranging herself to enhance what cleavage there was. "But sometimes you just have to let them *breathe*. Right?" she said, giving Rita a quick wink as she turned to her for confirmation, cupping what there was to cup with her two hands. Of course, what made it all the funnier was that Rita, one never to call attention to herself, made every effort to *de*-emphasize her substantial endowment. The "substantiality" of which Kit seemed to be openly fascinated with, which cracked Sabi up, and which in turn made Rita turn crimson each time Kit teased Sabi in comparison.

"Alright, you three," Claire intervened. "Rita, honey, I don't know why you let them get to you every time with this tit talk. And as for the bra-less bit, we know that Sabi does it to dazzle onlookers," she raised her eyebrows quizzically, "and Kit's only interested in comfort—and is *hardly* the flirting type, Sabi. Not to worry. So let's get

going. It's almost one." She looked back at Sabi with an evil grin.
" 'Breathe.' Right."

They set off for the pier, taking time to check out menus along the
way in preparation for lunch with Diane and Grant later. The street
was packed with tanned, relaxed, contented-looking people, plus a
fair amount, mainly of the gay male persuasion, who were more in
the alert and hungry-looking category—and *bronzed* rather than
tanned. They wended their way through the bodies and made the
turn onto the pier. It, too, was swarming, but with would-be whale
watchers and deep-sea fishermen as well as people waiting to take
the incoming ferry back to Boston. They had timed their arrival just
right; the ferry was just passing through the mouth of the harbor as
they walked up. In a few minutes it docked, and the latest crop of
seekers of summer-fun-in-the-sun streamed off the boat. Claire and
Kit, hands on their brows to shade the sun, searched through the
rush of faces for their friends.

"Hey!" Claire called, waving to another searching face walking up
the gangplank. "That looks like Grant!"

Grant waved back and smiled as the woman to her right looked
up and began waving, too.

"And there's Diane!" Kit said.

"My God. You'd think we were meeting royalty coming off the
friggin' Q.E. II after a trans-Atlantic crossing," Sabi said, only half quietly to Rita, who nodded in agreement. They just smiled at the dirty
looks they got in reply.

The two women soon joined them on the pier. After the requisite
hugging and kissing and initial introductions, they reviewed the luggage situation and decided to drop the bags off at Stella's, then head
back out for lunch and whatever else the afternoon held in store.
They parceled out the two women's luggage and headed back up the
pier to the street.

"So, did you get things straightened away at the Holiday Inn for
Diane?" Claire asked Grant.

"Yep. As if you doubted my powers of influence," Grant replied
with mock boastfulness. "You forget that I was *your* guide to the
wonders and workings of P-Town. Hell, woman, I've forgotten more
nights than you've spent here!"

"I know, I know. The voice of experience and all that crap." Claire glanced over at her as they were walking and winked at Grant. "But it is the height of summer, so I wasn't so sure you could pull it off."

"In all honesty, it's a good thing my guy Harry's still the manager there," Grant said, shifting her bag to her other shoulder. "Otherwise, it really would have been dicey."

"I had every confidence in you, old pal. I knew you'd pull it off."

"Damned right. When have I *ever* let you down, Griff?" Grant said, falling into their old habit of using last names, or versions thereof. Grant gave Claire the crooked half-smile that always seemed to charm people. That, the remnants of a Texas drawl, and a thick shock of sandy-red hair that refused to conform to any sort of hairstyle. Add to that the freckles that came with the hair and a gangly frame that gave Grant the air of being a permanently thirteen-year-old tomboy, and you could see why people couldn't help but smile when they met her. She was what she would have killed someone for saying: cute—in a rough-edged sort of way.

Behind them, Kit and Diane were doing their version of the same conversation.

"Damn! It is so good to see you!" Kit said, putting her free arm around Diane's shoulders and giving her a squeeze. "What's it been? Almost three years?"

"Yeah, I guess that's right. If you don't count that time I was in New York about six months after you guys moved in together." She looked at Kit out of the side of her eye and smiled at her look of consternation. "We didn't get to spend a lot of 'quality time' that visit, if you recall. You seemed *just* a little preoccupied with your new love."

"Oh, yeah," Kit replied, smiling sheepishly back at Diane. "I guess we were pretty much oblivious to anybody else at that point. Sorry. But at least we went out for a few beers and got more or less caught up."

"You're right. But I didn't get much of a chance to get to know Sabi, which I hope to do while I'm here. That reminds me—I really hope this isn't a major intrusion on your vacation. It just seemed ideal that we were both so close this week. Besides, I have plenty of work to keep me busy for most of the time."

"Oh, please! Stop it. I know you and your work, and I know you well enough that I can tell you if we want to do something on our own. We didn't live through three years of hell together in college for nothing!" Kit paused a moment, looking over at Diane. "Hmmmm. Something's different since I saw you last."

"Well, it took you long enough! I thought lesbians were supposed to notice other women. I only got practically all my hair cut off!"

Kit stopped and took a longer look at Diane. Indeed, the wavy hair that had been getting progressively shorter since the butt-length days of college was now a mass of sandy blonde ringlets that just covered her neck in back. And it looked great. It framed her face in an almost cherubic way. Truth be told, Kit had had a bit of a crush on Diane in those long ago days. Diane was the light and airy "femme" to Kit's then-unacknowledged "butch." Where Kit was the loud life of the party, Diane had been more the quiet, one-liner type. She was taller than Kit, an easy 5'7", with a slight, nicely shaped build and an easy, unforced air of confidence. A natural for the business management career she'd chosen. And while Diane wasn't what one would call a classic beauty, she was *very* attractive—sexy in that undefined but universally appealing way that some women are. That bit about guys not making passes at girls who wear glasses was way off the mark with Diane.

"It looks great," Kit responded with unfeigned admiration. "But you always looked great."

"Uh, oh. Just because I'm in this gay heaven out here, don't think you can lure me over to your side with your compliments!" Diane gave her a nudge in the ribs.

"No way! I've got my hands full with my wife up there!"

Leading the pack, Rita and Sabi were busy coming up with potential exit strategies if the "reunions" behind them got too carried away as the week went on.

When they got to the driveway, Sabi announced their arrival and dropped back to tell Diane about her first look at Stella's. By the time they all got to the deck and the picnic table, everyone was laughing at the well-told tale. Kit and Claire took the bags to Kit and Sabi's room and headed back outside.

"You guys ready for some lunch?" Claire asked the group. "We'll cook out back here for dinner, so you can soak up all the 'charm' of the place then, okay?"

Back out on the street, the consensus was that they'd stop at The Post Office Cafe, a tried-and-true staple of P-Town dining, just past the pier. The wait was only about fifteen minutes, which gave the newcomers a nice interlude to do some people watching and enjoy the local ambience. Not that it was a new experience for Grant— more like coming home. But it was fun watching Diane's reactions to the mélange of people teeming through the street.

"Wow. I see why you guys come here. This is incredible! I've been to San Francisco, the Village, even Key West, but never have I seen so many *different* people all together. It's amazing."

"Gee. For a straight chick, you've beaten *me* to the major gay strongholds," Grant said with a look of surprise.

"Me, too," Claire added.

"Well, it's not like that was why I went. I went to graduate school in Florida and had business trips to the other places. Does that make me an honorary member or something?" Diane asked with a sly smile.

"Sure. We'll take all the support from the straight crowd we can get!" Kit responded. " I knew there was a reason I liked you!" she added, giving Diane an affirming high-five.

Soon they were seated and perusing menus. A scarlet-haired young man glided over to take their drink orders. They couldn't help but notice his red-rimmed eyes, pale pallor, and distracted air.

Claire ordered a beer and her lunch and looked up at the waiter as he took her menu. "And we promise to not be a difficult table." He looked down at her with a puzzled smile. "It, uh, looks like you might have had a hard night."

"Oh, God. Is it that obvious?" he replied, running a hand through his bright hair. "You should only know. *Never* get involved with people you work with—especially when they're the summer help." He glared over his shoulder. "They keep you out to all hours and then break your heart," he said as he dramatically thrust his jaw upward, adopting a long-suffering air.

"I'm sorry," Claire said sympathetically. "I just hope his hangover is ten times worse than yours."

"I wish. But thanks for the thought," he said as he turned to the other women for their orders. "And I'll put in a good word to the cook for you." He finished with the orders and flew off to put them in.

"Good ol' Griff," Grant said, shaking her head slightly with a smile. "You never meet a stranger, do you?"

"Hey, it never hurts to be nice to the help. Besides, you're not exactly a shrinking violet yourself, honey."

"No, that I'm not. Except with the ladies."

"Oh, c'mon. Grant the lady-killer? Since when are you at a loss with some sweet young thing?"

"Since I broke up with Karen, it seems. I'm batting zero lately." She took a drink of her Bloody Mary. "I don't know. Maybe my heart's not in it. Karen really threw me."

"I was so surprised when Claire told me," Rita said, looking concerned and somehow doubtful at the same time. "We had such a good time when we were up at your place last fall. And when I was talking to Karen, she seemed perfectly happy." She paused and looked at Grant. "Not like Linda's attitude at all," she added, referring to Grant's previous partner.

"Oh, dear God, no. I mean, Karen certainly has her issues—and deciding she's straight again is *clearly* one of them. But, no, this wasn't like that other horrendous break-up at all. Actually, it was really very civilized. Which is maybe why it was so hard to take. It was *so* civilized, it was like it didn't bother her all that much."

"Oh, I doubt that," Claire said. "What was it? Three years you guys lived together?"

"Yep. And it may end up being more than that."

"What do you mean?" Rita asked.

"I mean, I'm such a good egg, I told her she could stay till she knows what she's doing."

"Jesus, Grant. You think that might have anything to do with your head being in the wrong place to meet other women, or what???" Claire asked. "Wait a minute—you didn't tell her it was okay to have that . . . *guy* over, did you?" She looked over at Diane. "No offense."

"None taken," Diane said wanly.

"Well, I didn't tell her she couldn't. I mean, she's paying half the rent."

"Oh, for Christ's sake, Grant. Talk about being masochistic."

"Yeah, I know. But I wanted to be understanding. Besides, maybe she'll reconsider if I play it cool and let her have some time and don't pressure her."

"Yeah, okay . . ." Claire said, half shaking her head.

"Hey, I'm still out there—looking and seeing what's what. Even if I am pretty much over the entire bar scene. That's *really* fun," she said with a grimace.

"Yeah, I'm glad we didn't have to go through all that," Kit added, putting her hand over Sabi's. "Sounds like it can get pretty brutal."

"Well, I'm sure there are other options," Diane ventured.

"Not a lot. And I'm not ready to go to the other extreme and join AA to meet somebody!" Grant said with a wistful smile.

"Well, it sounds to me like you're trying your best to be a decent human being—which I, for one, think is an amazingly admirable and loving thing to do under the circumstances," Diane said firmly. "Sometimes you have to make sure you've done everything possible before you can be ready for the next relationship."

"Thanks," Grant said, smiling over at Diane. "But Griff's known me a long time and knows my tendency to be a little self-destructive. Trust me, she's on my side."

Claire shrugged, a little embarrassed. "I just want you to be happy, pal."

"I know. I also know from our conversation over here on the ferry that this all hits a little close to home for Diane." She glanced at her across the table. "It hasn't exactly been your year either."

"So, what *is* going on with you?" Kit said, taking her cue. "When we talked around Christmas, it sounded like you and Paul were going great guns. 'Course, I also thought you and Michael were pretty serious, too, until I heard he was history."

"Yeah, well, at Christmas we were. But somewhere between then and May, things took a nosedive." She sighed and took a sip of her wine. "I guess it was around the first of the year, he started talking about moving in together. Which I wasn't totally against. It's just that I wanted to take things a little slower than I had last time around with Michael. Once you've been through the hell of breaking up with shared furniture and shit, you don't go leaping back in without thinking twice—or three times. So anyway, things were okay for the most part. And when he brought it up again in the spring, I told him I'd give him a definite answer when I got back from a trip I had to Chicago—which is when you were there, too, though we never managed to connect. Anyway, when I got back, things were different. I don't know if I'd waited too long or what, but he was very distant. And when *I* brought up the living together thing, we'd always somehow manage to get on another topic. One of *my* old tricks. Ironic, huh? Or I'm a good teacher. I knew something was up, but figured I was overreacting. Then Memorial Day came; we had plans to go away to Rehobeth Beach for the holiday." Diane looked over at Claire, Rita and Grant. "I live in Baltimore. So, I call the resort to check on directions and find out there's no reservation for us. And when I asked Paul, he said it had seemed pointless to go through the motions of a romantic weekend when he didn't feel like that about me anymore. Boom. That was it. I was so hurt, I just left and didn't even try to talk to him for a week or so. Then I called and suggested we get together to talk. We had dinner, but it was obvious it was over. Personally, I think there was somebody else. But he never did admit it. So, here I am, taking extra assignments and working my ass off. I guess that's why I admire Grant—I just couldn't be around him now, not after being that hurt."

"God, Di, I had no idea. Why didn't you call or come up and recoup with people who love you?" Kit asked.

"I really didn't want to talk about it for a while after. Not with my track record. And, besides, I didn't want to be some depressed wreck my next trip up, and I'd only met you once, Sabi, so I didn't want your next impression to be me at my worst."

"Oh, don't be silly. And don't ever think like that again. I would've understood."

"I know, but it worked out that I was up here now, so I didn't want to waste this opportunity to see you guys."

Sabi smiled at her, not without a slight look of embarrassment. She'd hardly been enthused at the prospect of Diane's arrival.

"Scarlet" approached the table. "My God, girls. This is P-Town— why the somber faces?"

"That's odd coming from Mr. Brokenhearted," Claire retorted.

"Oh, that was an *hour* ago. We're friends again and off to tea later!"

"Why couldn't I have been born a gay boy rather than a lesbian?" Grant moaned. "Oh, to snap out of it like that!"

They all laughed and got money out for lunch. Diane leaned over to Kit. "What's 'tea'?"

"I'll tell you all about it," Kit said. "In fact, there's a good chance you'll see firsthand before the week's over." After Kit gave "Scarlet" the money and everyone thanked him for elevating the mood at the table, Kit finished her drink and put her baseball cap on in a decisive sort of way. "I think it's time for a stroll along Commercial Street. I want Diane to see some of the shops, and, of course, the rest of the 'sights'!"

Out on the street, the activity had, if anything, increased. The tourists filled the sidewalks and the actual street itself, per the norm. But now the early shift of hawkers were out, too: boys in full regalia pitching this year's crop of drag shows, and reps for every comedy show, cabaret singer, play, and piano bar. Who were on roller skates, scooters, and high heels, all of them passing out little colored flyers for their acts. It was a show in itself.

By the time they'd gone a couple of blocks, Kit had a handful of little slips of paper.

"You planning on seeing them all?" Sabi teased her.

"Hey, I'm just glad it's not Claire collecting them as usual. For months after we're here, I'm still finding these little shits around!" Rita laughed.

"I figured it wouldn't hurt to take a look at them while we're getting dinner together tonight, just to see what we all want to catch."

By that point, they'd reached Sapph-ires, and Sabi wanted to show Diane the ring she'd been eying. By the time the rest of the party caught up to them, they were inside, getting a closer look. Grant mumbled something under her breath that Claire didn't catch. "What?" she asked her.

"I *said* you better watch your ass in here. I remember this place; it's basically an overpriced clip joint," she replied in a not-too-subtle whisper.

"Really!"

Claire looked up and saw Pat leaning against the counter not far from them. "Don't mind my friend. She's originally from Texas." She winked at Grant and chuckled at her having been caught in the act of being a jerk. "I've always told you you need to work on those social skills."

"Yeah, yeah," Grant mumbled, shoving her hands in her pockets and reddening a little.

"My God—you've done the impossible. You've made this big, ol' dyke blush!" Claire said to Pat, shaking her head in feigned amazement.

Grant gave her a dirty look. "I'll get you," she growled.

"Well, considering her origins, I'll let it go, I guess," Pat said, giving Grant a none-too-flattering once-over. She looked over at Claire. "Claire, right?"

Claire nodded and pointed at her friend. "And this is my newly-arrived friend, Grant."

"Oh, it's a pleasure, I'm sure," Pat said acidly, offering her hand. She looked back at Claire. "You seem nice enough, but some of your friends—!" She glanced over at Sabi who was immersed in jewelry talk with Diane and Rita, Kit standing behind them looking bored.

"I know. But they all *do* have their redeeming qualities, believe it or not. In fact, Grant here is the one who introduced us to P-Town."

"How nice," Pat said. "So, I take it in one of your previous trips you were a customer of mine?"

"Well, no. Someone I knew told me you guys were . . . a . . . little . . . high," Grant replied sheepishly.

"I see. Well, you feel free to look around and let me know what you think yourself." Pat gave them both a polite smile and moved back down the counter to the other group.

"Nice move, ace," Claire said with a laugh, giving Grant a pat on the back. "Though I have to admit I really never *have* seen you blush."

Grant answered with another grumble and likewise walked toward the rest of the group. As they both strolled up to them, Sabi was holding up her hand, admiring a beautiful lapis lazuli pinky ring. Kit looked stricken. Diane, however, was fully into the jewelry mindset.

"Oh, Sabi! That looks *gorgeous* on you."

"It does, doesn't it," Sabi replied approvingly, moving her hand around and admiring it further.

"Hey! I thought you were my friend!" Kit said tapping Diane on the shoulder.

"I *am*. That's why I'm helping *you* be the good partner I'm sure you are!" Diane had everyone laughing at Kit's squirming.

"Well, it *is* a nice ring," Kit said, resituating her hat on her head nervously. "But seems to me there was lots of other 'have-to-have' stuff we've seen. Maybe we should narrow things down a little bit before we blow a wad here."

"That's what I love about you, honey. You have such a delicate way of putting things," Sabi replied, taking the ring off and leaning around to give Kit a peck on the cheek. "But you're right. My shopping hormones are running rampant. Maybe we'll take a spin around after dinner and see what else is on my list."

"You guys are shopping tonight?" Pat asked the group, with a questioning little frown.

"Actually we hadn't gotten that far," Claire volunteered. "We thought about seeing Big Ed tonight. But I guess we'll have a pow-wow over dinner and see what sounds like fun."

"Is the dance cruise on your list?" she asked, giving Kit a quick look.

"They still do that?" Grant chimed in.

Pat gave her a withering look. "Well, your friend does know her P-Town, I guess," Pat said, looking back at Claire and the others.

"It's actually a lot of fun, as I recall," Grant added, trying to regain equal footing with the others.

"It's an annual thing. A moonlight lesbian dance cruise that the women's bars sponsor during Carnival Week. They do all kinds of music, and it's usually a great party. You might want to consider it," Pat said, putting the ring back in the case.

"What d'ya think, guys?" Claire asked. "Kinda sounds like fun. God knows, we never go dancing the rest of the year. And out on the water, with the moonlight and the music . . ." She put her arm around Rita and gave her a squeeze.

"It is supposed to be a gorgeous night," Kit added, looking lovingly at Sabi. "That is, if you don't mind, Diane. Think you can put up with a bunch of romantic dykes for a night?"

"I'm game," Diane replied.

"Hey! I don't remember the two of us agreeing yet," Sabi said, moving beside Rita.

"Well, maybe I'll see you guys there," Pat said. Again, she gave Kit a quick glance that, mercifully, Sabi didn't see. Kit did, however.

By the time they got back to Stella's, they'd agreed to do some "dancing in the dark," thanks in part to Claire's suggestion that it would be a good way to celebrate Grant's birthday, which had been the week before. Kit got the grill out and loaded it with coals while Claire helped Diane and Grant with their luggage, then set off for the car to drop them at the motel to check in. They'd already decided to walk back while the foursome got dinner together. Later, as they set the picnic table, Claire and Kit were relieved to overhear Rita and Sabi chattering away about Grant and Diane and their respective recent traumas—with concern and interest in their voices rather than the previous boredom and annoyance. Kit and Claire relaxed and sipped their cocktails as they monitored the glowing coals in their little portable grill, nestled down in the sand at the top of the beach. The girls had gone back inside to finish their preparations when they heard footsteps on the deck. Expecting to see Grant and Diane, Claire and Kit stood up to see Stella herself surveying the set table, complete with wine glasses and candles.

"Well! Looks like you girls are having yourselves quite a feast tonight."

"Sort of," Claire answered. "Some friends came up for a couple of nights, so we're having them over for some London broil and whatnot."

"They're not staying here, are they?" They could feel her scowl more than they could see it with the setting sun in their eyes.

"No. They have rooms at the Holiday."

About that time, Grant and Diane came strolling in, laughing and talking loudly. Actually, it was Grant who made for the loud part.

"Je-sus H. Christ! You shoulda seen me in those bad ol' super butch days! I'm tellin' ya, in Texas there was none of this 'just be yourself' bullshit. Hell, no! Darlin', you were the 'man' or the 'woman'—no in between. It was sick shit, but who had a choice?"

"You always know when Grant arrives," Claire said loudly enough for Grant to hear.

"Hell, yes! If you're gonna bother to show up, make an entrance, I always say."

"Ladies, I'd like to introduce you to the esteemed owner of this wonderful place, *the* Stella Dimitopoulos herself!" Claire made the introductions with great flair, all the better to flatter Stella's outsized ego.

As soon as names were exchanged around, Grant picked up on Claire's cue and launched into her P-Town past, making much of how sorry she was that, after all the years she'd been coming there, she'd never realized this charming little place was nestled down here on the beach—all of which Stella ate up with a spoon. And which, in turn, had all the others stifling their laughter, Rita and Sabi having joined the group mid-story. Before they knew it, Grant had invited Stella to join them for dinner, and Rita was off to the apartment to grab another place setting.

When Claire and Kit announced that the meat was ready, Stella excused herself and was back in a few minutes with two bottles of very decent red wine; she might be cheap about everything else, but when it came to her own creature comforts, it seemed she didn't scrimp, much to their drinking pleasure. As they sat down to the meal, Stella made it a point to wedge in between Claire and Grant, and then proceeded to launch into marvelous stories about P-Town over the last twenty years, always keeping an eye on Grant for the right reactions. Old, curmudgeonly Stella could be quite the charming raconteur—with the right audience.

CHAPTER

8

The evening was as perfect as the day that had given rise to it. The faintest breeze provided just the right balance to the still-warm summer air, the last rays of the sun deferring to the rising moon's silvery ascent. As Claire and Kit cleaned the spent coals and ash out of the grill, they heard Grant whistle and Diane giggle as Rita and Sabi made their grand entrances, finally.

"Well, these two look like they're ready for some serious cruisin'— and I don't mean by just bein' *on* that boat tonight!" Grant called over her shoulder. "You two better keep an eye on 'em."

"Oh, stop, you!" Diane added, giving Grant a tap on the wrist. "I've only known you for a day, but I'm guessing you're the troublemaker of the group!"

"Me? Nah. I just like to get Rita when I can. But she's always so calm and controlled it usually doesn't work anyway."

"Well, you'll certainly have to do better than that, Ms. Grant, to get a rise out of me," Rita said as she situated her jacket around her shoulders. "You forget I've lived with Claire long enough that I don't take the bait that easily. Now, Sabi, here, on the other hand—you probably should watch out for her!"

"Not tonight. After that dinner and wine, and with such a glorious night, *even* I'm too mellow to react."

"Man, you *must* be mellow," Claire said, walking back up onto the deck, brushing the soot off her hands. "I can't believe you let Ms. Casanova off the hook that easily."

"Aw, c'mon, Griff, give it a rest already," Grant groaned.

"I don't know—this is just *too* good." Claire sauntered over and put her arm around Grant. "It's not every day I get to watch you turn on that Texas charm and totally melt the heart of a crusty old dyke like Stella!" Grant shrugged Claire's arm off and sat down, ignoring her. "Now, is that any way to treat one of your oldest and dearest friends? C'mon—you gotta admit it was priceless. Not just watching Stella fall under your spell, but seeing you squirm like that! My God, no matter what you said to try to be less 'desirable,' she thought it was the funniest or cleverest thing she ever heard. I can't get over it . . . Stella, of all people." Claire chuckled to herself. "Looks like you got yourself a bona fide 'sugar mama' there, pal! Plaid sports jacket and all!" Grant groaned again and put her head in her hands.

"You're right, honey," Rita added. "She's got some nerve giving us a hard time! You really were turning on the charm," she said to Grant, with a skeptically raised eyebrow.

"I was just being *polite!* It's what you do when you're from the South. *Now* what the hell am I gonna do? Avoid her the rest of the time I'm here?"

"Nah. Just be a little *less* charming—if you can, that is." Grant scowled over at Claire. "That is, of course, unless you'd *like* to be heir to her millions."

"Whoa!" Kit exclaimed. "You really think she's worth millions?"

"Didn't you hear her talking about all those properties she owns? Villa in Mexico, two more places here, brownstone in goddamned Greenwich Village. Hell, yes, millions!"

"Can we maybe move on to another subject now?" Grant implored, looking genuinely miserable.

"Yes, we can," Claire answered giving her a consoling pat on the back. "I just have one more question: Which one of you *would* wear the sports jacket in the family?"

"To hell with all of you," Grant grumbled, getting up and grabbing her sweatshirt. "I don't know about you guys, but I've got a dance to go to." She stopped short and turned around with a pitiful look on her face. "*Please* tell me she won't be there."

"Not to worry, you're safe. And you're right. I think we better get moving or we're going to literally miss the boat!" Claire said as she threw her sweatshirt around her shoulders. "Are we ready?"

In short order they were once again among the milling crowd on the street. In the evenings, the throng was a little different though. If it was possible, people were strolling even more leisurely. And added to the mellow masses were the lines of people outside various bars waiting to get into shows. But even the added bottlenecking had little effect on the pervasive air of sated happiness; by that point, everyone was glowing too much from the sun of the day and a wonderful dinner to top it off, seemingly regardless of the choice of restaurant.

The six women turned down Standish Street to the wharf and noticed they'd joined a loosely organized parade of women heading the same direction.

"Jesus! Just when I thought I'd seen more lesbians than ever before!" Kit said with a genuine air of wonder.

"Down, girl," Sabi said, putting her arm through Kit's. "It's not that I'm jealous, honey. I just don't want you making a fool out of yourself drooling down your nice, clean shirt." Sabi leaned her head on Kit's shoulder as they walked. "It's not your most attractive look—and definitely a turn-off if I want to feel you against me while we're dancing," she said close to her ear, giving it a little lick.

Kit turned her head and gave Sabi a kiss on her nose. "Nice try, honey. But I can still look."

They reached the berth where the party boat was docked, handed over their tickets, and filed down the gangplank. The boat was normally used for dinner cruises, with a spacious interior outfitted with tables. At the front was a nice-sized dance floor backed by a small bandstand where a DJ was already at work sorting records and keeping the early mellow music going. First stop, of course, was the bar, where they all got a cocktail and continued their exploration of the boat. Narrow stairs on either side of the bar led to an upper aft deck, complete with speakers, seating, and another open area for dancing. Walking forward, they found a smaller fore deck, ideal for feeling the wind and catching the ocean spray once they were underway. At the moment, it was a perfect place to catch the sunset at its brilliant final burst before giving way to whatever rival show the moon and stars had planned for the night. As they all stood there, looking out over the town, they felt a small jerk and heard the deep rumble of the engines powering up for their departure.

"Better go down and claim a table before they're all gone," Grant said.

"Ah, the voice of experience," Claire teased.

Indeed, when they got back down to the main deck, most of the tables had been claimed. But they were lucky enough to find one with side wings they could pull up to convert it to a larger round table with room enough for all six of them. Granted, it was a little close to the DJ, but when she saw them looking apprehensively her way, she winked and angled the speaker closest to them more toward the dance floor and walked over to them.

"Sorry, ladies," she said with a warm smile. "I can't promise this is an ideal table for intimate conversation, but it's great access if you want to give me any requests!" She smiled again, even more broadly, her glance seeming to linger on Sabi. With her thick, short black hair, deeply tanned skin and dark eyes, she looked to be Hispanic, too. "Please. Don't hesitate to let me know what you want to hear." She winked and walked back to her equipment. Sabi quickly lit a cigarette and turned around to survey the room.

Claire grinned and leaned over the table and tapped Sabi's hand. "Hey, you. Turn around. I want to see if that's an honest-to-God blush on those well-tanned Puerto Rican cheeks!"

"What?" Kit said, turning from laughing with Grant in time to hear the end of Claire's comment. "What blush? What'd I miss?"

"You totally oblivious or what?" Claire said to her, grinning like a Cheshire cat. "Seems our friendly DJ took a liking to your honey's pretty Latina smile. And I think Miss Sabi here is a little flustered!"

"Well, I'll fix that," Kit said, scooting her chair back, her face clouding up into a scowl.

"Oh, for God's sake, Kit," Sabi hissed, pulling her back down to her chair. "It was nothing. She was just being friendly and apologizing for the music being so loud here." Sabi pulled Kit's arm around her and snuggled back into her. *"Sangana!"* she hissed in Claire's direction.

"Yeah, whatever about my mother. But, uh, it seems to me when

Pat the jeweler was 'friendly' like that with Kit, you got a little bent out of shape, too. No?" Claire continued relentlessly. "Ooh! Speaking of whom . . . talk about timing!"

They all looked, none too casually, in the same direction as Claire. Three or four tables back and across the floor was Pat, at what seemed to be two tables of friends. Fortunately, she was looking the other direction as she was scrutinized. As Claire looked along with the rest of them, someone caught her eye at the table behind Pat's. Dara was among the attendees, as well. Claire couldn't see who she was with, however, without being too obvious. She couldn't help but hope there might be another harmless, little dance floor encounter.

"Alright, alright. Touché. Point made. All that crap." Sabi scooted even closer to Kit and gave her a long, lingering kiss.

"My God," Grant said, fanning herself. "We're barely out of the marina and it's already gettin' pretty damned steamy in here!"

"Well, she's so sexy when she gets jealous, I just couldn't help myself," Sabi answered coquettishly. "Besides, we both are incredibly attractive, so I suppose these things are bound to happen," she said, batting her eyelashes and running her hand through her hair with a dramatic flourish.

"Oh, great. Now I have to put up with two oversized egos *and* a boatful of lovesick lesbians," Diane added with feigned exasperation.

As they'd been talking, the DJ had begun to gradually crank the music up. As the first upbeat dance tune ended, she picked up a microphone.

"LA-DIES A-N-D . . . well, LADIES!" she began, to a roar of laughter. "I want to welcome you all to the annual Carnival Week Lesbian Dance Cruise! I'm Carmen and I'll be your DJ tonight, though I'm sure as the night goes along, I'll wish I was out gettin' down with some of you gorgeous women!" She glanced at the table to her left. "But I promise I'll be good—and I'll do my best to make sure the music is, too! So, don't be bashful. We got lots of booze, lots of moonlight, and LOTS—OF—MUSIC!!!" At which point she cranked up the speakers and the music fairly shook the boat. "SO LET'S DANCE!"

As invariably happens with a good DJ and a good song, everybody was grinning when she finished and practically rose in unison to head to the dance floor, including the table of six. After shaking their "groove things" for three well-segued dance tunes, the group moved en masse back to the table for a short breather and some "refreshments."

"Looks like this is going to be a good group tonight," Claire shouted over the music. "Nothing worse than a being at a dance where no one dances!" She looked at her empty glass. "Unless it's being at a dance where no one takes your drink order!"

"I think our 'waitron' is working her way over," Grant said. "Next round's on me. It's a tradition of mine on my birthday."

"Wait a minute. Your birthday was actually last week, which means you probably already bought way more drinks than you should have! So, *we'll* get this one to toast the extension of the festivities," Claire countered.

"Well, actually, I really didn't do all that much celebrating. Not much in the mood, given recent events. Hell, I didn't even do my traditional shots of Jack. So, this one is definitely mine," she said, digging into her pocket.

"Oooh. Jack *Daniels.* Serious stuff," Diane said, crossing her arms and nodding her head in mock awe. "Well, nobody does shots of Jack around me without yours truly getting in on the action."

"Oh, yeah," Grant said, looking at Diane smugly. "You really look like the type who does shots."

Kit raised her eyebrows and shook her head. "You better watch yourself, Grant. Looks can be pretty deceiving with this one. She's not the frail girly-girl you might think. She used to raise hell in Raleigh when we were in school. I'm tellin' you, she was an animal when it came to partying."

"Really. You're not seriously thinking you can hold your own against me?" Grant replied, scooting her chair closer to Diane's.

"Do I hear a challenge?" Diane replied, hand up to her ear. "Bring 'em on! Only one condition."

"Here it comes. I knew she was bluffing," Grant said over her shoulder to Claire.

"I never do shots of Jack alone. Beer chasers. No chugging necessary, though. It's not like we're college kids anymore."

"Jesus, Grant. Kit wasn't fooling," Claire said, looking over at Diane with newfound respect. "This kid's no piker. You up for boilermakers?"

"Hell, yes!" She turned around in her chair and waved to get the server's attention. "You're on, Tarheel girl. No one drinks a Texan under the table."

"Thank God, we don't have far to go when we get back," Claire whispered to Rita. "'Cause it looks like we'll be carrying somebody!"

"The question is who," Rita whispered back.

When their drinks arrived, Grant paid the server and motioned for her to lean down. "Do me a favor, would you darlin'? Keep a nice, close eye on this table. I got a reputation to maintain here, and I'd hate to have it ruined by not havin' Mr. Daniels here when I need him. Know what I mean?" She slipped a generous tip onto the woman's serving tray.

"Yes, ma'am. Consider yourself taken care of." She stuffed the money into her tip glass and winked at Grant as she turned and headed for the next table.

Grant followed her with her eyes. "She's kinda' cute. This may turn out to be a halfway decent birthday celebration after all."

"Hey, you," Diane said, tugging on her T-shirt sleeve. "I suggest you keep your mind on the business at hand. I intend to give you a run for your money."

"Oh, you do, do you?" Grant replied, eying her questioningly. "Well, we'll just see about that, little lady. Bottom's up!" Grant downed the shot.

"*Sköl*," shouted Diane and did the same, and then reached for her beer, all the time smiling at Grant.

"Okay. I think I'm about ready for another spin," Claire announced to the table. "And I'm thinking the barroom babes here could stand sweating off a little of that demon rum!" Rita stayed seated as Claire got up to follow the others to the floor. "Aw, c'mon, babe. You never dance with me!"

"Go on ahead, honey," she said, stroking Claire's cheek. "I was a sport and danced first thing tonight, just because I knew you'd say that. *And* I danced at the Boatslip. Not bad for someone who's not a dancer. Besides, you've got the whole group out there. I'm going to sit this one out. Go on!" she said, shooing Claire on.

Claire joined the group and was soon fully absorbed in the music. As they all continued into the next song, Kit and Sabi pulled out their best dance moves—a little solo freestyle stuff, plus some couples moves that were very impressive. They were both good dancers, especially Sabi—something about that Latin hip movement gave anything she did an extra provocative kick. And it was evident that Kit enjoyed it as much as everyone else who slipped a look to see who the hot little number was. More, actually—she knew who was "dancing" with the "little number" at home that night. Kit was so engrossed in Sabi's show, she didn't realize she was edging into the person behind her—until, that is, she stepped on a foot.

She spun around to apologize and practically embraced Pat, who had likewise spun around to confront her "attacker." "Oh!" Kit said, totally taken aback, mainly at the fact that she was actually pleased to see her. "I'm sorry," she shouted over the din, composing herself as she did. "I didn't realize you were there."

"Apparently not!" Pat shouted back, initially indignant. Then she laughed, amused by Kit's wide-eyed shock and embarrassment, then sudden shift to attempted nonchalance. "Not to worry. It happens." She held her finger up to hold Kit's attention while she took a quick sip of the drink she'd brought on the floor with her. "Glad you guys decided to come tonight. Good idea?" she said loudly, looking smug.

"Yeah. I have to say, this is a great party!" Kit said. "I think everyone's having a great time." As they talked, their groups semi-merged, so that they were soon all dancing more or less together, "they" having shrunken a bit as Kit noticed Grant and Diane back at the table working on their second round. Pat followed Kit's eyes.

"Looks like it," Pat said.

"Oh, those two. Well, I don't know how much dancin' they're going to do. They're doing the Jack-and-beer thing. It's Grant's birthday."

"Gotcha. Looks like the celebrating is going well," Pat said, watching the two drinkers crack up with laughter.

Claire sidled over near Kit. "Hey, Pat! Thanks for the suggestion. This is great!"

"No problem. The more the merrier." She showed no intention of merging back into her group, and continued dancing with Kit. Claire

made it a point to make eye contact with Sabi and take her own dancing up a notch. Sabi's sidelong glances, however, made it clear that
she was well aware of the situation. She started to edge closer to Kit
when suddenly Grant and Diane joined them, clearly loosened up a
bit from their latest "toast."

"Hey, girl!" Diane shouted to Sabi. "I hate to admit it, but this
beats most of the dances I've been to with guys. You women actually
dance!"

"You bet, honey! That's one of the requirements to get into the
club!"

Diane smiled. "I guess so! Well, I guess I qualify on at least one
level!"

The music started winding down, and a different beat took over
as Carmen came back on the microphone.

"Buenos noches, senoritas y . . . senoras! I've decided I should ex-
pose you east coast girls—at least *most* of you—to some *real* music!
One of these days, I'm betting you'll be hearing this in all the clubs!"
She cranked up a salsa beat that momentarily stymied the dancers
but soon had them adapting their moves to keep up. Sabi, however,
didn't miss a beat—literally. Her face lit up, and with absolute
machisma (if one can call it that), cut in between Kit and Pat and
whisked Kit off. She pressed her close against her, positioned Kit's
hands appropriately and, with no verbal instruction needed, taught
her all she needed to know about *salsa* dancing. The crowd moved
back and clapped to the beat with them, watching as their hips,
shoulders and heads moved with the music of the islands. Sabi led
without leading so that they looked as though they'd been dancing
together like this for years. Soon others picked up the moves and
joined them, including Grant and Diane, with Grant clutching Diane
to her, trying her Texas best to get the same rhythm going that Sabi
and Kit did. Diane seemed a little taken aback, but was blithely trying
to be a sport about it. Carmen, on the other hand, looked decidedly
less than pleased. Poised beside a speaker, she had clearly hoped to
take a break from her booth and pick up where she'd assumed Kit
would leave off. As casually as possible, she edged backwards back
up to her turntables, changing what would have been the next
dance. Soon "Pump Up the Volume" was blaring away.

Grant and Diane headed back to the table and started in on round three—and began to look it. Grant had her arm around the back of Diane's chair and was hanging on her every word, all of which Diane seemed totally oblivious to. Claire rejoined the table by way of Carmen and took a deep drink of her bourbon and Seven, having resisted urgings from the "contestants" to modify her usual and join the "contest." Soon, Kit and Sabi were back to cool off. They sat out the next couple of songs, mainly teasing and egging on Grant and Diane. Kit, however, started to look concerned.

She scooted around the edge of the table towards Claire. "You did tell Grant that Diane's not really into this whole scene, right?"

"I *told* you I did," Claire said, patting Kit on the back. "They're okay. Hell, Diane's made it clear she's the token straight tonight."

"I don't know," Kit said, playing with the tab on her beer can. "Grant seems to be really into this one-on-one thing."

"You worry too much, my friend. Diane's a big girl. And Grant's not stupid. Re-*lax,*" Claire said soothingly, bouncing in her chair to the beat of the music. "Where the hell's my song?"

"What song?"

"My fave. You'll see."

As the current song wound down, Carmen got on the mike again. "Just to let you know, ladies, I am taking requests. Just stroll right on up and let me know. In the meantime, we have our first for the evening. However, our requestor has made it clear that we HAVE to have a full dance floor! So, let's boogie, ladies!"

At that, the beat merged seamlessly into a more insistent version of the same tempo, and a general whoop went up from the crowd as Natalie Cole's version of "Pink Cadillac" filled not only the room but seemingly the ocean depths surrounding them. The boat was rockin'. Claire grabbed Rita's hand, as Rita smiled in defeat and rose to join her on the dance floor.

"Good one, Claire," Kit shouted, all smiles, pulling Sabi, also smiling, behind her. Grant and Diane weren't far behind. And, indeed, *everyone* in the room was on the floor, united in the way that certain dance tunes can make of hundreds of individuals one gyrating organism. Claire wiped the sweat from her brow and looked around her as she launched into last-stage full dance mode, feet moving in steps, arms bouncing over her head in time with the music, and looked around at the packed dance floor. Moving towards them was Dara, eyes half closed, lost in the music. Subtly, Claire angled her body in unspoken dance language to create an access point to their corner of the floor. In unconscious recognition, Dara moved toward it, opening her eyes as she was almost in their sphere. She brightened and waved, as talking was useless at this stage of the night. She and the woman she was apparently dancing with faced Claire who then turned slightly so as not to exclude Rita. Dara waved at Rita as well, who waved back. Hey, if not in real life, why not have the best of both worlds on the dance floor, Claire thought to herself, and again abandoned herself to the music.

At the segue point into the next song, Claire leaned toward Dara. "So, how's it going?"

"You can't tell?" Dara said, glancing back at the woman she was dancing with.

"Well, now that you mention it, I guess so!" Claire forced a happy smile. "Any flack from the ex?"

"Not yet. But I've been playing it cool about my exact activities. Truth is, she's been awfully agreeable. I think she may finally be getting it." Claire nodded. "Anyway, she's here somewhere, too, and so far so good. Hopefully, I'll see you when it's not so loud, and I'll give you more of an update." Dara smiled at Claire. "In the meantime, thanks. I probably wouldn't be here if it weren't for you." Claire smiled back with an oh-it's-nothing kind of look. Then sighed and turned her attention again to dancing.

The grouping lasted another song, near the end of which people began drifting off the dance floor, including Rita, who headed toward the stairs to the upper deck. Claire debated about joining her or dancing one more dance as Carmen stepped to the mike. "And now, ladies, another request from the floor—one you might find a little out of the ordinary. Grab your partners, girls!" The music took an abrupt turn. A country beat replaced the dance beat and Grant's face lit up, along with a few scattered others. Claire grinned and decided this was worth sticking around to see.

"Whee-ha!" Grant whooped, in true Texas fashion. "Now, *this* is dancin'!" she exclaimed, grabbing a surprised Diane, who stopped dancing and looked at her, puzzled.

"This is a Texas two-step, darlin'. You can two-step can't you?" Diane shrugged her shoulders and bravely gave it a try. It was not a pretty sight. Grant doggedly tried to lead poor Diane in a totally unfamiliar dance that actually required knowing steps and moves. However, just beyond them, Pat was in a similar predicament, vainly trying to follow and lead at the same time with a tall woman who likewise had no clue what she was doing. They caught one another's eyes and maneuvered their partners nearer one another with a common goal in mind. Diane and the other woman caught on and deferred, gratefully, no doubt, to the opposite's partner. Soon Pat and Grant were off, spinning and stomping and having a grand old time.

"You know, I should've let you flounder around out here with that poor thing who didn't know a two-step from a hole in the wall."

"Ah, that's not nice," Grant said, expertly leading Pat around the floor in two-step fashion. "Besides, you didn't look to be in very good shape either. Though I guess you'd a had a right to leave me out there in two-step hell. Say, how *do* you know how to two-step?"

"I suppose you think you're the only Texas lesbian to ever make it this far north, huh?"

"Apparently not—much to my good fortune at the moment." Grant paused and cleared her throat. "Uh, I guess my little comment this afternoon was pretty tacky." She twirled Pat and pulled her back, a little closer this time. "I hope this means you forgive me. Even though I can't really show you my best form since I don't have my boots on!"

"Well, I don't know if I'm at total forgiveness level yet. But I have to say you dance a mean two-step—in boots or not—which could go a long way toward my getting over your big mouth!" They both laughed and stomped even harder.

Carmen obliged the five or six couples who actually knew how to dance the two-step and played one more before shifting to a slow song. As the tempo slowed, Grant stumbled a little as she went to pull Pat closer to dance the slow dance.

"I'm thinking I need a drink after all this energetic leaping around," Pat said, eying Grant dubiously. "No doubt we'll see each other around."

Grant steadied herself, a little wobbly as she regained her standing legs. "We okay?" she said, offering her hand.

"Why not?" Pat responded shaking her hand.

"Hey! It's my birthday! Come on over and have a dirthday brink with me," Grant said, trying to square her shoulders and then realizing what she'd just said. "You know what I mean," she said, taking her hand and pulling her over to their table. Kit and Sabi, however, were on their way to the dance floor to enjoy the romantic musical interlude as Grant and Pat arrived back at the table. As Claire greeted them, Rita reappeared and pulled a pleasantly surprised Claire towards the floor

While Grant and Pat had been two-stepping, Diane had ordered the next round. Grant waved the waitress over and ordered Pat a drink over her protestations to the contrary. The three of them attempted conversation over the din, to no avail, and waited for the waitress to return since Grant refused to go the next round until Pat was duly served.

"Oh! By the way . . . I hope I didn't break up anything out there," Grant said, straining to keep her eyelids from drooping.

"Nah. Just someone who asked me to dance. Hell, I don't even know her name." Pat sighed. "You'd think living in P-Town you'd be bound to find *someone* interesting, if only for a week's fling. But not when you have to *work* in P-Town. Puts a real crimp in your social availability."

"You single?" Grant said, surprised.

"Yeah. Broke up about six months ago with not only my romantic partner but my business partner as well. Let's just say it hasn't been the most fun six months of my life."

"I'm sorry. I know the drill. Same story. Not fun," Grant tried gamely to explain, almost monosyllabically given her focus on trying desperately not to slur her words.

The foursome reappeared at the table about the time the waitress arrived with Pat's drink. As Grant and Diane started in on the next round, looks circulated around the table with the same unspoken question in their eyes.

"Hey, you two," Claire said to Grant and Diane. "I say we call it a draw. Given what time it is, we probably only have fifteen or twenty minutes before we dock."

"Draw, hay-ell!" Grant *tried* to snap. Instead it came out much slower, the south Texas drawl thick as syrup. "Di-yan said she wanted another gahh-damned round, and I'll be da-a-amned if shum little straight shick ish going to say I couldn't keepupp!" she slurred, punctuating the final statement with an emphatic hiccup.

Kit looked at Diane pleadingly, but Diane was far enough in her cups that it was evident she wasn't going to fold now either. They both picked up their shot glasses and downed the bourbon. Only Diane reached for the beer. Grant, on the other hand, insisted she wanted to dance another dance and grabbed Diane by the hand to lead her out. Pat sat back, puzzled but amused.

Grant and Diane's dance lasted maybe two minutes before Grant attempted a spin of some sort and ended up on the floor, nearly taking with her the women who had been behind her. Kit and Claire headed to the floor to "escort" their friends back to the table.

Once there, Grant's head sank down onto her arms on the table, while Diane, hanging on to her dignity by a thread, bobbled in her chair, head up, finishing her beer. Mercifully, Carmen announced the last dance and that the boat would be docking in a few minutes.

"You know, you guys can just crash on our floor for the night," Claire offered, much to Rita's surprise.

"No," Diane said, losing her winner's air and mellowing. "I think we both need to get to our own beds and crash." She stopped for a minute, frowning with thought and swaying as she sat there. "The question is, of course, how we're going to *get* to our beds." It was her turn to hiccup.

"Not to worry," Pat said. "I really didn't drink that much tonight. I've found out the hard way over the last few months that drinking and being depressed don't mix all that well. My car's up at the shop. Where is it exactly you guys have to go?"

After they brought Pat up to speed on the Holiday Inn arrangements and room keys were located in advance, the general consensus was to start the migration toward the door now, before the last dance finished. Grant, all but passed out, put up no resistance to

Claire and Pat's arms on either side of her, lifting her up and then "assisting" her feeble attempt at walking. Diane, stiff-lipped and determined, insisted she'd make it out under her own power, despite Kit's attempt to provide the same assistance. "You can't shay you won," she slurred, "unlesshoo make it out onurown." The walk up the gangplank was less than dignified. Fortunately, they were not alone in that respect.

CHAPTER
9

Thursday morning arrived much too soon—and was much too bright—for at least three of the four women. Rita was up at her usual early hour and, this particular morning, had *lots* of quiet time for her private reverie. Around nine o'clock she heard a crash and a string of expletives. She smiled to herself and looked up toward the door of their apartment. Sure enough, a few minutes later Claire came stumbling out, her face twisted in a scowl. Rita waited patiently at the picnic table, pretending to read her book.

"Who the hell had the bright idea to rearrange the kitchen so damned early? I practically killed myself tripping over the chair!"

"And good morning to you, sweetheart," Rita replied calmly.

"Yeah. Whatever." She rubbed her face and then held her head for a moment. "Jesus. Why'd you let me drink so much?"

"That's my fault, too, I suppose?"

"Well . . . yeah." Claire looked over at Rita, trying hard to maintain her pout, but finally succumbing to the smile that was working its way out. *"Yeah,"* she repeated emphatically, walking over to Rita who was just sitting there, arms crossed, regarding her patiently. "That's part of your job as a devoted, caring partner." She kissed Rita lightly. "Trust me. That's all the kiss you want right now." Claire sat down beside Rita and yawned. "So, any other counties heard from yet?"

"No. Shockingly, you're the first party girl up."

"What time *is* it?"

"A little after nine, I think."

"Hmmm. Well, this won't do at all. In my awakening stupor, I thought it might be a good idea—not to mention therapeutic—to do the Boatslip this morning and, uh, dry out a bit. After some sustenance, of course. And a little hair of the dog."

"Oh, for Christ's sake, Claire. Surely you had enough to drink last night."

"Honey. Since you're the first to boast about never having been drunk even once in your life, I don't think you're all that qualified to know what a first-class hangover demands. And it does demand a Bloody Mary the morning after. Trust me." She rubbed her temples again. "Not on an empty stomach, of course. The breakfast I assume you were setting up for is the other necessity."

"Well, I should make you all deal with cold cereal."

"Ah, you wouldn't do that to your honey, would you?"

"I haven't decided," Rita said, turning back to her book, pretending to dismiss Claire.

"Then there's hope, I guess." Claire sat quietly for a moment, staring out at the bay. "First, though, some desperately needed caffeine." She got up to head back upstairs for coffee when a door on the ground floor squeaked open. Out stumbled both Kit and Sabi, looking no better than Claire. "Well! Two more rays of sunshine! You guys narrowly avoided my little wake-up visit that was on the agenda just after my first cup of coffee. Interested in some?"

"Oh, my God, yes," Sabi groaned. "Isn't vacation supposed to be fun? My head doesn't feel like it's having fun." Kit just slouched her way to the table and grunted a greeting to Rita.

"Three coffees coming up."

Soon Claire was back with a tray laden with steaming cups and the requisite sides.

"Here you are, ladies," she said putting the tray on the table. "And, yes, Sabi, I remembered the half-and-half."

Sabi tried to manage a smile. "Oh, thank God. Coffee."

They sat silently for a moment, letting the caffeine gain a foothold in their systems. Then Kit started chuckling to herself.

"Man. That Grant is a real pisser. I was just thinking about her out there doing that two-step thing, half-drunk out of her mind."

"Ouch. If we think we're hurting, can you imagine what she's gonna wake up to?" Sabi added. "*And* Diane. I had no idea quiet, professional Diane was such a party girl at heart."

"Oh, yeah," Kit replied. "In school, no one could drink her under the table. This buttoned-up bit is new since she started doing her high-powered business thing. Last night was the Diane I remember."

"Well, they were a riot. So, should we call and let them be as miserable as we are?" Claire asked.

"I'm in no shape to do anything yet," Kit said. "Let's give 'em a break and wait until we've eaten. Then we'll roust them out."

"Breakfast does sound pretty good," Claire said, leaning toward Rita and resting her chin on her shoulder. "You gonna have mercy on us after all?"

"Oh, alright. But you all deserve a little pain after acting like such children last night." She stood up and looked down at them. "And it looks like you've got it."

"Ooh. Not so loud," Kit said, grimacing.

"So, did Rita tell you guys about my idea?" Claire asked.

"Yeah," said Sabi. "Sounds good to me. A day in the sun sounds like about all I can manage at the moment."

"Ditto," replied Kit. "Did we say anything about that last night? The last couple of hours are a little hazy."

"I don't think so. That's the other reason I figured we should give the girls a shout, so they could get a move-on if they want to join us."

"Yeah, you're right. Want me to go with you?" Kit said, shielding her eyes from the sun as she looked up at Claire.

"No, I'll let you wake up a little bit more. But when I get back, you can assist me in rounding up some Bloodys to kick-start our engines."

"Oh, God. Let me get some coffee down first," Sabi said, now holding her head.

Claire patted her gently on the head and left to make the call.

"Jeesh. I really didn't think we drank that much last night. Maybe it was the ocean air," Kit said, yawning.

"Oh, no, sweetie. We *all* were definitely drinking—except Rita, of course. Thank God. We'd be up shit's creek if we didn't have her to take care of us."

Kit sat quietly for a minute. "I hope those two got to the motel okay. They were *really* turned around. Even for Diane. But I guess after the year she's had, she deserved a good blowout. I get the impression she doesn't have fun like she used to. She's gotten so intense and serious the last few years. I'm worried she'll be burnt out by thirty."

"Not if she lets go like that every now and then," Sabi answered. "Didn't look to me like she'd forgotten how to have a good time."

"Yeah, but with her it's one extreme or the other. Oh, well. I guess she's a big girl by this point."

"Exactly. Relax." Sabi reached over and massaged Kit's shoulders. "Speaking of having fun, you, my little *chica*, were very impressive out there doing salsa for the first time. We're definitely going to have to make time for more of that in the future. 'Course, the problem is finding a lesbian bar that has salsa music!"

"I'll leave that to you, honey. I'm sure you'll find one if it exists."

"Well, that was surprising," Claire said as she rejoined them at the table.

"What?"

"No answer in Grant's room. I didn't remember Diane's room number, so I left a message for Grant that we'd be at The Boatslip by 10:30 or so. I hope there are enough chairs to claim by then. There should be, though. First things first—Bloodys and breakfast. Let's go up and see how Rita's doing with the food side of things. I'll get to work on the other part. You guys got a lime?"

Forty-five minutes later they'd refueled, donned their suits and shorts, and were headed down Commercial Street, albeit more slowly than usual. As they passed Sapph-ires, Kit looked in.

"Wonder how Pat's feeling this morning? I know she said she hadn't done that much drinking, but I bet she's not looking forward to a day dealing with haggling tourists."

"How about you don't worry so much about your *friend* Pat," Sabi said coldly.

"Oh, stop it, Sabi. She hardly said ten words to me last night," Kit said in a bored tone. She walked toward the window and cupped her hands around her eyes to look in.

"Well, even so." Sabi adjusted her sunglasses and squared her shoulders, her body language completing the thought. Then she noticed what Kit was doing. "Since when are *you* interested in jewelry?"

"I'm not. I just wanted to see if Pat was busy; thought it might be a good idea to see how the final chapter of the night went since we couldn't reach Grant earlier." She peered a moment longer. "But I guess we'll just have to wait till the girls meet us. She's got customers waiting. Oh well."

As they were turning to head on to The Boatslip, Pat glanced over at the front window and caught a glimpse of Kit pulling her baseball cap back on, after having reversed it to look in the window. She left her current customers to decide which of the four styles of lambda necklaces they wanted to see and rushed to the door.

"Hey! Kit! Guys!" she yelled up the street. Kit turned and waved and jogged back toward the shop with the other three women trailing behind.

"Great," Sabi snarled to Rita. "Just what I need with my head feeling like an overripe watermelon and my disposition less than fucking sunny."

"Shhh!" shushed Rita. "You need to get a grip, sweetie. Even *I* think you're overreacting—and you know I wouldn't tell you that if I didn't love you. Lighten up a little. Kit adores you and you know it!" she hissed under her breath.

"Oh, alright."

As they approached the store, Pat and Kit were already in conversation.

". . . so I hope everything was okay after I finally left. Man, they were in sad shape. Not that I feel exactly chipper myself at the moment. You guys hear from them yet today?" Pat said.

"No, not yet. Claire called but didn't manage to rouse Grant. Shit. Now I'm getting worried," Kit said, shoving her hat up and rubbing her forehead.

"Aw, I don't think there's anything to worry about," Pat replied. "They were drunk, all right, but I'm sure they both promptly passed out and are paying royally for it today."

"Yeah, you're probably right. Anyway, we left a message for 'em that we'd be at The Boatslip for the day, so they'll probably show up in a couple of hours."

"Well, if I see them wandering around, I'll point 'em in the right direction."

"Thanks. And thanks for taking them home last night."

"Hey. No problem." She looked back in the store. "Gotta go. Enjoy the day, ladies. I sure as hell wish *I* was spending the day in the sun." She rolled her eyes, took a deep breath, and went back in the store.

"I bet you do," Sabi muttered under her breath. Kit gave her a dirty look as they started back toward the club.

"So, what'd Pat have to say?" Claire asked.

"Not all that much, really. She decided she should walk them to their rooms when they all got to the motel. Seems Grant was in rare form by the time they got to Diane's room—your basic mad dash for the bathroom. Pat waited around a while, but when it sounded like Grant would be, uh, busy for a while, Diane told her there was no reason she had to hang around, she'd make sure Grant was okay. So, she waited a little while longer, then decided to head on home. And that's when you guys walked up."

"Well, I think she's right. I'm sure there's nothing wrong that some aspirin, sleep, and caffeine can't cure," Claire said. "Which they've both had experience at. We'll give them until noon-ish and then start calling again. And we'll have lounges waiting for them if they show up sooner."

While the morning had again started off typically overcast, the sun was already burning off the clouds by the time the hunky pool boy had the six pool lounges set up; The Boatslip was never short on outstanding looking male employees to keep the tanning crowd happy and ordering drinks. And, amazingly, most of them were genuinely friendly and not as self-absorbed as one might expect of such Adonis types—at least the "body" types the women were used to from the New York Village scene. The waiter for their section timed his arrival to coincide with the last smoothing of their beach towels on the lounges. They ordered and then finished getting situated, sunscreen and shades on, books out, and bags stashed. Of course, just as they'd gotten comfortably stretched out, the waiter arrived with their drinks. As Kit and Claire sipped their second Bloody Marys, they sat up and surveyed the increasingly crowded deck.

"I still can't believe we missed doing this the first years we came," Claire mused, shaking her head. "Thank God, Dean told us about it. Hell, he'd found out about the pool routine the first year he was up here!"

"Dean . . . Have I met Dean?" Kit asked.

"Only briefly that first night you came with me to Broadway Baby. He's the guy that knows *everything* there is to know about movies. You want to know who the key grip was for *Invasion of the Body Snatchers,* Dean'll tell you!"

"Oh, yeah! I remember now. Well, I'm glad he clued you in, too. This is the best. To Dean!" Kit raised her glass to Claire, and they clinked.

"Like you two need a toast to drink," Sabi muttered from behind the book she was reading.

Rita raised her glass of Pepsi to Sabi. "Cheers!"

"Ha, ha, ha," Claire said, tolerantly. "I don't remember addressing either of you lovely ladies. Now, if you don't mind, I think I'll finish my *New Yorker* while I wait for Sabi to finish her trashy lesbian novel so I can read it!"

"Better be nice to me," Sabi said, peering over her sunglasses.

By eleven, the sun was downright intense. Claire abandoned her magazine to take in the warming rays. As she laid there feeling her body absorb the sun, her mind started to drift. She smiled at the various images of the boat ride that passed through her mind, linger-ing first on one then another, until she came upon the picture of Dara dancing. Mmmmm . . . that woman could dance. The image took her back to their encounter here earlier in the week, and then back to seeing her the first time on the beach at Stella's. God, she was a striking woman. Claire had been absolutely dazzled, which hadn't happened for a very long time. Really, not since she'd been with Rita. But Dara was totally unlike Rita—worldly, sophisticated, tall, and handsomely beautiful in that Candice Bergen sort of way, a look Claire had always found irresistible. Chalk it up to the influence of forever lusting after Candice/Lakey once she'd seen *The Group* at an impressionable age!

She simply couldn't help but notice this woman . . . and imagine what life might have been like had she met her first. She imagined running into her at a bar in New York, Dara being there . . . oh, on a business trip. They'd talk, chairs scooting closer as conversation became more involved and they learned they were both unattached. Knees would brush and stay touching as Claire put her arm around the back of Dara's chair. As the bar got noisier, Dara would lean closer to talk, and the conversation would pause as they looked at one another a little too long and then slowly, naturally lean into a soft, testing kiss. Wordlessly, they would get up, leave the bar, hail a cab, and be in Dara's hotel room, locked in an embrace that was punctuated by slowly, sensually disrobing one another, one piece of clothing at a time. Collapsing onto the bed, Claire would reach up to stroke Dara's face, her hands slowly moving down her neck to caress her perfect, waiting breasts. Claire could almost hear the quick gasp as her fingers found their marks. Then Claire would lean up and take each small focal point of sensation into her mouth, sucking and nipping them to hardness while Dara's knee ground slowly, insistently into her. Claire would suddenly rise and literally throw Dara on the bed, kissing her hard while her hand searched lower down, finding her warm wetness and teasing her with light, uncommitted touching. Then she'd start the slow, maddening, unrushed kissing down the length of her body, stopping when she was just at the place Dara so wanted her to be. Open to her kisses, Dara would beg and Claire would simply blow lightly, with an occasional quick dart of her tongue, until, sensing Dara was at the peak of desperate wanting, Claire would suddenly take all of her into her mouth . . .

"Oh, my God!" Sabi blurted out.

"Jesus Christ, honey! I was just dozing off. You scared me to death!" Kit groaned.

"I can't believe what trash this book is! I'm so glad I bought it," Sabi giggled.

"Well, at least that means you'll be zipping right through it, so I won't have too long to wait," Claire said, getting up from her prone position, sighing at the thought of the fantasy moment Sabi had just unwittingly destroyed. She sat there and realized how hot the morning had become. She was dripping wet.

Claire wiped her face with her beach towel. As she put her sunglasses back on, she turned to see if anyone had ventured into the pool yet. Indeed, four or five people were in, a couple of them languidly swimming laps and the others bouncing around in the shallow end getting cool.

"Well, I think it's time for a first dip," she said, having decided it would be a good idea to leave the world of what-if for a while—and cool off. She swung around to look for her flip-flops under the lounge. "You ready?" she said over her shoulder to Kit.

"Whoo! Yeah. I was just going to ask you the same thing. Girls?"

"Not yet," Rita said, not moving from her reclining position. "I'm too comfortable at the moment."

"Did you put enough sun block on, honey?" Claire said, leaning over and patting Rita's leg. "Ooh. I hope so, 'cause your skin is really hot."

Rita reached down and patted Claire's hand. "Yes, dear. I'm fine."

"Okay. Let's go!"

They walked toward the pool, Claire sucking in the little belly that she always imagined was too large. Even with only gay guys around as far as she could tell, there was that twinge of vanity that wearing a bathing suit always brought out. Kit, on the other hand, couldn't care less. She was one of those lucky, unselfconscious people who was totally comfortable in her own skin.

That first step into the pool sent shivers through both women. But as soon as they dove into the water and swam a few strokes, it was evident the pool was actually pretty warm—it was just their sun-seared bodies that were hot. After a couple of laps, they rendezvoused at the side of the pool and watched the other bathers for a while. One guy seemed to be demonstrating his swimming prowess to whomever might be interested in looking, swimming lap after lap with strong, muscular strokes. Four men on the other side of the pool chatted, cocktails balanced on the deck beside them. And there were two women who were totally oblivious to the fact that they were steadily edging their way into deeper water since they were locked in a long kiss, which they broke momentarily to just smile and look at one another.

"Ah . . . young love. Ain't it grand?" Claire said.

"Guess so. I'm just wondering if they'll even realize it when they're both under water," Kit replied with a chuckle.

About that time, the taller of the two broke away and laughed, realizing the imminent reality of that very thing. She picked up the other woman and tossed her backward into the deep end, quickly turning to jog back into shallower water, clearly expecting retaliation. As she did so, Claire squinted against the sun bouncing off the surface of the water and, with a jolt to the pit of her stomach, realized it was Dara. Having a marvelous time, it seemed. After her recent interlude, she tried to rid her mind of irrational feelings of jealousy. She squinted more, trying to see better.

"Isn't that the woman from Stella's who was on the boat last night?" Kit asked.

"Yeah, I think so," Claire said, trying to make sure she sounded nonchalant.

" 'You think so'—ha! C'mon, I've seen you checking her out."

"I have not!" Claire replied indignantly. She glanced over at Kit who was just looking at her, eyebrows raised. "Well, not really 'checking her out.' We've talked some." Kit cleared her throat and started whistling tunelessly, looking up in the air patiently. "Alright, alright. I think she's hot. But there's no rule against admiring the sights." She almost felt as though Kit had been spying on her earlier daydream.

"Ah, ha! I knew it!" Kit exclaimed, smacking the water for effect.

"Shut up, you. I'd rather the whole pool not know."

"Not to worry, pal. I know you're not the screwing around type. And you're right—no harm in looking."

"Yeah. You should talk."

"Hey! That's not nice. I haven't done a thing."

"Okay. I suppose you haven't been enjoying the attention from Pat *at all*," Claire shot back with a smirk.

"Alright, you got me. It *has* been fun being a little bit pursued. But I'm not gonna *do* anything about it."

"Hell, no. Not if you want to live to see thirty, you're not!"

"Damned straight about that. My little honey'd have my ass!"

"So, this little conversation is between us."

"Absolutely." Kit extended her hand and Claire shook it with a wink and a laugh.

When they looked back out at the couple, Dara and her friend were wading over toward them.

"Hey, Claire! And . . . I'm sorry. I forgot your name."

"Kit. Kit Summers."

"Hi. I'm Dara and this is Trudy." Kit shook Dara's outstretched hand, then Trudy's, Claire doing so next.

"Well, looks like you guys had the same idea after last night," Claire said.

Yeah, I guess so. We, uh, weren't feeling too energetic this morning," Dara said with a little smile. "And a little baking in the sun seemed like a good idea."

"Exactly," Kit said with a knowing laugh. "Hope you started your day with a Bloody Mary like we did. Gotta come down off a night like that kinda' slow!"

"Well, we opted for lots of water and juice. But I'm thinking it's about time to get daring again," Trudy offered.

"I don't know," Dara said, smiling warmly at Trudy. "I may need a few more laps to work off last night's imbibing before I start again." She put her arm around Trudy. "But don't let me stop you, honey. I'm just not used to all this partying. I'm used to, shall we say, a more low-keyed nightlife."

"Aw, I don't believe that," Claire said. "You said you were from Washington, right?" Dara nodded. "And, as I recall, there are some *pretty* happening ladies' bars down there, no?"

"You know D.C.?" Dara asked.

"A little. Or, at least I used to—I spent a couple of summers there in college doing the intern thing at the State Department. *And* I managed to get around a little bit on the weekends. It's a great town."

"Yes, it is. But when you're putting in twelve- and fifteen-hour days, you don't hit the hot spots too regularly. Not to mention, when you've been in a relationship as long as Becca and I were. Actually, I work for State. I'm an attorney there."

"Yeah, I guess not," she responded to the first part of her statement. "But, speaking of State . . ." Claire went on to see if Dara knew any of the people she had known back in her days there, which led to more conversation about Washington, and how Claire had considered the law route once, and eventually led back to Becca and Dara's relationship. Fortunately, Kit and Trudy seemed to be equally engrossed in their conversation.

"So, it was all very mutual, thank God. Nothing's worse than these vicious break-ups that lesbians seem to specialize in."

"That's for sure."

Dara looked over at Kit and Trudy talking and smiled. "By the way, I want to thank you again for the chat we had here, when was it? Monday?"

"I think so. I always lose track of days when I'm here."

"Anyway, I really don't know if I'd have even said hello to someone like Trudy if you and I hadn't talked. Really." Dara smiled warmly at Claire. Claire swallowed hard and muttered some blandishment. This was getting hard. "And I think it's been good for Becca, too. She was pretty psyched about someone she was talking to last night. Who knows? We may finally have something to talk about on that long drive home this time!"

Claire smiled, genuinely and yet still innocently, she hoped. "I'm glad it helped. You never know. Sometimes free advice can be dangerous. You just looked so unhappy that I figured you couldn't do too much worse trying another approach."

"Well, it was the right advice at the right time." She paused a moment and looked hard at Claire. "I hope your lady knows how lucky she is."

"Oh, I'm sure I'm the luckier of the two of us," Claire said, her heart beating a mile a minute, trying to sound nonplussed and wondering if she was blushing. Thank God she was already on the red side after all the sun of the last few days.

"Well . . ." Dara looked at her a moment longer, and, for just an instant, Claire met her gaze. Then Dara took a breath and splashed some water up on her shoulders. "Man! That sun's getting intense. I think it's time for another dip and then maybe that drink." She turned to catch Trudy's eye, then turned back to Claire. "You guys coming tonight?"

"Tonight? Oh! The Carnival party! Right. Yeah, I think so."

"I figured. Our schedules seem to have overlapped so far, and, God knows, this is the event of the week."

"Well, then maybe we'll see you guys."

"Great." Dara walked over and gave Trudy a kiss on the cheek, and they swam off toward the deep end. Claire watched them for a moment—well, watched Dara. In addition to being gorgeous, she swam the length of the pool with absolute athletic grace. Oh well, Claire thought. Another time, another place.

"Alright, put your goddamned tongue back in your mouth," Kit said joining her.

"Stop it," Claire said with a small frown. "Besides, we have a deal. Remember?"

"Yeah, I remember. But you better get that moonstruck look off your face before we join the girls, or you're going to be in deep shit, my friend."

They compared notes about their respective conversations as they too swam a bit more and then headed out of the pool.

"So, I'll be curious to see who Dara's ex, Becca, has hooked up with," Claire said as they got back to the chairs.

Rita and Sabi were chatting away and sipping two fresh drinks when they walked up.

"Hey! Where are ours?" Claire asked, looking wounded.

"Well, you guys were so engrossed in your pool conversations, we figured you'd have ordered poolside by now," Sabi said with an arched eyebrow.

"You can do that?" Kit said, looking disappointed.

"Don't worry. I'm sure our lovely waiter, Bobby, will be cruising by momentarily," Rita said, smiling a little too benignly.

"Oh. We're on a first-name basis already?"

"Of course," Sabi replied. "You know how we love these little gay boys. They're so much friendlier than the lesbians around here."

"Well, not *all* the lesbians, apparently," Rita said, giving Sabi a conspiratorial look.

Oh, please," Claire said, sitting down and scanning the deck for Bobby. "Dara was telling me all about her new girlfriend, if you must know."

"Oh, I don't need to know," Rita said, leaning back on the lounge.

"Sure you don't. Anyway, seems my 'meddling,' as you accused me of, has proven quite helpful—for both of them. Seems Becca's met someone, too."

"Who's Becca?" Rita asked, sitting up again and looking over at Claire.

"Dara's ex."

"Really." Rita took a sip of her piña colada. "I think that was the name of the woman I met last night when I went out for air." She lay back down and proceeded to read her book.

CHAPTER
10

The sudden stop of The Boatslip's ever-present music and the sound of a whistle broke the dozing all four women had slipped into.

"Alright, all you beautiful boys and girls!" The pool boy was up on top of the stack of unused pool chairs, one hand on his hip, the other casually swinging the whistle on its lanyard. "Time to turn your chairs and follow Mr. Sun!" he shouted, emphasizing the sibilant "s" and gesturing dramatically toward the blazing orb with both hands like an airport ground crew member on the tarmac. He leapt down off the chairs and flitted back over to his stool at the shaded poolside bar. The music resumed as the sixty or so sun worshippers, most used to the midday ritual, roused themselves and practically rose as one to hoist the lounges around to face the sun that was just edging toward the westward side of the sky.

"Well, I guess that means it must be around noon," Claire said as she helped Kit finish situating the last of their six lounges. "Where the hell are those guys?"

"Hey! No need for profanity, young lady!" Grant said as she ambled up to the chairs. Grant never walked faster than an amble, a stroll, or a saunter, and certainly not today. Diane, as well, was walking with a little less spring in her step than the day before.

"Well, nice to see you girls were able to join us," Claire said in greeting, peering over her sunglasses. "Decide to sleep in a bit this morning?"

"Very funny," Diane replied, looking up from where she had immediately plopped down on one of the extra lounges. "Yeah. After that incredibly stupid college kid stunt we pulled last night, neither of us was exactly ready for an early start on the day." She looked over at Grant with a strained smile. "And some of less than others of us."

"Oh, *yeah,*" Kit said, looking over at Grant. "Word has it that *someone* was feeling a little under the weather last night. Doin' a little praying to the porcelain god, Grant?" Kit asked with an evil grin.

"Aw, hell! I thought you said you hadn't talked to anyone yet," Grant half mumbled, looking over at Diane, who was already reclining on the lounge.

She leaned up on one elbow. "I didn't. Looks like this town's even smaller than it appears."

"Nope. Wasn't Diane. Just your basic 'little birdie,' " Claire answered.

"Pat. It was Pat, wasn't it?"

"Oh, alright, yes. We stopped by to make sure you two lushes made it to your rooms okay. We were worried when you didn't answer this morning. I gather you got my message, though."

"Yeah, yeah, yeah. I wasn't exactly a pretty sight last night. Got a little carried away, I guess."

Diane looked over at Grant but said nothing, rearranging herself in her chair and stretching out to take in the sun.

"Thank God Diane's a decent human being and took pity on me. Hell, I barely remember even getting to the damned motel." She paused to rub her temples. "And, yes, I got your message and here we are. A little worse for the wear, but all in one piece. Now, can I get a goddamned drink to take the edge off this miserable, shittin' hangover?"

"Ooh. A little testy, aren't we?" Claire teased. The only reply was a dirty look from Grant. "Alright, alright. We have a very lovely waiter who should be prancing by any minute now."

As if on cue, Bobby appeared and took drink orders. After inquiring about food options, sandwiches were added to the order.

"Sorry if I'm a little on the cranky side," Grant added as an afterthought. "Truth is, I actually had a great time. Shit, I haven't done any two-stepping for a helluva long time. Guess I shouldn't be too pissed at Pat. She's really not too bad—for a Yankee gal."

"I'm sure she'll be glad to know that you're still in the land of the living—and so magnanimous in your revised opinion of her," Claire said with a chuckle. "Actually, she was a little concerned, too, leaving you in, uh, less than good shape."

"Really?" Grant said, perking up a bit. "Well, that's nice of her." She paused and looked around the deck. "Where the hell's that pretty boy with my drink? You could die of thirst out here!"

"Sounds like Grant's back to herself," Rita said, glancing over Grant's way. "How about you?" she said, looking to her side where Diane was still quietly sunning herself.

"Huh? Who, me?" she said, seeming to rouse from a short doze and turning her head to look over at Rita. "Oh, I'm fine." Then she turned her head back toward the sun.

"Well, good," Rita replied simply, a little taken aback by the abbreviated response. She looked in the other direction at Sabi, who was up on one elbow to hear what she, too, thought would be some embellishment to a good drunk story, and shrugged. Sabi shrugged back, equally puzzled at the lack of response.

Bobby arrived with their drinks and lunch, and they proceeded to eat and chat about other events from the night before, as well as about events from the earlier part of the week. Soon, the mood was definitely lighter, especially after Kit and Claire told them the tale of the killer beach mosquitoes.

"Well, I'd still definitely like to try to do a day at the beach, if you guys think it's safe!" Diane added, finally entering the conversation.

"Shouldn't be a problem. We'll make a list over dinner and figure out the rest of the week," Claire said. Almost simultaneously, Rita and Sabi looked over at her with raised eyebrows. Fortunately, neither Diane nor Grant saw them. Claire took a deep breath. "And if there are things you guys want to do on your own, feel free. We can always meet up later."

Her attempt at casualness seemed to work, since Grant and Diane each simply nodded while finishing their sandwiches. They all laid down, a little groggy from the sun and food and drinks. Their reverie, however, was short-lived. Squeals and shouts from the pool piqued Claire and Kit's curiosity. They looked over to see a group of guys playing with a couple of beach balls, seemingly starting up a combination of pool volley ball-dodge ball. When the pool contingent saw the two women looking their way, they motioned for them to come join them. Claire and Kit each smiled and motioned no and turned back around. Soon, one of the guys was standing before them, dripping little puddles on the concrete.

"Aw, c'mon girls! We need a couple of lesbians to make the game *fun!*" He stood there a second, tapping his bare foot. "Those pansies over there have a one-track mind when it comes to playing with balls."

By this time, the other four women were sitting up to see what the commotion was about.

"How about it, girls? The sun's brutal and it probably wouldn't hurt to work off some of that lunch," Claire asked the group.

"I'm game, if you are," Kit answered.

"Me, too," added Grant.

"You guys going?" Diane asked, addressing herself to Rita and Sabi.

"Hell, you know they're going to bug us until we do," Sabi sighed, only half annoyed. "Besides I feel a little crispy. It's about time to cool off, anyway."

Soon the whole entourage was in the pool, getting used to the cool water on their toasted skin. The game rearranged itself to accommodate the six women, and before long they were all laughing and splashing around, flinging the oversized beach balls around the pool. A couple of would-be swimmers left, annoyed at how the game had commandeered the entire shallow end. However, others good-naturedly joined in, including Dara and Trudy, who were among the onlookers, much to Claire's delight. While she was busy being inclusive but casual with the new players—Rita had definitely taken note of their arrival—she noticed a couple of occasions when Grant would make funny little asides in Diane's direction, only to be barely acknowledged. Of course, since Diane was on Rita and Sabi's "team"—very definitely the losing side—her focus could understandably have been on redeeming their less-than-athletic attempts to stay in the game.

When a couple of the boys decided it was cocktail time, Rita, Sabi, and Diane likewise decided it was enough pool for them and headed back to the chairs. Claire, Kit, and Grant decided to stay in and enjoy having the pool to themselves for a while. While getting their breath at the far end of the pool after a couple of laps, Kit and Claire noticed Grant hanging on the side of the pool, looking uncharacteristically pensive.

"Hmmm. Looks like there's trouble in Texas," Claire said quietly to Kit as they swam over to her. Claire dove under the water and shot up in front of Grant. "Hey, par'dner! Why the long face? Look around you, girl—beautiful, half-dressed women as far as the eye can see! Just itchin' for some of your Southern charm, I'm guessing."

"Yeah, right," Grant said despondently. "That's what got me into this mess."

"What mess?" Claire asked, frowning a bit as she gave Kit a quick look.

"Ah, shit, I think I've really fucked things up. I don't know why the hell I had to go and get totally shit-faced last night—first damned night I'm here. You guys letting me come out and all . . ." She paused and shook her head. "I mean, I can be an asshole anyway when I've been drinking, but lately, I get really turned around. And of all times to get wasted and pull such a stupid stunt."

"No fucking way," Kit said with a cross between disbelief and menace in her voice. "Tell me you're not saying what I think you're saying. Jesus Christ."

"Oh, no, Grant. Surely to God you didn't come on to Diane," Claire said in a low, careful voice.

Grant simply shook her head yes, continuing to look down into the water as she'd been doing since she started speaking.

"Now I get it. No wonder she's been avoiding you like the plague all day," Claire said, shaking her head. "I suppose I don't have to re-mind you that I told you she was straight before you even got on the damned ferry."

"I know, I know, I know!" Grant hissed back at them under her breath, trying to avoid making the confrontation too obvious. "It's not like I planned some grand seduction. And, truthfully, I really don't even remember how everything happened. I just remember getting to the room with Pat and trying to keep my eyes open and not pass out right on the floor. Then, as you *know*," she looked up at them with a hint of a smile, "I kinda' took a little detour to the, ahem, facilities. By the time I got out, Pat was gone, and Diane was sitting on one of the beds, giving me the ol' tsk-tsk-tsk routine and shaking her head. She wasn't really pissed or anything, just tired and probably annoyed and actually very caring. That's what I guess I sorta misinterpreted in my blurry state. She even went out and got me a soda from the vending machine. Oh, what a jerk." Grant hung her head with her hand over her eyes. "Anyway, when she got back, I was already laying on the bed, trying not to focus on the goddamned flowers on the wallpaper that were spinning out of control. She gets me a cold washcloth for my head, then kind of strokes my hair while I'm layin' there, moaning like a damned puppy. I think I was telling her some typically sad story about my tragic love life, and I think I was holding her hand, getting all stupid and teary. She said something nice and comforting and leaned over to turn the washcloth over on my head. And that's when, like a moron, I lean up and plant one on her. Jesus. As soon as I did it, drunk or not, I knew I was screwed. At least I think I brushed my teeth before I came out of the bathroom."

"Oh, good. I'm so glad you were considerate and thought ahead," Kit sneered.

"Aw, c'mon, Kit. I didn't *plan* it. Really I didn't. And I am so sorry. I know she's your friend, and you gotta believe I feel like a total ass."

Kit softened at how pitiful the tough Texan sounded. "I know, I know. That's how Sabi and I got together, truth be told." She gave Grant a wistful smile. "But my instincts were a helluva lot better than yours. So, what'd she say?"

"Hell, I don't remember. I just remember her jumping back like a snake had bit her and mumbling something about it being late and maybe I'd better try to get to my room. I vaguely recall trying to get up, tripping on my shoes or something, and then making another mad dash to the bathroom. I guess I passed out in there, 'cause the next thing I knew, she was helping me up and walking me to the bed. And I'm pretty sure she lay down with me. But that's all I remember till this morning. I think somewhere in there she mumbled something about me not looking too dangerous. Just the impression you want to leave, right? Anyway, I woke up, and the other bed wasn't made and there was a note saying she'd gone to get some coffee and donuts down at the front desk. Of course, I felt like a friggin' Mack truck had run me over and left me for dead; but I managed to pull myself together and leave her a note saying I was going to my room to get showered and whatever. When I was getting out of the shower, I noticed the message light was on on my phone and called and got your message. So, I screwed up my nerve and called Diane. She was nice enough—a little distant, but that's understandable—and told me she'd be ready in a half hour or so and that my coffee and donuts were in front of my door, which they were. Talk about *really* feeling like a heel. I met her downstairs to wait for the shuttle bus into town and tried apologizing, but she pretty much brushed it off and said not to worry, it was a long drunken night and let's forget it ever happened. And here we are."

"Whoo. Well, my friend, when you step in it, you really step in it," Claire said, giving Grant a consoling hug around her shoulders. "But you can't change it now. And, while I'm thinking she probably isn't likely to spend any quality time with you any time soon, maybe you should take her at her word and assume it was a dumb mistake she's willing to take in stride. I mean, she's obviously been around the whole gay scene more than once. And she's certainly a nice looking woman. Maybe she's used to fending off lovelorn lesbians."

"Very funny," Grant said.

"No, I'm serious. She doesn't strike me as some totally naïve type. I think you should let it go and proceed as normal—uh, normal being, of course, that you look elsewhere for your next romantic encounter."

"You know, I think Claire's right," Kit said. "I mean, I could kick your ass for putting the moves on my friend, don't get me wrong." Grant looked up, a little cautiously. Kit smiled back. "Don't worry. I'm not into the macho fight thing. But I've known Diane a long time, and if she said it was okay, it's okay. Of course, I also know how careful she is with emotional stuff under the best of circumstances, so I wouldn't be looking to be her best friend right away. I say just give it time and maybe try another apology somewhere down the line. Just be careful you don't do anything to make her think there's gonna be a repeat performance."

"Oh, you don't have to worry about that. Truth is, I think she's great, and she's definitely attractive, but what I did and didn't want to tell her this morning—talk about adding insult to injury—was that I'm not even that attracted to her. It really was all about being drunk out of my mind."

"Well, thank God, you didn't launch into that comforting spiel," Claire said, rolling her eyes. "Kit's right. Just play it cool. The less said at the moment, the better, I'm thinking." She looked up toward their lounges. "So, wha'dya think *they're* talking about?!?"

By the time the three women got back to the lounges, the other three women were talking a mile a minute and laughing like old friends. Grant, Kit, and Claire looked at one another with looks of deep relief.

"Well, the bathing beauties have returned!" Sabi announced. "We were beginning to think you guys were going to spend the whole day in there."

"Pool's great," Kit said, leaning down and giving Sabi a soggy kiss. "But I missed you."

"Aw, Jesus, Kit. Give it a rest," Claire teased.

"It wouldn't hurt you to act like you even know I'm here," Rita said with a diffident air.

"See what you got me into?" Claire said, giving Kit a push onto her lounge. She walked over to Rita's lounge, swooped Rita into her arms, and kissed her long and dramatically. Then she pulled back, looking into Rita's eyes, and gave her another kiss. "I *always* know right where you are."

"Okay. Now who's laying it on?" Kit shot back.

"Please, ladies. You're making me feel *very* lonely," Diane said with a laugh. "And from the looks of things, I don't have much hope of that changing any time soon."

There was a just a moment of uncomfortable silence. As Claire was looking around, trying to think of a conversational shift to turn the mood around, she visibly brightened.

"Hmmm. Now that you mention it, we actually might be able to do something about that," she said out of the corner of her mouth in Kit's direction. Kit looked at her, puzzled but shrugged as Claire winked at her. Claire then looked over at Diane and frowned. "Whoo! I'm guessing you haven't been in the sun much yet this summer."

"Well, no, not really. Why?"

"Because you're gonna be glowing in the dark come nightfall if you don't get out of the sun pretty soon."

"Shit." Diane poked her arm and watched the skin pop up white. "You're right."

"I think you should be the advance guard and go find us a nice table by the pool under the umbrellas."

"Good idea. I really don't want to be out of commission for the rest of the week nursing third-degree burns."

"Here." Grant got up off her lounge. "Let me help you with that stuff."

Claire gave Grant a questioning little frown, to which Grant responded with a don't-worry-I-know-what-I'm-doing look. Kit likewise nudged Claire, who gave *her* a not-now look.

As Grant and Diane made their ways to the poolside tables, the conversation at the lounges erupted practically on cue.

"I don't know what the hell you think you're doing," Rita said sharply to Claire. "Do you know what's going on with them?"

"Aha! I knew it! You guys *were* having the same conversation up here that we were having in the pool."

"Well, if you know, why did you practically orchestrate this little tête-à-tête of theirs? Hasn't poor Diane been through enough already with your *friend?*" Rita continued, still pissed.

"Honey," Claire said patiently, "first of all, I didn't expect Grant to do the helpful thing. But I think she just wants to apologize one more time now that everyone's fully awake and in the light of day. I actually had a whole different plan in mind, which we'll go over and help along once Grant does her thing."

"I don't know what the hell you're talking about, but it better not involve Grant or upsetting Diane any more than she already is."

"I'm with Rita," Sabi added. "I still can't believe Grant would pull such a stupid, mean trick on somebody who was trying to help her."

"Babe, it may have been stupid, God knows, but even I don't think Grant did anything mean or malicious. It was just a drunken, dumb thing." Kit paused. "Besides, sometimes those dumb, drunken moves can turn out pretty good." She leaned over to kiss Sabi.

"Oh, please. This situation is totally different than ours was. Grant *knew* Diane was straight." Kit raised her eyebrows questioningly. "And Diane was just doing what anyone would do when someone's that drunk. You certainly can't call it any kind of a 'come on.' " Kit raised her eyebrows again, this time with a grin. "Kit, stop it! It's not like there was anything leading up to something like that."

"Hmmm. Let me see. I seem to recall a night a few days before our big concert date. Granted, we didn't have a moonlit cruise going for us, but I remember something about being out with a bunch of friends dancing and drinking and talking the night away, getting pretty polluted and *somebody* suggesting I lie down for a minute— which I *very* nearly took to the next step right then. Except, of course, I promptly passed out. And while nothing happened *that* night, it certainly had a lot to do with, uh, 'developments' not long *after* that."

"Alright. Point made," Sabi said with annoyance and frustration. "But I still say it's different!"

"You're right, sweetie," Rita said, patting Sabi's arm. "It is different. But I guess I do see their point—though I *still* think the being drunk excuse is always a lame one. Even so, I don't think Grant did it deliberately. I don't know her as well as Claire does, but that doesn't seem to be like her."

"Soooo," Claire interjected, "I think we should all do our best to try to resume an appropriate air of summer fun and frivolity and help them get back on track again. Agreed?"

With assents all around, Claire looked back toward the pool. "Well, we wrapped that up in the nick of time. Here comes Grant." Each of them grabbed the book or magazine they'd been reading.

"Alright, you guys. It doesn't take a brain surgeon to know what you've been talking about." They all looked up sheepishly. "Not to worry. Everything's okay now. We talked, and we're pretty much back on good terms. Though I think your friend's getting a little lonely over there watching beautiful men she can't have strut their stuff."

"Actually, I think I'm getting a little too pink for my own good as well," Rita said.

"I think that's our cue, pal," Kit said to Claire as she sat up and started searching for her deck shoes.

In short order, the full entourage was packed up and trundling over to the table Diane had claimed for them. As they approached, however, Claire started chuckling to herself. "The game, as they say, is afoot."

Kit looked over at the table and also chuckled. "Excellent thinking!"

"I just hate it when they get smug," Sabi said quietly to Rita.

As they all arrived at the table, Diane looked up, grinning ear to ear. "Hey, guys!" She looked back at the waiter she clearly had been having a conversation with. "I want you to meet the rest of the group. This is—"

"Hey, girls! I was hoping I'd see you all back here."

"Hey, Tom," Claire said, raising her hand in a high-five sort of wave. "We were starting to think you were off today."

He shook his head and sighed. "No, no rest for the weary, as they say."

"I see you've met our friend, Diane."

The rest of the group greeted Tom and sat down.

"I sure have," he said, looking back at Diane and giving her a wink.

Rita leaned over and whispered to Claire, "You think you're *so* slick!" Then she kissed her on the cheek and gave her thigh a little squeeze. Claire looked even more self-satisfied than before, which wasn't easy.

"So, I guess you've figured out that you two have something very unique in common—at least unique here," Claire said, smiling at Diane.

"Well, it would appear that I managed to stumble onto the only straight waiter in the place—maybe in all of Provincetown!"

"I don't know about *that,* but the first part I'm pretty sure is on target," he said, flashing that perfect smile that had so dazzled Jimmy, and likely countless others. He glanced over at the bar. "But the waiter part will be in deep trouble if I don't start showing up over there with drink orders. Ladies?"

As Tom departed to round up the order, Diane turned to the group. "Oh my God. Is he drop-dead gorgeous or what?"

"So, is good old P-Town a little more to your liking now?" Claire teased her.

"Uh, yeah. *Definitely.*" She looked over at Claire, eyes squinted. "Hey . . . did you know he was over here? You obviously know him."

"I'm taking the fifth on that one—that is, till I see how things work out!"

"Don't worry. No matter what, you definitely score on this one!"

The chatter went on for a while as they all agreed on Tom's obvious charms and reverted to high school level plotting about Diane's best plan of attack to reel in her catch.

"Aw, you guys. I say she should just let nature take its course and see what happens," Grant finally added, having been more or less silent during the plotting conversation.

"I don't know . . ." Diane answered, giving Grant a sidelong look. "That kinda backfired on me recently." Then she broke into a grin at Grant's horrified look back and gave her a gentle punch on the shoulder. "Lighten up, girl! That's all ancient history now." Grant sighed in relief, smiling wanly.

Tom reappeared with the drinks and leaned against the fence, clearly in no hurry to leave.

Claire took a deep swig of her beer, then looked up at Tom. "You know if Jimmy shows up, you're in deep shit."

"Who's Jimmy?" Diane asked, trying to mask her concern.

"Oh, God. I don't know if this poor, young thing is any match for his claws!" Tom laughed and then noticed that Diane didn't. "Don't worry, hon. I don't swing both ways—though nothing would delight Jimmy and some of my coworkers more. Jimmy's a harmless old queen who's talked himself into pursuing the unattainable. Definitely more act than reality. In fact, after he made the usual four or five attempts to seduce me, he's turned into my biggest defender around here. I mean there's no *way* you can be a halfway good looking guy—or girl, for that matter—and not expect to get propositioned by same in P-Town." Even sunburned, Diane's blush was visible. She gave a Grant a sheepish look. "Anyway, I knew the score when I came up here during college looking for a summer job. My family came up here for years when I was a kid, and I always loved the place. I mean, it's the perfect place for a straight guy to really focus on making money—it's not like you're going to be distracted romantically. And if you are," he looked down at Diane, "you're sure as hell not going to have any competition!" He stopped to push his sun-streaked brown hair out of his eyes. "Actually, working here has been one of my easier gigs. Management frowns on the help getting, uh, shall we say, involved with the customers. But . . ." he leaned down to pick up the bevnap Diane had dropped, "sometimes you just have to take your chances." Looks were exchanged around the table as Tom and Diane continued looking at one another. Tom suddenly gathered his composure. "And now it's back to work. You guys staying for tea?"

The women looked around at each other and all nodded their assents. "Yeah, for a while," Claire answered for the group.

"Good. I'll see *you* later." For the second time, Diane blushed. She turned to watch Tom walk away, then turned back around, giggling and fanning herself.

"Hey, down girl!" Kit said to her friend. "Jesus. I haven't seen you like this since college."

"Well, I haven't met a guy that hunky since college!"

Sabi and Rita exchanged glances. "I have to admit, he is beautiful—and charming," Sabi started. "But you might want to be a little on the careful side. Gay *or* straight, it is your basic summer fling setting, you know."

"Oh, for God's sake, Sabi. I'm hardly a teenager." Sabi looked at her over her sunglasses. Diane sighed. "Even though I *know* I'm acting like one." She smiled broadly. "And you know what? Who cares? A fling sounds just about right at the moment."

"Yeah, you, Miss Casual." Kit took a drink of her Corona and then smiled warmly at Diane. "You never had a casual bone in your body. So, watch your ass, girlie. Sabi may have a point. Though, nothing says you can't have a good time."

"Thanks, Kit. Nothing like mixed messages," Sabi said with an annoyed sigh and a dirty look at Kit.

"No, I hear you all. But nobody needs to worry. Kit's right—I can be very uptight and intense. But after the past few years, it's time I learned that very thing: how to just have a good time. Which, with a little effort and half-good sense, I think I can pull off. To a good time!" She raised her drink in a toast.

"To a good time!" they all responded, and clinked glasses.

"And to being with friends," Diane continued. "Old ones," she said looking at Kit and Sabi, "and new ones," she continued looking first at Claire and Rita and then, smiling, at Grant. "Cheers!" After they'd drunk a second toast, Diane scooted her chair back. "Well, if we're going to be dancing any time soon, I really think I need to find the facilities."

"I'll show you. Its always a good idea to have someone keep an eye on the door when you have unisex johns," Kit said getting up with Diane.

"Actually, that sounds like a *really* good idea after a couple of beers," Claire added.

"Ditto," said Grant.

"And they always complain about us girly-girls having tiny bladders," Sabi said over her shoulder to Rita.

"So, is it me or is everybody but us totally fucked up when it comes to relationships?" Rita asked Sabi once the rest of the table had departed.

"I'm right with you there, darlin'," Sabi answered. "I mean, I certainly sowed my share of wild oats. But that was when I was a lot younger than this bunch. And if you're basically in the market for something real, I really don't think this is the ideal setting."

"Well, I suppose it *is* me, to a great extent. I really never even did the wild oats thing. I've just always believed that the whole point of all the flirting and dating and ultimately making love was about being with the right someone—someone special and some*thing* lasting. Not just anyone to do anything. But I know I'm pretty alone in thinking that."

"Oh, I don't know if you're all that alone. I think everyone *wants* that. It's just how you go about getting there. Not everyone's as, oh, I don't know, centered and serious as you are about it."

"But how can you *not* be serious about the most important thing—person—in your life?" Rita replied, her sincerity palpable in her face.

"Aw, honey. Because not everyone you meet or find attractive *is* the most important person. You've been lucky—or amazingly in tune, I guess—to know when you met the right one. For the rest of us sad schmucks, we had to go through the whole draining and, more times than not, disappointing rigmarole to find out who the right one was. Jesus, I was still *engaged* when I met Kit. Which, I'm sure, you would have found entirely unacceptable had you known me then and known I was flirting with a woman. Though I would have denied that was what I was doing. But thank God I did—imagine having gone through with it and then finding out it was all wrong? Dear God, what if we'd had kids and all?"

Rita silently took a sip of her drink.

"Oh, I'm sorry, honey. I totally spaced it there." Sabi patted Rita's hand and lit a cigarette. "But that's my point. You might have saved yourself all the heartache of the fucked up life you had with Rick if you'd been a little less sure just because you felt *something*. Sometimes fun is just fun. But it's also how you find out about people. Of course, screwing around just to screw around is hardly the way to go either. But everybody's got to figure it out for themselves." She smiled lovingly at Rita. "But I have a feeling that's why there are people like you—to remind us if we've forgotten the point."

Rita smiled, too. "Thanks, Sabi. Though I guess I'm not *exactly* innocent given how things worked out with Claire . . . me still being married and all." She sighed and looked at Sabi, conceding the obvious. "But I didn't do what I did to have a fling, for God's sake. I just feel pretty out of touch with how lightly everyone takes these things. And I know I can get pretty judgmental. Just give me a swift one in the ribs if I get out of hand."

"Promise." She held her glass up.

As they were toasting, Tom took a swing by and leaned over the fence. "So, where's my girl?"

"Oh-h-h. Already she's your girl, huh?" Sabi said with only a trace of a smile.

"You know what I mean. So'd some dyke sweep her off her feet already?"

"Careful, son. Don't let the lipstick fool you," Sabi retorted with a warning glare.

"Sorry," Tom replied quietly.

"No, she's still on your side of the fence," Rita answered. "She's just 'powdering her nose.' "

"Well, do me a favor. Tell her not to stay inside too long. I'll be looking for her out by the railing."

With that, he was off to deliver the drinks on his tray. Not long after, the girls were back. After the message was delivered, they all decided that it was time to do some dancing, though Diane was more in favor of not losing their claim to the table and the vantage point it offered her.

"Listen, honey," Sabi said as she donned her shorts over her suit, "the first rule in the game is not to appear too eager. Put those shorts on and come in with us for a while. Trust me. If he's interested, he'll be checking you out through those big damned windows around the dance floor. You don't want to disappoint him, do you?"

By the time they inched their way through the crowd inside, things were hopping. This time, they wasted no time observing from the sidelines and jumped in the middle of the grinding bodies on the dance floor. Sabi kept watch, and sure enough, Tom made a couple of trips by the side window, searching the crowd inside. After a couple of dances, Sabi gave Diane the high sign and sent her off to linger by the railing, with explicit instructions to keep her focus on the seascape out in front of her. Tom should, and would, find *her*.

The dance contingent kept it up for another dance or two and then took a breather on the sidelines. Sure enough, there were Tom and Diane doing their gazing-out-at-the-ocean thing. Her earlier comments notwithstanding, Grant seemed less than pleased by the afternoon's turn of events.

"I thought she wasn't your type," Claire shouted over the music.

"She's not," Grant shouted back. "But no one wants to be tossed aside *that* fast."

"You idiot! You can't be tossed if you were never anything to begin with!"

"I know," Grant said dejectedly, taking a swig of beer. "Guess I still don't like the idea of *totally* striking out."

"Give it a rest, ego girl," Claire said, giving her a hug. "Keep your eyes open. You never know."

As the temperature inside continued to climb, Rita announced she needed a *real* breather and the group headed outside, making it a point not to be seen by the spooning couple. As Kit and Sabi went back inside for what they'd agreed would be their last dance, Tom and Diane moved away from the railing and strolled over to where the other women were perched.

"Nice try, guys," Diane said, smiling. "We saw you come out and hide yourselves over here. But Tom's got to finish working tea, so we decided we'd take you off the hook."

"Hey, you're all coming to the big Carnival party tonight, right?" Tom asked.

"Wouldn't miss it," Claire answered. "We were here last year and it was a riot."

"Great. I'm working tonight, so I'll see you all here." He turned to Diane. "I'll especially be looking for you." He pulled Diane a little closer and kissed her lightly. As he moved back, he smiled. "You get to see a whole other side of me tonight."

"I'm counting on it," Diane replied. She grabbed his shirt and pulled him even closer, and gave him a kiss she hoped would guarantee he found her later.

CHAPTER

11

The walk back to Stella's was a long one for Diane; the parting scene at the Boatslip had been too good not to rib her unmercifully about. But she bore the other five women's good-natured teasing nobly, simply smiling tolerantly at each new joke and witty—or not—aside. After all, she was the one with the hot date for the evening. And while she was, indeed, usually far more tentative and cautious about the usual dating ritual, she'd decided while baking in the sun that maybe her days of practicality and reticence had been for naught. Here she was, almost thirty, with only a string of failed attempts at finding Mr. Right to show for it. Clearly, her previous *modus operandi* hadn't been exactly successful. Granted, this hardly seemed to have the makings of any sort of real relationship, but what the hell. It was time to have fun and relax—work could wait and good sense could take a back seat to a good time. Besides, this wasn't a situation of rockets and fireworks; that hadn't really ever happened yet in her experience. This was just your basic cute guy, definite interest, and perfect opportunity. The least a serious, hard-working girl deserved. The bells and whistles jazz would happen someday. Besides, you never know . . .

When they got back to Stella's, everyone automatically headed for the table on the deck while Claire and Kit went inside to grab some sodas and beers for the group. The sun was still blazing and no one was quite ready to start gearing up for the evening.

"Anybody up for a dip in the bay?" Kit asked as they returned with the beverages.

"I'll join you in a minute," Claire said as she plopped down on the picnic bench beside Rita. "Think I'll just sip my beer and relax for a minute."

Everyone sat quietly for a minute, simply looking out at the boats and the shimmer of sun on the water, when suddenly Sabi burst out in laughter.

"What's with you?" Kit asked her.

" 'Relax for a minute'? What the hell have we *done* to relax *from?* Walk five blocks after an exhausting day of laying in the sun and drinking?!?" She started to cackle again. "And the worst part is, I was thinking to myself, 'Yeah. That's a good idea. I'm fucking exhausted.' This is downright depraved and totally self-indulgent. And I love it!"

"I think this is what happens when every damned bone in your body is relaxed," Rita said, chuckling with her. "I feel like you'd need a crane to lift me off this bench!"

"Ah, hell. We all deserve it," Grant added. "From what we've all been saying about our jobs and lives back home, it sounds to me like every one of us needed exactly this. Kick back and chill."

"Here, here!" Claire shouted, raising her beer bottle, everyone chiming in.

The laughter died down, and Diane leaned back and stretched, a little yawn escaping as she did so. "I hate to say it, but I could actually do with a little nap."

"Oh-h-h!" Kit intoned, giving her a conspiratorial wink. " Are we expecting a busy evening?"

"Alright, alright. I knew as soon as I said it I was leaving myself open," she said, with a smile. "But last night *was* a late one, and I, uh, was sort of busy playing Florence Nightingale even later." She smiled playfully at Grant, who maintained her focus on her beer bottle.

"She's right, you know," Grant said, looking tentatively over at Diane. "And this whole Carnival thing can turn into a pretty big party, as I recall. I think heading back and grabbing forty winks sounds like a good idea." She drained her beer. "And I *promise* to be a perfect gentleman, as it were." She nodded her head deferentially with a slight smile and got up. "Ready?"

"Yep. So, what's the plan for the evening?" Diane asked.

"Well, let's see." Claire pulled her watch out of her shorts pocket.

"It's only a little after four. Thank God, it was an eager dance crowd this afternoon and we didn't have to wait for things to get hopping. Anyway, you guys should plan to be back here by 6:30 if you want to see the parade, and I heartily recommend you do. It's really a riot. I still can't believe these guys schlep all these gowns and shit up here just to play dress-up for the week, but they do. And they *definitely* expect an audience. If you get here a little earlier, you'll be able to see Stella's own contingent strutting up to take their place in the festivities on the street. And after the parade, we'll go somewhere and grab dinner. In fact, ladies," she turned and addressed her three compatriots, "we can go through the magazine and already have a place in mind by the time they get back."

"Sounds like a plan," Grant said. "We'll see you in a couple of hours."

As Grant and Diane left for the motel, Claire put her arm around Rita. "You know, that nap idea didn't sound too bad, actually." She gave Rita a squeeze and kissed her on the cheek.

"Uh, you know, you're right. It didn't at that," Kit said, taking Sabi's hand and kissing it softly.

"Okay. See you guys back out here at six-ish," Claire said, already half up from the table.

Rita and Sabi looked at each other. "Excuse me?" Sabi said pulling her hand away, teasingly. "I don't remember Rita or me saying we felt like naps. Did you say something, sweetie?"

"No, I don't remember saying a word," Rita answered, trying to hide her smile. "Besides, I thought we were going to check the magazine for restaurants. And weren't you guys going for a swim?"

"Oh, come on," Claire replied, pulling Rita up from her seat and playfully slapping her backside. "Swimming can wait."

Claire reached over and gently stroked each of Rita's eyebrows. Rita stirred a little, brushing Claire's hand away as though it were an annoying mosquito, and nestled closer to her. For a minute, Claire just looked at her. Every now and then, it surprised her all over again that she had ended up with someone so totally unlike all the women she'd known before Rita, *and* someone so wonderful in so many ways. She was definitely worth all that they'd been through: the crazed, possessive husband, raising three kids, dealing with no money—thanks to the vindictive part of the crazed, possessive husband—and all the rest. It was all worth it to have this woman lying beside her who was as deeply loving, dedicated, and committed as Rita was—not to mention beautiful and passionate. That was the dessert that came with such a marvelous main course. Speaking of which, there was also the added bonus of her being an unbelievable cook! Yes, every now and then, Claire had to simply smile at her amazing luck. Or maybe blessing was the better word.

Claire did just that and leaned over and kissed Rita lightly. Rita smiled in her sleep and moaned a little, reaching over and pulling Claire into a long, tender kiss.

Claire pulled herself up on one arm. "Asleep, my ass!"

"Mmmmm. Now where were we?" Rita whispered, still smiling, eyes still shut.

"If we go back to where we were, we'll never get out of here tonight."

"Aw, don't make me get up," Rita said, yawning. "You'll definitely regret it." Rita slowly opened her eyes and looked at Claire.

"Don't give me that look," Claire said, pretending to shield her eyes. "You know I'm defenseless against 'the look.' "

Rita leaned up and started nibbling on Claire's ear, lightly tracing its outline with her tongue. "That's what I'm counting on," she whispered, as Claire shivered at the sensation. Rita reached over and pushed Claire back down onto the bed. "Don't worry. We won't be late—if you're cooperative, that is."

Claire especially loved this side of Rita; a side no one else would have believed could also be part of the quiet, unassuming woman they thought they knew. The side that was hers alone to know. When the countless obligations of the day were behind her, the bedroom door was shut and she was lying beside Claire, a strong, confident, in-control woman appeared; a woman who, in this private world, was verbal and insistent and far from reserved about her wants and needs. Sometimes it became an exciting, arousing battle of wills to see who would prevail as the dominant partner of the moment. And, other times, Claire very willingly tossed aside *her* knowing, worldly, controlling persona along with the clothes she equally willingly tossed on the floor beside the bed.

Claire didn't answer. Instead, she stretched, cat-like, out on the bed and looked up at Rita. Rita looked down at her with a teasing smile and slowly leaned closer to Claire, her breasts just within reach, in an unspoken command. Claire reached up and caressed them, slowly working her way to the ultra-sensitive concentrations of sensation. Rita shuddered, the sharp intake of breath between her clenched teeth signaling to Claire that she was, indeed, cooperating. Rita got her breath and began telling Claire in luscious detail what she wanted her to do. Claire passively complied, moving onto her knees to begin kissing her partner lightly along the length of her body until she'd reached her feet, then reversed course, continuing to kiss and lightly nibble as she retraced her way backwards up Rita's legs to the soft skin of her inner thighs, finally stretching out when she'd reached the point that their bodies were aligned and she could feel Rita's lips kissing her thighs. Rita opened her legs, inviting—no, demanding—the attention she needed and Claire, in response, did likewise. Tasting the familiar tastes, breathing in the familiar smells, and relaxing into the long-ago learned rhythms of one another, they each and together gave themselves over to the probing, knowing, loving, patient, driving, attentive, demanding ownership of the other's body. Years of exploring and finding and memorizing each satiny contour and crevice, each hidden pulsing guide to the throbbing center of the other gave way to the crashing arrival of two-as-one at a unique, brilliantly lit spot in the universe that only they could take each other to.

Taking one last taste of her that sent a final convulsive shudder through Rita's body, Claire moved back up on the bed, facing her partner, and pulled Rita close, cradling her in her own less dramatic cleavage and stroking her hair until they both dozed off to the sound of the buoy bells in the distance.

Claire woke with a start and looked at her watch. "Damn! It's after five thirty. Come on, babe. We gotta get our shit together. Diane and Grant'll be here in less than an hour."

"Hey! It's not me that takes forever to get ready," Rita said with a lazy yawn. "Go ahead, draggy ass. Get in the shower. Even so, I'll be ready before you."

"Yeah? Wanta make a bet?"

"Sure. What do I get if I win?"

Claire leaned over and kissed her again. "Win or lose, it's the same. If you think you've got the stamina."

"Promise?"

When Claire finally made her way down to the deck by about six fifteen, Rita, Sabi and Kit were all posed facing the stairway, legs crossed, fingers drumming the table, vainly trying to whistle.

"Very cute," she said, lighting a cigarette and pointedly sitting on the other side of the table from them. "Frankly, I'm pretty impressed with myself making it down in here in under an hour! You all know I can't pull my tits together in less time than that."

"And, if you ask me, there's not a helluva lot to pull together," Sabi said in a stage whisper to the other two.

"Hey! That's not nice. They're perfectly fine, in my book. Besides, you know what they say . . ."

"Claire!" Rita said, reddening a little.

"More than a mouthful's a waste!" Kit blurted out in her stead.

"Oh, Kit. You're so vulgar," Sabi said, chastening her. "And you know Rita gets embarrassed."

Kit chuckled deeply. "Yeah, I know. And I love it when she does. How the hell do you put up with us? You know one of us is gonna come out with something totally tasteless at any given moment."

"It's not easy, you know," Rita said, laughing. "I was raised a nice, Catholic, Italian girl."

"Yeah. And look at you now!" Claire said, laughing with Kit.

"You're right. And the worst part is, I love it!"

"Whoo! Our little Rita is getting pretty frisky!" Kit said, raising her eyebrows.

"You shoulda seen her a couple of hours ago," Claire said, doing the same stage whisper bit.

"Alright, Claire Griffith. That's enough out of you," Rita said, out and out blushing this time.

"Yeah. Must be the air up here. My little chili pepper was—"

"Uh, little Miss Catherine Marie Summers. You may want to quit while you're ahead," Sabi interjected with a semi-menacing scowl.

"Catherine Marie? What the hell kind of name is that for any self respecting dyke?" Grant was laughing before she even got to the table.

"Never mind," Kit half mumbled into her beer.

"Well, we made it! And pretty much on time, I'd say. Though, dragging my sorry ass out of that bed once I fell asleep was truly painful," Grant said, perching herself beside Claire.

"Oh, my God. You can say that again," Diane added, joining the group. "It may *not* have been such a brilliant idea to suggest the nap thing." She yawned and plopped her head onto her upturned fists.

"Oh, I don't know about that," Claire said with an evil grin.

"Hey! Sounds like someone enjoyed their naps," Grant added with an equally evil chuckle.

"Alright, girls. Enough," Sabi interrupted before anyone could add fuel to the fire. "Jesus. You give 'em a little, and they're like teenagers!" she said to Rita. "So, what's happening out on the street?" she asked the newcomers.

"Well, I think we may want to move this little confab up there pretty soon," Diane said. "The sidewalks are getting pretty crowded."

About then, they heard whoops and hoots from the other side of the complex.

"Hey! It sounds like the boys are ready to strut their stuff," Claire said, extricating her long legs from the picnic table. "Let's go see the girls, girls!"

The group made their way to the small, bricked entry area to Stella's. There they found six "ladies" decked out beyond beyond— the whole megillah. *Tons* of make up, wigs for days, stiletto heels, boas, and dresses that would knock your eyes out: beaded, fringed, satin, lamé, rhinestones, feathers—you name it. The women stared for a moment and then gave them a round of applause.

"Outstanding!" Kit shouted.

Sabi ran up to a 6'4" "lady." "Where *did* you get those shoes?" she said, genuinely entranced.

"Oh, these old things?" "She" fluttered her spider-like false eye-lashes. "Unless you wear a size twelve, I don't think my place'll work for you. But I saw some almost like them in a Niemann-Marcus cata-log. I took a picture in to try to match them."

"My God." Diane couldn't stop staring. "I've seen my share of drag queens. But these guys are really *good.* And that black . . . 'woman' is *amazing.*"

"She ought to be. She does a show up here, and knows these guys from all the years they've been coming here for this."

"Amazing. These guys really come up just for this, huh?"

"Damn right. High point of their year, from what I've gathered." Claire said, smiling at Diane's amazement. "But this is nothing. Come on. Let's go see the *real* show."

They strode up the driveway and edged their way into the crowd gathered along the sidewalk. However, as soon as they'd gotten po-sitioned, they heard hoots behind them and acted as a human gate-way for their fellow guests to make their grand entrance onto the street. The crowd roared, which of course only encouraged them. The boys gave the gathered onlookers a little pre-show, prancing and voguing to show their frocks to full advantage. Just as they were run-ning out of novel poses, the sound of an approaching siren pulled the general attention of the crowd up the street.

The parade had begun, complete with the flashing lights of a po-lice escort.

"Jesus. They really take this stuff seriously," Diane said, again amazed.

"Smart thing. Who do you think keeps this place afloat? These over-mascaraed faggots, that's who," Claire said. "I hate to admit it, but my fellow lesbians don't always do their part."

"What do you mean?" Diane asked.

"Well, let's just say that we get a lot of very grateful thank-yous when we leave your basic good-service twenty percent on the table. I know women make less than men and all that stuff. But, please. Cheap is cheap—and it's always tacky. It seems like it's starting to change, thank God. But it's these guys that keep this place well oiled with *lots* of cash."

"Wow." Diane looked out at the street and the first float, boom box blaring with dance music, muscle boys spinning their drag queen partners, skirts flaring. "Hell, let's give 'em a hand!"

As they watched, floats of *all* shapes and sizes—ditto for their sequined passengers—passed by. Flatbed trucks with dancers, walking contingents from the various cabaret shows, drag queens on minibikes, drag queens on bicycles, drag queens singing harmony, drag queens in comic drag, serious drag, bad drag, elegant drag, thrift shop drag, even bona fide women in what could only be called drag (!) came by. And interspersed between the various permutations of drag were rainbow flags, rainbow bunting, rainbow balloons, rainbow scarves, rainbow shorts, tops, hats, even a poodle dyed in rainbow stripes!

In true P-Town style, the crowd loved it. The applause and the cheers just got louder as a new contingent outdid the one before it.

Claire turned to Diane. "The best is, I bet half these people have never been and probably would never *go* to a Gay Pride Day parade, let alone a gay bar. But they get here and it's like they forget the fucked-up, repressed people they are at home—the straight half, I mean. Look at all the baby carriages stopped watching the parade!"

"Yeah." Diane was focused on the group of women passing by doing their supportive drag thing in tuxes and suits.

"Oh, that's rich," Claire said, half to herself.

"What?"

"That's not a bunch of butch dykes there, you know. I recognize some of the women from the bar. They're the lipstick lesbian waitresses."

"Wow," Diane said quietly.

Claire looked over at her. "You okay?"

"Yeah. I'm fine," Diane said, sort of coming out of a pensive moment. "I'm just a little overwhelmed. I had no idea this was, like, a real parade."

"Definitely."

Finally, the last contingent, a kazoo band, passed by. The women all gathered, laughing and comparing notes at who and what had just passed by and made their way back down the driveway.

Leaning up against the gate was Stella, puffing on the little pipe she sometimes indulged in, the perfect compliment to her *own* regular butch drag get-up. Not that it was in any way intentionally so. That was just Stella. The rich smell of Captain Black tobacco wafted up the driveway.

"Well, ladies. How was the big show?" she said with as much of a smile as Stella ever really mustered.

"Didn't you see?" Claire asked.

"Nah. Seen dozens of 'em. One pretty boy in those ridiculous high heels looks pretty much like another, if you ask me. I can't for the life of me figure out why the hell they'd torture themselves like that. Hell, I don't know why women do it. Personally, I never liked women who were all tarted up in that frilly stuff." She looked over at Grant, but Grant was intently studying the fence.

Sabi gathered herself together to rebut Stella's assessment of the virtues of feminine adornment, but Kit caught her eye before she could launch into her spiel. Kit shook her head slightly with a little frown. Sabi sighed and crossed her arms.

Diane, however, jumped in. "Oh, they're just having fun. Though, I have to admit, I've never seen anything quite like it. Jeez, half those guys made me feel like a real plain Jane. I could take lessons! They were gorgeous."

Before Stella could answer, Claire jumped in. "I say we take this little discussion down to the deck and decide what we're doing for dinner."

"I thought you guys were going to have that all figured out by the time we got back," Grant said, with a little smile at Claire.

"We, uh, got distracted."

"I bet you did."

Stella started to turn back to go into her apartment.

"Want to come down for a drink?" Claire said to her.

"Well, I, uh, I've got some work to do in the office. I really shouldn't," she answered less than convincingly.

"Ah, you can take a break. It's Carnival, for God's sake!"

"Well, maybe for a minute," Stella replied, tapping her pipe on the sole of her boot. Stella had to be the only woman—person—in P-Town to wear boots in August.

When they were all settled around the table and Kit and Claire had gotten beverages for the group, Claire made a toast to Carnival. The conversation then moved from a final appraisal of the parade to the more pressing issue of dinner plans.

"Any recommendations, Stella?" Kit asked. "I bet you've tried out all the hot spots in town."

"Well, I don't go out like I used to. All these new trendy places. And not cheap either."

"C'mon, Stella. You haven't been out at all this summer?" Claire prodded.

"No, I have," Stella said a little defensively. "But usually just my regular places like The Mayflower or the Lobster Pot." She puffed a second on her refilled pipe, thinking. "And now that you mention it, I did try one of the new places. Over at The Gifford House. I think it's called 11 Carver. Not bad, and not too pricey either." The women tried to stifle the grins that threatened to slip out at Stella's notorious cheapness.

"Sounds good to me," Rita offered. "Do we need reservations?"

"We didn't when I went."

"Yeah, but there's six of us. It might not be so easy to seat us together if we just walk in," Sabi said.

"Alright, alright," Claire said tolerantly, with a dramatic sigh. "I'll go up and call them."

"I gotta get back to the office anyway. You can use my phone," Stella offered.

"Well, thank you. I am starting to run a little low on quarters," Claire laughed. As Stella started to get up, Claire looked quickly around the table, a question in her eyes. Little nods all around—except for Grant, who frowned and shrugged her shoulders.

"So how long you gonna be working?" Claire asked lightly.

"Oh, I don't know. It's not like you're ever really finished running a place like this," Stella answered gruffly.

"Well, then, just save it for later and have dinner with us. We'll even treat. Consider it a late birthday present."

"Oh, you don't have to do that. I'm sure you girls have big plans for the night. You don't want to be dragging an old broad like me around with you."

"That's it. You're coming. I'll go in and call, and you get what you need to come along."

"Well, I don't know . . ."

Claire took her by the arm. "Let's go."

In ten minutes they were back down. "Okay, girls. Let's get going. They can take us in fifteen minutes, which should work out perfectly. Just take what you need for the evening, 'cause we'll head over to The Boatslip from there. Chop, chop!"

It was another spectacular evening in Provincetown. Though the sun had started its descent into the western sky, the air was still warm—hot, even—from the perfect summer day that was winding down. The group leisurely strolled along Commercial, allowing Grant and Diane to do a little window-shopping. As had become part of the ritual Commercial Street promenade, they stopped in front of Sapph-ires to see if there was anything new. Sabi spotted it immediately. Front and center in the display window was a truly dazzling sapphire pinky ring. Unlike the typically overblown pieces Sabi had fancied thus far, this was a truly elegant ring; a small but brilliant, emerald-cut sapphire, set into a fairly wide gold band, with small diamond baguettes on either side of the sapphire. Sabi was silent, just staring at the bauble.

"Uh, oh. You're in big trouble now, my friend," Claire said to Kit. "I've never seen her actually rendered speechless by a piece of jewelry. God help you, kid."

"Oh, honey," Sabi said, taking Kit by the arm and pulling her closer to the window. "It's perfect. Can we please go in and see it?"

"I thought you wanted the lapis. Besides, I thought you were trying to avoid my friend Pat," Kit said, hoping against hope for a reprieve.

"I thought so, too, until I saw this."

"O-o-o-okay. Let's go."

While they inspected the ring, Pat sauntered over to the rest of the group. "You guys going to the big event tonight?"

"Yep. Wouldn't miss it," Claire replied. "You?"

"Sure. I'll let the help watch the store tonight. It'll definitely be quiet—my clientele will be at The Boatslip. Amazingly, Gayle agreed.

God knows, that's one of the only things we've agreed on lately." She glanced over to see if Sabi and Kit were ready for her help. Sabi was holding her hand up, admiring the ring at different angles. Kit looked pained. "Where you going for dinner? I assume that's what brought you out on the street this early."

"The new place at The Gifford House," Grant answered. "Stella here recommended it."

"Good choice. I've been a couple of times. Not bad. But then, it really is hard to find a bad restaurant here."

"Yeah, you're right," Grant said. "Used to be, when we got bored with the places in Beantown, we'd hop in the car on a Friday or Saturday night and buzz out here just for dinner."

"You from Boston?" Pat asked Grant. "I don't remember you mentioning that last night."

"I didn't, huh? Guess it didn't come up with all that Texas two-steppin' going on." Grant smiled easily.

"Well, me too. In the off-season, anyway. I'm surprised we haven't run into each other before."

"Well, I haven't been all that social the last couple of years. Doin' my stay-at-home bit. Thought it'd keep the little lady happy."

"Tell me you don't really call your partner 'little lady,' " Pat said, looking up at Grant with a bored look.

"Not all the time. Actually, that was one of the few things it seems she *didn't* criticize me for," Grant replied, her expression falling a bit.

"Oh, right. Forgot you were doing the recovery-from-the-ex thing, too."

"That's okay."

"Well, when you get back, you should check out one of my favorite places, Smiley's. It's a great restaurant and a pretty decent crowd. You'd like it."

Grant's face darkened. "Thanks, but no thanks. I've been there. That was Karen's idea of a perfect setting to tell me she was screwin' her 'friend' Chris—a guy. Yeah, I had a great evening all right. And the food sucked, too."

"Whoa! I'm batting a thousand here. Sorry again. But maybe you weren't exactly open to its charms. Give it another chance. A good friend of mine's the chef, and she's gotten great reviews. Trust me."

"I don't think so," Grant snapped, totally out of character for the mellow, laid back Texan. "I hate that piss elegant crap. Overpriced and overrated. An expensive lesson, that's all."

Pat stared at her a minute, considering her response. Her jaw tightened as she excused herself and went back to check on Sabi and Kit.

"Jesus, Grant. Get a grip. She was just being nice," Claire said under her breath.

"Ah, fuck it. What do I care what she thinks? She should've just left it alone." Grant walked over to a counter on the other side of the store where Diane was trying her best to make conversation with Stella who was leaning against the counter, bored by the whole detour.

"I hope those two are about ready. I think it's about time to make our exit," Claire said to Rita.

"You may want to get her alone and talk to her," Rita said. "She's obviously still pretty bent about this whole Karen thing. I feel bad for her, but she's got to get beyond it. Not to mention that it might have been good for her to make a new friend in Boston. I never hear her talk about any real friends there."

"Yeah, I know. I'll try to get to her before she leaves."

Kit and Sabi walked over to them. "You guys ready for some grub?" Kit asked.

"What? No pretty little bag to take with?" Claire teased Sabi.

"We're going to *think* about it," Sabi answered, her voice controlled but annoyed. "And she'll probably *still* be 'thinking about it' as we're driving home."

"Honey. First of all, we can't get it now 'cause we'll be out all night. And, like I said before, let's just be sure there's nothing you want more while we're here," Kit said consolingly, trying to smooth things over.

"Fine. Are we ready to go?"

"Boy, are we ready to go," Claire said, heading over to get Grant and Stella. As they reached the door, Claire turned around to say good-bye to Pat. She waited as Pat turned to go to the cash register and saw Claire standing there. "See you at The Boatslip!" Claire said as cheerfully as she could.

"Yeah. Whatever," Pat said as she absently nodded her head and went back to what she was doing.

On the way to the restaurant, Rita updated Sabi and Kit on the scene they'd missed while Grant, Diane, and Stella walked on ahead. Clearly, they had their work cut out for them in trying to get the evening back on track. Jewelry would *not* be a topic of conversation.

Fortunately, the restaurant helped. The décor was warm and inviting, as was the help. They were immediately seated, and, by the time their drinks arrived, conversation was back on track about what the newcomers could expect at Carnival later on. Stella had the table rolling with laughter, telling tales of Carnivals past, when it was considered far more exotic to see hordes of men in dresses and tottering around on heels. What was more hysterical than the stories was Stella trying to imitate guys trying to imitate women. There wasn't a feminine bone in her body.

As they were finishing their cocktails and finalizing their dinner choices, their waitress approached the table with a tray of refills.

"Wow. That's what I call service!" Grant said, her earlier mood washed away with the last drops of the vodka martini she'd just sucked dry.

"I guess I could let you believe that and boost my tip, but I'd be in deep shit if I did. Actually, they're from the gentleman over there." She motioned to a corner table. They all turned to see Jimmy waving madly at them. They waved back and motioned him over.

"What a guy!" Claire said, getting up to give him a hello and thank-you kiss. "And what a pleasant surprise. I assume you're also setting down a good base for all that partying later on."

"*Absolutment, ma cherie!*" Jimmy replied with a limp-wristed flourish. "So, who are the new additions to your little Sapphic group?"

Claire made introductions around, noting that he was only partially right, Diane being the token straight of the night.

"So, *you're* the one," he said, squinting his eyes and raising one eyebrow. "You've absolutely *ruined* my grand plan for the night, you know."

Diane was understandably taken aback. "I'm terribly sorry, but I'm afraid I have no idea what you're talking about."

"You don't, huh?" Jimmy sighed. "Look at your drink, darling." Diane frowned and looked down at the strawberry daiquiri in front of her. The paper from the straw was artfully curled around the straw as it had been on her first one. But as she looked closer, she saw there was writing on the paper. She unwrapped it and spread it out and then looked searchingly around the restaurant. Her face broke into a smile, and she excused herself from the table.

Everyone at the table followed her with their eyes. Standing behind the small service bar, arms crossed, looking smug, was Tom.

"Well, that explains everything, including your little pout!" Claire said, laughing at Jimmy's attempt at giving Tom the evil eye.

"Who told you to bring one of *them* with you? I know I could've finally broken him down tonight."

"Okay, Jimmy. Whatever you say," Claire said, patting his arm. "Now, be a good boy, and go eat your dinner and try not to make more of a scene. We owe you a drink later. Or will we be able to recognize you later?"

"Just look for the most dazzling queen there, *not* in drag. Why would I want to camouflage all this natural beauty?" He snapped his head around and made a grand retreat to his table, with a look back and a smiling wink at them.

Diane rejoined them as their entrees arrived. "Amazing," she said, looking back at the bar one more time. "Not only is he good-looking and charming, he's an absolute workaholic. I can't believe he works here in between shifts at The Boatslip. I think I'm in love," she said fanning herself.

"Relax, you," Kit said, looking a little worried. "You just met this guy a couple of hours ago, you know."

"I know. I'm just playing. But it's fun to play. Besides, you were always the one bugging me about lightening up. Well, better late than never!"

"Just be careful," Grant added. "I feel a little protective now that I've been thrown over for this gigolo!"

Stella gave Grant a dirty look, and quickly picked up where she left off in conversation.

Dinner wound down and, as the evening darkened outside, the women finished their coffees and prepared to join the second parade of the evening that was headed to The Boatslip.

CHAPTER

12

By the time the crew slowly worked their way down to Commercial Street, there was already a noticeable flow of people heading in the direction of The Boatslip. The women paused and watched the crowd for a few minutes, taking in the splendor of some of the costumes and get-ups already in evidence. Diane, ironically, was dubbed the official whistler since she was the only one of the group able to pull off a bona fide wolf whistle. Initially, her attempts were decidedly half-hearted since she could *really* whistle, and people always turned to see who the "admirer" was. But as she started spotting "women" that she was almost convinced really *were* women, her whistles got markedly louder and throatier. You couldn't *not* appreciate such artful presentation!

After one such piercing outburst, the lady in question spun around and gave them a full curtsy right in the middle of the street, soaking up the adulation. When she hoisted her six-foot-something frame back up, they realized it was another of their fellow guests from Stella's. She sauntered over to thank them properly.

"So, you like?" She twirled to show off her ensemble in its sequined splendor. The women all laughed and gave her a round of applause. *"Merci tres beaucoup.* It's not every day a girl gets whistled at." As Diane reddened a bit, the *madame* cooled herself with the also-sequined fan that she snapped open with a flourish. "You girls on your way, too?"

"Yeah. In a little while," Claire answered. "No hurry. It's only a little after eight. The show starts around nine, right?"

"Sweetie, if you want to see *anything,* you may want to get your little buns down there *tout de suite.* Hell, honey, half the fun is watching all the queens make their grand entrances. The show's absolutely secondary."

"Well, then, I guess we better get going. Ready to join the promenade, ladies?"

"You girls have fun," Stella said. "I think I'm going to head back and make sure some damn faggot hasn't left her curling iron on."

"Aw, c'mon, Stella. It should be a blast," Diane offered.

"I've been watching gay boys in their boas for thirty years, honey. And, frankly, I'm bored. Strutting around like a bunch of two-bit whores. Huh."

"Alright, alright. We just wanted you to know you're more than welcome to join us," Claire added with a smothered chuckle. "You're sure now," she added emphatically.

"I'm sure. Besides, they're saying we might be in for some rain tonight, and I don't fancy getting chilled to the bone. Have a good time. Just remember I've got other guests, you know. So don't come in all hoopin' and hollerin' at some ungodly hour."

"Not to worry."

With that, they were on their way with the rest of the Carnival merrymakers.

"You know, last time we were here for Carnival, I told myself I was going to bring Dad's old tux next time and do the lesbian drag thing," Claire said, shaking her head, annoyed she'd forgotten.

"That's okay, honey. There was a reason I left a man, you know. I really don't need the substitute version," Rita said, giving Claire a patronizing pat on the back. A dirty look was the only response.

They only fully appreciated the size of the gathering crowd as they neared The Boatslip, and the street throng merged and slowly funneled into the entrance gate. All of gay P-Town—a redundancy at best—had turned out, it seemed, for the evening's festivities.

The six women shuffled along with the crowd until things opened up once everyone poured out onto the deck. Where there were normally the rows of lounge chairs, people were already claiming patches of deck to sit on for themselves and expected later arrivals. At the far end of the deck, in front of the seated spectators, was a long stage, complete with a vast backdrop decorated in giant pink and lavender paisley swirls. A huge sign adorned the center of the backdrop, with gold and silver iridescent lettering: "Welcome to the 1988 Carnival Queen Pageant." Already spotlights were swooping around the entire deck area, just visible in the beginnings of dusk.

"Wow. This is like something out of Vegas—or, more aptly, Atlantic City, I guess," Diane said, with a slightly bewildered and at the same time impressed tone.

"Damn right," Grant answered. "I'm tellin' ya', this is a big damned deal up here. Oh!" She turned to Claire. "Do those two guys who dress up like twins still come to this thing? I remember them from years ago."

"Yep. They were here a couple of years ago when we came. With the giant headdresses—God knows, they're too big to call hats!— and the whole bit. You can't miss them if they're here." She looked around the rapidly disappearing deck. "But we're not gonna see very damned much if we don't grab some deck space pretty soon. That guy was right. It's definitely filling up. We can stand up wherever we perch and see what's going on."

They worked their way through the milling crowd past little bunches of chatting, laughing people—some dressed up, some simply admiring. About two-thirds of the way to the stage, they saw a patch of unclaimed deck that looked about right, not too far into the seated crowd. They inched past people seated on the outside edge who had staked out spots that would give them good vantage points to watch the bedecked attendees, who clearly had no interest in—or conceivable way *of*—sitting on the deck floor. They were there to be seen.

The women flagged a passing waiter and ordered drinks. As they waited, they, too, joined in the people watching. More glittering gowns, more carefully applied make-up. The best were the guys who really were just having fun—gorgeous gowns, lacquered wigs, *and* beards and mustaches. As they were all taking in the sights, Claire squinted to see something more clearly. For a minute or two she said nothing, since the woman she was watching was turned at an angle, talking to a group of people. Then she turned to put her arm around the woman with her. Yep. It was Dara. And Trudy. And Dara looked great—plain black tee that showed off her deepening tan, honeyed hair casually swept back, khaki shorts that fit her perfectly. And that smile. Damn, that was one terrific smile.

"I see your friend showed up," Rita said quietly.

"What friend?" Claire answered, she hoped not too quickly after the words were already out of her mouth.

"Come on, Claire. You're not exactly subtle, you know. Put your tongue back in your mouth."

"Oh, for God's sake. I was just checking out the crowd like every-body else."

"Yeah. And this is the senior prom."

"Hey, whose ear was I whispering sweet nothings in this after-noon? Yours or Dara's?"

"Damn right. If you want to live to see New York again," Rita said, taking Claire's hand territorially. "Remember who cooks you those nice dinners. Just see if *she* brings you coffee in the morning and makes your lunch for you." She smiled slyly at Claire and then kissed her. "You do know I'd have to kill you if you ever did anything stu-pid."

"I know, I know. I have no interest in seeing just how much Sicilian there is in you," Claire replied with a smile. "Nothing to worry about, honey."

About then Dara noticed them standing in the midst of the crowd and waved. As Claire *and* Rita waved back, Kit waved, too, but in a slightly different direction.

"Hey! There's Pat."

"Oh, now you're starting, too?" Sabi said with thinly disguised sar-casm.

"Who?" Grant asked.

"Pat. You know, two-steppin', jewelry-store-Pat?"

"Of course, I know. The one I keep locking horns with. What, is she looking to crash our little party?"

"I don't know. She's over there—by the bar." Kit was pointing her out as Pat turned and saw them and waved. She started in their di-rection in an unhurried stroll.

"Oh, great," Grant grumbled.

The waiter reappeared with their drinks and was turning to respond to a hail from another thirsty customer, when Diane spoke up.

"Excuse me?" The waiter turned back. "Is Tom working tonight?"

"Uh, yeah. He *better* be."

"Could you do me a favor if you see him? Would you tell him Diane's here?"

"Oh, I'm sure you'll see him. But if I see him first, I'll tell him."

"Thanks," she replied, frowning a bit as he walked away. "Not exactly Mr. Warm-and-Friendly. Must be another disappointed suitor. I hope we do see him first. Something tells me this guy's not real interested in being helpful."

"Ah, he's probably just crazed trying to water this horde," Grant said comfortingly. "I'm bettin' ol' Tom'll be looking for you, honey. And we'll all keep an eye out, right guys?"

"Aw. How sweet. You guys were looking for me?" Pat, hand to her throat acting flattered, had just reached the group as Grant finished her comment.

"Not exactly," Grant sniffed.

"Ah, c'mon. You're not still pissy about that whole restaurant conversation, are you? Hell, you're the one that practically ripped my throat out. I was just making small talk. If anyone should be pissed, it should be me, don't you think?" Pat said quietly, an eyebrow raised in question and a half-smile on her face.

From behind, Grant felt a little nudge in her back. "Hang tough," Sabi whispered.

Grant thought for a second. Actually, she *had* overreacted, and Pat was clearly trying to make amends.

"Hey, don't blow a circuit over it," Pat said. "I just figured I'd say hi. I'm starting to feel like we're all old buds as much as I've seen you guys. And I'm determined to get a ring on the finger of that one." She leaned around Grant to catch Sabi's eye. Sabi forced a smile.

"I'm just workin' on tryin' to swallow my pride so an apology can make it out," Grant said with a sheepish smile. "You're absolutely right. You didn't do anything. I was just being an ass. Let me buy you a drink."

"Sounds like an apology to me." Pat brightened and flashed a beautiful smile that took everyone by surprise. Since they'd run into her early in the week, it had seemed that every encounter had been somehow less than pleasant; even on the boat there'd been a certain tension. But as they all looked at her standing there, smiling, it was as though they were seeing a new person. The smile revealed what an attractive person she was beneath the gruff, acerbic veneer. It was a pleasant and unexpected surprise.

"What? Is everybody that shocked to hear an apology out of the Texas Two-step Queen?" Pat asked.

Claire regained her composure first. "Nah. She's pretty good with that hard-bitten act, but she's a pushover once you get to know her."

"Ah, thanks. There's goes my whole hard ass image," Grant replied breaking into a smile, too.

"Well! That's better," Pat said, taking a deep breath. "Now. Where's a damned waiter? Next round's on me. Actually, despite our some-times strained encounters the past few days, I've had one of my best weeks ever. I think you guys are good luck."

"Well, I don't know if that's mutual. We'll see how much lighter my wallet is by the time we leave!" Kit quipped back.

"And I'll see if anything actually does end up on my finger," Sabi said, finally surrendering a genuine smile.

"So, who *are* you keeping an eye out for?" Pat asked. The conversation returned to Tom and soon shifted to more dazzling arrivals. Pat edged her way round the chattering group until she stood beside Sabi. She moved her head close to Sabi's ear when no one was looking. "By the way. Your lady there is definitely a cutie. But not to worry—you've got nothing to worry about from me. Never did, re-ally. I just have a bad habit of flirting. Besides, I would *not* want you to turn on me! I've seen the damage a pissed Puerto Rican *chica* can do." As she moved back to her original spot, she winked as Sabi looked back at her, skeptically. Pat raised her drink. "Okay?"

Sabi regarded her a moment longer, then raised her glass in re-sponse, a smile slowly replacing her semi-frown. "Okay."

"Whoo. Glad we got that straightened out. And just in time. Yo! Sweetheart!" A waiter edging his way through the crowd looked up and nodded. Pat looked back at Sabi. "Ready for that drink?"

After the waiter took their order, a piercing shriek made them all turn in the direction of the sound. Not one but *three* Elizabeth Taylor look-alikes were scurrying as best they could in their spike heels in their direction.

"Pat, honey! We are in desperate need of your help," the tallest of the bunch said breathlessly. "Now," she said, smoothing her satin aqua gown, "which one of us looks most like the real Liz?" All three of them struck poses to await Pat's verdict.

"Do I *look* that stupid?" she said, shaking her head. "No fucking way I'd risk the wrath of two of you."

"Aw, c'mon. We'll be good, we promise," another one said. "But keep in mind, *I* even have violet contacts on. If Monty were here, he'd choose me in a heartbeat."

"Honey, if Monty were here, he would most certainly *not* be looking at any of you. The hunky guy over there in the muscle shirt, maybe. But I'm sure he'd agree that you all look spectacular."

"Talk about weaseling out," the third member of the trio said with a bored tone. "Come on, girls. Let's go find someone who's got *real* balls!"

"That shouldn't be hard," Pat said with a laugh. "Have fun, girls!"

The tall one leaned over and gave her a peck on the cheek. "You, too, honey." Then he leaned back. "Besides, I know you'd pick me!" he whispered and blew her a kiss.

"You gotta love 'em."

As they continued looking around, they realized the crowd was starting to encroach on their deck space. They all sat down, trying to subtly push their circle out a bit to gain as much space as possible. Once they were settled, the music suddenly changed to the MGM fanfare and the spotlights swooped crazily over the waiting audience, then focused on the stage. A debonair man bounded up onto the stage and introduced himself as the emcee for the evening. During his patter about the evening's program, a different waiter returned with their drinks. Diane leaned over to get a better look at him as he squatted down to not block people's views while he passed the drinks out. Not Tom.

Kit noticed the maneuver and squeezed Diane's arm. "Don't worry. We'll find him."

With fresh drinks in hand, they settled in to enjoy the show. Grant tried in vain to light a cigarette, the evening breeze complicating the task. She leaned behind Pat, using her as a shield. In the process she managed to topple Pat's drink, which had been perched beside her—and that was *now* soaking into Pat's jeans.

"Shit!" Pat whispered, scooting over to avoid what she could of the spreading puddle. "You really do have it in for me, don't you." Fortunately, she was smiling.

Amidst 'oh shits' and annoyed sighs as the liquid spread further to their neighbors, Grant gamely tried to mop up what she could off Pat and the deck with woefully inadequate bevnaps.

"Forget me," Pat said. "Get what you can off the deck. I'll go to the ladies room and see if I can undo any of the damage."

"Wait. I'll go with you. The least I can do is help—and buy you another drink," Grant offered.

"So, *go* already," someone behind them hissed.

"But hurry back, guys—you'll miss all the acts," Claire whispered as they hunched down and tried to scoot out of the crowd as unobtrusively as possible.

The show began with teaser bits from all the shows in town. For almost an hour, many of the names Rita and Claire had raved about to Sabi and Kit entertained the audience. Gay comics like Big Ed and Lea DeLaria; lesbian singers Chris Williamson and Tret Fure; the Dyketones; various other singers and cabaret acts; and the *pièce de résistance,* Jimmy James, Marilyn Monroe impersonator *par excellence,* who was joined by the members of a drag act known as Legends. As they finished their segment of the show, the emcee joined them on the stage and led the audience in the cheering and applause.

"Well, I don't know if it was such a great idea to end this part of the show with the most beautiful men to ever put on dresses and wigs! Aren't they utterly *gor*-geous?" The crowd gave the impersonators another round of applause as they waved and left the stage. "Because now our esteemed judges have a very important task at hand—judging between our eager entrants to choose this year's CARNIVAL QUEEN AND HER COURT!" The audience erupted in whoops and cheers.

"This is a riot!" Sabi shouted over the hollering. "I'm so glad we came this week. Except that they're all so beautiful, I'm starting to feel downright unfeminine!"

"Yeah. Like they look hotter than you," Kit said.

Sabi leaned over and gave her a long, lingering kiss. "I'm so glad you decided to save me from a life of heterosexual boredom." She squeezed Kit's hand and snuggled up against her.

"Shit," Kit said as she caught her breath. "I'm glad we came this week, too!"

The parade of entrants began. For the next half hour, the stage was alight with the cream of the would-be Queen crop, leavened with the occasional novelty entrant, including the two men Grant remembered: both had thick black mustaches, and each was arrayed in a tangerine gown, gigantic Carmen Miranda headdress, three-inch platform sandals, with a toy flamingo under one arm. The girls whistled and cheered for their friends from Stella's as well as Pat's Liz Taylor pals. Finally, the last entrant—another Marilyn that actually gave Jimmy a run for his money—sashayed across the stage. The emcee bounded back up on the stage and announced that the judges needed about fifteen minutes to make their decisions.

Dance music blared out of the speakers, and waiters appeared en masse to make one last sweep before the evening's end. The breeze had picked up, so that they were holding the bevnaps on their trays as they walked. The women ordered and got up to stretch, putting their jackets on as they did so. Diane, Rita, and Sabi flew to the ladies room to try to beat the crowd. The other women were chatting and laughing about who the winner would be when Pat suddenly got quiet and abruptly grabbed Grant by both arms to position her in front of her.

"What's this all about?" Grant said, surprised.

"Just keep talking and don't move," Pat answered, putting her head down, a frown on her brow. "Gayle, my ex, is over there talking to the Lizes. I already ran into her once tonight before I saw you guys. Actually, that's one of the reasons I kind of latched on to your little group. She was busy trying to make me jealous flirting with a mutual friend of ours. It didn't work, because I really don't give a shit. Jesus, I'm the one that broke up with her! But it's annoying as hell. Not only do I have to work with her, I have to put up with these stupid games when I'm out trying to have a good time. Then I saw you guys . . . and thought I actually might have a good time—if I could manage to get *you* to laugh and that *other* one to not want to poison my drink or something."

Grant chuckled and crossed her arms, obstructing any onlooker's view even more. "Well, though I never expected to say so, I'm glad you wandered over. Now, as for the ex, we could play her game, you know."

"What do you mean?"

"Watch. Just follow my lead." Grant moved to Pat's side, and put her arm around her and walked her over to where Claire and Kit were talking, a little closer to the Lizes and Gayle.

"Well! What have we here?" Claire said, looking more than a little shocked.

"Nothing. Just look casual. We're trying to fuck with her ex's head." Grant motioned with her head to the other group. "Turnabout's fair play, I always say."

The bathroom contingent walked up, all with puzzled looks on their faces. "How long were we gone?" Rita asked, half laughing. "Things have certainly changed since we left."

"It's a long story," Pat answered. "Grant's just helping me even a score with my ex. I'll tell you all about it later."

"My God. Things do happen fast in P-Town," Diane added.

A gust of wind blew in off the bay, and the women huddled together. "They better get this crowning thing going pretty fast or they may lose their crowd," Kit said, holding Sabi close.

"I don't know. With as much as everyone's had to drink, I'm thinking they're not feeling the breeze. Though it is getting a little nippy," Claire said as she looked around at the flapping pennants strung between the balconies and the awnings.

The music stopped and the emcee took the stage. "Ladies and gentlemen! Our judges have reached a decision." The crowd quieted and sat back down to await the announcement. "After much serious deliberation, the judges are ready to announce the new 1988 Carnival Queen and her court! First, the court."

He began reading off names, and thrilled winners took the stage to receive their plastic tiaras. The crowd cracked up as "the twins" shared the last runner-up spot and cheered each of the other members of "the court." After the emcee announced the first runner-up—the Marilyn look-alike—and got to the final name, that of the Queen, he paused, looking puzzled.

"Hmmm. This is most irregular. It seems we have a mystery winner—a stunning vision of feminine beauty that the judges spied on the sidelines. And they have decided that she will be our 1988 Carnival Queen. Ladies and gentlemen, I am proud to introduce your new Carnival Queen!" He gestured to his left.

A raven-haired beauty with a black spangled gown mounted the steps, strutted to center stage, and curtsied to the crowd.

"Oh. My. God." Claire was the only one who could speak.

CHAPTER
13

"One of The Boatslip's own," the emcee continued, "QUEEN THOMASINA!"

The crowd roared their approval as the new Queen glided confidently across the stage in her heels, hands on her hips, head held high with the rhinestone-encrusted crown glittering in the spotlights, waving at her adoring fans. Six bare-chested, well-muscled guys clad in bowties and tux pants ran up on the stage behind her and hoisted the Queen onto their shoulders and paraded her around the stage.

"Dear God. Tell me that's not who I think it is," Diane whispered huskily to Grant who was standing beside her, everyone now on their feet for a standing ovation.

"Uh, I don't know. Who the hell can tell with all that makeup caked on."

Diane looked at her sullenly. "That's not exactly the answer I was looking for."

Claire and the rest of the group moved around Diane. "Oh, honey. Don't get all bent out of shape. It's *Carnival.* We told you, everyone gets in on the act around here. I bet all the little faggots here conned him into doing this just *because* he's the only straight one. And practically everyone knows him, so it was bound to get a laugh. Actually, it is pretty funny—and he does look fabulous."

Rita smacked Claire on the arm. "For God's sake, Claire. Shut up," she whispered angrily.

"Oh, stop it. I'm telling you, this whole thing's a joke."

"Even so. It just doesn't strike me as all that funny," Diane said, taking a deep breath and crossing her arms, holding herself together.

"Di, come on. Claire's right. What's the big deal? He's just being a good sport," Kit offered, putting her arm around Diane.

"Maybe so. I know this doesn't sound very enlightened, but it just kind of creeps me out. I mean, it's one thing for a bunch of flamboyant gay guys to play dress-up, but a straight guy? For a bunch of gay guys? And to look so . . . *authentic* doing it?" She shook her head and took another deep breath. "It's just that I was hoping Tom would be your basic normal guy for a change. I needed him to be."

The other women looked around at each other, genuinely thrown and at a loss for words at what they all tacitly agreed was Diane's overreaction. As they waited for one of them to come up with the next wise, comforting thing to say, the emcee walked back to center stage, still laughing with the rest of the crowd.

"Alright, alright! Settle down out there. As you've probably guessed by now, we decided to have a little fun with one of our more popular waiters here. Tom, come here." Tom was placed back down on the stage by his bearers and regally strolled over to the emcee, still waving to the crowd.

"I hate to have to do this to you, but there *are* certain, uh, qualifications for this whole queen business." He looked over his shoulder at the crowd and raised both eyebrows in mock surprise. The joke had the crowd roaring again. "And, sadly, one of those rules is that the winner has to . . ." he paused dramatically, "have actually *been* in the competition!" Tom feigned a big pout and hung his head. The emcee reached up and removed the crown. "Sorry, buddy. But just think of the story it'll make when you get home to Chicago! Let's give Tom another big hand for being such a truly *fab*-ulous queen for a . . . minute!" The crowd cheered Tom again, at which point he bowed and yanked off his wig as he stood back up. He bowed again and made his way off the stage. The emcee went on to crown the first runner-up, "Marilyn," the one, *true* Carnival Queen. The semi-clad boys reappeared and presented the new-*est* Queen to the approving crowd.

"See? What'd I tell you," Kit said, laughing along with the crowd despite herself. "It was just a big goof. And, personally, I'm impressed he's that cool with the whole thing to even do it. Sounds secure in his sexuality to me."

"I know. You're probably right. But I just feel like the joke's on me. It's stupid, I know. But I can't help it." She picked up her jacket. "Do you think one of you could drop me off at the motel? I know you all probably want to go out or something, but I'm just not in the mood."

Grant, torn between wanting to stay and still feeling a little protective of Diane, hesitated a moment. "No problem. I'll take you, if I can borrow the car." She looked over at Claire who nodded yes.

"Want some company?" Pat said.

"Uh, sure," Grant replied, surprised but not displeased at the offer. "I could probably use a resident's help making it back through the Saturday night crowd. Where you guys going to be?"

As the group was deciding on the rest of the night, they heard laughing and whistles next to them. The crowd beside them parted and Tom strutted in, wig and heels in hand. He stopped, hand on hip in front of the group. "So? Surprised? Told 'ja you'd see a different side of me tonight!" he said, laughing and slapping his wig back on at a cock-eyed angle.

Diane looked at him coolly. "Yeah. That's not exactly the side I expected. You were definitely the biggest surprise of the night." She turned to kiss Kit and the others goodnight.

Tom, in all his broad-shouldered beauty, looked thunderstruck. He frowned, looking around at the other women, and walked over to her. "What's this? I thought you, of all people—doing your own straight-among-the-gays thing—would think this was hysterical."

Diane just looked up, on the verge of tears.

"Oh, Jesus. This is great. Come here." Tom took Diane by the arm and led her over to the railing.

"Well, I guess we're not going anywhere at the moment," Grant said, as she tossed her sweatshirt over her shoulder. "Drink, anyone?"

In the meantime, the crowd had quieted down as the real queen and her court were officially presented *en masse* and were serenaded by all the vocalists of the evening. Suddenly, in the middle of a rousing chorus of "I Am What I Am," a gust of cold wind blew off the ocean and sent the Carmen Miranda twins reeling as they grabbed at the masses of fruit piled on their heads. The emcee came back with a riposte about angering the gods, as the queen and her court shuddered, grabbing their bare shoulders. He was gamely waving his arms at the audience, in a sing-along gesture, encouraging them to join in the unofficial gay theme song. But the crowd was paying more attention to what was going on behind him. As the gusts continued, the entire backdrop began to sway crazily. Drinks that were sitting on the deck while people clapped blew over and hundreds of cups went skittering across the deck. Then the speakers started crackling menacingly.

"Well, folks it's a helluva finale, but that's it for our Carnival Queen pageant." The emcee stood gamely center stage, trying to end the evening with a modicum of decorum. He waved at the crowd, still smiling, as the queen and her court made for the stairs off the stage. "Thanks for com—" A violent gust blew him back a bit. Then a loud crack made him whirl around. A member of the "court" grabbed him around the waist and pulled him toward the steps just as the backdrop crashed down onto the stage. The queen was the last off, still smiling and waving at the top of the steps, until the next gust brought with it a sudden, lashing rain.

"Jesus, Mary, and Joseph!" Rita shouted. "Where did *this* come from?"

"When Stella mentioned rain, she didn't say anything about a fucking hurricane!" Kit shouted over the wind.

"Not a hurricane," Grant shouted back. "It's what we up here call a nor'easter, and they can feel a lot like a hurricane. We need to get the hell out of here!"

The crowd was practically stampeding toward the exit. People were clutching jackets around them or pulling them over their heads against the stinging rain. Heels and wigs came off, and people scurried in all directions.

"Hey! Where's Tom and Diane?" Kit shouted, as they jogged along with the mass of people moving in the direction of the exit. They turned around and made for the canopied area of the deck that led to the dance floor. It provided at least a little shelter in which to reconnoiter and try to distinguish separate forms in the horde of people.

They each peered through the rain in different directions, trying to spot the couple when Pat suddenly stopped short.

"Shit!" she said.

"What's wrong?" Grant asked.

"My damned animals are stuck out in the back yard of the house where I'm staying. And they're probably scared shitless. That is, if the cats haven't bolted the fence by now. I gotta go. I can't leave them in this."

"I don't blame you," Sabi said. "I'd do the same thing if it was our dogs. Go ahead, hon. It doesn't take all of us standing out here getting soaked to find those two idiots."

"Thanks, guys. I really hate to bail on you in this mess, but I just have to." She looked at Grant. "Come on. I could use some help— I've got three cats and a dog." She grabbed Grant by the arm and pulled her with her out into the rain before Grant could answer. Grant looked back at the four women huddled under the canopy and shrugged and waved as Pat pulled her onward toward the exit.

"Well, *that* was certainly interesting," Sabi said as they disappeared into the crowd. She looked around at Kit for a response.

Kit just stared at her, shaking her head. " 'Hon'? You called her 'hon'?"

"Oh, stop," Sabi replied, smacking Kit on arm. "She's not as bad as I thought. And I feel bad for the animals."

Kit looked around at Claire and Rita who were smiling, stifling their own bemusement at this other sea change of the night.

"Hey. People change their minds, right?" Claire added with a little snorting laugh. Kit rolled her eyes with an oh-brother look at Claire's attempt to put a positive spin on the moment. "Anyway, we have more pressing business at the moment. We can talk about this new development when we get back to our nice warm rooms. You guys see anything?"

They stood huddled together, scanning the fleeing crowd for some glimpse of the couple. "Hey!" Sabi shouted over the increasing roar of the rain. "Is that them over there?" She pointed to one of the last few couples. The four women went running over to them, calling their names. The couple stopped and looked up, stunned to see anyone running out from under the canopy. When they did so, it was evident even through the running mascara of the more femininely bedecked of the two that it wasn't Tom. And the delicately featured guy with him certainly wasn't Diane.

"Sorry," Kit shouted. "We thought you were someone else. Did you happen to see a guy and a girl out where you were?" The two guys looked at them like they'd blown in with the storm. "Well, not exactly. The guy is Tom—you know, the first queen tonight?"

The couple shook their heads and ran on toward the exit, giving the women annoyed, puzzled looks.

"Shit!" Kit said in frustration. "Where the hell are they? There's practically no one left."

"Let's move up by the exit," Claire suggested. "It's covered too, and we might have a better shot at seeing whoever *is* left a little more clearly than out here in the pouring rain."

They waited another fifteen minutes or so by the exit, to no avail. Finally, a woman staffer came over and told them they'd have to leave since they were getting ready to close things up. Claire asked her if she'd seen Tom since the storm hit.

"Actually, yes, I did. He and some woman ducked into the bar about the time the stage started falling apart. But there's no one in there now. Like I said, we're closing up."

"Well, they're obviously not here," Claire said with a sigh. "And we have to get out. We can figure out a plan when we get back to Stella's."

"I don't know," Kit said, shaking her head. "I don't like this."

"We don't have a choice, honey," Sabi said, putting her arm around Kit. "It's not like Diane doesn't know how to find us. Besides, they probably weren't done talking and couldn't find us to tell us. Diane's a big girl. She'll be fine."

"Ladies . . ." the staffer said, clearly impatient with the lingering group.

"Sorry," Rita said tersely, spinning around to look the woman straight in the eyes. "We're just worried about our friend. We're leaving." Something about the flicker of anger in Rita's eyes elicited a mumbled apology from the woman. There was something definitely frightening about quiet Rita getting to such a point that even a stranger could see.

"Don't mind my honey," Claire said, putting her arm around Rita and pulling her close. "She gets a little testy in nor'easters. We're outta here." She turned to Rita as they all took a deep breath and started out into the pouring rain. "As I've said before, I always want you on *my* side. That half-Sicilian thing is definitely scary."

Already soaked, they didn't bother trying to stay dry and walked at a normal pace down the middle of Commercial Street, searching the faces of passersby for the two they were still hoping to see. Not that there were that many faces to see. Understandably, the storm had cleared the street of the usual post-Carnival party crowd. Actually, though, they were surprised to see as many people as they did, most, like them, having resigned themselves to being soaked and making the best of an unexpected walk in the rain. That is, until the wind picked up; then even the drunkest of the committed party-ers ducked for cover in a shop entrance.

By the time they reached Stella's, the wind started blowing steadily, the temperature dropped further and the four women were shivering. They stopped quickly at the front of the deck to see how high the water was on their beach. Small waves were crashing onto the deck.

"Come up to our room," Rita said to Sabi and Kit. "I'll make some coffee and you can wrap up in the extra blankets we have for the sofa bed." Kit and Sabi nodded silently, and they all trooped up to the second floor.

Soon they were all wrapped in blankets sitting around the kitchen table, sipping mugs of hot coffee. Claire checked along the baseboards and found the controls for the radiators that, mercifully, the room was equipped with.

"God, I hope we have heat, too," Sabi said, looking concerned.

"Not to worry. I know for a fact that you do," Clare said reassuringly. "When we had your room one year, we had a plain old rain storm and had to turn on the heat. Something about being out here on this little point makes the temperature drop like that," she said as she snapped her fingers.

"Thank God." Sabi looked over at Kit. "Jesus, you must be cold. You never drink coffee at night." Kit just looked up at her, still shivering.

"I know what's missing," Claire said, scooting her chair back from the table. She reappeared with the bourbon bottle. "Hell, this doesn't even count as a nightcap—I don't know about you all, but I'm sober as a judge at this point."

Kit held her mug out for a shot of spirits. "Definitely," she said. "I don't know when I've been this chilled. And certainly not in August." Sabi, and even Rita, likewise held their mugs up. Kit took a sip of the spiked coffee. "I just hope they're okay."

"I'm sure they are. It's really not all *that* late, you know," Rita offered. "And I agree with what Sabi said earlier. They probably went out to talk and figured we'd assume as much. And don't forget— Diane would need a ride back to the motel when she didn't find us. Tom no doubt knows someone with a car or has one."

"You're right," Kit said, assuming a look of certainty. "In fact, she's probably there now. I'll go down and call."

"Oh, no you don't, little lady," Sabi said, reaching up and grabbing Kit's shoulder to pull her down as she was getting out of her chair. "I'm not having you go out and stand in the rain again to use that damned pay phone. If she's there, she's there. And, who knows—if she is, maybe she's *busy* and wouldn't even answer. And if she doesn't, you'll just worry. So I vote for *not* assuming the worst and checking things out in the morning—when hopefully it'll be dry and warm and back to being the *un*-scary P-Town we've come to love." There was a finality in her tone that made Kit stay seated and just nod her head.

"Good. I agree," Claire added as a sort of seconding voice, indicating that the case was closed. "Should be a good story, I'm guessing. Actually, make that stor-*ies,* plural."

"Ooh! That's right," Sabi said, brightening. "I almost forgot all about Grant and Pat. I'm thinking that might be the better story!"

"Did you see the look on her face as Pat dragged her away? Talk about a deer in the headlights! Or, I guess tonight that would be fog lights," Claire added with a laugh. "But she sure as hell didn't put up any fight. Man, I didn't see that one coming."

"Oh, for God's sake! Who says anything's going on?" Rita said with a little scowl at the other three chuckling women.

"How long did you say you've been a lesbian?" Sabi asked her, one eyebrow cocked. "My God, honey. All that sparring and baiting with the two of them. I, for one, wondered how long it would take."

"Well, I still say you're jumping to conclusions. I just hope they made it to Pat's okay. That wind is really nasty." At that, another gust rattled the shingles of the building.

"Speaking of which . . ." Kit said, looking over at Sabi. "I think it's time for us to make a dash for our room before another one of those blows through. I'm ready for some serious cuddling." She leaned over and gave Sabi a quick kiss.

"Cuddling. Right." Claire got up, smiling, and went in the living room area. "Here." She handed Sabi and Kit each a tee shirt and gym shorts plus an umbrella. "Wear these down so you don't have to put on those nasty, wet clothes. We'll hang them in our shower to dry. And I'm sure we won't be needing the umbrella tonight. Okay? Come up when you get up. I'm thinking it's a hearty breakfast day tomorrow."

CHAPTER
14

The nor'easter howled through the night. A couple of times Claire felt Rita jump, awakened by a thunderclap or an especially heavy gale wind that blew through. It was rare for Claire to ever awaken in the middle of the night, but when Rita cuddled in especially close to her one of those times and kissed her softly, Claire was glad she was awake. Rita decided she wanted to collect her "winnings" from the bet earlier that evening, winner and loser both coming out ahead in the deal. Afterwards, they both slept soundly until somewhere in the middle of Claire's dream about being late for work, she realized Rita was shaking her.

"Wha'?" she said, trying to rouse herself. She sat up, still in a daze. "What's wrong?"

"I don't know if it's still the storm, but I keep hearing a banging, or knocking or something."

Claire rubbed her eyes. "What time *is* it, anyway?"

"Not quite five, I think," Rita answered groggily, checking the travel alarm.

Claire listened a minute. "Shit. I think someone's at the door." She leapt out of bed and shivered a little since it was still definitely not feeling like summer. When she got to the bottom of the ladder that led up to the sleeping loft, it was evident that it was, indeed, knocking.

Rita listened up in the loft to hear whoever it was that had awakened them at such an ungodly hour. Suddenly she heard Claire crack up with laughter.

"Honey! Get down here. We have visitors."

Rita climbed down the ladder and padded out to the kitchen.

There, still standing just outside the doorway, were Kit and Sabi, huddled together under the umbrella, looking absolutely and utterly pathetic. "We got a leak," Sabi whined, dolefully.

"Oh, my God! What happened? Get in here, you two." Rita started bustling around the kitchen, flipping into Mom mode at the sight of the dripping twosome. "And you, you idiot. You make them stand there in the rain while I come down?"

"It was just too good," Claire said, still laughing. "The two of them, looking like drowned rats. You just had to get the full effect."

While Sabi and Kit pulled off their jackets, they told Claire and Rita the saga of *their* night.

"You remember that whole bit last night about cuddling?" Kit said, as she lit a cigarette. "Well, by the time we got dried off, found the heater, found the extra blanket, and got settled, the whole evening caught up with us and that's really all we *did* do. I mean, we passed *out*. No biggie. But then one helluva thunderclap hit"—Rita and Claire couldn't help but smile—"and we both jumped. Well, since we were both awake at that point . . ."

"Gotcha," Claire said, still smiling.

"Oh. OH! Woke you guys up, too, huh?" Kit returned Claire's sly grin. "Well, anyway, we both seemed to have the same idea. So, I roll over a little closer, and after a minute or two notice that my side feels wet. I figured, oh well, and, ah, continued, as it were. We got a major lip-lock goin' on, when all of a sudden this humongous drip hits us both in the face. So, we figure we'll scoot to one side and try to ignore it for the moment. I feel *another* drip hit the back of my head. So, we take a time out and turn on the light and look up at the ceiling. As we're lying there, we watch little beads of water race each other along not one but three beams on the fucking ceiling! We feel the middle of the bed and realize the mattress between us is practically soaked! Well, by now we're both cracking up at how ridiculous the whole stupid thing is."

"So, what does this one do? Horny, little fucker gets the umbrella you gave us, props it on the bed so it's over us and goes at it again," Sabi says with an annoyed air.

"And did *you* object? I don't think so," Kit said with a raised eyebrow. She continued with the story.

"So, there we are, lying there, when all of a sudden we both burst out laughing at the same moment at the sound of the drops bouncing off the umbrella! Not to mention how ludicrous it would look if someone were to walk in on this sight—two dykes, after-sex cigarettes in their hands, lying under an umbrella in bed! I'm surprised she didn't wake you both up with that cackle of hers."

"Well, we tried to find a dry spot on the bed to go back to sleep, but it was useless. So up we get, take some of the pans in the cupboard and position them on the bed to catch the water. Then we remembered the sofa bed up here, and decided to throw ourselves on your mercy."

"No problem," Claire said, wiping tears from her eyes from laughing so hard. "Of course, the question is whether any of us can fall back asleep after all this laughing."

But after everybody got situated, they did, indeed. The smell of fresh-brewed coffee and bacon finally awakened Kit and Sabi. True to form, Rita had gotten up first and was quietly preparing breakfast while the other three slept. Kit rolled over with a grumble, but Sabi got up to help Rita.

"How long you been up," Sabi whispered.

"Oh, about an hour or so, I guess."

"And you've done all this already?"

"Yep. And I've been to the bakery for rolls and donuts."

"*Dios mio.* Rita, girl, you are a wonder." Sabi yawned and looked around. "So, can I do anything? Or is everything in the oven warming?"

"No, I'm not that good. But there's really nothing to do until the sleepyheads get their asses out of bed. Then you can rustle up some eggs."

Sabi took a sip off coffee. "So, is it still bad out there?" She got up and peeked through the curtains at what appeared to be a fairly constant rain.

"Well, as you can see, it's still raining. But it seems like the wind has calmed down a lot. Wait till you go look at the bay—I think there's a cruise ship or something that's either docked or grounded here. They must've had to *literally* find the nearest port in the storm."

"Wow. That really was some storm. I wouldn't tell Kit, but I was getting scared last night. Especially when we were outside at The Boatslip. I don't like that heavy wind shit."

"Me neither. But it looked like everything weathered it okay. At least, as best I could see on my early walk."

"What walk? Who'd be stupid enough to go out in this shit for a walk?" Claire stood in the entryway between the kitchen and the living room and yawned. "No, don't tell me. Lemme guess." She frowned, pretending to consider the question. "My honey!"

"Ha, ha, ha. Yes, your honey—going to get *you* your Portuguese doughnut thingies."

Claire stumbled around the table to Rita and gave her a kiss. "You're the best, honey."

"Yeah, yeah." Rita smiled up at her despite her effort to play the wounded party and kissed her back.

"Okay. Now, that you've saved your ass again, why don't you go get your friend up, and we'll eat this lovely breakfast Rita's made for us," Sabi said, making a shooing gesture toward the living room.

Kit was already half awake and sat up at hearing Sabi. "I'm up already. Jeez, you guys are loud."

"Sorry, pal. But they woke me up, too." Claire dodged Rita's hand that came up backwards over her head and then swung around to connect with her ass in a nearly double-jointed maneuver that only an experienced mother could manage. "Not that it wasn't time to get up, mind you," she added with a quick look back over her shoulder.

Kit stumbled out to join them, and after she'd had a quick wake-up cup of coffee, they proceeded to dive into the breakfast feast.

"Damn, I was hungry," Claire said, taking a deep breath. "But that should hold me for a while." She took a sip of coffee. "Well, I guess it's time to start figuring out the whereabouts of our lost friends. And from the looks of it out there, we have the whole day to do it, since I don't think this is a beach or pool day. But I think the first order of business may be a trip to that Army/Navy store and see if they have any cheap sweats. God knows *that* wasn't on my summer packing list. Better to lay around in if we're gonna be inside most of the day."

"Sounds good to me," Kit replied. "But first I want to call the motel and see if we can solve at least one of the mysteries right away." She finished her last swallow of coffee. "On the way, we better go see if our whole damned apartment has floated away. *And* tell Stella. You want to come with me and see if Grant's in her room?"

Kit and Claire left to do reconnaissance on the room, their friends, and some sweatpants while Rita and Sabi cleaned up the kitchen.

A quick look in the room convinced Claire that the girls had not been exaggerating about the night before. "My God. How'd you guys sleep as long as you did in this soggy mess?"

"I'm tellin' you, we were wiped when we first laid down. I'm surprised the thunder even woke me up. But I'm glad it did," she said with a wink. "So, should we dump these pots?"

"Actually, no. I think Stella should see this mess just the way it is. Let's go get her."

They returned with Stella in tow, having given her a brief overview of the entire night before, but being very sparse with details about Grant's disappearance.

"Those shiftless sons-a-bitches!" she exclaimed as she looked the room over.

"Who?"

"The bastards that repaired the upstairs walkway this spring. I *told* them it looked to me like the whole damned thing was canted back toward the building rather than toward the ground. But no-o-o. *I* was crazy. *I* was always finding fault with the work people do. Well, this is why. Just wait till I get Joe Sampson on the phone. He better be over here tomorrow figuring out how he's going to make this right. Own a business and let this kind of shoddy workmanship get by. Bah!" And without a single word to either of them, still muttering to herself, Stella was off to do battle.

"And what about our room?" Kit moaned, standing there surveying the soggy mess, stunned at the unspoken dismissal.

"Don't worry. We'll check in with her later today. I really don't think this is the best time to try to have a rational conversation with her. If worse comes to worse, you guys can always sleep upstairs. And we'll make her give you a refund."

"Make her. Right." Kit said, grabbing her baseball cap and walking out the door. "Well, on to the next crisis." Kit strode across the deck and out the gate to the phone, not even waiting for Claire to catch up with the umbrella.

Claire stood watching the poncho-clad crowds pass by up on the sidewalk as Kit called Diane's room. It was evident by Kit's silence that no one was answering. She then waited none too patiently for the receptionist to get back on the phone, and left a message for Diane to leave a message on Stella's business line, where they all got messages, as soon as she got in.

"Your turn," she said, handing the phone to Claire with the receptionist still on the line. However, Claire's attempt at contacting Grant was no more successful than Kit's. So, she left the same message—reinforcing that it was imperative they get the messages.

"Well, that's two strikes. I suppose the damned store'll be out of sweats by the time we get there. That'll make it three for three," Kit grumbled as they started off down Commercial Street for the final errand of the morning.

"Hey!" Claire trotted up the driveway to catch up with Kit who'd taken off ahead of her, taking giant strides entirely out of proportion with her small body, oblivious of the rain. "Relax, Kit. We'll track down the two delinquents, Stella will get the room fixed, and everything'll be fine. Really."

Kit slowed a bit and rearranged the baseball cap on her head as she did when she was deep in thought. "I know all that. It's Diane— and Grant, for that matter. The one thing the girls *didn't* want to happen was have our time here end up being about *our* friends when they got here. So, what happens? This."

"I'm tellin' you, relax. They didn't seem pissed this morning. Hell, we both got lucky last night. Doesn't sound like anyone's pissed off to me."

"Well, you got a point there," she replied, slowing down even more as her pique began to fade. "I mean, it's not like we did anything to make all this shit happen."

"Not at all. And to prove it, I'm betting that there *will* be sweatpants left when we get to the store. It'll be a sign."

The gods were, indeed, smiling, albeit through the rain. They not only found not-half-bad cheap sweats, they also stumbled on another barrel near the back of the store filled with rain ponchos, the one in the front of the store having been empty. As they browsed, they found some fun candles in hurricane-style holders, which seemed very apropos, and a ship's life preserver that Claire wanted for the backyard, *and* which completed their storm-themed buying spree.

The girls made their way back along Commercial, keeping an eye open for their missing-in-action friends. The question was what kind of action.

By the time they arrived back at Stella's, the rain had tapered off to a drizzle. They put the umbrella down when they were about halfway there and relied on their newly purchased ponchos for protection, the umbrella being a hazard in the crowded street, rain notwithstanding. As a result, when they got back to Stella's they noticed the havoc wreaked by the storm out on the beach that they hadn't earlier, huddled under the umbrella. They also saw two figures standing by the railing, beach towels over their heads.

"Ahoy, mateys!" Claire yelled. The two towel-covered figures spun around. "What did I tell you? Who the hell else would be out here in get-ups like that?" Claire said to Kit. Sabi started hooting with laughter at the sight of them. Not only did Claire and Kit look more like Mutt and Jeff than ever in their new bright red ponchos, they had taken it to the next level with Claire sporting the life preserver slung around her neck and Kit holding a hurricane lamp in each hand.

When they joined the other two at the railing, however, they stopped laughing. Boats were literally strewn everywhere along the beach, as though some giant toddler had had a temper tantrum and thrown its toys about. The boats' owners were out, pants rolled up, working together to right overturned boats and bail water out of ones that had managed not to be overturned. Masts were snapped in two, sails ripped. And out in the harbor was a cruise ship, listing a little to port, where it clearly was partially grounded now that the tide was out.

"Shit."

"You can say that again," Claire said in answer to Kit's one-word summation of the sight. "Man, oh, man. That really *was* some storm. Imagine coming out to find this if you owned one of these boats?"

"Not really. I think I'd just sit down and cry."

"You wouldn't have time," Rita replied quietly. "These people have been out here working since who knows when."

All of a sudden, Sabi burst out in laughter.

"What in the name of God could be funny in the middle of this?" Kit said, annoyed and embarrassed that some of the people down on the beach would hear her guffaw.

"Look!" Sabi pointed down on the beach toward the pier. Their gazes were met with one of the most incongruous sights they'd ever seen, or might ever see, for that matter. What looked to be a family of seven or eight—mother with a bundle that looked like a baby in her arms, father, maybe a grandparent, and four kids—were walking along the beach back and forth, restricting their stroll to a fairly deserted strip of the beach below the pier's boardwalk. What made the sight so odd was that they looked to be Amish.

"Oh, my God," Sabi said, covering her mouth with her hand, smothering the urge to burst out laughing again. "Can you even imagine what they must be thinking? Talk about the wrath of God! They must be from that ship that's stuck out there. God knows, they're not day-trippers. Here they not only get hit with a nor'easter while at sea, they end up stuck in, of all places, Province-fucking-town! Could *anything* be closer to Sodom and Gomorrah to them? You can almost see the panic on their faces from here. Now I've seen everything. Can you imagine the stories they're gonna tell when they get home?" She looked back at the two newcomers to the deck. "And look at you two. You're almost as weird looking, but you really can't top the visitors down there! Hmmm . . . judging from the bags and your new duds, it looks like you did some shopping."

"That we did, matey," Claire replied, sticking to her seafaring voice. "But maybe we should throw the life preserver to your friends down there!"

"What's so damned interesting on the beach?" It was the unmistakable growl of Stella. She walked up to where they were standing and scanned the beach. "Damned fools should have listened to the short wave if they have boats. They were saying since yesterday afternoon we might get hit with this."

"And you didn't tell us?" Kit said in unconcealed anger and exasperation.

"Well, you didn't have a boat that might get blown to bits. Besides, I figured it'd blow out to sea and we'd only see a little rain. Damned if they weren't right."

"Uh, next time you hear that something like this *might* even happen, tell us, okay?" Claire said, trying to remain controlled. "And, by the way. What's the story on Kit and Sabi's room?"

"Well, there's not much that can be done about it until next week. But the storm's over, so leaks shouldn't be a problem."

"Yeah? What about our sopping wet mattress?"

"You have a choice about that one. I have a few in storage, but that lazy college boy helper of mine is off for the day; isn't due here until tomorrow. So, you can stay up with your friends for a night or the rest of the weekend. I'll credit your full room rate for every night you stay up there. It's worth it to me to let the thing dry out on its own and not have to haul another one up here."

"Hmmm." Kit looked at Sabi who shrugged in response. "Let us talk about it, and I'll let you know later today. We have to stay up there tonight anyway, right?"

"Unless you want to sleep out here on the deck," Stella replied with her usual tact.

"Like she said, they'll let you know later on," Claire intervened. "It's still pretty nasty out here. How about we go up and sort through our purchases?"

Once upstairs, Sabi and Kit retreated to a corner of the living room for a quick chat about their circumstances. In the meantime, Claire pulled out the sweats ensemble she'd gotten for Rita. Sabi, naturally nosy, glanced over to see what Rita got and was soon digging through Kit's bag, the conversation temporarily on hold. Playing into the response she knew her public expected, she started bemoaning the less-than-chic look of the sweats Kit had picked out for her. Once she had them on and was nestled cozily in the couch, though, she seemed to care little about the fashion statement aspect of the ensemble.

Rita was in the process of making another pot of coffee to warm up the intrepid shoppers when there was a knock on the door. She put the can down on the counter and went to the door.

It was Grant and Pat, hand in hand.

CHAPTER
15

"Well, well, well!" Rita said, as she slowly shook her head and stood looking at the two women, her hand still on the doorknob. Neither of them said a word, but instead both shrugged as if on cue and smiled sheepishly at Rita, raindrops dripping off the hoods of *their* red ponchos.

Claire walked up bedside Rita and chuckled at the sight of the chagrined couple. "Well, looks like you managed to tear yourselves away from . . . *whatever* to trek out for ponchos. I'm surprised we didn't bump into you." She turned toward the living room. "Hey, girls. We got company!" she yelled. She turned back to the visitors. "Jesus, get in here, you idiots. Don't you know it's raining out there?!?"

The other two were already up and in the kitchen when Claire made her announcement. They started helping Grant and Pat out of their rain togs as Rita headed for her usual station in the kitchen to finish making the fresh pot of coffee.

"My God. You two look like hell," she said as she looked over after pouring the water in the coffee maker. "Want something to eat? I've got some breakfast stuff left I can warm up for you."

Grant walked over and hugged Rita. "God love ya', woman. You're such a gem. Though I still can't figure out for the life of me how that pain in the ass over there's managed to hang on to you. We really do have to talk one of these days," she said in a conspiratorial whisper, with a sidelong look in Claire's direction.

"You know, you can drink your coffee outside if the company's not to your liking," Claire quipped making a quick turn back towards the door. "Aw, hell. C'mere, you goofball." Claire gave Grant a big hug. "It's good to know that at least half of the missing-in-action are present and accounted for."

"What are you talking about?" Pat asked with a frown, sitting down at the table and taking the cup of warmed up coffee Rita offered while the fresh pot brewed.

"Oh, that's right. You guys missed all the end o' Carnival trauma," Sabi noted, sitting down beside Pat. Kit looked over at Claire and shrugged, eyebrow raised at this latest display of camaraderie on Sabi's part. "Well! Let's see . . ." And Sabi launched into the missing Diane and Tom saga, complete with Kit's attempt to reach her, and Grant, this morning.

"The bottom line," Kit interrupted as Sabi digressed into dramatics about the storm, their leak, even the damned sweatpants, "is that we don't have a clue as to where they are. No call, no note, no messages here or at the motel, nothing. And it's practically fucking noon!"

"Honey, relax. This isn't exactly the inner city or the wilderness here. I seriously doubt they've been abducted by rival gangs or attacked by a pack of wolves. Odds are good they were out late and haven't even woken up yet," Sabi offered by way of comfort. "Besides, we haven't heard these guys' story yet. And I'm *dying* to hear it!"

Pat sat quietly for a moment, holding the warm mug in her hands, still looking concerned. Before she could comment on the Diane/ Tom situation, Grant launched into their story.

"Well, I'm not surprised at all you lost 'em in that mess last night. I swear to God, that was some nasty nor'easter. A couple of times walking to Pat's, I had to grab her and duck into a doorway, or I seriously thought she was gonna get swept up and blown back to Boston!" She took a sip of the fresh coffee Rita put down in front of her. "But, anyway, we finally made it, dodging blowing trash and all kinds of shit. Hell, we only had to go a few blocks from The Boatslip, but I bet it took us twenty minutes to get there.

"So, we went in to her apartment and checked to see if by some stroke of dumb luck her next-door neighbor—her landlord—had thought to bring the animals in and to see that there was no damage to windows or anything. Luckily, everything inside was intact, but no animals. So, we got all poncho-ed up—so no, smart ass, we didn't have to go out this morning!" she said, sticking her tongue out at Claire "—and started the animal rescue portion of our evening. Not only would it take too long to tell, it definitely took too long to actually do. Lots of looking under steps, porches, blown-in rubbish, climbing through bushes, shining flashlights up trees, you name it. Finally, we managed to hear the dog whimpering when the wind calmed for two seconds and followed the sound back to Pat's back porch. There's the poor little bastard, wedged behind the barbecue grill, his head stuck up under the cover. So, we got him in and semidried off and headed back out for the *cats*. Two we found pretty quick; we backtracked and took another look under the front porch, and there they were, huddled right to the left of where we looked before, while we were busy shining the flashlight back all the way under the house! But that last little fucker! Jesus H. Christ. I thought we'd never find her." She turned to Claire and lowered her head and her voice. "And I half wish we hadn't—little bitch clawed the shit out of me." She glanced back over at Pat, who was sitting quietly, arms crossed.

"Care to continue or shall I?" she said, with a tolerant smile. "Actually, I *will* pick it up from here," she said, scooting her chair into the table and getting resituated. As Grant started to jump back into the story, Pat put her finger on Grant's lips. "No, no, no, dear. *I* get to do this part." Grant sat back in her chair, arms crossed, pouting. Pat smiled and gave her a quick peck on the cheek. "Don't worry. I won't make you sound too foolish.

"So little Miss Hard-ass here overrules my suggestion that we leave Pisspot—I know, but if you knew this cat, you'd understand my odd choice of names—to her own self-protective, animal instincts and take cover from the now *driving* rain." Pat turned to Claire. "Did you ever try to talk this hardheaded woman *out* of doing something she'd put her mind to?" Claire nodded and cleared her throat. "Yeah, then, you know why we continued on our merry little search.

"I live in the west end, a couple of blocks past The Boatslip, in a great little house *across* from the oceanfront houses, sadly. But the cats have the run of the neighborhood and love to hang out by the water. When I told Grant this, she decided we had to go down to the beach to check. Now, I don't know if you guys took a look at *your* beach when you got home," to which everyone silently nodded with appropriate looks of oh-my-God, "but if you did, you know what it was like as we went clambering down my neighbor's side walkway, down the beach stairs, and started slogging through the soggy sand and damned waves that were crashing." She gave Grant a sidelong look. "My big, strong heroine here decided I should go back up the stairs lest I get dragged out to sea. Do I need to remind you who's lived here the past five summers? Anyway, she climbed up the embankment, looking behind rocks and bushes, to no avail. When she turned to look up and check on me, she sees the cat come skittering out from behind a rowboat that she'd just flashed the light behind a second before. Then she trips and takes a header down the embankment, face first right into a tide pool on the beach. I go running down the steps, *genuinely* afraid she might get dragged into the ocean if a breaker hits while she's down, the cat goes bounding under the dock, and I drag Grant back toward the tide line just as a nasty wave hits."

"Aw, shit, Pat. I was fine. Soaked to the skin and spittin' sand, but fine. You make it sound like I was some helpless female flailing around in the water."

"Dear God, Grant, no one here would mistake you for a helpless female!" The group smothered their laughter as Grant sniffed and tried to regain her dignity. "Anyway, as I was saying, my new friend here pulled herself together and was more determined than ever to get that cat, which was huddled against one of the pylons of the dock. She was down there coaxing the cat, and as she reached for her, Pisspot gave her a nasty swipe and, unfortunately, connected. She headed straight for me when she saw me, and this one slips and falls *right* in the water this time!"

The four women burst into laughter at the visual of this last scene. Pat smiled and chuckled along with them, giving Grant a pat on the arm as she sat there, scowling, though with a hint of a smile at the corners of her mouth.

"The cat and I crab walked down to where poor Grant was sitting, up to her tits in water now, and dragged her to her feet, slogged our way back up to level ground, and made our way home. And that, ladies, was *our* night!"

Everyone, including Grant, had a good laugh and traded teasing jibes at the would-be rescuer, who took it all in good stride. Suddenly, Sabi stopped laughing and looked hard at both Grant and Pat. "Wait a minute, you two. Something tells me you're leaving out some pertinent details. What do you guys think?"

"Ye-e-ah. Sabi's right," Claire said, giving the new couple a scrutinizing look. "C'mon, you two. Give it up."

For the second time since Claire had known Grant, she flushed scarlet. Pat just smiled and sat back in her chair. "You wanted to tell the story, honey. So, go ahead. Finish the story."

"Never mind. You go ahead," Grant said, still blushing.

"Oh, my God!" Pat said suddenly. "Actually, there *is* more to the story." She turned to Grant. "We almost forgot to tell them about our visitor."

"Visitor?" Claire said. "Sounds juicy and mysterious."

"Yeah, maybe more than we would have liked." Everyone around the table exchanged puzzled and somewhat concerned glances as Pat took a deep breath and continued with the story.

"So, where was I? Oh, yeah. Back at my humble abode. Well, we made our way back to my place, got the animals and ourselves dried off, and brewed up a pot of coffee. Clearly, there was lots of laughing and rehashing of the story going on at that point, and we were both anything but ready to call it a night. Fortunately, I had a bottle of brandy to go with the hot coffee."

"Looks like we were all on the same wavelength at that point of the evening!" Claire interjected, chuckling.

"Yeah, well, we were chilled to the bone," Pat continued. "Medicinal purposes, only, you understand! So, we sat on the couch, the kids— my runaway animals—decided to join us, with Pisspot all *over* Grant. It was the funniest thing, since Grant was understandably a tad leery of that bad cat. But she warmed up to her, and the cat wouldn't leave her alone—which shocked the shit out of me since that cat won't have anything to do with anybody." She paused a moment and looked at Grant warmly. "Actually, it didn't shock me, to tell the truth. In case you hadn't figured it out, I sort of had, shall we say, designs on your friend when I grabbed her and dragged her off with me. But I wasn't totally sure she was on the same wavelength. She can be pretty innocent, you know." Claire smiled and nodded. "Something about Pisspot being the center of the rescue effort cinched it for me. They're kinda alike, Grant and that cat: ornery as hell, not easy to know but pretty cute. And cuddly as hell."

"C'mon, Pat. You're killin' me here," Grant said, coloring again.

Aw, you love it and you know you do," she said, taking Grant's hand. "So, we sipped our coffee and brandy, put on some music, got cozy and . . . well, went with the moment. And about the time 'the moment' was going to shift to other quarters, as it were, there's this thud-thud-thud on my door. Scared the shit out of both of us. So, I go to the door with this one right behind me—again, my fearless protector. I opened the door and there's Gayle, my ex, soaked and hanging on to the doorjamb, swaying like a drunken sailor, which she clearly was . . . the drunk part anyway. Great. Just what I needed. Of course, as soon as she saw Grant, she started cursing and threatening and being a genuine asshole. And I suppose that was the final confirmation about Grant. Having known Gayle all these years, I'm assuming Grant's going to go at it with her and I'll have this big macho dyke brawl on my hands at nearly two o'clock in the morning. But, instead, Grant calmed her down, told her she was there to help me with the animals, walked Gayle over to the kitchen table, poured her some coffee, and talked shit with her for like fifteen minutes or so. I'd forgotten what civilized behavior was like after all these years.

"Grant left her there for a minute to whisper to me that it might be a good idea to get Gayle on her way before the liquor caught up to her again. Then she offered to 'go to the bathroom' for a while so I could ask Gayle to leave without embarrassing her in front of someone else. What a sweetie." Pat gave Grant's hand a squeeze.

"Unfortunately, it didn't go quite as planned, since Gayle had the drunken idea that she was going to pop over and pick up where we left off—six months ago! After I made it *very* clear that that wasn't going to happen, she threatened to wreck the store, take care of the bitch in the bathroom, and prove to me she still loved me! You gotta love drunks; seems she'd forgotten that little detail about her being the one screwin' around. At that, Grant came storming out of the bathroom and told Gayle to walk out on her own or," here she shifted to an imitation of Grant's Texas drawl, " 'or it mat not be quite so easy to be walkin' at all when I'm through with ya.' Can you believe it? Mellow, two-steppin' Grant! You'd have been proud of her—never even raised her voice!"

"Grant??" Claire said in genuine disbelief. She looked at Grant. "You?!?"

"Well, Griff, you've never seen me really pissed off. And I was *really* pissed off!"

"Apparently," Claire said, shaking her head with a bemused smile.

"I think Gayle would've taken her on, except when she took a step toward her, she slipped on the rug and had to catch herself on a hat tree I have by the door and would've ended up in a less-than-dignified heap on the floor if Grant hadn't caught her before she pulled the thing over on herself.

"Fortunately, that seemed to take the fight out of her. She grabbed her jacket and slurred something about not needing my shit anymore and being sorry she hadn't taken her chances with the hot chick she left at the bar, and maybe she'd just go back and see if her new Carnival friends were still there. Now, after your story, I'm wondering just who those so-called friends were—and who the 'hot chick' was.

"As for us, let's just say we finally fell asleep to the sound of birds chirping." She winked at Grant who picked up their clasped hands and kissed Pat's. "Which is why we look like hell this morning or afternoon or whatever the hell it is."

"As well you should," Sabi replied, giving Pat a combination congratulatory/comforting pat on the back. "You earned it—on all counts, it sounds like."

"Well, so far your evening wins the best story of the nor'easter competition," Claire said. "Ours was certainly boring by comparison. Now the sixty-four thousand dollar question is what the remaining saga turns out to be. And I don't know about you guys, but I'm getting more curious as time goes on."

"Actually, though our main reason for coming over was to let you know we were okay, we also wanted to see if you guys wanted to come over to my place for the afternoon and watch movies or something, since it looks like this weather isn't letting up any time soon. I've got everything we need—booze, food, music, popcorn, the works," Pat said.

"Yeah. Pat's got a great little place—fireplace and everything," Grant added, clearly excited at the prospect of having her friends become part of her new relationship. "And today's the perfect day to fire it up."

"Assuming you have some dry wood," Claire added.

"I don't think that's our main concern at the moment," Rita said quickly before Claire got caught up in planning the day. "Did you forget about Diane?"

"*No,* I didn't forget about Diane," she replied in a sarcastic, simpering reply to Rita's chastising tone. "But if this all resolves itself as simply as I suspect it will, I thought it sounded like a fun way to spend the *rest* of the day."

"Chill out, you two," Grant said. "Rita's right; first things first. And let's *hope* Claire's right. Honey, you're the resident expert on all things P-Town. Any suggestions?"

Sabi leaned over to whisper to Rita. "My, my. We're at the 'honey' stage already."

Pat gave them a smile rather than a dirty look. The change in twenty-four hours was truly impressive. "Actually, I've been thinking about the best thing to do since you guys told us what happened, and I think I may at least have a place to start. I know a guy who works at The Boatslip. I'll give him a call and see if he knows anything, including where Tom lives. Regardless, though, there's really not much difference sitting here or sitting at my place. And Grant's right. I do have a killer fireplace. We can leave a note on your door and let Stella know where we are in case Diane calls here."

The other five women looked at each other at the mention of Stella's name.

Claire smiled ruefully. "Uh, oh. Well, Heartbreak Kid, something tells me Miss Stella's not gonna be thrilled about this new development. Maybe we'll bag the Stella part and just leave the note."

"What the hell are you talking about?" Pat asked with a look of puzzlement mixed with distaste.

"It's a long story," Sabi said. "We'll fill you in on the way to your house."

"So, you guys are coming," Grant half stated, half asked.

"Honey?" Claire asked Rita.

"Why not? I suppose Pat's right. And if we find out where Tom lives, we can stop by on the way."

"Sounds like a plan," Kit said. She'd been conspicuously quiet throughout the debate.

"Don't worry, honey," Sabi said. "Diane's fine. She better be. She's gonna need all her strength when we find her and I kick her ass right down the middle of Commercial Street!"

CHAPTER
16

The rain hadn't slowed the gathering weekend crowds on Commercial Street. The troop slogged along through the puddles and the people and the continuing drizzle, en route to the address Pat's friend had given her. They stopped briefly at the jewelry store to check on the leak that had caused the store to close for the day—and had made for the unexpected day off for Pat.

A back corner of the floor was wet, the drips from the ceiling just missing the glass watch cabinet. The ceiling hadn't sagged, so it appeared the store could re-open in a day or two once the roof was repaired and the ceiling and floor had dried out.

"Well, it could be a helluva lot worse," Pat mused, looking over the damage. "It's a damned good thing I'm responsible since it doesn't look like my late night visitor/business partner has managed to show up yet to survey the damage. I bet she hasn't even woken up to get the message from our cleaning guy who called me. Oh well. I'm actually grateful for her irresponsibility today. I wasn't looking forward to running into her. There's plenty of time for that. And the time off is an extra bonus . . . and a well timed one at that." She took Grant's hand and leaned up to kiss her. "Shit. I never do this kind of stuff. I'm starting to scare myself!"

Grant was grinning from ear to ear. "You don't hear me complaining."

Pat locked up the store and paused in front to check the notes she'd made during her phone call. "According to Shawn, Tom's sharing a place up off Bradford, way the hell at the other end of Court Street. Okay, girls, let's go see what we can find out."

As the women made their way along Commercial to Court, Sabi

and Pat continued a conversation they'd started in the store about
the new sapphire ring Pat showed her the day before. Claire took her
chance to catch up to Grant and slow her down so that they were at
the back of the group.

"So, what's the story, pal?" Claire asked.

"What's the story about what?" Grant replied, trying hard to adopt
her usual wide-eyed, clueless look.

"Oh, yeah, right. Do it with somebody else, okay? But don't kid a
kidder, kid."

"Alright, alright. What d'ya want to know?"

"I don't know exactly. I guess how you feel about this whole thing
is a good starter."

"Jesus, Claire. I'm as shocked as you are. Totally bowled over. I
mean, you always come to P-Town hoping to score; your basic summer fling, anyway. But I'm feeling more than fling-y about this one.
And I'm as scared as I am happy." Grant stopped to light a cigarette.
For a moment she just stood there, smoking it and saying nothing. "I
swear to God, I never expected this. Hell, this time coming out here,
I really was totally focused on seeing you and Rita and *not* on finding
a woman. But she's really special, I gotta tell you. Even when you
guys first introduced me, I got that . . . you know . . . that . . . stupid
feeling, like everything you say matters and you *know* you're gonna
fuck it up because it does!" Grant smiled, more to herself than at
Claire. "But she told me last night that she felt the same way when I
came in the store that day. And speaking of last night—Lord God
almighty. Granted, it's been a while. But unless I'm gettin' senile
awful young, I don't remember anything like that with anybody before. Un-fucking-believable. Literally."

"Jesus, you must have it bad. First of all, you *never* call me 'Claire,'
and, secondly, I have never seen or heard you like this. But you may
want to take a deep breath, my friend. I mean, it's only a couple of
days you even know this woman."

"Oh, I know, you don't have to tell *me*. Why do you think I've
been so quiet today? But the way I figure it, what the hell! The worst
that can happen is that it is a fling, I'll be crushed for a while and no
worse off than I was before. Except I'll have had one helluva good

time!" She paused. "And, if it's real . . . well, if it's real I'll have even more reason to be grateful you're my friend."

"Oh, stop. If it was meant to be, you guys would've run into each other sooner or later. How ideal—she even lives in Boston. Just watch your ass, sweetie. No matter what, gettin' burned's no fun."

"Thanks. It's good to know if I'm not watching it, you will be." Grant gave Claire a hug around the shoulders. "Now, if you'll excuse me, I think I'll jog on up and see if my little saleswoman is done with her pitch!"

"You. Jogging. Incredible. It must be love." Claire watched as Grant did, indeed, jog—uphill, no less—to meet Pat. Rita was waiting as Claire made her way more slowly to the top of Court Street.

"So, anything you'd like to share?" she said, putting her arm through Claire's.

"Not really. Except that she's got it bad. And she's happy as a pig in shit. Your classic lesbian leap to cloud nine."

"Well, the good news is that Sabi came back with the same report from Pat. Which makes her doubly happy, since that means she won't have to unleash her Puerto Rican wrath on her for flirting with Kit."

"So, now all we have to do is track down Diane to get Kit out of her funk, and we can get on with our vacation."

"And the sooner the better."

"I couldn't agree with you more, honey. Let's catch up with the rest of the group."

They were waiting for Rita and Claire on the other side of Bradford. "Hey, you slowpokes!" Sabi shouted. "It may not be pouring, but this still isn't my idea of strolling weather!"

"We're coming, we're coming." Claire hollered back, as she scanned the traffic and grabbed Rita's hand to make a dash for it when there was a break. "You are *such* a pain in the ass!" she said to Sabi. "We're usually waiting for you while you take an hour staring in every damned window we pass on Commercial Street!"

"Well, I'm on a mission now, so let's get movin', girls!"

They continued on along Court, checking numbers as they went. Finally, after a healthy hike, they saw the house. They headed to the back, as Shawn had told Pat to, Tom's apartment being in the rear on the third floor.

"My God, can't anything about this be easy?" Rita panted as they finally mounted the landing.

"Let's hope the rest of this is as easy as knocking on the door," Kit answered, looking grim. "If not, Sabi's gonna have help kicking Diane's ass when we find her." She strode purposefully up to the door and pounded on it. While she waited for an answer, Pat leaned over the landing railing, trying to see in a side window.

"Anything?" she asked as she cupped her hands to peer in.

"Not yet," whispered Sabi, not wanting Kit to hear.

"Well, I can see pretty well, and I don't see any lights or movement. But it's definitely Tom's place. I can see his uniform on the couch. Ooh! I can also see his outfit from last night. So, he's been here since we saw him last. Wait a minute—I think I see someone coming."

The door opened and a bleary-eyed guy with sleep creases on the left side of his face stood there rubbing his eyes. "Yeah?"

"Hey. Is Tom around?" Kit asked brusquely.

The guy looked at her, clearly annoyed at her tone. "Who wants to know?"

"Listen, pal—"

Pat jumped over to the door. "Hi. You must be Phil. I'm Pat Williams. I own the gay jewelry store in town." Pat explained. Phil said nothing. "Anyway, we're actually looking for a friend of ours who we think was with Tom last night, and we can't find her. So we figured we'd try here. We tried calling, but it seems there's something wrong with the phone."

"Yeah. I took it off the fucking hook 'cause I'm trying to get some sleep, which you all just totally screwed up. And as for Tom, how should I know where the fuck he is? We just split the rent, man. He does his thing, I do mine."

"I see," Pat said, looking back at the group and rolling her eyes. "So, I guess that means he's not here now."

"Do you really think I'd have gotten my sorry ass out of bed if I didn't have to?"

Sabi came flying around from the back of the group and launched into a string of Spanish expletives. "Listen, you sonofabitch. You don't even want me to translate what I just said. But you *do* want to go check in his room and make goddamned sure he's not in his bed if you don't want a really pissed off Puerto Rican dyke to come in there and claw your macho bullshit eyes out!"

Phil grumbled something and disappeared for a minute. He reappeared, looking a little more awake this time, but keeping his hand on the door as though he wanted to be able to slam it quickly if necessary. "No. Looks like he stopped by at some point, but, like I told you, he's not here. Sorry if I'm not exactly Mr. Charming, but I was out all fucking night—and *didn't* get fucked," he said in a tone dripping with sarcasm, giving them an annoyed smirk. "So, if you *ladies* will excuse me . . ." He started to close the door, but Kit jumped up from behind Claire, putting her foot in the door.

"Excuse me, Phil," she said, with equal sarcasm. "Could you at least put this note on his door?" He took the note and again started to close the door. "And one more thing." He opened it a crack. "If I *don't* find my friend soon, I'm calling the police. So, you might want to clean up your fucking act in case it's them who wakes you up next time."

As he slammed the door they heard him mutter, "Goddamned dykes." Kit started back at the door, but Claire got to her first.

"Whoa, killer. He's bigger and nastier than you," Pat cautioned. "And we have some detective work to do. Let's leave Phil to another day. We know where he and Tom live. That's all we need at the moment."

"Prick!" Kit said, half at the door. "Now what?" she said, squaring her hat on her head as she turned back to the group. The anger had quickly abated and her tone had shifted to one bordering on desperation.

"Okay. Plan B," Pat said, taking a deep breath. "First, I think Kit should try the motel again. It's been a while since you guys called, right?" Kit nodded. "Okay. Then, if there's still no answer, we'll stop by The Boatslip and see if we can find anybody who might have seen them leave. It's on the way to my house anyway."

The rain had all but stopped by the time they got back down to Commercial Street. Hoods went down, the better to keep an eye out to spot the truant couple in case they were out strolling along, oblivious to time and weather. Kit called the motel, only to listen to the sound of unanswered ringing. She left another message and confirmed with the desk clerk that no one had picked up the earlier one.

Given that it was only about 1:30 and the weather had been rotten, The Boatslip's usually packed deck was deserted. Waiters slumped against each of the three bars, bored and, most likely, hung over. The couples fanned out, each taking one of the bars to see what they could find out.

Rita and Claire struck out at the pool bar and headed for the deck bar under the canopy to rendezvous with Kit and Sabi who'd had that assignment. Grant and Pat checked out the main bar by the dance floor. Kit paced and smoked up a storm, while her partner and friends simply looked at one another, not knowing what to say at this point. Granted, it was actually early in the day, but it seemed as though they'd been searching for hours.

"You know, we got this all wrong. It's not Diane's ass we have to kick when we find her, it's that asshole Tom's. That whole enlightened-eighties-man-working-at-a-gay-bar bit—it's probably a big fucking act to try to score with a dyke . . . or some dyke's unsuspecting straight friend."

"Honey, quit beating yourself up over this. This is only the second place we've even asked. We'll find her, I promise," Sabi said consolingly, putting her arm around Kit—but not without a questioning look to the side at Rita and Claire.

As Kit lit up yet another cigarette, Pat and Grant came bounding out of the main building. "Finally! Good news!" Grant said, turning to Pat to continue the update.

"Well, first we thought we were striking out yet again—only two guys at the bar were even working last night, and neither one of them remembered seeing Tom after his grand crowning. But then one of the senior staffers walked by and heard me asking and stopped. Seems you talked to her last night when you were leaving?"

"Oh yeah! I remember her," Sabi said, brightening.

"Big deal," Kit said. "She only remembered seeing Tom and Diane leave."

"That was last night. Today, when we told her we still hadn't found Diane, she said the more she thought about it, she thinks they stopped out by the exit and ran into a group of people that they then left with. And one of them was Gayle!"

"How in the hell does she know Gayle?" Grant asked, clearly annoyed at even the mention of her name.

"Trust me, honey—*lots* of women in this town know Gayle. That was a big part of the problem."

"Oh. Sorry." Grant stuffed her hands in her pockets and *again* turned a color that clashed with the red in her hair.

"Anyway, I couldn't care less about that. At least we have a lead. Let's head to my house and I'll give her a call. Maybe she'll even have the good sense to apologize for that little scene last night. Though, on second thought, that'd definitely be out of character."

They arrived at Pat's house and instantly knew why Grant was so keen on them coming over. It was a charming, classic Cape Cod decorated in fun, warm, bright colors with all sorts of interesting, as opposed to cluttery, tchotchkes. A beautiful fieldstone fireplace took up the better part of one living room wall, with comfy, inviting overstuffed chairs on either side of it. A wonderful Deco-style couch sat between them, looking directly at the fireplace.

"Oh, Pat. This is wonderful," Rita said, still looking around at all the eye-catching antiques and accent pieces tastefully placed around the room.

"You like it?" Pat replied, clearly pleased with the impression her home had made. "I do. It's certainly enough for me when I'm here. And there's plenty of room to entertain, down here *and* upstairs." She winked at Grant. "I'm actually trying to angle a way to buy it in the next year or two when the couple that owns it moves to Florida. It's two guys who have an antique store in town, and they're at the point where they've had it with the summer rat race and the cold winters. We're trying to work it so I get a reduced price and they have a place to come on vacation in the summers if we convert the attic to sort of an efficiency apartment. Keep your fingers crossed."

"Sounds good to me," Claire said. "It's always been our dream to own something out here. God bless you, kid. Hope it works out."

"Feel free to wander around and look the place over. I'm going to call Gayle right now. With any luck, she's home, still in bed with a hangover like Mr. Personality at Tom's."

Rita and Sabi took Pat up on the offer to look around, while Kit and Claire made Grant take them outside and show them where she took her late night "swim." When they got back, Rita and Sabi were admiring a Victorian lamp in the living room and Pat was in the kitchen on the phone. She leaned out the doorway and motioned for Grant to start a fire.

"Shit! I'm from Houston; we don't do fires down on the Gulf Coast. Help me out here, guys. I got a reputation to maintain."

"Not to worry," Claire said. "I grew up with a fireplace. Let's just find some wood—preferably dry—and we'll see what we can do."

They hunted around outside and found a woodpile protected by a tarp. After each lugged in an armful, Claire set about making a fire. In five minutes, the beginnings of a blaze were underway. The five women got comfortable in the living room, gazing at the small flames, mesmerized with willing the fire to grow as people seem to do in front of a fireplace. Claire got up every minute or two to add kindling and fan the flames a bit to keep the blaze on track.

Pat came out of the kitchen with chips, a plate of cheese and crackers, and a bottle of red wine. She put them on the coffee table centered between the couch, chairs, and fireplace and sat down with a look of deep thought.

"Grant? Want to do the honors with the wine?" Grant proceeded to open the wine, while Pat cut some slices of cheese. She took one with a cracker and sat down on the floor against the chair where Grant was sitting.

"Well? You gonna share those deep thoughts or do we have to guess?" Kit finally asked.

"Oh! Sorry. I do that sometimes when I get stuck on a thought," Pat apologized. "Well, we know more than we did and yet somehow we don't." Puzzled looks filled all the faces focused on her. "Here's the deal. Gayle, indeed, went out with Tom, Diane—at least I'm *assuming* it was Diane, whom she referred to as that 'stuck up bitch Tom was with'—and at least two other people. And they went to The Pied Piper—I *think*. The problem is that Gayle was already drunk when she left The Boatslip, and, as it turns out, she wisely chose not to rejoin them when she left here."

"Ri-i-i-ight! You were talking to her before you came over by us,"

Grant said, the bigger picture taking focus. "Guess last night was re-ally a continuation of earlier in the evening."

"Yeah, pretty much. Anyway, she knows they went to a bar, drank some more, danced, apparently pissed *someone* off since she started referring to the group as a bunch of 'fuckwads,' and only knows that everyone was still there when she left. Including someone whose name reminded her of the guy who sang 'Mack the Knife.' "

" 'Mack the Knife'? What the hell does that mean?" Claire asked, looking around the room at equally baffled faces.

CHAPTER
17

After a few minutes of quizzing Pat about any other hints Gayle might have even inadvertently dropped, and some tentative guesses about the mystery person, the women lapsed into silence. They sat watching the fire for a good ten minutes, saying nothing, all deep in thought at the new but hardly illuminating piece of information they'd just received. Claire had taken up a more or less permanent station squatting in front of the fireplace, shifting the logs around as they started to finally catch fire. She grabbed a back log with the poker and shifted it slightly forward, making the others resting on it fall like puzzle pieces into a configuration that kicked the sporadically igniting separate logs into one common, steady blaze. She sat down on the tiled hearth, momentarily content, and lit a cigarette, then took a long drink of her wine.

"Well, like I said before, the obvious reference is to Bobby Darin, which I guess still hasn't set off any alarms for the rest of you, 'cause it sure hasn't for me."

"Shit! That's the guy's name!" Kit burst out, slapping her leg in frustration. "You and Rita kept talking about who 'Bobby' could be, and I didn't want to admit I couldn't remember the guy's name."

"Oh, come on. Surely the rest of you knew that much," Claire said in a bored tone.

"Well, as the oldest in the group, *I* knew that, but apparently our younger friends didn't," Rita said with a little smile. "But even so, I'm still drawing a total blank about anybody we've met named Bobby or whose last name is Darin."

Sabi brightened. "I'll bet you anything it's Tom's asshole roommate!"

"No, sorry, honey," Pat said. "He's definitely Phil. Phil Robbins. I know, because he's notorious around here. He's a townie who moved out of his family's house when he had a minute-and-a-half fling with one of the gay boys a couple of summers ago and decided to live the P-Town gay life. He joined the ranks of the prancing waiters, but it didn't take long for him to realize he didn't exactly fit in. I'm not so sure he *isn't* gay, but *he* doesn't think so anymore, and he sure as hell couldn't keep up with the pretty boys from New York and Boston. So, he's the resident fag-hater . . . and fag *baiter,* as you found out. Tom felt sorry for him and agreed to share a place with him this summer; thought he could mellow him out. You see how well that worked." She took a sip of her wine. "But whatever he is or isn't, he ain't no Bobby Darin, however you figure it."

"C'mon, guys," Grant said, exasperation in her voice as she looked at Kit, who was sitting with her head in her hands, kicking at a pull in Pat's rug. "There's got to be someone we've met, or that you guys met earlier in the week, who fits the bill." As she finished, a calico cat, with a hint of reddish hair reminiscent of Grant's thrown into the furry mix, bounded out from an unseen spot and jumped up on Grant's lap. She smiled and crossed her legs to give the cat room to stretch out. "By the way, this is that damned little Pisspot."

"Told you they were buddies," Pat said, smiling at the pair.

"Hmmm . . . I wonder if Jimmy would have any idea who it is?" Claire said, half to herself. "Honey, what did I say his last name was?"

"I remember it's Irish . . . Riley? No . . . McGee? No, that was my neighbor in Flushing. Shea! That's it. Jimmy Shea."

"Yep. That's it," Claire said, stubbing her cigarette out on the bed of the fireplace. "You got a phone book handy, Pat?"

Pat got up to retrieve the phone book and came back with it and a portable phone. She handed them both to Claire. "Here's hoping he knows something."

Claire took both and started looking up the name. "Here he is." She looked at the phone a moment and then back at Pat. "Alright. How the hell do I turn this damned thing on? We peasants in New York aren't quite this advanced yet." Pat showed her how to work the phone and Claire dialed the number. All faces were trained on her reaction as she sat quietly listening to the phone. She shook her head in frustration and cleared her throat. "Hey, Jimmy. It's Claire Griffith. Uh, I was calling to see if you could help me out with a little problem we've got. Seems we've sort of lost one of our friends. But we have managed to stumble onto a clue that involves a name we don't know. Thought you might be able to help identify him. When you get this message, try me at . . ." she put her hand over the phone. "What's your number here?" Pat gave her the number and she repeated it into the phone. "Okay? Thanks, Jimmy."

She turned the phone off. "Okay, kids. Anymore bright ideas?"

No one spoke up right away. Sabi scooted closer to Kit and put her arm around her, which Kit shrugged off. She got up and started pacing in front of the fireplace.

"I don't know about you guys, but I can't just sit here and do nothing. Gimme that phone. Maybe she's finally back at the motel. And if she's not, maybe she came back and didn't check her phone for messages and left a note on your door, Grant. Or maybe there's a note on our door and we haven't been there to get it." She grabbed the phone and dug in her pocket to find the motel's number. "Damn her! I figured after all this time she finally figured out how to take care of herself without me running interference all the time. This is just like our fucking junior year."

She stopped short as the receptionist at the motel apparently answered. They heard her go through the same litany of questions she'd asked the previous two times, and heard the same despondent response to the negative answer. She punched the phone off and thrust it in Pat's direction.

"Shit! She pulled something like this that year. Took me two days to find her. Thank God she was just bummed about some jerk she'd been dating and holed up with a friend of ours who promised not to tell anyone where she was."

"Who?" Sabi asked, brows knit in question.

"Kim."

"Oh, *that* one. I can't stand her."

"Oh, for God's sake, Sabi. That's just 'cause you have this stupid jealousy thing going on. I told you nothing happened between us."

"Yeah, well, I'm sure it's only because you were too naïve to know a pass when someone made one in those days."

"Anyway, I can't believe this is happening again." She shook her head, half annoyed and half upset. "I really hoped that by now Diane would've found a nice, smart, all-round good guy."

"Ha. From what all my straight friends tell me, that's not such an easy thing to do," Pat said.

"Yeah, well, I know that. But once she was in the business world— and she travels in some pretty decent circles—I figured she'd run into all those MBAs who waited till after school to settle down. And over the last couple of years it sounded like she had met some okay guys. But she's got *really* lousy judgment with men; who's screwing around on a wife, who's neurotic, who's just plain old fucked up. Now she runs into this turkey whose idea of ambition is waiting tables on a bunch of faggots. I don't know . . ."

"Relax, Kit. We'll figure this out," Claire said. "And I didn't get the impression that Tom was any kind of major loser." She moved closer to the fire again to stoke it now that it had shifted on its own as it burnt. "Bobby, Bobby, Bobby. I just don't know. Or . . ." she said slowly, arching her eyebrow and shaking her head thoughtfully, "maybe this guy's *first* name is Darin."

"Eww," Sabi said, wrinkling her nose. *"Nobody's* named Darin— certainly not the gay boys who come here."

"Think!" Claire commanded.

"I don't have to think about that," Sabi grumbled under her breath. "I *know* I'd remember some dorky guy named *Darin.*"

"But maybe it's not a guy," Rita said, slowly shifting her gaze to Claire with an almost accusatory look.

"What's *that* for?" Claire said defensively.

"Think about it," said Rita. "You know anybody with a name that sounds like Da-a-r-in?" She said the name slowly, drawing the two syllables out.

"Oh, shit! I guess I do," she said sheepishly. She cleared her throat. "I guess Dara sounds a lot like Darin, huh?"

"You mean your friend we keep seeing around who's at Stella's, too?" Kit said, surprised at the connection but excited at the lead it might provide.

"Well, it's as close as we've been able to get," she replied, throwing Kit a quick, silencing glare.

"I don't know," Grant said. "Seems kind of a stretch to me. You'd think Gayle would have said something about *part* of the name being like Bobby Darin or just have mentioned the last name being like a first name."

"You don't know Gayle," Pat interjected. "I didn't say she was inclined to be all that helpful or that reliable. Remember, she was pretty blasted last night. It seems like at least something to go on."

"Otherwise, it's a helluva coincidence," Claire concurred. "There's nobody else any of us can come up with a name that even comes close. I mean, she was definitely at the pageant, and I assume she knows Tom. I saw her laughing and talking with him at the pool. And her name does sound close."

"Alright. Let's assume that's who Gayle meant. Now what?" Pat asked.

"Well, I'm afraid staying here isn't going to get us any closer to figuring this out—much as I'd love to lay down right here on the floor and take a nap right about now," Claire said, smiling.

"You can say that again," Sabi added, yawning.

"So, my suggestion is that Pat and Grant stay here, since we've left this number with Jimmy, at Tom's place, and as one of the numbers on the messages at the motel. We'll go back to Stella's and check for notes and messages. And we'll try to track Dara down and see if she was part of the party crowd last night."

"Yeah. And we can check in at The Boatslip on the way, just to see if he's called in or anything. Hell, we could smack right into 'em on the street," Kit said, having perked up a bit with a new scent to follow.

They were a somber, not to mention tired and bedraggled, looking foursome as they made their way along Commercial Street. There had been no word at The Boatslip, even after waiting for a couple of waiters from the night before to come on shift to see what they might know. Though they were anxious to get back to Stella's to see where the Dara connection might lead, no one in the group could muster much more than a plodding walk. The edge they had earlier in the day when there was some sense of adventure to their search was long gone. The dead ends and the fatigue, given the previous night's interrupted sleep, had caught up with them all. As they started to pass The Post Office Cafe, Claire stopped by the signs for the shows upstairs in the cabaret room.

"Oh, for God's sake, Claire," Rita said crankily, "who the hell's interested in shows at this point?"

"I just thought I'd check to see what the times were just in case we want to go. It is our last night, you know."

"Thanks for reminding me," Rita snapped.

"I'm so sorry guys," Kit said, tears welling up in her eyes. "Guess you two were right. We never should have invited anybody up here. Now our last fucking day is ruined, we're exhausted, and we still have no clue where that damned Diane is."

"I'm sorry, Kit. I didn't mean it like that," Rita said. "Really." Claire looked at her and shrugged. Rita glowered back and continued. "We couldn't have gone to the beach or anything today, anyhow. And you couldn't have known something like this would happen. Don't be upset. Please."

"It's okay. I guess I'm just tired and frustrated and everything's starting to get to me. It's just—"

"Hey, you guys! Come here!" Sabi shouted excitedly, looking in the window of The Post Office. "Am I totally losing my mind, or is that Tom in there? Near the back. See? I'd swear that looks like the back of his head."

The other three women looked in. "Could be," Rita said, squinting against the reflection of the glass. "Let's go find out."

"Wait a sec, guys. If it is, there's not enough room in this place for all four of us to even sit down and hear what he has to say. And if it's not, all of us trooping in and out seems pretty silly. Why don't you two go on back to the room and check for notes and messages like we planned, and Kit and I will see what the story is here."

"Oh, yeah. Send the little women on back to the house," Sabi sniped back.

"Honey, Claire's right. Besides, if that is him, I'm genuinely afraid you might cause a little bit of a scene," Kit added.

"Scene? You betchur ass I'm gonna make a scene when I get my hands on that *hela gran puta!*"

"That's exactly what I mean. Rita?" Kit looked imploringly at Rita.

"Come on, sweetie. They've got a point." She put an arm around Sabi and started to walk her away from the restaurant. "We'll go look for Dara while they check this out."

Sabi let Rita lead her away, still sputtering in Spanish. Kit and Claire went in, sidling along past rushing waiters and crowded tables until they got to the table in question. They walked to the far side of it to look back at the face of its occupant. Sure enough, it was Tom— looking decidedly worse for the wear.

He looked up from the coffee he was gingerly sipping and smiled. "Hey, girls! What's up?"

" '*What's up?*' " Kit's face was red with rage. "What's up is that I'd like to know where the fuck my friend is! And, I swear to God, if anything's happened to her, I'll fuckin' kick your ass all the way back to . . . to wherever it is you're from!"

"Kit. Kit!" Claire raised her voice to snap Kit out of her growing rage. She put her hand on Kit's arm. "Calm down, babe."

"What the hell are you talking about," Tom asked, genuinely baffled. "You mean Diane?"

"Of course, I mean Diane, asshole!"

"Hey, ladies, relax. You gotta tell me what's going on, 'cause I don't have a clue what this is all about." He stopped a passing waiter. "Yo, Bill. Can you grab a couple of chairs? I know it's tight, but this is important. I have to talk to these women." The waiter sighed and nodded, and went off in search of chairs. While they waited, Kit and Claire alternately told him the missing Diane saga, their search for the better part of the day, ending with seeing him sitting here. As they neared the end of their story, the waiter showed up, as did Jimmy, who was the other party sharing Tom's table.

"My, my, my! It's a veritable party!"

"Hi, Jimmy," Claire said offhandedly.

"Oops. Bad night, huh?" he said, shaking his head in mock sympathy.

"Yeah, Jimmy. You could say that. It seems my 'date' of last night has gone missing," Tom said, looking at Jimmy pointedly.

"Oh, please," Jimmy said, making a shooing motion. "This is P-Town, boys and girls. People go missing for the night *all* the time. I really don't think this is cause for such grand theatrics."

"Jimmy. Stop. They're really worried. And so am I."

"Well, have you told them about *our* evening?" Jimmy winked at Tom. "Or are we a little too hung over to be verbal yet?"

"No, I think I can manage that." Tom took a deep breath and a sip of a Bloody Mary he was nursing. "Well, your facts are right, as far as they go. Diane and I didn't see you guys anywhere, so I suggested we go for a drink and finish our talk. When we went off together at The Boatslip, I'd started in trying to convince her that the whole 'queen' bit was a big joke some of the other waiters had talked me into. Nothing more. *I* didn't have a problem with it; I didn't know why she should. But she just didn't seem to find anything funny about the whole thing. The storm blew up, we looked around for you guys, and made a dash for the exit where we saw Jimmy and one of the women that owns that jewelry store talking to Dara and her new girlfriend." Claire and Kit looked at each other and nodded at the mystery name being confirmed. "We joked about the storm and the real queen nearly getting blown away as we waited to get out with the crowd. And before we knew it, we'd all decided to stop at the first bar that was open and wait the storm out while we had a drink. As it so happened, that turned out to be The Pied—which I joked about at the time as being appropriate. Balance out the gay guy thing. Diane didn't seem thrilled but went along with the crowd.

"We got in and Dara laughed when she looked around at the bar. Seems her old girlfriend, I can't remember her name—"

"Becca, I think," Claire offered.

"Yeah, Becca. Anyway, she was there hanging out at the bar by herself. Dara went over to see what happened to her fling-for-the-week, and Trudy, *her* summer vacay girlfriend, got all bent out of shape. Jimmy and the other woman decided to play referee on that one while Diane and I talked.

"I picked up where I'd left off explaining, and she finally started to calm down, and we laughed and joked for a while like everything's okay. *Then* I get this whole big story about all the fucked up boyfriends she's had, including one who was gay."

"Gay?" Kit blurted out. "Who? Which one was that?"

"I don't know. It was a *long* story. And, frankly, the whole thing was beginning to seem like a whole lot of trouble for just a date."

"Listen, pal—" Kit started.

"Forget it, Kit. Go ahead," Claire said, trying to keep the situation in check.

"Anyway, *then* she tells me that when she saw me doing the queen bit, she figured it was happening again, and started wondering, like she had before, if maybe there was a reason she kept picking gay guys. Like, maybe there was something going on with her. Well! I figure this is something I can deal with now. I put my arm around her and tell her not to worry, I'll make sure she doesn't have any doubts about whether she's a real woman." He looked up from under his lowered eyes at the two women at the table. "No offense. It just seemed like the thing to say. And I meant it—you know, in the right way." Kit and Claire didn't bother to comment.

"She gives me this shocked look, and I tell her it's true; that there was this girl last week going through a whole 'am I gay/am I bi/am I straight' thing and that I made a believer out of her!" He smiled to himself, apparently recalling his manly charms.

"Oh, that's just great," Kit said, disgusted. "Did it occur to you to try a little more understanding, sensitive approach?"

Jimmy looked over at her and put his hand up beside his mouth. "Don't forget—he's *straight,*" he said in a stage whisper.

"Gee, thanks, Jimmy. At least you finally figured that out." Tom turned back to the two women. "I guess you're right, though. I didn't count on the reaction I got, that's for sure. I think I also said something stupid about that being the best part of P-Town—you know, being one of the only straight guys around when someone like her needed me. She stormed out to the back deck without saying a word."

"Oh, man, Tom. You're a real charmer," Claire said, rolling her eyes.

Tom shrugged and went on. "Gayle—the jewelry store chick—I think it was, went out to see if she could calm her down. I was really pissed, so I ordered a shot of something, which was not a great idea.

"About fifteen, twenty minutes later, she comes back—Gayle—all pissy and leaves. Never did like her. Anyway, I'm pretty drunk by that point and getting more pissed at Diane for walking out. So, I figure it's my turn to fix things, and *I* get up to go out on the deck. Jimmy stopped me and said he thought it was better if he went, so he did. About ten minutes later, he comes back and tells me he thinks we should leave, that Diane doesn't want to talk to me. All I remember after that is trying to get up to go out there anyway, and Jimmy catching me as I went down. Next thing I know, I'm waking up at Jimmy's."

"So, what the hell happened to Diane?" Kit said, starting to get riled up again.

"I honestly don't know. Really." He shook his head slowly and gave a little shrug. "I'm sorry . . . I really am."

"You didn't even ask Jimmy when you came to this morning?" Claire asked, joining Kit in getting agitated at his almost blasé attitude.

"Oh, give the boy a break. He had a hard night—way too much tequila and rejection to boot." He saw them gearing up to jump all over him. "Down, girls. I'm more than happy to tell you what I know, though it's not much more than what you know already.

"When I went out to check on your friend, she was talking to . . . is it Dara? There were so many women coming and going from that table, it was hard to keep track of who was who. Yes, it was Dara— she's the classy-looking one of the two from Stella's, right? Claire nodded. "So, they're standing by the railing talking. Seems Gayle, in her own inimitable way, had tried to 'comfort' Diane. You know Gayle?"

"Not personally—thank God, I think," Claire said. "But we've talked to Pat today, and it seems Gayle was just getting warmed up when you guys were with her."

"Oh, Jesus," Jimmy said, taking a drink of his Bloody Mary. "Tell me she showed up at Pat's. Christ. Pat's a good girl. But that Gayle—! So, I'm guessing Gayle had made a total ass of herself, which Dara overheard and ended. They didn't give me all the juicy details. But by the time I got out there, they were talking and laughing about what asses people are. I asked Diane if she was okay and did she want to talk to Tom. The answers were yes and no, respectively. She said she wanted to stay for a while and to tell Tom to go on without her. I figured she was a big girl and went in to tell Mr. Suave and Debonair. Then he passed out, like he said, and I simply did what any good friend would do in a similar situation: opened my home to the poor boy and took—or, rather, *put*—him to bed. Just to keep an eye on him, of course . . . in case anything else should, uh, arise during the night." He sniffed and sighed. "But, like the rest of the ill-fated evening, that didn't go according to plan either."

Tom smiled at Jimmy and put his arm around his shoulders. "Sorry, pal. I'm flattered, as always. But I'm just not a man's man—at least not like that. I am glad you're a friend, though."

"Yeah. It's nice to have friends when you're in a tight spot," Kit said sarcastically, though with less anger than before.

"You'll forgive Kit if she's less than warm and fuzzy at this point," Claire said. "All we know is we still have a friend missing—and no idea where she is."

CHAPTER
18

For a few seconds everyone was silent, even Jimmy, there being no clever or witty riposte to Claire's last comment that wouldn't have seemed callous and entirely inappropriate. Finally, it was Jimmy who spoke.

"Listen, girls. I'm telling you, just as sure as I'm queer as a three-dollar bill, Diane is fine. I just don't have that oh-my-God feeling I get when a situation is truly dire—and, trust me, I know that feeling." He paused and thought for a moment and then looked around the table at each of them. "Well, it looks like the deposed Queen here can get herself home this time under her own power, thanks to the miraculous therapeutic benefits of the blessed virgin *Bloody* Mary, so I'll cruise home—you should pardon the expression. There are a couple of phone calls I think I'll make. I suggest you go on to your rooms and see if your girlfriends have any news. If any of us comes up with anything useful or newsworthy, we'll pass it along. You've got my number, right?"

Claire nodded. "Yeah, I think so. I'll check my stack of notes when I get home."

"Never mind—here." Jimmy grabbed an extra bevnap from the table and stuck his arm out to waylay a passing waiter. He smiled and snatched a pen from the waiter's apron. "Thanks, honey, I'll just be a minute." He jotted the number down, replaced the pen from whence it had come and sent the young man on his way, with a quick pinch on his ass and a wink.

"Okay, honey. Here you go. I know it's a pain in the ass to call from Stella's, but if you find out something, CALL ME. You understand? And if I come across anything, I'll either hike over or call Stella's private phone. That old bag wouldn't dare blow me off—I've got too much on her. Okay?"

Claire and Kit both nodded silently, a bit taken aback by this other serious and very capable Jimmy.

"Oh, for God's sake. Don't look so shocked. Believe it or not, underneath this flaming exterior beats the heart of a cold, calculating businessman. Now, go! I don't want too many people to see me in this altogether too intense mood; it'll utterly destroy my hard-won party boy image. Scoot!"

The two women got up and each gave him a kiss on the cheek, which totally flustered the imperturbable Jimmy. They turned to Tom, who stood up and gave them each a hug. "When I get back, the first thing I'm gonna do is kick the crap out of that asshole Phil. Then I'll see what I can find out. Jimmy's right, though—I'm sure everything's okay. Really."

"Yeah, well, I sure hope so," Kit said, her brow still knit in concern. She turned and headed for the door.

"Thanks, guys," Claire said quietly as she got ready to follow Kit out. She stood looking at them for another moment. "I don't know . . . maybe your gut feelings aren't at the flashing red light level, but mine are getting pretty damned close." The two men simply nodded as she turned and left.

"Fuck," Tom said as he plopped back down in his seat. "This really sucks."

"Yes, Thomas, darling, you could certainly say that." Jimmy looked at him a moment and then sighed. "Thank God you're not one of us."

Claire and Kit walked in silence until they got to the top of the drive that led down to Stella's. Kit stopped, her hands in her pockets, staring out at the street. Claire stood beside her, quietly waiting.

"So, what if we go down there and they know nothing?" she said, her eyes starting to brim with tears. "What do we do then?"

Claire put her arm around her friend. "Then we figure something else out. That's all. But before we worry about what that something else is exactly, let's go down and find out if we even have to go there."

Claire took a deep breath and turned Kit around. Her face was res-
olute and set. "Ready?"

"Guess so," Kit replied, pulling her hat off and running a hand
through her shock of unruly hair.

They strode purposefully down the driveway and through the
gate. As they walked out onto the main deck, they heard familiar
voices and laughter coming from down by the picnic table but saw
only tops of heads above the backs of the deck chairs that were lined
up looking out on the bay. They looked at each other, shrugged, and
headed to the table.

"Well, I'm certainly glad they're enjoying the last day of vacation,"
Kit said almost bitterly. Claire said nothing and kept walking.

They came around the picnic table and stopped short. Indeed,
Sabi was hooting and slapping Rita's leg as she rocked with laughter.
Beside them, in the other two chairs, Diane and Dara were sitting
back, clearly enjoying their appreciative audience. Rita looked up
and saw Kit and Claire. She cleared her throat and nudged Sabi.
Diane and Dara looked up at the two new arrivals. Diane smiled
wanly and started to get up out of her chair.

Kit ripped her cap off her head and threw it on the deck, her face
contorted with a mix of rage, relief, and raw emotion. "YOU FUCK-
ING SON OF A BITCH!" she bellowed. "Do you have any goddamned
idea what I've been through the last . . ." she sputtered, looking
around, "I don't know, it seems like days! Jesus Christ, Diane. We've
been looking for you since last night. Where the hell have you
been?!?"

Diane had not made it to her feet, the blast of Kit's anger and
worry having almost physically knocked her back. Before she could
respond, however, Sabi was up and had her arms around Kit.

"Honey," she said soothingly. Kit pushed her arms away and
turned around to wipe the tears from her eyes. "Honey!" Sabi said
loudly, taking Kit's head in her two hands and turning it around to
look at her. "Re-*lax*. I know you're upset—and you have every right
to be—but calm down. Everything's fine now." She looked at Claire.
"I'm thinking a beer—or bourbon if you've got any left—would be a
really good idea right about now." Claire nodded and turned to go

upstairs, but whirled back around. "But don't anybody say one damned word until I get back!" She jogged off on her mission of the moment.

Kit took short, broken breaths as she put her hat back on and sat down where Sabi had been sitting. Sabi, sitting on the arm of the chair, handed her a cigarette and lit it for her, giving her a kiss on the cheek as she handed it over, while everyone else sat quietly and waited for her to compose herself.

Kit looked over at Diane and started to get teary again. "You asshole," she said quietly this time, so that it almost sounded like a term of endearment. "I've been scared sick." She wiped another tear away.

This time Diane made it up out of her seat and knelt in front of Kit. She hugged her and Kit grabbed her and squeezed her so hard Diane started laughing.

"I know you want to kill me, but don't squeeze the life out of me!" she said, laughing as she put a hand on Kit's cheek and looked her in the eyes. "I am so sorry, Kit. The story is so stupid, you probably *will* kill me when I tell you." Kit looked at her, one last tear trailing down her cheek. "Oh, honey," Diane groaned, pained at the pain in her friend's face. "Sabi's right, everything's fine. *Really* fine. In fact, even though it's been hell on you, this has very likely been the best twenty-four hours of my life." Kit looked at her as if she were speaking another language. "Just hang on a couple of more minutes till Claire gets back down. You both should hear the story together."

Not thirty seconds later, Claire appeared with a small cooler and a shopping bag. "I didn't know what you guys had down here, so I figured I'd bring down supplies so we didn't have to interrupt the story." She unloaded liquor, Pepsi, glasses, ice, and chips on the table and two beers and koozies from the cooler. She leaned against the railing, beer opened, cigarette lit. "Okay, kid," she said looking down at Diane. "Let's have it."

Diane took a deep breath and looked at Dara, who gave her a wink of encouragement and took her hand. Kit shot a stunned look up at Sabi. Sabi smiled at her and put her finger to her lips. Claire smiled and shook her head, shifting her weight to a more comfortable stance.

Diane looked at Kit. "Well, I guess that pretty much ruined the whole suspense about the end of the story, huh? Must be something in the P-Town air, I figure."

"Holy shit!" Kit said, rubbing her head and pushing her cap up off her forehead. "No fuckin' way."

"Way," Diane answered, smiling at Kit. "Okay. Here's the story."

"Actually, you can probably save your breath about some of it," Claire interrupted. Now it was Sabi and Rita's turn to look surprised. "We just spent the last half hour with Tom and Jimmy—you were right, Sabi. That was them in The Post Office Cafe. And they told us most of the story, up through you being out on the deck with Dara after Tom made a total ass of himself. Did you get that far with these two?" she said, gesturing toward Sabi and Rita.

"Yep. So, you guys know that at least the beginning of my disappearance was a perfectly innocent situation of having gotten separated from everyone when the storm kicked up and deciding to hang out with Tom until I could get home. And, yes, I was also interested to see where things would go."

"Guess you found out, huh?" Kit said. "But how in the hell did you get from him being an asshole to . . . to this?"

"I don't know how much Tom told you, but he freaked me out with that queen bit way more than even *I* could explain. Truth be told, by the time we got to the bar, I just wanted to go home and sort out this weird bunch of feelings I was having. I knew as well as everyone else that there was no reason to have reacted the way I did, but what I couldn't figure out was why it really didn't have all that much to do with Tom. The truth of the matter is that I really was never that attracted to him; he was gorgeous and funny and all that, so it certainly seemed like I should be interested. But I realized in the bar that it was more of a game than anything else: could I get—and keep—this hot guy interested in me. Once I did, it was more a curiosity thing than a real interest or sexual kind of thing. Did he tell you about the talk we had in the bar?" Claire and Kit both nodded. "Well, I'm sure he thought it was all about him, but I was really talking more to myself than anything else. I was trying to make sense of my less-than-successful romantic history, including all the gay guys I'd ended up dating since—"

"Guys? Plural?" Kit asked incredulously.

"Yeah, Kit. I never told you 'cause it just seemed too weird. And I didn't want you to think I was anti-gay or anything."

"Apparently not," Claire added.

"Yeah, well . . ." Diane gave Dara a smile. "Anyway, I was sitting there trying to figure out what the hell was going on with me. I certainly didn't tell you guys, but I'd been noticing some of the women since I got here—I mean *noticing*. But I shrugged it off as being open-minded and normally curious. And every time *you*," she looked up at Claire, "got in trouble for looking at Dara, I took notice. I thought she was definitely one of the most handsome and attractive women I'd ever seen." She paused a moment and smiled. "Wow. There's a phrase right out of all those years of being careful and objective. The truth is, every time I saw her, I'd almost forget to *breathe*. You guys know. That whole heart beating so hard you think it's going to explode, tingly all over—especially in places that took me *totally* by surprise—and then fantasizing ways we might casually run into each other again. I mean, the whole nine yards. So, imagine my delight when she ended up in our little group last night! Which, now, I think was more the reason I went than Tom. But back to the story."

"So, I'm sitting there, basically thinking out loud talking to Tom. The quiet moments when he thought I was going through my big sexual questioning thing, he was right—except I wasn't all that upset and worried at the moment about *that*. I was trying to figure out how I could get rid of *him* and talk to *her!* Thank God, he proved true to form and came out with that utterly stupid, macho 'saving me' bit! It was a godsend. So, out I go to the deck, having lost sight of Dara and hoping *desperately* she was out there. Which she was—busy trying to calm down that woman she'd been *playing* with all week." Diane gave Dara a sidelong glance.

Dara spoke up for the first time. "Hey! Don't make me out to be the bad guy here. I was your basic single-lesbian-on-vacation, doing what single-lesbians-on-vacation do! How should I know I'm getting cruised by women who seemingly have no reason to be cruising me?" She looked first at Diane and then up at Claire. This time, it was Claire's turn to do the scarlet face thing. She tried to muster a smile, cocking her head with slight shrug. Rita and Sabi were doing their best to swallow their laughter.

"Alright, you two," Claire said in mock menace, trying to lighten the embarrassing moment.

"Relax, Claire," Dara said, jumping in to take her off the proverbial hook. "It's summer, it's P-Town, I'm flattered. Go on, honey."

"Anyway, I'm outside, trying to be casual *and* stay relatively dry, when that woman—Gayle, is it? I can't believe Pat was ever with someone so . . . obnoxious. Anyway. Gayle comes out to pick up where Tom left off being an asshole. Suffice it to say, I was *not* interested in the least. But, as it so happens, I actually have to be grateful to her—if she hadn't started getting loud and obnoxious, Dara might never have even known I was out there. But, thank God, Gayle was as drunk and loud as she was. Dara came over, sent Gayle on her way, and we started talking. *Her* 'friend' finally got fed up and stormed off the deck, hoping, I'm sure, Dara would follow her. But, lucky for me, she didn't."

"Not just lucky for you," Dara said, squeezing Diane's hand.

"We started talking, and I'm doing mental cartwheels trying to figure out exactly what's going on and how the hell to handle it. I explained the whole Tom thing, which she interpreted as my being upset at losing a potential boyfriend. We got into each of our recent disappointing romantic histories and proceeded to talk nonstop for at least another hour. At one point, I tried to lighten things up by laughing and saying that at least I wasn't missing out on any hidden advantage she had being on the gay side of things if we were *both* out there pouring our hearts out. To which she replied, 'No, we don't have any more guarantees than anyone else. Fewer, in fact. But at least I know when my hurt is about losing love—*or* about not ever having found it yet. Do you?' And that was it—I looked at her and absolutely fell. My stomach jumped, and I felt like I could stand out there and watch the ocean with her forever. If I thought I got butterflies before, that was *nothing* compared to how I felt as she stood there, inches away from me, looking at me with such tenderness and concern. I couldn't move. I had no idea how she felt about me, how to interpret that look, let alone what to do *next*.

"So, I decided, what the hell. The whole night's been bizarre from the beginning, might as well go for it. I screwed up my nerve and told her what I'd never been able to bring myself to tell anyone else—that

I'd had a, I guess you'd call it a dalliance, with a woman in college and had never put it altogether out of my mind. And I *don't* mean in a negative way . . . even though at the time it scared the hell out of me. It was just too intense. And way too *sinful* and dangerous given my good Catholic upbringing. But standing there with Dara so focused on comforting me when she'd been dealing with Becca and a real relationship ending, and me just dealing with an asshole simply *being* an asshole, not to mention letting her date for the evening walk out, well . . ."

"Whoa, whoa. Wait a minute. You never told me?" Kit said, hurt and disappointment mixed in with the surprise on her face.

"No, Kit, I didn't. In college, I had my doubts about you, but since I didn't really know, I was afraid it might freak you out if you weren't sure about yourself. And after you and Sabi got together, I was even happier for you both than I think I would have been otherwise. I could watch you both be happy in a way I just didn't believe was mine to choose. And I didn't say anything then because I guess I was almost afraid you'd try to talk me into, I don't know, joining the club or something. And I just wasn't ready to take that leap—until now."

"That's a pretty big leap," Kit replied. Are you sure about this?"

"Uh, excuse me? Aren't you the one that got involved with a certain *engaged* lady you only knew for a few weeks, for God's sake? And wasn't that a first for both of you?"

"Wel-l-l . . . yeah, but—"

"Yeah, but. Don't worry. I'm a big girl. And for once, I'm going to follow my heart instead of my brain—which hasn't had a great track record so far. I figure it's time I took a chance."

"Hey! You two can hash that out later. I want to hear the rest of the story!" Sabi said, intervening.

"Right. Well, we just kept talking, and then it got colder, and we scooted closer together, and pretty soon she had her arm around me, and then . . . well, let's just say I've been around the block a time or two with guys. And I absolutely felt like I got kissed for the first time."

"Honey," Dara interrupted, "it does my ego good hearing you tell this, but I'm afraid our audience may not be interested in all the juicy details."

Sabi, who had been leaning on her knees, hanging on Diane's

every word, sat straight up in her chair. "Are you kidding? Go ahead, honey. Don't you leave out a *thing.*"

Dara smiled. "Well, I might have some objections to that."

"Oh, you know what I mean." Sabi waved dismissively at Dara as she maintained her focus on Diane. "Go on."

"We heard the DJ call the last dance and the bartender announced last call. Fortunately, we'd switched to sodas at the outset of the conversation, so we were totally sober by the time we left the bar—after dancing together . . . for the first time, which was wonderful, too, but I won't bore you with all that. You guys know. Anyway, we didn't know whether Becca was in their room or not, so we walked all the way to the Holiday Inn in the storm, which was another thing I'd never done. It was amazing. We took hot showers and then kept talking and dozing and just holding one another till morning—something I've *never* done with a guy. We woke up again about nine or so, grabbed coffee down in the lobby and walked down to the beach right in front of the motel. Then we headed into town for breakfast and stopped by here on the way. When you weren't in your room, we left a note on your door. We figured you were out to breakfast and kind of thought we might run into you. I guess it blew off since you guys didn't find it. Anyway, we got breakfast, walked around Commercial for a while and came back here a couple of hours ago and hung out in Dara's room, checking every now and then to see if you got back. And then we saw Claire and Rita's door open and here we are."

"A couple of hours up in the room, huh?" Sabi said with an evil smile.

Diane returned the smile with one just as evil. "Remember that bit about there being no advantages to being a lesbian? Well, I've definitely changed my mind!"

"Ah ha!" Claire exclaimed. "Let me be the first to welcome you to that club you were talking about before!"

"Wow. You *have* been busy," Kit said, shaking her head. "Jesus. This certainly isn't the story I was expecting. But you always did have a way of shocking the shit out of me when I least expected it. Like that time in college when you disappeared—" She stopped short and looked over at Diane. "Well, I'll be a son of a bitch—that was it, wasn't it? That's why you were with Kim. And I didn't have a fucking clue."

"Knowing you guys were friends at the time and how Sabi felt about her later, well, you can see why I didn't feel real comfortable telling you."

"Makes sense to me," Sabi said, as she yawned and stretched. "And what also makes sense to me is that before we all pass out in these deck chairs, I think it's time for a nap. We've got the rest of the evening to talk about old times—*and* certain people who were a part of them. If we must."

"Oh, stop," Kit said, giving Sabi a playful whack with her cap. "It looks as though Kim may be an unwitting good guy in this whole saga."

"Wait a minute—let's not get carried away here!" Sabi replied.

"Well, I second Sabi's motion," Claire said. "All in favor?"

"I agree—but aren't you guys forgetting something?" Rita asked. "Like the fact that we've got half of Provincetown on high alert looking for these two?"

"Oh, shit!" Claire said. "You're right, honey. I think I've got all the numbers. I'll go call Jimmy and Pat. Be right back."

"What about you guys?" Rita asked Sabi and Kit. "You want to check to see if your bed is still a raft?"

"Raft?" Diane asked, frowning in question. "What else happened while I was gone?"

Kit headed to check the room and Sabi proceeded to tell the tale of the night before, their day so far, and why *they* were more than ready for forty winks. By the time Kit got back with the good news that Stella had left a note saying she'd found someone to bring the extra mattress over and they now had a nice dry bed, Sabi had finished the story and Claire had returned.

"So, *now* what are we all laughing at? I swear, it's dangerous for anyone to disappear for more than fifteen minutes without missing out on something!" They all reassured Claire that she hadn't missed out on anything except a recounting of their recent adventures. "Thank God. I couldn't imagine what could possibly top the Diane/Dara saga. As for the rest of our merry band, everyone is informed *and* relieved. And we now have tentative plans for our final evening, assuming we're all in agreement. Pat suggested that, given all these happy new couplings—as it were!—that we should all go out to dinner tonight. So, I suggested one of our all time faves, Franco's. And I took the liberty of making reservations since there are so damned many of us at this point. We can always cancel if you guys aren't into it."

"Sounds good to me—honey?" Sabi said, looking over to Kit, who nodded her assent.

"And you guys?" Claire asked the newest couple.

"Well, Franco's is one of my regular stops here, too. So, I'm fine with it if Diane is," Dara volunteered, looking over at Diane for confirmation.

"Oh, God. They really are a couple already," Sabi said, rolling her eyes and smiling.

"You guys okay in Dara's room or is there still an issue with your ex?" Claire asked.

"No, we're okay. When we got back today, she'd left a note. I still don't know the details, but there must have been something in the air or the stars or something last night; it seems Becca has found 'alternative accommodations,' as it were, too. So, we're fine."

"Oh, we're definitely fine," Diane added, leaning over and giving Dara a kiss.

"Jesus. This is definitely gonna take some getting used to," Kit said, shaking her head wearily but smiling as she took Sabi by the hand and headed for their room.

CHAPTER
19

Grant suddenly sat straight up and started chuckling. "Unbeliev-able . . . we've both been out here practically every summer, both been living in Boston for years, both even hanging out at the same damned restaurant, and only *now* do we manage to connect?" She shook her head in wonder.

"You know, if I were the sensitive, easily-offended type, I'd be re-ally bent out of shape right now." Grant looked over at Pat with a puz-zled expression. Pat got up on one elbow. "Usually the reactions to my lovemaking are along the lines of a sigh or two, a little cuddling, maybe even your basic all-out collapse—you know, that whole after-glow stuff. But someone popping up not thirty seconds later, totally naked, and launching into conversation, makes me wonder a bit if I'm losing my touch!" Fortunately, for Grant, this was all said with a tolerant smile.

"Ah, shit, honey. I'm sorry." She leaned over and kissed Pat long and lovingly. "There. *That's* my reaction to you as a lover—and a pre-view of things to come, in case you were wondering. I guess I was just overcome by the whole thing—you, me, us . . . together like this. It's because it *was* so wonderful that I was lying here amazed—and a little pissed—that we didn't find each other sooner. Jesus, how many nights—and afternoons—of this have we missed out on?"

"Boy, you really know how to pour on that Southern charm bit." Pat fell back onto her pillow. "But I'm sorta surprised you're 'the glass is half empty' kind of gal. Actually, I was thinking about pretty much the same thing. But *I* was lying here smiling at the fact that we found each other at *all*. Hell, honey, Boston's a big town; and how many hundreds of people are there milling around on the streets here all week, every week? It's a wonder we *ever* found each other. And it's not like we're *fifty* or something. We probably met at the perfect moment: old enough to have made our mistakes with other people—God willing!—and young enough to get to enjoy life without all that earlier shit." She looked deeply into Grant's eyes. "That is, if we want to see where this takes us."

" 'If'? What do you mean 'if'? What'd I do?"

Pat laughed, jumping out from under the covers, and threw herself on top of Grant. "You didn't do anything, dopey. It's just that we haven't talked about what comes after P-Town—when we're both back in Boston and life goes back to normal. Remember, I live here half the year, and I've seen *lots* of vacation romances. I'm the one who makes a living on all those spontaneous, passion-inspired jewelry purchases, don't forget! Something about the heat, the ocean, the sunsets—those lesbian dance cruises!" Pat smiled and pushed Grant back down on the bed as she started to get up. "I saw you checking me out. You think you're so clever!"

"Aw, c'mon. I was *not* 'checking you out'! I didn't even like you at that point."

"Bullshit. You are such a *liar!*"

"Wel-l-l-l, maybe when we were dancing I noticed you a little bit," Grant said with a begrudging tone and a sly smile. She looked at Pat long and hard, her smile fading into a serious, searching look. "No, you're right. Of course I noticed you. And you're right about this probably being the ideal time in our lives for us to bump smack dab right into each other, having been under each other's noses all this time. And you're *also* right about P-Town romances—there *is* something about being here that makes it pretty damned easy to do that whole head-over-heels thing." She took a breath and ran her hands through her hair. "On the other hand, this business about overlapping lives sure makes it seem as though we were supposed to meet, one way or the other. But I have to tell you, I'm a little tender around the edges these days."

"I know," Pat said softly, pushing Grant's unruly hair back out of her face. She scooted around behind her and put her arms around Grant's waist, holding her and rocking her ever so slightly. "I know, baby. Me, too. But I surprised *myself* when I grabbed your hand last night. I honestly didn't plan it, but it just felt, I don't know . . . natural and *right*. And you took it and followed me. No questions. I don't know if anyone's ever trusted me like that. For my part, I decided right then and there this was worth the risk."

Grant smiled again. "God knows, I've never been one to walk away from a pretty lady whisking me off to her beach house—or *almost* beach house." She stopped and thought for a moment. "You know, you're the first woman to ever 'whisk' me off anywhere. It's always been me who stuck my neck out and made the first move." She leaned back into Pat's arms. "And no one's ever held *me*. It's a little weird, but I like it. I like it a lot . . ."

"So do I," Pat whispered in her ear. "I think all that matters is that we both seem to be on the same page at the same time. And I'm kinda looking forward to seeing how this book ends." As Pat continued rocking Grant, she let her hands roam along her lean body, stopping on her small, almost teenage breasts. Grant moaned and leaned back into Pat, indulging in the newness of being the recipient of such deep pleasures.

Grant looked around at Pat. The sincerity, tenderness, and desire in her face, the beauty of her body, the potential for happiness were all too much for her. An unexpected tear slipped out of the corner of one eye and rolled down past her ear onto Pat's chest. Pat looked down at her, concerned by the sudden change in attitude and gently wiped away the damp trail on her cheek. Grant smiled and turned her head to kiss Pat's cheek, reaching around at the same time to pull her down onto the bed and kiss her hungrily. She looked deeply into Pat's eyes as she began caressing her breasts, coaxing them both back into a state of readiness. "It's way too early to talk about the ending. We're just at the beginning . . ." She moved her hand down, her fingers exploring the warm dampness just within her reach and slowly started again at the beginning.

Kit and Sabi closed the door to their apartment and both simultaneously collapsed on the bed. For a few minutes, neither of them said a word. The combined effect of the previous night and the stress of the events of the last nearly twenty-four hours had drained them both. Kit finally rolled over to get up.

"Where ya' goin', hon?" Sabi asked.

"I need a beer." Kit slouched to the refrigerator, grabbed a cold one, popped it open, and plopped back onto the bed. "Besides being fucking exhausted, I think I'm still in shock."

"I know, *mamita*. I can't say that I was at all expecting this particular end to Diane's little mystery disappearance. But, if you think about it, it's really not all that shocking. The bad relationships, her total acceptance of us—never any curious questions, not even privately to you—and that sad, sort of lost look she's always had. It makes sense."

"Not if you'd known her for almost ten years like I have," Kit said disconsolately.

"Honey, there's no way you would have known. It's not something you were looking for. Hell, *she* didn't know."

"Ex-*act*-ly. And now she's acting like she's some sort of full-fledged lesbian. I don't know . . . I just don't think it happens that fast. Maybe she's just trying to fit in with the rest of us."

Oh, stop now, Kit. Fast? At least she *had* some sort of experience before this. Look at us—we both jumped into this without either one of us having so much as kissed another woman." Kit stared at the ceiling. "Right?"

"Oh! Of course, honey. You know I would have told you. But right now I really hate admitting that."

"Listen. I know you've always felt like Diane's protector—more worldly, more practical, more aware of what's going on. And I think you liked that role. But that doesn't mean you get to decide, or approve of, what she chooses to do." Kit said nothing. Sabi went on: "Besides, I kind of have a good feeling about this. For the first time since I know Diane—or have heard your stories—she seems genuinely happy and . . . I don't know . . . comfortable and truly at ease with herself. I know it's soon, but I think the early signs are good. Besides, even if it's not her thing in the long run, she wouldn't be the first woman to have a good, old-fashioned fling with another woman. Can't hurt in my book; at the least, she'll have a whole new perspective on gayness and relationships in general."

"My, my, my!" Kit said, leaning back and looking at Sabi with exaggerated astonishment. "Aren't we Little Miss Shrink! But, I suppose you do have a point." Kit chuckled to herself. "Guess it's true what they say: careful what you wish for. How many times have I complained about Diane being a workaholic and wishing she'd loosen up, be more spontaneous? Man, oh, man—looks like I don't have to worry about that one anymore! Nothing to do now but sit back and see what develops. No matter what, I'll always be there for her."

"Yes, my darling, I know you will." Sabi looked at her and caressed Kit's cheek. "I knew there was a reason I loved you." She leaned over and kissed Kit softly and pulled her down on the bed. "Now, I don't know about you, but I thought that nap thing sounded like a *really* good idea." They settled in to do just that, Sabi on her back and Kit snuggled against her on her side.

Suddenly Sabi broke out in laughter. Kit opened her eyes and looked over at her. She followed Sabi's gaze up to the ceiling and then likewise started laughing uncontrollably.

"You gotta hand it to Stella. If there's a way to fix a problem on the cheap, she's the one who'll figure it out!" Above them stretched a blue tarp, affixed to the first dry beams on either side of the offending damp ones, that stretched from directly above their heads down to the two windows that fronted onto the deck. About a foot away from them, the tarp had been split to allow each end to hang out the opened top of each window, creating a makeshift drainage system for any other untimely leaks. Tacky, but ingenious—and, hopefully, effective.

"Aw, I wanted to spend our last night gazing up at our wooden beams, with the little red light creating that sleazy, bordello effect." She took Kit's arm and put it under her head, pulling herself close to her. "I kinda liked that harlot on the high seas thing, with you as the quiet but passionate cabin boy—who's really a girl!—who secretly ravishes me every night and steals my heart!" She leaned over and turned Kit's head toward her, pulling off the baseball cap she hadn't yet removed and kissing her hard.

"Whoa!" Kit said, coming up for air. "So that's what was making you such an animal earlier in the week! Hell! Let me rip that damned thing down. I don't give a shit about a soggy mattress if wooden beams are what it takes! Besides, who says it's gonna rain again anyway?" She pushed a still laughing Sabi down on the bed and reached down to strip off her own tank top before turning her attention back to Sabi. Slowly she lifted Sabi's tank up over her belly and then slower yet to reveal the familiar but always exciting sight of her breasts, rising and falling with her quickening breath. Sabi sighed and raised her back to make it easier for Kit. Kit threw the shirt on the floor, easing herself down onto Sabi, and picked up the kiss where they'd left off. As she moved so that nipples rubbed against nipples, their hands found and removed the clothing that remained the only barriers between bodies that hungered to touch.

No shipboard fantasy was necessary. Just the proximity of bodies, the knowledge of one another's deepest desires, and the intense passion that had marked their union from the beginning. As they simultaneously collapsed onto the bed for the second time that afternoon, Sabi again started laughing.

"For Christ's sake! *Now* what's so damned funny?"

"I wonder who else is 'napping' right about now?"

"Yeah, right!" Claire said, as she pulled a laughing Rita back down on the couch where they'd been sitting. "Like anyone else is actually back in their rooms *napping*. I'm warning you right now, you go up in that bed, don't expect to get any sleep!"

Rita waited until Claire relaxed her grip, then sprang up and made a dash for the ladder up to the sleeping loft. Claire chuckled at the attempted escape and slowly got up off the couch to follow her. She yawned and stretched. "Shit. I actually *am* sort of wiped out. Guess the adrenaline's back down to normal after all the excitement. You want anything to drink before I climb up?"

"Yeah, bring me a glass of Pepsi when you come up. And don't think you're pulling that tired bit on me now," Rita called down.

While Rita waited for Claire to make her way up to the loft, her thoughts drifted to the various scenes and dramas of the week. As the oldest in the group and the only parent, she was always inclined to view events from a more cautious, sometimes even skeptical, perspective. Plus, her youth had unfolded at a time not given to the same sort of free-spirited and freewheeling behavior her friends had experienced—not to mention that her young adulthood had been spent being a "good" wife and mother. As a result, she often had a hard time reconciling her friends' behavior with how much she loved them as people. That went for Claire as much as for Sabi, Kit, and the now extended group of friends. Sometimes they all seemed just too reckless and focused on, well, *fun* rather than considering the consequences.

But then a recollection popped into her mind. She smiled to herself, despite the previous thoughts. It was the image of Claire's face staring down at her in the middle of the night, during the week she had visited Claire in Ohio at her folks' house—a totally irrational, spontaneous decision on Rita's part. At the time, neither of them knew if Claire's return to Ohio would be permanent; she knew she simply *had* to go see Claire. All that mattered was finding a way to not lose touch with this young woman. The fact that she had grown so deeply attached to someone she'd worked with for less than a year and known as a friend for only a few months *was* disconcerting and out of character. But, oddly, it didn't seem to matter to her. So, despite never having so much as gone away overnight without her husband or family, she made the trip to Ohio—if for no other reason, as a gesture to reassure Claire that her coming out to Rita just a few weeks before she left had no impact on their friendship. But something had been happening between them from the moment Rita arrived. Nothing overt, but subtle and intense. Every look or touch or comment seemed charged and meaningful. And that night she awoke to see Claire staring at her with a look that not only didn't frighten her, it deeply excited her.

Rita had returned the gaze and asked Claire if anything was wrong, though she knew full well that nothing was. Claire immediately became embarrassed, apologized for waking her, and rolled over to go back to sleep. Rita, much to her own surprise, put her arm around Claire and gently pulled her back over to face her. She asked Claire what she'd been thinking while she was looking at her. Claire made the requisite excuses about not being able to sleep and just lying there drifting in her own thoughts. Rita said nothing, left her arm draped over Claire, and continued to look deeply into Claire's eyes, which had somehow become much bluer than she remembered, the hint of moonlight coming through the window reflecting off them. Claire had hesitantly reached over to run her fingers through Rita's tousled brown hair. And suddenly, with no prior plan or consideration for consequences, Rita reached both hands over to Claire's face and pulled it to hers.

Rita sighed contentedly at the memory. She remembered that first sensation of a woman's lips on hers, so unlike the aggressive, presumptuous kiss of a man. But soft, searching, comforting, and arousing all at once; as though lips could ask—and answer—questions that were beyond the power of spoken words. It was a kiss that seemed to last an eternity. Or maybe it was a succession of kisses that felt like one. All Rita knew at the time was that she had never wanted it to end. And she had instinctively conveyed that; again, words were unneeded as hands and mouths hungrily began seeking, bodies began to learn the textures and contours and responses of the other, and sighs and moans said all that needed to be said.

She had never felt so alive and loved and fulfilled. She'd known then that something she'd yearned for, for as long as she could remember, something she'd never given a name to had entered her universe—finally. And irrevocably. She had no intention of losing it, or the woman who had revealed a world of pleasure and desire she'd never imagined.

Rita nuzzled deeper into her pillow, back from the warm moment that felt like yesterday despite the years. Her thoughts drifted through the events of the week, the women following their hearts and making leaps similar to hers, though, frankly, probably far more considered and informed than hers had ever been. *I wonder if they'll make it? If they've thought of what could happen? If they'll find themselves as in love and as happy as . . .*

Claire reached the top of the ladder and stopped. She'd intended to leap on the bed and ravish her waiting partner as a bit of a change to their usual romantic encounters. But instead, she crept quietly to the bed in deference to the deep, contented breathing and occasional little snore that was coming from Rita's side of the bed. Claire slipped into bed and carefully got herself comfortable, trying hard not to disturb the dreams being woven beside her. She propped herself up on one elbow and watched the beautiful face on the pillow next to hers. She smiled and thought back to the first time she'd watched Rita sleep . . .

*   *   *

Dara reached the top of the dune first. She dropped the roll of blankets and towels she'd lugged up the precipitously sloping dune. She closed her eyes and stretched her arms out to better breathe in the crisp ocean air that had been scrubbed clean by the powerful storm. After another deep breath, she turned to look down the sandy hill to see how Diane was doing with her ascent. She smiled to herself as she watched Diane's head bobbing along as she scrambled up the last few yards. Dara felt a little bad about the extra effort involved in getting to this particular part of Race Point, but she knew that the view was magnificent and that not many people ventured this far beyond the regular swimming areas. Especially today, when there was no one at the beach anyway, with the rain lasting as long into the day as it had. She, however, was prepared; knowing the sand would be wet, she'd "borrowed" a large piece of blue tarp that had been rolled up in an out of the way corner of Stella's. She couldn't imagine what the hell Stella needed a tarp for, but it certainly came in handy for what she and Diane had decided to do with what remained of the afternoon.

Like everyone else, they had retired for a nap after the grand confrontation. But, despite being the ones needing sleep the most—especially Diane who, between dealing with Grant after the dance cruise and then meeting Dara, had yet to enjoy a full night's sleep—they found themselves fully awake and eager to take advantage of the fact that the rain had stopped. Without saying so, they both seemed to realize that time was short now and that if they were to have any P-Town memories of their own, it had to be today. When Diane asked what they could do other than make the now less-than-exciting Commercial Street promenade, Dara brightened and told Diane to grab some sweatpants and be ready to go in fifteen minutes. In half an hour, they were at the beach, slogging through the sand, with Dara reassuring Diane it wasn't much farther.

As Diane finally crested the dune where Dara was waiting, she wiped the mist off her glasses and looked out at the ocean and audibly gasped. The waves were still responding to the roiling currents produced by the wind and rain of the night before and pounding the sandy shore as the tide reached its zenith. The sky was a purplish pewter, brooding and yet somehow comforting, with wispy breaks here and there that held the potential of a beautiful sunset. As they stood there, silent in the presence of such raw beauty, they could almost feel in the air itself the surging power and energy pulsating beneath the swells as they slowly, calmly expanded and undulated toward the shore, gaining size and momentum, until they finally crashed magnificently onto the beach below them. They silently reached for each other's hand and made their way down the beach side of the dune. About three quarters of the way down, they found a spot that was reasonably dry—at least free of puddles and tide pools—stretched out the tarp, and quickly threw the blanket on top of it before the windy remnants of the storm could blow it away. They stationed portions of their gear at the four corners and lay back on the blanket, each propped on both elbows, looking out at the ocean.

Diane spoke first. "So, how do you think it went?"

Dara chuckled to herself. "Compared to what? I can't say as how I've ever been in that exact situation before. And I have this unshakable feeling that I'm somehow the grand seductress in all this." She leaned over close to Diane's ear. "And you sort of left out that part about *you* grabbing *me* on the deck and planting a big sloppy kiss on me," she said softly, moving closer to Diane's ear and biting the lobe, then the sensitive skin of her neck just below.

Diane shivered and smiled at Dara. "Oh, my God! I can't believe what that does to me." She shivered again and scooted closer to Dara. "I'm sorry . . . it really didn't come up, and I guess we got off the subject at some point."

"Nice try, cutie. I just hope you eventually make sure they don't think that predatory lesbian Dara swooped down on poor, confused Diane and led her down the lavender path. Not that I guess I mind all that much—they're your friends, not mine. Or not yet, anyway. But I'd hate for them to hold that against me someday." She got quiet and looked out at the waves.

"What's wrong, baby?"

"Nothing, honey, really. I'm getting way ahead of myself."

"What are you talking about?" Then Diane abruptly sat up, her eyes getting moist. "Oh, my God. It's 'someday'—you're not ready for that with someone again so soon. That's it, isn't it?"

Dara's first response was shock at the intensity of Diane's emotional outburst. But then her face softened into a bemused smile. She put her arm around Diane and pulled her close. "No, baby, no, no, no. Just the opposite. I was worried that *I* was moving too far ahead in my thinking, imagining your friends being mine—ours. I've been afraid to talk about whatever comes next for fear I'd scare you away. I know how new this whole thing is to you. But we don't really have a lot of time to do it later. I mean, today's pretty much it."

Diane rolled over into Dara's arms. "Don't even say it. I know. Oh, how I know. But I don't want to think about it—not right now."

Dara hugged her close and lightly kissed her neck as Diane held on to her even tighter. "Okay, honey. We don't have to. I just don't want you to think that this was some sort of lighthearted seduction on my part or any kind of summer fling. I . . . I don't want to scare you off, but I hope we get the chance to see if this could turn into something."

Diane blinked the tears out of her eyes and broke into a grin. "Now *that's* a definite difference in this side of things." She took a deep breath and got a tissue out of her pocket to wipe her eyes and nose. "With practically every guy I've dated, it was always me worried about whether I was coming on too strong, too committal, too something. And now I'm the one hearing that. Amazing." She picked up a piece of a shell and threw it down into a lapping wave a few yards below them on the sand. "Don't worry, honey. I think we're pretty much in sync. On lots of levels. First, we both need some time to get our shit together after our last relationships. And we both care about our jobs and careers. And, most importantly, I think we feel the same about each other—and I've never really known how that felt. So, yes, I'm just as eager as you are to find out if this could be something; better yet, to work on making it something."

"Thank God," Dara said with a deep sigh. She kissed Diane's hand and held it against her chest. "And for starters, I need you to promise you'll *talk* to me. Especially given your, well, novice status in all this. With Becca, even after all the years we were together, she rarely trusted me with how she really felt, what she needed. And, given what you were saying last night about years of not being, shall we say, very forthcoming, I want us to be clear on that right from the outset. I guarantee you that'll end any relationship, let alone one that's starting on the basis of a couple of days."

"I promise. You're right, I'm not great at it, but I'll do my best. But you have to promise not to be afraid to call me on it if you sense I'm holding back. Old habits are hard to break, you know. But I want to—I absolutely want to." Diane leaned over and kissed Dara.

Dara pulled back a little to look at Diane. She shook her head and sighed.

"What's wrong *now?*" Diane asked, a guarded, concerned look on her face.

Dara smiled and shook her head again. "Nothing's wrong. Not really. I was just thinking of a promise I made myself in college—the *last* time I got myself involved with a virgin . . . lesbian-wise, that is."

"Let me guess," Diane answered, lying back down on the blanket and taking her glasses off. She closed her eyes as she stretched and spread out full length on the blanket. "I'm guessing you promised yourself you'd *never* get into that situation again." She raised her head to shake her short curls free. Without looking at Dara, she asked, "So, are you sorry this happened?"

"That's why I was smiling. Nothing like happily making a liar out of yourself. 'Course, it's really up to you whether I was wrong about the risks involved."

"Ah, but what about the perks?" She stretched again, her nipples jutting up against the material of her tee shirt. "Like having such a willing student."

"Why, my dear Ms. Anderson. If I didn't know better, I'd say you were coming on to me," Dara answered, scooting closer to Diane. She ran one hand through Diane's sandy blond curls, burying her nose in them and losing herself in the scent, while with the other she began to lightly rub the hardening nubs with the flat of her hand.

"And if *I* didn't know better, I'd say you brought me out here to this deserted beach to have your way with me," Diane said, as she began to breathe harder.

"Not really. I just figured it was a soothing setting for that nap

we're supposed to be taking. That, and it also seemed the ideal setting for . . . continuing your education." She smiled slyly, grabbed the
other blanket they'd brought, and threw it over their legs. Then she
lifted Diane's tee shirt and began kissing her belly, slowly moving upward.

"Don't forget—we have to make it back by dinner," Diane said in
a hoarse whisper.

"Don't worry. We'll be back in plenty of time—and maybe even
worn out enough to take that nap beforehand. Besides, I somehow
doubt we'll be the only ones running late." As Dara talked, she kept
kissing and lightly nipping the tender skin below Dara's breasts.
"Ready for your next lesson?"

"Mmmm. So, any instructions you'd like to give me for this one?"
Diane moaned at the feel of Dara's mouth as it finally arrived at its
first destination, and then moved to its partner.

"Not really," she said, replacing the attentions of her mouth with
those of her fingers. "But, as with all worthwhile learning experiences, I think we should first review our earlier lesson," Dara whispered into Diane's ear. "And since you're in the accelerated program,
this might be a *multiple* lesson day."

"Whatever you say, Ms. Winston." Diane shivered, partly from the
cool, damp breeze, but mainly from the feel of Dara's hand slipping
underneath the elastic of her sweatpants and easing them down her
thighs. As Diane bent her legs and pulled them down the rest of the
way, Dara deftly and easily slid her fingers into her, Diane having
knowingly opted not to wear anything underneath. Even so, she
gasped at the sudden, welcome feel of Dara inside her. She began
rocking slowly against the expert pressure of Dara's fingers and
thumb, holding back as she reached over and roughly pulled Dara's
sweatpants down and began lavishing the same attentions on her.
Rather than the tender, initiatory moments of earlier that day, this
was hard, needy, possessing lovemaking, inspired by the wild, crashing sea below them. It wasn't long before throaty cries of release
mixed with the roar of the surf.

"Hoh," Dara exhaled as she collapsed on the sandy bed beneath
her. "Lord have mercy, you're a quick learner."

Diane slowly rolled over to face Dara. "But isn't that the mark of an excellent teacher?" They slowly leaned into one another, their lips touching ever so lightly, the slightest initial physical contact making them each flinch elsewhere with remembered intensity. Then again, a little more insistently. Then again, hungrily.

Dara pulled back, catching her breath. "You know, you definitely have the makings of an 'A' student."

"It's all about the subject matter," Diane whispered huskily, picking up the kissing where it had left off.

"I think you're ready for that next lesson," Dara said, shaking herself free of Diane's embrace and starting to kiss her way down Diane's belly.

"I *know* I'm ready," Diane said with certainty, as she opened her legs to Dara's body now positioned between them, and surrendered to the exploding sensations of Dara losing herself in that other set of sandy blond curls.

CHAPTER
20

Claire and Rita looked at each other, genuinely puzzled. Claire had made the reservations, but she had no recollection of having said anything about any special occasion—that there had even *been* a reservation for eight available on a Friday night seemed occasion enough. Yet, when they arrived at Franco's and gave them Claire's name, the maitre d' checked it off with hardly a glance at the reservation book, smiled knowingly, and said they'd been expecting them. Then he asked if they'd like to wait upstairs at the bar for the rest of their party and have a cocktail—on the house. Claire, certainly not one to pass on a free cocktail—in an elegant bar with an ocean view, no less—nodded happily, and they strolled upstairs to the lounge, Tallulah's.

They chose a small table that afforded them a perfect vantage point of the last rays of sun winking off the easy swells in the bay. The waiter took their order and delivered it to them with a smile and the universal sign for gratis spirits: "Cheers, ladies!" Then he added an enigmatic parting shot: "Here's hoping we can provide a fitting end to what I hope was a wonderful—if eventful—week in P-Town." Then he was off to take care of the new arrivals waiting for tables near the bar.

"Hmmm. Curiouser and curiouser," Claire said, as she picked up her Tanqueray Gibson and took an initial, appraising taste. "Ah! That wonderful first icy sip of gin. How's your Cape Codder, honey?"

"Good. *Very* good, as a matter of fact. Which is saying a lot for a non-drinker." Rita took another sip of the drink. "So, what in the world is going on?"

"I haven't a clue. But I'm likin' it, whatever it is! Guess we'll have to see if any of the rest of the crew have any idea." She lit a cigarette and gazed out at the water. "Speaking of whom, it's 7:45—you think *any* of them will manage to make it by eight? Not that I really mind at the moment. It's nice just being here with you. And I could use a drink and a few moments to recover from that exceptionally *lovely* wake-up call you gave me." Claire leaned across the table and kissed Rita lovingly. "Unfortunately, you fell asleep this afternoon before I could put *my* little plan in motion. And then you absolutely wore me out, you animal!"

"That's okay. The night's not over yet," Rita answered, looking up provocatively over the rim of her glass as she took another sip of her drink.

"Damn right."

"But you've got a point about the rest of them. Even with our little 'interlude,' we managed to get here on time. Think anyone else had similar ideas?"

"Are you kidding? After the night we all had, I'm sure everyone was exhausted. We'll be lucky if they all don't sleep right through and forget we even had dinner plans."

They sat quietly for a while, holding hands and enjoying the view and the music. The Deco theme of Franco's carried through from the general chrome- and rosewood-appointed decor to the table settings and glassware to the waiters' tuxes to the music. Billie Holliday serenaded them as they sat, soaking it all up. They'd just started reflecting on the week when the waiter approached them and told them other members of their party were waiting downstairs.

"Well! Guess someone's made a liar out of me," Claire said happily as she and Rita scooted out from the table to go back downstairs. As they started to pick up their drinks, the waiter stopped them.

"Allow me," he said graciously. "I'll take these down to your table. Which, by the way, will be The Algonquin tonight."

Claire raised an eyebrow, duly impressed. All the tables and booths at Franco's were named for celebrities—mainly period movie stars—of the time, except for one: a large, round table that bore the name of the famous New York hotel where, at a similar table known simply as The Roundtable, a celebrated collection of literary personalities and other members of the New York intelligentsia of the day gathered. Granted, their little group could hardly hope to compare to the likes of Dorothy Parker, Robert Benchley, Bennett Cerf, or the rest of the regulars at that former table, but for Provincetown, Claire figured they'd do.

When they got downstairs, they saw Grant and Pat waiting patiently by the maitre d's station. Claire couldn't help but smile as she watched Grant rather solicitously help Pat off with her jacket, practically radiating happiness, not to mention a touch of pride at being with such an attractive and capable woman. It was *very* nice to see for a change; virtually all the years Claire had known Grant she'd been either alone or with someone clearly, at least to Claire, not her equal. This pairing, however, had definite potential.

After Rita hugged the arrivals, Claire followed suit and then, so as not to linger too long in the entrance to the dining room, turned quickly to the host. Before she could ask if their table was ready, he nodded and led them into the main dining room. Sure enough, he led them to a large, round table more or less centered in the room that could accommodate ten, let alone eight, more than comfortably.

"Lord have mercy! This is some spiffy restaurant," Grant said, when Claire told them about their noteworthy table. She craned her neck around to check out the rest of the room, which at this prime dinner hour was filled with murmuring patrons. "I'd heard of it, and Pat told me she loved this place. Now I see why. Food's good, too?"

"The best," Claire replied, Rita and Pat nodding in agreement. "Italian-Continental-ish, with sauces and specials to die for—and Franco himself is still the head chef. We always try to make it here when we come up. Ever since we wandered down that little alley beside the Army-Navy store years ago and discovered his first location. God, it was tiny; maybe held thirty people, max, in those days. But absolutely charming. Obviously word got around, and he moved up to this place. And judging from our visit last year, size hasn't compromised the charm *or* the food. It's also nice that Franco himself is gay, as is most of the wait staff, in case you couldn't tell! Nice to keep it in the family, so to speak."

Their waiter arrived and delivered Claire and Rita's drinks then took Pat and Grant's drink order. He returned with the drinks as well as a tray of assorted olives, artichoke hearts, chunks of aged Parmesan cheese, and various other raw and pickled vegetables. Claire and Rita looked at each other again and shrugged.

"What?" Grant asked, noticing the exchange.

"I don't remember a spread like this coming with drinks, do you, Pat?" Rita asked.

"Now that you mention it, no, I don't. Maybe it's something new."

"I don't know," Claire said, frowning a bit. "It seems we're getting some sort of VIP treatment, and Rita and I can't figure out why." She looked at them suspiciously. "So, you don't know anything about this?"

"Sorry. Wish I could take the credit," Grant said with a shrug. Pat shook her head in agreement. "Hell, why question it? Suits me fine," Grant said as she reached over and snagged a piece of cheese.

Claire looked at Rita and shrugged, too. Then she cleared her throat dramatically. "Ahem! Even though the rest of our party's running a little late, I think we should at least *start* the toasting." She paused to think a minute. Everyone waited, glasses poised. "To rocky beginnings that turn out to be stepping stones in disguise—leading to what I hope will be much happiness for both of you." They all clinked their glasses.

"Aw, Griff," Grant said, looking down and fidgeting with her silverware.

"Thank you, Claire. That was beautiful," Pat said warmly, her eyes a little moist. She turned to Grant. "And I hope exactly the same thing." She took Grant's hand in hers and gave it a squeeze.

Claire knit her brow, looking at the two of them. "So, is it the booze already or do you two have that, uh, special *glow?*"

"Claire!" Rita said, smacking Claire's hand.

"I just—"

"Man! You must have clout!" Kit said a little too loudly, prompting the people at the surrounding tables to look up at the new arrivals. "Best table in the house and comp drinks upstairs. Jesus, girl. Who do you know?"

"*Dios mio!* Would you shut up, you? This isn't some two-bit sports bar, Kit!" Sabi said. "Can you believe her?" she said, turning to Dara and Diane who had come in with them.

"So you guys have been boozin' it up upstairs while we're down here waiting for you?" Claire said, a little annoyed.

"Well, we got here about ten till, and figured you'd be up there, too. So, while the bartender had the waiter check to see if you were here, we ordered drinks and watched that amazing view." Everyone instinctively turned to the big picture windows to see the colors of the sunset reflecting off the water, a blaze of golds, purples, reds, and oranges. "Then when he got back to tell us you *were* here, and I went to pay him, he told us our drinks were on the house. I think I like this place!"

After everyone was situated, their waiter, Eric, reappeared on cue and delivered Grant and Pat's drinks as well as the other drinks from upstairs. He returned a few moments later with menus and ran through the list of unbelievably sumptuous-sounding specials for the evening.

As they scrutinized their menus, conversation flowed easily around the table. There was the expected ribbing over the now-amusing recent series of events and laughter at recalled moments of earlier ones that had presaged the new unions at the table. By the time the waiter returned to take their orders, they were all laughing at what everyone now agreed was the ludicrous and hysterical sight of Tom as the Carnival queen and the actual queen looking like Dorothy about to be snatched up for her trip to Oz.

After much hemming and hawing and repetitions of specials, they all finally ordered. Diane sighed audibly.

"What's wrong, honey?" Dara asked, putting her arm around Diane.

"I was thinking about Oz."

"Oka-a-ay, but I'm a little confused." Dara looked around at the other equally clueless faces.

Diane laughed quietly. "Gee. I figured you'd all get that. I was feeling a little like Dorothy—when it's finally time to go home to Kansas. Except in *this* version, I really *don't* want to go home. There's no place like P-Town."

The table got very quiet, as various of them flicked cigarettes or toyed with their swizzle sticks or gazed out at the lights on the bay. Finally, Grant broke the silence.

"Well, actually, we were talking about that this afternoon—just before we dozed off."

Without a word, everyone's eyes met. Suddenly the entire table burst out laughing, knowing looks darting from person to person.

"Aw, come on," Grant said. "Not *everyone!*"

Hands that weren't already being held were grabbed, as everyone nodded wordlessly and burst out laughing again.

"Well, aren't we a bunch of horny little fuckers!" Grant said in her reliably delicate way.

"Exactly!" Kit burst out.

"Anyway, as I was saying . . . We really *were* talking this afternoon—at one point! And Pat and I decided that this little party of ours got goin' kinda late. So, we were thinking that maybe there was a way we could stretch things out for at least another day. There's no reason I have to be home tomorrow, and Pat figured Gayle could be *persuaded* to cover for her after her little scene last night."

It was as if someone turned a light on in the room. The other six women literally brightened at the prospect of extending their stays.

"Shit! That'd be great!" Claire said. "But there *is* this nasty little detail of where we'd all stay."

"Well, I think I could talk my pal at the Holiday into extending the two reservations there. Hell, we've already more than put in our two-night minimums." She flashed a grin at Diane, who nodded in agreement. " 'Course, I'll be at Pat's, and she's got an extra bedroom. So we could all have our own rooms. The bottom line is we've got places for all of us to stay, if you guys want to."

Claire looked at Rita, Kit looked at Sabi, and Dara looked at Diane.

"Well, honey. Who *says* we have to leave Oz? At least right now? We've even got our very own wizard!" Dara looked over at Grant and bowed her head in deference, raising her glass at the same time in a toast. "To Oz?"

In unison they all heartily replied, "To Oz!"

"With apologies to L. Frank Baum," Dara said, raising her glass to her lips.

"Okay, then!" Claire said, with a confirming tone to her voice. "We can move our stuff out of Stella's in the—" She stopped short. "Shit. Stella. I wonder if Jimmy told Stella we found Diane?" She looked around the table, her eyes coming to light on Grant and Pat. "A-a-and there's still the little detail about her, shall we say, 'favorite person' not exactly being 'available' anymore." She raised her eyebrows and took another sip of her drink. "Well, I don't know about anybody else, but I sure as hell don't want to be the one to break the news."

"Honey, how about we enjoy our meal and deal with Stella when we have to," Rita suggested. "I, for one, don't think we have to solve every problem before it is one. Besides, she didn't come with us to Carnival, which you'd think she might have done if she were all *that* interested."

"God bless clear-thinking Rita," Grant said, with palpable relief. "She's right. Let's enjoy the evening and deal with tomorrow tomorrow."

As they raised their glasses in agreement, Eric approached the table. "Ma'am, since you hadn't gotten around to ordering wine with your dinner, may I recommend a nice red?" He showed the bottle to Claire. She looked around the table, and silently confirmed with everyone else that wine would be a good idea.

"Certainly! I guess we should start with a couple of bottles," she said to him.

"It's already taken care of," he said, heading back to the kitchen and soon returning with another bottle of the Bordeaux he'd shown her. He opened a bottle, poured a taste, and gave it to Claire to sample. She tasted it and nodded her approval.

"Uh, Eric. How exactly do you mean 'taken care of'?" she asked him.

"Well, I'm not at liberty to say at the moment. But, as with your cocktails, the wine has been taken care of."

"Okay," she said, shrugging in concession to whatever or whomever they owed their good fortune as Eric made his way around the table pouring wine in all their glasses. "To our generous benefactor," she said, raising her glass. They all followed suit and toasted. As they put their glasses down, Eric returned with their appetizers.

For the next hour or so, conversation diminished to satisfied sighs, moans, and various inadequate adjectives. The table was jammed with treats from Franco's kitchen: giant mushrooms stuffed with crab meat, mussels Posillipo, calamari, veal Oscar, steak Diane, pastas, shrimp, lobster, wine sauces, red sauces, filet mignon, delicately sautéed vegetables—all cooked to perfection. It was a true feast. Finally, one by one, the women slouched back in their chairs, drunk on food far more than the wine or any of the other spirits. Eric reappeared and looked satisfied at the clean plates in front of each of them.

"So, ladies, should I assume you enjoyed the meal?"

"Oh, my God," Kit groaned. "I don't think I can move for the rest of the night."

"I should say not," Sabi said, shaking her head. "I don't know when I've seen you eat like that. You know, you didn't have to scarf down every last bite."

"I don't blame her," Dara groaned. "I couldn't bring myself to leave anything either. It was just too good."

"Well, I trust you left some room for dessert," Eric said.

"Dessert? You must be joking," Diane said, loosening the belt on her slacks.

"Well, how about some coffee in the meantime? I'll leave the dessert menu here and you can think about it."

They passed the menu around the table to the sound of more groans and moans as they read the offerings, one more delectable than the other. Eric returned with coffees, espressos, and cappuccinos and asked if they were ready to order.

"I think we need a couple of more minutes, my friend," Kit said, taking a deep breath as if to try to find a vacant space somewhere inside her. Eric encouraged them to take their time and moved off to another table.

"Well, I suppose if we're staying another day, we should try to hit the beach. Hardly seems right you guys come out here and not even get to dip a pinky in the actual Atlantic," Kit said, looking from Diane to Grant. "Our little bay hardly counts. Besides, fighting the waves'll work off some of this food!"

"Sounds good," Pat said. "I haven't managed to make it there much at all this summer—the downside of a good season for jewelry-hungry lesbians, I guess," she said with a jaunty smile. Kit registered a look of sudden awareness and shifted in her seat.

As the rest of the table started planning the beach excursion, Kit leaned over to Pat and whispered something in her ear. Pat nodded and smiled. The two of them listened to the conversation for a little while longer, then Pat excused herself to go to the ladies room.

"Whew! Good idea," Kit said, pushing her chair back. "That is, if I can manage to move!"

After they'd left, Sabi's mood shifted and a pout settled over her features. "Well, what the hell is *that* all about?"

"Now, now. Down, girl," Claire said, a hint of a smile at the corners of her mouth. "I don't think there's any reason to let the green monster out of the cage. There are times jealousy is definitely the wrong tack to take. Besides, they'd have to deal with you *and* Grant, and I can't imagine anyone wanting to take on the wrath of Texas and Puerto Rico combined!"

The rest of the group agreed, most vocally Grant, and Sabi calmed down, more or less. The two women reappeared at the table in short order, and the conversation resumed where it had left off. Soon, Eric returned and the women gave him their orders. They'd decided to share three desserts, zabaglione, fresh fruit with *crème fraiche,* and a sinful sounding chocolate mocha mousse torte. Eric had hardly been gone before he was back, toting a champagne cooler. This time, however, all eyes turned to Pat and Kit.

Sabi leaned over and kissed Kit on the cheek. "Aw, honey. How perfect."

Kit shook her head and looked over at Pat who was doing the same thing. "Sorry, babe. Wish I could take the credit, but it wasn't either one of us."

Claire turned to Eric, who was grinning as he twisted the wire from the neck of the bottle while another waiter put champagne glasses in front of each of them. "Alright, now, young man. Don't you think we've been patient enough?" she said, trying to muster up a stern, demanding look.

"Just a little longer, then all will be revealed. Actually, it's been fun watching you guys enjoy this little mystery. And having fun as a waiter on a busy Friday night is a welcome change!" He began pouring the champagne. "My last duty is to tell you that another bottle will be waiting for you up at Tallulah's when you're finished. Drink up, ladies!"

"Well, girls, I guess this is the week for intrigue! Seems there's nothing to do but enjoy the bubbly," Claire said, again resigned to let things play out as *someone* had planned. "But I think this latest surprise calls for a toast."

"Just a minute, Claire," Kit said, putting her glass down. "I actually *had* planned on ordering a bottle of champagne. But for a special reason." She cleared her throat and took a drink of water. Then she took a deep breath and picked up her champagne. "One of the reasons we decided to take Claire and Rita up on their invitation to come here with them was as a belated anniversary celebration—two years last May." A collective ah-h-h-h arose from the table and even a couple of tables around them. "Last year we could only afford a bottle of wine and a couple of steaks. So, this year I figured we deserved a little spiffier time—especially, you, honey." She looked at Sabi adoringly. "I know it hasn't always been easy, babe. But you've made my life complete—and happier than I ever thought it could be. Happy anniversary, honey . . . I love you with all my heart." She lifted her glass to Sabi who clinked her glass, then put it down and grabbed Kit in a seemingly life-threatening embrace and proceeded to cover her face with kisses. The rest of the table followed suit—in the toasting *and* the kissing. Then Kit raised her arms to signal quiet again. "And . . . well . . . here." She reached under the table and pulled out a small, beautifully wrapped package and placed it in front of Sabi. "Something to remember what I hope will be the first of many summers in P-Town—and a lifetime of being together."

Sabi was beyond words, tears rolling down her cheeks and spattering the tablecloth, which was getting a little damp for the same reason elsewhere around the table. She alternated brushing them off her face with unwrapping the box. Inside was a small velvet box; and inside that was the sapphire and diamond ring she'd been eyeing hungrily the last two days, but had given up any realistic hope of owning.

"Oh, Kit . . ." She slipped it on her finger and held it up in the candlelight. The people at the surrounding tables broke out in spontaneous applause as Kit kissed her again. She started crying anew and hugged Kit yet again. Then pulled back and slapped her arm. "Look what you've made me do! You've ruined my whole hard-ass, smart-mouth image, you!"

"So, *now* are you over the whole jealousy thing?" Kit said, turning to grin and wink at Pat.

"You two were in cahoots about this the whole time, weren't you?"

"Well, in all honesty, not the whole time. I *did* think she was pretty cute at first," Pat said, snuggling a little closer to Grant. "But after that first evil eye bit from you—and seeing how you two were together—I knew I didn't have a chance. And look what I'd have missed out on," she said, patting Grant's knee. "But, you gotta admit, it doesn't suck knowing someone in the jewelry biz!"

"But how'd you . . . when'd you . . ."

"Relax, babe. There's time to go over all that," Kit said, putting her arm around Sabi. "Just remember that I can be just as sneaky as you if I need to be! Now, I think we should finish what we can of this gorgeous stuff," Eric placed the desserts on the table as she spoke, "and get upstairs to see who else is so good at bein' sneaky."

Soon they were all dragging themselves up the stairs that led to Tallulah's, having left a well-rewarded and *very* happy Eric behind. The lounge was veiled in the romantic dusky light of candles on the tables and in amber sconces on the walls. They stood, trying to figure out where they were supposed to go, when Dara spotted a champagne cooler beside a grouping of cocktail tables by the windows. They headed over and sat down, looking back and forth at one another, half expecting one of them to finally come clean. Instead, two men approached the table, towels over their arms, to serve the champagne.

"Well, well, well! What have we here?" said the shorter of the two, as he tossed the towel over his shoulder. "It's a veritable gaggle of gay girls! All tanned and happy and paired up like it's prom night! Our own girls of Provincetown, all together, in one place. Thank God!"

"Jimmy, you conniving son-of-a-bitch!" Claire blurted out. "Is this all your doing?"

"Well, my darling, I must admit I was the brains behind the whole scheme. You actually touched this crusty, old heart of mine when you were all so distraught over your friend here." He patted Diane on the shoulder. "So, when Claire called me and told me all was well and asked me if I thought you could get a *large* reservation here—Jesus! Do lesbians always have to travel in packs?—I called first to make *sure* you would. And since I got my old boyfriend Franco when I called, I told him about the whole thing. We faggots just can't resist juicy, romantic stories, you know, not to mention happy endings. So he came up with the table and the comp cocktail bit. Then I decided that my friend here needed to pony up and do something, too." He turned to the person next to him, whom nobody had even focused on yet. Tom looked up and waved sheepishly. "That was your wine. So, that left me with the champagne—and I hope you noticed that it wasn't some cheap swill, by the way."

Claire kissed the bunched tips of her fingers in the French gesture of approval. *"Magnifique, monsieur."*

"Good. I'm glad you approve," he said, tossing his head and sighing in satisfaction. "But the final touch—this bottle—came from a most unlikely source." He looked over at a table in the far corner. "Girls!" He clapped his hands as if summoning a genie. "Come, come!"

Four women approached the table. Before they could see, they *heard* who one of them was: "Leave it to a damned pretty boy to make a big, damned deal out of nothing," growled Stella.

"Stella?" Rita asked, in an uncharacteristic outburst.

"Well, you don't have to be *that* surprised. I'm not a crotchety old bitch all the time!" For a moment, it almost looked as though she was smiling. "Truth is, I was pretty relieved when I heard everything had worked out. But then, after I called Gayle to tell her—"

"My God! How many people were looking for me?" Diane said in wonder.

"Honey, when Jimmy Shea says he's calling out the Mounties, I leave no stone unturned," Jimmy said proudly.

"As I was saying," Stella continued, a little miffed at the interruption, "when I called Gayle, we got talking and she invited me to dinner with her two new friends." Standing with Stella and Gayle were Trudy and Becca. "So, I went." She finally looked over at Grant. "God knows, *you* weren't ever going to get around to buying me a drink!" Grant's face took on the reddened hue that, by now, was becoming a regular part of her features. Stella, this time, did, indeed, smile. "And, surprisingly, we had a . . . pretty good time." A positive, pleasant attitude was clearly a less-than-familiar situation for poor Stella. "We decided to come up here for a nightcap—which we started much earlier, I might add—and ran into this fairy boy. And pretty soon I found myself roped into springing for more damned champagne! Been a while since I've had champagne. We just might need another bottle!" Clearly, the champagne was agreeing with her and was no doubt partly responsible for this new, improved Stella.

Jimmy popped open the bottle in the cooler and signaled the real waiter for another bottle while chairs and tables were rearranged to accommodate the expanded crowd. Once they were all seated, the room was abuzz with laughter and various conversations all going on at once around the bunched tables. At one end of the grouping, Dara managed to gracefully handle the potentially awkward situation of having two exes and a new lady at the same table, while at the other end, Claire tried to not look shocked when Rita went to greet Becca—whom she had, indeed, met and, apparently, got to know rather well on the dance cruise. In between, Pat and Gayle managed to exchange reasonably cordial hellos, and Diane seemed perfectly at ease talking to Tom, who looked a little crushed at seeing her and Dara so obviously enamored of one another. That is, until he spotted the barmaid. When a darkly handsome, middle-aged man entered the bar, Jimmy lit up like a Christmas tree and quickly introduced his new beau, Richard. Claire remembered to propose a belated toast to Stella's birthday, much to her embarrassment—and veiled satisfaction. That simple gesture also may have helped bring about what seemed like the final proof of the extraordinary nature of the evening; either that, or it was the champagne—or possibly divine intervention. When Stella heard about the proposed extra day of vacation, she magnanimously offered the use of a beach house she also owned in town—no charge! As she so aptly put it, "No use making the competition at the motel any damned richer!"

Claire cleared her throat, to no avail. Finally, she stood up.

"Excuse me! Everybody! PEOPLE!" The din subsided. "I definitely think a toast is in order." She looked around at all the faces looking up at her. "Here's to P-Town and a wonderful week . . . despite a minor setback, shall we say! But, more importantly, to friends—without whom it would just be another place: old and dear ones, who have a permanent place in our hearts and souls, and new and unexpected ones for whom it's a pleasure and a joy to make room there. Cheers." Added to the glow of the candles was the greater glow of smiling, happy faces.

CHAPTER
21

Claire toted the first of their bags out to the van. Inside, the grand Sunday brunch that had coalesced earlier that morning was still breaking up.

The day had started painfully early, Rita, Claire, Sabi, and Kit having literally dragged themselves from their comfortable beds in Stella's beach house to finish the packing they'd only half-heartedly begun the evening before. They'd had all good intentions of finishing the job before going out for one last night on the town. But the events of the day had caught up with them and packing had fallen by the wayside.

Saturday's beach outing was therapeutic as well as great fun. Drying out from the Franco's bash—*and* the final bottle of champagne that Stella produced later for a final toast to the moonlit bay— was much enhanced by the beating sun and bracing ocean water. The majority of the Franco's group ultimately showed up, albeit not at all as early as they had gamely planned during that last champagne toast. Instead of bright and relatively early at ten a.m., the first intrepid beachgoers—Grant and Pat—had staked out a spot a little before noon. Close behind them were Dara and Diane, who got a relatively early start in their move from Diane's motel room to the extra room at Pat's, Dara having more or less packed up the room at Stella's the night before when Becca announced *she* needed the room. Pat and Grant had left the door unlocked with a note saying they were going ahead to the beach to find a decent spot before the weekend onslaught left little choice in the matter. The other foursome made it around one, followed in dribs and drabs by Jimmy, Richard, Becca, and Trudy. Stella was expectedly absent. Loosening up and getting a little bit rowdy under cloak of darkness was one thing; showing up in a bathing suit was quite another. And somehow appropriately, given their respective bad behavior on Thursday night, Gayle and Tom both had to work.

The day—warm, sunny, with just the right hint of a breeze—had passed in a pleasant blur of conversation, waning hangovers, picnic lunches, occasional dozing, disguised beers (alcoholic beverages being officially *verboten* on the national seashore), and grand plans for the months ahead and summers to come. Along the way, the swimmers among them ventured into the chilly Atlantic waters to get their dose of the ocean, floating and bobbing in the buoyant salt water and body surfing as breakers eased their way into the cove and carried the willing swimmers to shore. It was a day of true relaxation; the stories were easy, unforced, and the bonds that were new to the week were not so much forged as slowly melded into sturdy links that just might hold through the long nights of fall and winter yet to come.

By four or so, the sun and the previous night had taken their toll. The plan was for everyone to retire to their respective housing to relax and then to rendezvous later at a comedy show by a local favorite, Lea DeLaria, and then go from there. Mercifully, they had a few hours to recuperate, as the show didn't start till 8:30. The four women began the unpleasant task of gathering their things together to start the packing process; the move to Stella's beach house had been a matter of literally throwing things in duffels and boxes and assorted shopping bags so as to make it to the beach at a reasonable time. Now it was down to the real work of sorting and packing and making room for what they'd started the week with as well as the various purchases they'd accumulated along the way.

Sabi was the first to sabotage their forward momentum. She had just dumped her duffel bag on the floor to re-sort it, when she suddenly plopped herself down beside the mess and then flopped back, prone on the floor.

"I can't do it," she groaned.

"Aw, come on, honey," Kit said, throwing a bra at her. "Yes you can.

You don't even have to repack your bag. Just get everything together and I'll pack it all."

"No, it's not just that. I don't *want* to pack. Because I don't want to *go*. Don't make me go," she said, pulling herself up slightly and throwing herself on Kit who was sitting cross-legged on the floor doing the actual packing. "Besides, I've got a boo-boo on my lip from the sun." Kit sucked in her breath as she looked more closely at Sabi's lip; not one but a cluster of nasty-looking fever blisters were starting to erupt.

"Sucks, doesn't it?" Claire said from across the room where she was slowly working on the same task.

"Claire and I usually hardly speak when it's finally time to pack," Rita said, as she slumped onto the couch. "I hate this part. It's like the whole week never happened." She slid down and turned her body to lie down on the couch.

"Oh, no you don't," Claire said. She got up from where she was kneeling and went over to pull Rita back up into a sitting position. "Besides, the week *did* happen, and I, for one, had a great time. Now, come on. We still have an evening ahead of us, and I'd like to have the majority of this done before we go out."

"I can't," Rita groaned. "I'm exhausted, honey. Just let me doze a couple of minutes, and I promise I'll get up and help you finish."

Claire stood above her, smiling and shaking her head. "Go ahead. I'll get as far as I can without your stuff, then I'm going to wake you up. So, don't get mad at me when I do."

Kit looked down at Sabi's head on her shoulder. "You want to take a little nap, too?"

"Can I? I don't think I'll make it tonight if I don't."

"Sure. Why don't you go in the room and get comfy. Maybe I'll try to catch forty winks once I get a handle on this."

Claire tapped Rita's shoulder. "You, too, honey. You'll be more comfortable in the bed." Rita dragged herself up without a word and disappeared into their room.

Claire folded and arranged a few more things, then looked over at Kit. She was folding in slow motion. "Yeah, boy, you're really making headway there," she chided. "Maybe the girls are right. Truth be told,

I can feel myself nodding just trying to decide what should go where."

"I'm so glad you said that," Kit said with a tone of evident relief. "The sun and the water really wiped me out."

"Okay. We'll sleep for an hour or so, get up and pack, then head out. I think there's an alarm clock in our room. I'll set it and get everyone up."

There was an alarm clock in Claire and Rita's room, equipped with a snooze button and all-too-easy off switch.

"Honey. Honey? Honey! You have to get up. I think we all over-slept."

Claire awoke to a half-dark room. "Shit! What time is it?" She leaned over and turned the lamp on. "Aw, man! It's 7:30 already. We have to get the girls up, shower and get ourselves out of here. We're supposed to meet everybody at the Crown and Anchor. Thank God Grant said she'd get the tickets—that is, assuming *they* didn't do the same thing."

In a blur of half-awake stumbling and muttering and tearing through clumps of clothes to find outfits, the women managed to get showers, dress, primp (to lesser and greater extents), and get out the door by eight—an almost superhuman effort.

When they arrived at the Crown and Anchor, the entire party was standing out front waiting for them. They, too, had also napped, but with better clocks. While hardly the first in line, they were surprised to find three cocktail tables near the front that they managed to all squeeze around. As the show progressed, they realized why the tables had been vacant. In addition to *very* bawdy, loud lesbian and gay humor, Lea loved to find an unwitting target in the audience. Tonight it was Sabi. She teased her about being from New York; she teased her about being Hispanic; she *really* teased her about being a "lip-stick lesbian," even coming out in the audience to see "how many inches thick that makeup is or if that's *really* a Puerto Rican tan you're sportin'." Then she made the error of teasing her about being a "fashionable, Upper East Side, lip *gloss* lesbian." She ended the bit with a comment about needing to see if that helped in the kissing de-partment and swooped down on totally unaware Sabi, planting one right on her. Unfortunately for Lea, it *wasn't* lip-gloss—and it was clear from the shocked look on her face that she hadn't been prepared for a mouthful of Carmex. The audience roared with laughter at the tables having been turned on loud, obnoxious Lea—who, it turned out, could get as good as she could give. Sabi rose to the occasion and stood, puckering up her swollen lips and putting her arms out to invite Lea to give her a follow-up buss. Lea laughed and, instead, gave her a hug and continued on with a wickedly funny wrap-up to the show.

Given the lingering fatigue from two full days of partying, it didn't take much for the group to quickly decide to forego a rowdier venue and simply migrate out to the club's deck bar.

After rehashing the show a bit—and Sabi's minor star turn—the conversation began to dwindle down to short comments, quick replies, and then intermittent silences. Everyone knew what everyone else was thinking: the end of the week, the return to "normalcy"—whatever the hell that really was—the departure from Oz. And farewells to the newly discovered friends who'd made the journey of the last few days such a memorable one.

"Jesus Christ, guys. This isn't a fucking wake," Kit finally blurted out in one of the silences. "I mean, hell, we've all got phones, three of you live in Boston, and the rest of us are all stretched out along the damned Eastern seaboard. If we can't manage to keep in touch, well, shame on us." She pulled the ubiquitous cap down even more firmly on her head.

Jimmy brightened a bit. "I'd forgotten these two lovely ladies are fellow Beantown residents," he said, looking over at Grant and Pat. "Well, I'm practically famous for my little soirees during those nasty cold months. And we could use a little lesbian levity. Just don't expect lots of sports talk—and *do* expect lovely hors d'oeuvres and show tunes. Who's got a pencil and paper? I ran out tonight without my favorite bag!"

Claire smiled at the turn the conversation had taken. She held Rita's hand and watched the connections branch out to take root in various directions. Soon the table was buzzing with addresses and phone numbers being recited, paper being torn into pieces to share with those who hadn't any, and tentative get-togethers already being planned. Claire knew a good exit opportunity when she saw one. She looked at Rita and rolled her eyes toward the door. Rita nodded back.

"Well, kids, it's been real, it's been fun, and it *has* been real fun. But the scene after this is liable to get real sloppy. So, we're going to split—packing beckons." Kit and Sabi nodded their agreement.

The rest of the table groaned with disappointment, but the four women pushed their chairs back and everyone got up as well for the round of hugging and kissing and farewelling. When Grant got to Claire, she hugged her and whispered in her ear, "I don't like this public good-bye stuff. We'll stop by in the morning. Can't promise you New York bagels, but I can rustle up a mean breakfast, complete with Bloody Marys."

"You got a deal. And we'll be up early. Something tells me not much packing is going to get done tonight."

On the other side of the table, Kit and Diane were having a similar conversation.

"Why don't you guys stop by in the morning?" Kit said. "We'll have some breakfast before we all hit the road. Hell, maybe I can talk Claire into a final round of Bloody Marys for the road!" Diane and Dara both agreed, and the hugging circle continued on around the table.

Claire had been right about the packing. When they finally got back to the West End house, it was after twelve, and they all agreed early packing beat late packing. They adjourned to the back deck to take in one more P-Town summer moon reflecting off the water.

Claire hoisted the overstuffed duffel bag up into the back of the minivan. Soon Kit had joined her with their largest bag, the two acting as a base for the rest of the stuff that had to somehow make it into what now looked to be an extremely small space.

"They still yapping in there?" Claire asked.

"Oh my God, yes! You'd think they all just met and were comparing life stories."

"It's that last crammed in bonding fix; one final hit of new affection. Not that I blame them. It's not often you meet people you hope you're gonna know all your life." She and Kit looked up at the same time and locked eyes for a moment. Then Claire reached over and pulled Kit's cap down over her eyes.

"Don't you worry, we're not goin' anywhere. No, sirree. You're stuck with us for a *long* time to come."

"Good. Now let's get this shit packed so we can finish those Bloody Marys."

In twenty minutes, they'd gotten the back loaded. All that was left was what they were keeping with them in the front of the minivan. Kit and Claire went around to the deck at the back of the house to join the others.

"You girls done with your chores?" Rita asked, smiling a little wickedly as she relaxed with her cup of coffee.

"Yes, ma'am!" Claire snapped to attention and saluted. "But no thanks to you two lazy-asses."

"Hey. You know the vacation rules. I *only* cook. And vacation's not over until we pull into our driveway."

"Ditto," Sabi said, nodding at Rita.

Claire rolled her eyes and sat down to reclaim her drink. "So, what's on your respective agendas for the day?" she asked the other two couples.

"Hmmm . . ." Grant said, flashing a smile Pat's way. "I think this horribly intense sun out here has pushed this fair-skinned, freckled girl almost to the brink of heat stroke. I just might have to call in sick tomorrow. What do you think, hon?"

"Oh, I don't know," Pat said, shaking her head with a look of deep concern on her face. "I think you may be right. What if you passed out on that ferry and no one knew what to do with you? Which is certainly *not* a problem with me around." She put her arm through Grants.

"And you guys?"

"Well, Baltimore's pretty much on the way to D.C., don't you think?" Dara said, looking over at Diane. "You by any chance interested in saving that plane ticket and hitching a ride with a lonely lady who's an excellent conversationalist?"

"Hmmm . . . well, let me see," Diane said, holding her chin in an attitude of deep thought. "Yes!"

"I thought you might say that. Lucky for us, Becca seems to have made her own plans. And you just never know about this heat stroke thing—could hit you at any time. Especially after a long, exhausting drive."

Diane laughed and smacked Dara on the arm. "You just might be more trouble than you're worth!"

"I don't think so," Dara said, putting her arm around Diane and giving her a squeeze. She turned to the rest of the group. "Maybe we'll follow you guys out. The long drive part's no joke."

"The potential heat stroke better not be either!" Diane retorted.

"Well, then, I guess the time has come," Claire said, draining her glass and standing up. "I, for one, am not going to do any major good-byes since I *know* I'll be seeing you," she said looking at Grant, "and I know you'll be seeing Kit," she said looking at Diane. "And I certainly hope we'll be seeing you ladies," she said, looking first at Pat and then Dara.

"I got a good vibe about all this," Sabi said. "And the first thing I'll do when I get home is light some incense and a candle for Santa Barbara and make sure we keep any negative shit away from you two," she said, meaning the two couples.

"Aw, for God's sake, Sabi. Not that Puerto Rican hoo-doo voodoo stuff," Claire sighed, with a little wink over at Rita.

"I'm telling you, little-Missy-Griffith-from-Ohio," a pet name Sabi reserved for moments calling for special emphasis. "You are definitely gonna get zapped one of these days making fun of the saints," Sabi said, shaking her head.

"What the hell is she talking about?" Dara said, looking at Diane with a puzzled look.

"That's definitely a story for another day," Claire said. "Suffice it to say, even though I tease her, she's got some powerful mojo working, and I bet you guys'll benefit from it. Just watch."

"Whatever you say," Dara said, picking up her backpack. "I'll take all the good vibes we can get." She kissed Diane on the head and grabbed her bag as well to take it to the car.

"You guys about ready?" Kit asked Rita and Sabi who were putting the last dishes away.

"Guess so," Rita said. She hung up the dishtowel and stood by the sink with her hands on her hips. "That's it. Did you leave the card for Stella?" Claire nodded. "Then let's hit the road, ladies."

" 'Til next time," Claire said as she hugged the other two couples. "And it better be soon."

"Hell, Griff. You know me. Just like a bad penny, I always turn up."

"I promise," Diane said, hugging Kit, "it won't be so long again."

The three departing couples climbed into their vehicles and pulled out, waving at Grant and Pat standing in front of the little house.

As they drove down the remaining stretch of Commercial Street on their way to the highway, the foursome said nothing, taking in the last sights of P-Town: the stone breakers that led out to the lighthouse, the marshlands, Herring Cove, then on past the magnificent dunes.

"Bye," Sabi said, looking back at the dunes as they sped by. "See ya next year."

"Ah. So, you think you might want to come back?" Claire said quietly.

"Hell, yes!" Sabi popped back. "Don't think you're *ever* coming up here without us!"

"Sabi," Kit said, turning around in the "co-pilot" seat and giving her a slightly dirty look.

"Wha-a-a-at? They're not allowed anymore. Those other times they came, that was just getting ready for when they brought us."

"Maybe they don't always want company."

"Me cago en na hijo! My God, Kit—you're so . . . white! We're not 'company' after this week. This was like those family vacations in the movies, where something goes majorly wrong and you make it through it and end up having a great time anyway. And being closer than ever."

"Oh, I am so glad to hear you say that," Rita said, turning in her seat and grabbing Sabi's hand. "I was afraid after these last few days that you guys'd never want to go away with us again."

Oh, stop," Kit interjected. "Granted, it doesn't seem like there's ever a dull moment when the four of us get together."

"And would you have it any other way?" Claire offered from the driver's seat.

"Not at all," Kit said firmly, situating her cap on her head. "So, what's next on our agenda? We gotta plan something or leaving's gonna kill us."

"Ooh, ooh, ooh!" Sabi was bouncing in her seat. "I know, I know! We'll have a big Halloween party—invite the new couples and make a weekend of it."

"That's sounds interesting," Claire said thoughtfully. "But if we do, we have to come up with some dynamite costume for all four of us."

The car was quiet as they all thought.

"How about the Fruit of the Loom fruit?" Kit offered.

"Good one!" Rita said. "But it might be hard making the fruit for the heads."

"Yeah, you're right."

"I got it! We could go as the Three Musketeers, since there really *are* four," Claire suggested.

"Ooh! I like that," Sabi squealed. "And I can borrow the ears from my niece and nephew."

There was total silence in the car.

"What?" Claire asked, totally lost.

"The ears, you idiot! They got 'em when they went to Disney World."

First Claire started quietly chuckling, then Rita, then Kit.

"*I'm* the idiot? The *Musketeers*—not the MOUSEketeers, you dope! 'One for all and all for one'?"

"Oh," Sabi said in almost a whisper. Then "the laugh" started. Slowly at first, and then it gained momentum, getting louder and more raucous every time she thought about her blunder. "Ears!" she said between snorts. "MUSketeers!" The cackling got louder. "Oh, my God. I'm gonna pee my pants!"

"Isn't that where we came in?"